EX LIBRIS

VINTAGE CLASSICS

MY AMERICAN

Stella Gibbons was born in London in 1902. She went to the North London Collegiate School and studied journalism at University College, London. She then spent ten years working for various newspapers, including the *Evening Standard*. Stella Gibbons is the author of twenty-five novels, three volumes of short stories and four volumes of poetry. Her first publication was a book of poems, *The Mountain Beast* (1930), and her first novel *Cold Comfort Farm* (1932) won the Femina Vie Heureuse Prize in 1933. Amongst her works are *Christmas at Cold Comfort Farm* (1940), *Westwood* (1946), *Conference at Cold Comfort Farm* (1959) and *Starlight* (1967). She was elected a Fellow of the Royal Society of Literature in 1950. In 1933 she married the actor and singer Allan Webb. They had one daughter. Stella Gibbons died in 1989.

STELLA GIBBONS

My American

VINTAGE BOOKS
London

Published by Vintage 2013

2 4 6 8 10 9 7 5 3 1

First published in Great Britain by Longmans, Green & Co. Ltd in 1939

Vintage
Random House, 20 Vauxhall Bridge Road,
London SW1V 2SA

www.vintage-classics.info

Addresses for companies within The Random House Group
Limited can be found at: www.randomhouse.co.uk/offices.htm

The Random House Group Limited Reg. No. 954009

A CIP catalogue record for this book
is available from the British Library

ISBN 9780099529347

The Random House Group Limited supports the Forest Stewardship
Council® (FSC®), the leading international forest-certification organisation.
Our books carrying the FSC label are printed on FSC®-certified paper. FSC is
the only forest-certification scheme supported by the leading environmental
organisations, including Greenpeace. Our paper procurement policy can be
found at www.randomhouse.co.uk/environment

Typeset in Bembo by Palimpsest Book Production Limited,
Falkirk, Stirlingshire

Printed and bound in Great Britain by
CPI Group (UK) Ltd, Croydon CR0 4YY

PART ONE

1

It was autumn. Kenwood House, the eighteenth-century mansion
on the edge of Hampstead Heath, had been recently opened to
the public by King George the Fifth and its beauties were still
sufficiently unfamiliar to attract crowds of Londoners, as well as
foreign visitors, to stare at them and admire the collection of
pictures inside the building.

But on this Saturday afternoon it was so cold that all but
a few people had gone home. Showers of leaves drifted from
the gigantic copper beech below the terrace in a slight icy
wind, and the grass bank was alive with their dark running
shapes. The sky was covered with a low pack of violet-grey
clouds, moving slowly. Soon it would be dusk, but there was
still a yellow gap in the west, looking wonderfully far away
and peaceful.

The paved yard in front of the mansion was lighter than the
terrace because it caught some of the glow from the west, and
the chauffeur of a big car waiting there could see comfortably to
read his newspaper. The soft noise of his leather gloves slapping
together as he struck his cold hands to shake the blood into
them was the only sound in the courtyard. When he stopped,
all he could hear was the rustling of leaves over the stone. A
black kitten was pouncing and darting after them. Suddenly it
ran behind one of the four high columns in front of the house
and did not come out again.

The front of the house had some domestic details to break
its bleak elegance; two old lampstands of wrought iron, painted
cream, and two flights of area steps, one on each side of the
lofty columns. Against the railing of the steps on the left a boy

3

of about thirteen was leaning, hands in the pockets of a loose fawn overcoat, one heel tapping softly, boredly, against the railing. A big fawn cap pulled over his eyes showed only high cheek-bones, fair-skinned cheeks, a childish mouth and firm chin, but his clothes were so un-English and his pose so assured that two late visitors hurrying out through the door under the columns five minutes since had turned to stare curiously at him. He kept looking towards the door as if waiting for someone to come out, and whistling softly through his teeth.

The courtyard was lonely, under the late afternoon sky. It looked across a lawn to a high barrier of beech trees, almost bare of leaves, moving slowly to and fro with a sighing sound, the yellow light showing through them. The chauffeur began to slap his hands again, bending closer over his paper.

Suddenly, from behind one of the columns, a little girl slowly walked out and advanced on the boy. She looked about twelve years old, and was dressed in a shabby brown coat with a white beret and black shoes and stockings, and in her arms she clasped the kitten, struggling and mewing thinly, pulling its claws down the front of her coat. She held it firmly with her little hands, hidden in rather dirty white woollen gloves. Her face was small and pale and pointed and seemed to have no features but large light brown eyes. The boy took no notice of her until she was at his side, then he looked up, surprised.

'Excuse me,' she said very quietly in a thin, faintly cockney voice, 'but please could you lend me sixpence?'

He stared at her. She returned the stare with a steady, polite look while her hands stroked the struggling kitten.

'What for?' he inquired at last, in a fresh charming drawl.

'To get home with.'

'Haven't you got any money?'

She shook her head. The kitten made a violent movement, and suddenly scratched her thin wrist where glove and coat sleeve met and drew blood, then wriggled down and darted off sideways over the courtyard, tail on end. Both children turned their heads slightly to watch it go.

'Mean to say,' he demanded incredulously, 'you came out without a dime in your pocket?'

'Oh, no,' she explained eagerly, coming a little nearer and sucking her scratched wrist while her light brown eyes looked at him across her glove. 'I did have a shilling for my birthday but I spent it.' She held up a packet of the postcards sold inside the mansion. 'I got these. I've only got a penny left now, and I live at Highbury and it costs twopence to get there and I thought I'd get some hot chestnuts on the way back, as I'm rather hungry. I didn't have any tea. Or any dinner.'

'Gosh!' he interrupted, admiration and pity in his voice. 'You must be hungry, I guess.'

'Yes, I am,' she said. She added proudly, 'I feel sick, I'm so hungry.'

He looked impressed at this but also rather embarrassed. The chauffeur had put down his paper and was staring idly across at them.

'Haven't your folks any money?' muttered the boy, diving into his pocket and not looking at her.

'I've only got Dad. My father, I mean. He gave me the shilling. I haven't got any mother.'

She said the last words in the quietest possible voice, looking down at the ground.

'Gee, I'm sorry. That's bad. Say, you'd better have a shilling so's you can buy something to eat as well. Oh, go on . . .' (as she shook her head, murmuring: 'Sixpence'll do, truly') . . . 'do have it!' And he held out a coin to her between the forefinger and thumb of his thick fur-lined glove.

She took it, and peeled back her own glove and carefully fitted the coin into her palm and pulled the glove over it once more, but all the time she kept her eyes fixed on his face.

'Thanks *very* much. I'll send it back to you. You give me your name and address, and I promise honour bright I'll send it back, you see 'f I don't.'

'I don't want you to do that, honest I don't. You must be a crazy kid spending your birthday money on a lot of old postcards. I'll give it to you, that's what. For a birthday present.'

'Thanks. I'm most awfully bucked,' she said carefully, as though repeating something she had heard someone else say. They stared at one another for a second or two in silence. Then she said:

'I say, what's your name? And where d'you live?'

'Robert Vorst. And I live in America and I'm going back home there to-morrow, and am I glad! Oh, boy!' He did a quick little double-shuffle, expertly neat and pleasing to watch.

'What part of America?' she persisted.

'Vine Falls. That's in Paul County, New Leicester. Say, I must go. There's my mother. Hope you get home safe. G'd-bye.'

He was running off to join two ladies who came out through the doors of the mansion at that moment, and who were looking round the courtyard as if in search of him, when he turned back. The little girl, who had half-retreated behind the column again, saw the last of the daylight on his fair face as he called to her:

'What's *your* name, Limey?'

'Amy Lee,' she called softly, putting her own little face round the column so that it caught in its turn the last of the yellow light. A plait of dark hair slipped slowly over her shoulder and hung there, swinging, as she leant forward.

'Bob!' called one of the ladies, in a slow sweet drawl, getting into the car with a display of apricot silk stockings above the knee, 'How many times have I told you not to use that word? Where have you been? We've been looking for you all over. Come right along now, this minute.' But she did not sound cross.

Amy Lee heard the boy protesting something that sounded like: 'Dan says it,' and then he followed the two ladies into the car, and the chauffeur shut the door and reseated himself. The car began slowly to move.

The boy sat opposite to the two ladies. He was looking across at Amy where she stood with one arm round the column and her plait swinging over her shoulder, and as she watched him, he pulled off his cap and waved it to her and for the first time he smiled. His hair was thick and fair and longer than an English boy's and one lock fell over his forehead, but at that distance she could not see the colour of his eyes.

The car turned the corner, and was gone.

At once the courtyard was twice as lonely and quiet. The kitten was over in a far corner by one of the grey brick wings of the house, chasing a leaf, and Amy went over and made one or two attempts to catch it, but it easily avoided her. She stood and watched it for a little while, the leaves whirling round her feet with their dry sound. A man came out of the house and locked the door, glancing indifferently over at her as he did so, then went away towards the old stables that had been turned into tea rooms.

The yellow gleam in the west had gone, and it was beginning to get dusk. She carefully turned up the collar of her coat round her thin little neck, murmuring something, then put her hands in her pockets and walked quickly away.

She went round to the right of the house, past the garden with dead brown roses on the bushes, and through a tunnel covered with ivy. At the end of this tunnel, in the valley, the lake gleamed dully. One swan glided slowly over the water, hardly seeming to move. She stopped in the twilight of the tunnel, where the wind blew coldly, to stare for a while at the swan, then walked on.

Along the empty terrace she went, where the beech leaves were blowing. The long windows of the house were shuttered now, and against the white wood it could be seen that some of them had pale purple glass. That was pretty; she stopped to admire it, then went on. She was not exactly hurrying, but she was such a light-stepping child that it was difficult to imagine her walking slowly or dawdling; her movement was like that of the running leaves themselves. Sometimes she stared at the wall of beeches beyond the lake, where flocks of pigeons, dark against the sky and pale against the trees, were settling down for the night. There were two people walking along the path by the lake, but that was all. The scene was as lonely as it was beautiful; it might have been in any romantic, faraway place rather than on the edge of London slums. Amy stared at the swan again, then at the low, slow-moving clouds, then suddenly drove both hands into her pockets, shook her plait over her shoulder, gave an excited little prance, and began to run. She held the coin the boy had given her tightly in her palm, and as she ran she whistled very softly in time to her running, a tune she had heard at the pictures and named to herself, 'The Cowboy's Rescue.' Down the terrace she flew, feeling her feet pushing the ground away behind her. *She* was the cowboy, riding to rescue someone, and behind her rode the enemy on fiery mustangs! She glanced sideways at the grass, temptingly green in the low evening light, but shook her head, muttering again.

When she came out of the grounds of Kenwood House she turned away from the Heath, which now lay spread beneath her. The valleys and hillocks were blue-green and the trees were dark brown on this dull yet clear evening, above the lights of London already sparkling in the valley far below. She went on until she came out into a quiet road where big houses stood back in large gardens, and then up a steep hill, skipping as she went along under the darkening sky with the shilling and the penny safe in the palm of her glove.

It had been a nice day today, and the nicest thing that had happened had been speaking to that boy from America. Now I've spoken to an American, she thought. I know how they talk. She tried to imitate the way he had spoken, repeating *Robert* (Somebody; the unfamiliar name in the unusual accent had defeated her), *Vine Falls, Paul County, New Leicester*, but found the intonation too difficult. When I get home, she thought, I'll have my supper, and read *The Gold Bug*, and look up Vine Falls on the atlas . . . *oh*! It's Saturday. Father'll be home. I can't. The disappointment made her stop dead for a moment. Then she murmured a few words, as though reassuring an invisible companion, and went slowly on, past the playing fields of Highgate School, up to Highgate Village.

She had been fascinated by the unfamiliar American voices as the party got out of the car, and had followed the two ladies and the boy as they toured the mansion. There were some other people going round as well, and no one took any notice of Amy, who was not a pretty or attractive child. Unnoticed in the little group, she had been able to stare at the Americans as much as she liked. The ladies were not a bit English-looking. Their feet were so small and pretty, and their clothes were different, somehow, from English clothes, and they asked so many questions and seemed more interested than anyone else. They were quite old, but the one the little boy called Aunt Carol was awfully pretty, with the biggest blue eyes Amy had ever seen. The boy's mother was not so pretty, but she looked very kind. She called him 'son,' and once she put her little hand on his shoulder when she wanted him to look at one of the pictures.

But he soon got tired of going round, and loitered behind. Once he had poked a bed with one finger, and said 'Gee!' Amy waited until he had dawdled into the next room, then she emerged from an alcove where she had been lurking and poked the bed in her turn, but could not see why he had said 'Gee!' She would have liked to ask him, but was afraid to.

They all three seemed so happy and rich-looking (the Aunt-Carol-one had a lovely diamond brooch on her blouse) that Amy could not stop looking at them, and when the boy at last slipped away and out into the yard, she had followed him. His queer clothes and handsome untroubled young face had attracted her so strongly that she felt she must speak to him. He looked so happy! I'm sure he has a lovely time, thought Amy, watching him from behind the pillar. He's looking cross now, because he didn't like the pictures, but he has a happy look, really. I expect he goes coasting, and lives in one of those old brownstone houses they have in my American books at home.

Then she began to imagine herself asking him to lend her sixpence to get home with, and before she knew that she meant to . . . moving forward as if in a dream . . . she really *was* asking him.

She often imagined herself doing things, and then did them, like that.

Here was Highgate Village, with all the little old shops lit up. It stood on the highest hilltop for miles. Amy was always glad when the Number 11 tram got to the bottom of Highgate Hill in case it ran away faster and faster, and fell at last into the twinkling, sparkling mass of lights at the bottom.

There was a Number 11 waiting now. She ran, and climbed hastily up to the top; and then of course it did not go for quite a long time. She was the only passenger, and she was content to sit there staring out of the window, now dashed with big rain drops, in a dream. Her head felt funny, but that was only because she was hungry, and it was all right, there was a cold fried herring at home, and some milk and four uncooked sausages. I shall fry up the herring and buy a bottle of Ka-Ola, she decided, with my shilling. He did say I was to buy something to eat. I should like to keep it, really, as it was a present from the only American I've ever spoken to, but I did ask him to lend it me so's I could get home and buy some chestnuts, so it wouldn't be fair to keep it. But Ka-Ola would count as chestnuts, really, because it's a sort of food. She rolled down her glove to make sure the shilling was still there.

It was there, but it was not a shilling. Instead of the King's Head, an utterly unfamiliar one confronted her . . . the savage profile of a Red Indian, his plaited hair dressed with feathers, and above his arched nose the tiny word LIBERTY. Bewildered, she turned the coin over and stared at the humped shoulders of a bison with horned and bearded head, bent towards the words Five Cents. And over the bison's back, in a curve, the words UNITED STATES OF AMERICA.

Amy's first feeling was bitterest disappointment, but not because she would now have to walk half-way home and go without her Ka-Ola.

'He did it on purpose!' she muttered furiously, tears rushing to her eyes. 'It was a horrid, beastly *joke*. Just the kind of thing a *boy* would think funny!'

She dashed the coin on the dirty floor.

'Here . . . here . . . what's all this?' demanded the conductor, who had come up unseen behind her. 'Throwin' money about. What's the matter with it?'

'Someone gave it me, and I thought it was a shilling,' she muttered, stooping to pick it up.

'Serves you right for not lookin' at it when they gave it you. Always count your change, always look at a bit of money before you put it in your bag, then you can't go far wrong. Here, let's see.'

She held it out, not very near. She did not want him to handle it. Already she felt sure that the American boy had only made a mistake, not been unkind.

But he took it from her and turned it round in his tired-looking, dirty hands.

'Kind of an American coin, that would be,' he said at last. 'Who gave it you?'

'A friend,' she said, looking up at him with a polite, steady expression. It was the look she always put on when she was lying. 'A lady,' she added, not too hastily.

'Sure it wasn't a gentleman?' snapped the conductor, suddenly cross. 'Now you get off my tram, and quick. Tryin' to get a ride for nothing, I know your sort. Go on, be off with you, or I'll fetch the inspector.'

She got up, without hurry, and followed him down the stairs. She would wait for the next tram and take a penny ride to Holloway Arcade and walk the rest of the way.

In a few minutes she was rocking down the hill through the rain that dashed furiously in crystal streaks against the glass. This conductor was all right, he took her penny without a word. She had waited until the first tram had gone so that the cross conductor should not tell any other conductor about it.

She loved riding on top of trams, but now she was so very hungry that the movement made her feel sick. Never mind (she murmured), I'll soon be home. If only Dad isn't in.

The coin was again tucked in her glove. Now I shall keep it, she decided, because it won't be a temptation to spend it. And after all, it was a present. He said so.

She got off the tram at the Holloway Arcade and set out on the walk along Holloway Road to Highbury Fields, where she lived. It was not far, and she walked along so quickly and lightly that she almost ran, the cold rain beating in her face. No one bumped into her—she saw to that—but it was tiring dodging people, and once a car nearly ran her down when she crossed a road. Everyone shouted at her, looking frightened and furious. Her head felt queerer and queerer, but she took no notice of that, and as usual, enjoyed the walk. She took in the golden windows of the shops, the cold winter smell of the celery piled outside a greengrocer's, the lovely face of Dolores Costello gazing out dreamily from a cinema hoarding. Amy loved walking in London; yet hardly knew that she loved it. She never said she did, or walked when she might ride, but when once she drifted into one of her long walks through the streets she was utterly happy. Unnoticed as a leaf, hands in pockets, she moved lightly along, in a dream, but a dream in which she noticed a thousand funny or frightening or pretty things and people.

At the pub called The Hen and Chickens she crossed over,

turned down Corsica Street and left the trams and buses and bright shops behind, went along Calabria Road, then through Baalbec Road into Highbury Place. Here the Fields faced her, their tall trees behind a railing shining silver with the wet.

The Fields are an open space shaped like a half-heart, and surrounded by Highbury Crescent and Highbury Place, two rows of tall, early nineteenth century houses of dark brown brick with elegant details in their fanlights, railings and balconies. There is plenty of life in the Fields, for the National School boys play football there and babies are brought from the poorer streets to sun-bathe and enjoy the bit of green, but the houses have the spell of the past on them.

Amy went down Highbury Walk, where there are two or three quiet little shops, and stopped at one with 'D. Beeding, Baker and Confectioner' over it. This was where she lived.

She peered in through the window of the shop before going on to the door at the side, which was ajar. Mrs Beeding was there, leaning forward over the counter with her hands spread out on the bleached wood and talking to a pretty, dark woman who was just going out carrying a wrapped loaf. Amy slipped in as the woman came out.

'Hullo, Amy . . . good night, then, Mrs Flower,' said Mrs Beeding, sitting down again on a broad chair close to a brightly burning oil stove and starting to knit. ''Ave yer had a nice birthday, luv?'

'Very nice, thank you, Mrs Beeding. Is Dad in?' She looked intently at Mrs Beeding.

'He's oopstairs. It's all right, luv.' Mrs Beeding glanced up, nodding calmly. 'I've got the rent. He gave it to me the minute he come in, and he's all right, too. You go on oop. Here's a few cakes for you. Custard tarts, they are, for your birthday.' She nodded towards a paper bag on the counter. 'Did yer see the pictures, luv?'

'Yes, thank you, Mrs Beeding.' Amy picked up the bag, opened it and sniffed delicious hot vanilla from the warm tarts. 'Thank you *very* much for these.'

'And were they pretty?'

'Yes, very pretty.'

'That's right. Now you run on upstairs, Amy. Mona'll bring up the letters if there's any for you. Good night, luv.'

'Good night, Mrs Beeding, and thank you *very* much for the tarts.'

The shining cleanliness of the shop, the bright flame of the oil stove, the lightness of the pastries, the calmness of Mrs Beeding's pink face and the neatness of her bobbed hair and fat body were all explained the instant that she spoke by her voice. It was a patronizing yet comfortingly competent voice, subduing rebellion almost before it had started, dismissing ghosts, looking Life straight in the eye and asking it what it thought it was up to now, taking obedience, cleanness and self-respect for granted like the daylight. It was the voice of Yorkshire.

Mrs Beeding was within two months of having her fifth child. She was forty-seven years old, thickly built even when she was not going to have a baby, with straight yellow hair, a firm little mouth and small bright grey eyes. She was not pretty to look at, but she was surprisingly satisfying. She wore a dark blue dress and a large concealing print overall, with a white collar that set off her pink cheeks. Her complexion was her only weakness. She put Stuff on it at night. None of her children knew what the Stuff was. Gran up in Yorkshire had given the recipe to Mum years ago, and Mum made some more Stuff whenever she wanted it. Mona, the younger girl, who had spots, was as sarcastic about Mum and her Stuff as she dared be.

Mrs Beeding, strong as a horse, was pleased about the new baby, for the youngest boy was now five and the Beedings were beginning to feel the lack of a baby in the house. Dora, who was nineteen and worked as junior typist in a firm of sherry importers in the City, had said at first that it really was the limit,

Mum having another at her age; but now even Dora was more pleased than shocked about the baby. The Beedings enjoyed babies.

Amy went slowly up the dark stairs. Her head felt so swimmy that she had to hang on to the banisters to keep herself from falling down while she carefully, without hurry, packed her mouth with custard tart. As soon as she had swallowed one she crammed her mouth again, walking slowly upstairs all the time, past long windows showing the dark brown sky of London's night, and closed doors whose white handles glimmered in the dimness. The house smelled clean, but stuffy and old. On the top landing as she finished the last tart, she opened the door of the three rooms that were her home.

Her father was dozing over *The Star* in an armchair by the gas stove, and started awake at the sound of the door opening.

'Hullo, where've you been?' he asked, flinging his arms above his head, his long legs out, and the paper all over the floor in a tremendous, savage, prolonged yawn. 'I came back specially to take you to the pictures. Want to come?'

'Oh, yes, please, Dad!'

'Don't call me Dad, there's a dear, good girl.'

'Father, I mean. Sorry. Yes, I would, please, only I'd like my supper first.'

'All right. It's only . . . what is it?' glancing down at his bare wrist and then frowning. 'Did you notice the shop clock as you came up?'

'It's half-past five.'

'Plenty of time. We'll have supper and get to the Majestic (God help us) about seven. What's on there, d'you know?'

'It's *Beau Geste*,' she answered at once, pausing at the door of her room and looking round at him, her face pink and her eyes bright with excitement.

'Not too bad. Get the supper, will you, there's a good monkey, I'm hungry.' He picked up his paper again.

Amy hurried to change her frock. It was nearly a month since she had been to the pictures. This was certainly being a good birthday! At breakfast he had given her a shilling (of course it had come out of his watch-pawning money, and that was worrying; it meant he had been betting on that dog-racing again, but he would get it out again next Friday when he was paid), and now *Beau Geste*!

When she came back she wore a teacloth tied firmly round the waist of her dark blue gym tunic and the sleeves of her white blouse were rolled up. She had changed into rubber shoes and brushed her hair, parted in the middle of a high round creamy forehead, and put on a worn but still brilliant silk necktie striped with dark red, pale blue, and rich dark green. Presently her father stopped skimming the paper and sat watching her as she went between the living-room and the tiny kitchen opening off it; a plain, queer little gnome of a girl.

She's too small for her age, he thought. Wants feeding up. Oh God, I can't help it. She'll have to take her chance. Millions of children grow up and get themselves through life. She's Edie's responsibility, not mine. I never wanted a child.

One of the horrible waves of misery that burst over him when he thought of his dead wife came on him now, and he got up, because it was not possible to bear it if he sat still, and went into his room and drew the curtains and pulled the quilt over the rumpled bed. He had been asleep all the afternoon.

He was a tall, fair, slim man of thirty-eight, but looking much younger, whose face was so weak and desolate (as though he had not one strong idea or happy thought behind it) that he was hardly attractive any more. But it was plain that ten years ago he had been beautiful, when his curly mouth had laughed instead of looking sulky, before his blue eyes became bloodshot. His profile was still fine and his gilt hair, receding rapidly now from a high forehead, kept its curl.

He had been born a gentleman; and to keep him a gentleman

and to fit him to get himself through life, some two thousand pounds had been spent. He now earned six pounds a week as a seller of advertising space on that old-fashioned but modestly prosperous paper for boys, *The Prize*, and nothing was left to show for the two thousand pounds but this: he was a gentleman still. This fact was a comfort to no one but himself, and not much to him. It helped him to get a job with *The Prize*, where the quality was valued, but it did not help him to sell advertising space and it made him dislike being called Dad in Amy's thin, faintly cockney voice.

He always thought about Amy's voice immediately after a wave of wretchedness had drenched him, and he was thinking about it as he came back into the sitting-room. It's the people she's always with, he thought, sitting down again. Nasal little rats at that appalling school, Mona Beeding always in and out of the place . . . she never hears a decent accent except mine from one year to the next. Oh, well . . . I can't help it. Or I suppose I could but I'm—if I've got the energy.

Amy had fried the sausages with some bread and put the kettle on and opened a tin of loganberries. Now she would have a nicer supper than she had planned, because, if he had not been in, she would have had to save the sausages for his breakfast. If only nothing awful happened, this would be almost the nicest day since Mother . . .

She breathed in, quickly, exactly as though she had bitten on an aching tooth, but continued to pour the boiling water steadily into the teapot. Just for a minute she had forgotten. She went across to the cupboard and got out the milk jug and rinsed it, very carefully and slowly to stop herself from thinking that on her last birthday her mother had been alive.

'You still hang on to that old thing of mine,' said her father, noticing her necktie with some amusement. The colours were those of the rowing club at his old college. 'It's in ribbons.'

'It's pretty,' she said. 'Prettier than ours. The school one, I mean.'

'Christ, so I should hope.'

'The Old Girls is quite pretty. It's dark brown and light brown and pale yellow.'

'Charming,' he said, yawning and staring at the window with a dreary, bored expression.

'It's ready,' said Amy, in a few minutes.

They sat down and began to eat.

The room was long and low, with two big windows and a cheap creamy wallpaper. The floor was stained and inadequately covered by three long Persian rugs, their colours almost worn away. The table they sat at was a good piece of late Victorian mahogany, stained with hot plate marks, but the sofa and two swollen armchairs were Early Hire Purchase; and the smaller chairs were imitation ladderbacks, varnished shiny brown like the ugly circular bookshelf beside the gas stove. There was not enough furniture in the room, and the bright orange curtains over the windows increased the desolate, temporary look.

But the pictures had been chosen by someone who had liked them. There was a reproduction of a crowded, brilliant battle scene with much red and blue in it by some Italian master, a branch laden with flowers, birds and snow against a grey sky by a Japanese, and a large coloured print of ladies and gentlemen in Victorian dress skating against a yellow sunset with a bonfire burning.

The house was very quiet. The gas stove hissed and faint cries came up sometimes from the distant streets.

'Well, what was Kenwood House like?' he asked at last, making conversation with an effort.

'Very pretty,' said Amy, her cheeks exactly the colour of a pink cyclamen petal from the hot tea and sausage and good bread and butter. 'It's very big, you know, and there are a lot of famous pictures there.'

'You're an extraordinary child. What made you want to go off there by yourself?'

'They told us about it at school,' she explained, 'and Miss Eckeridge, the drawing mistress, said we ought to go and see it.'

'They ought to have got up one of their highly cultural expeditions. More fun for you than going by yourself.'

'P'raps they will next term,' she said, giving him her polite, steady look instead of answering that they had, but that she had purposely not gone with it. He would have paid for her to go if she had asked him, but she hated going to places with a lot of people. She liked the sound of Kenwood House; but had decided to go there alone on her birthday, which was most fortunately a Saturday, and that was exactly what she had done. She hoped he would say no more about it, and he did not.

While they were eating the loganberries Amy began to think about *Beau Geste* and how lovely it would be. (She always enjoyed only one nice thing at a time, so as to get the best out of it in case something dreadful happened and spoiled it.) Supper was nearly over without a row or him saying anything about her cockney accent, and there would not be much to enjoy on the walk to the cinema, so now she could allow herself to think about *Beau Geste*.

Nothing could stop them going to it, now, surely; it was nearly seven o'clock and in ten minutes, after she had cleared away, they would go. Nothing . . . (she went quickly in her mind through all the things that might stop them going) . . . nothing . . . *Oh, suppose that beastly, horrible old Mr Porteous is home this week?*

It would have surprised Mr Porteous (known to the Boys as Porty) even more than it would have enraged him to hear himself called horrible, beastly and old, for he was only sixty and saw himself as a rich-natured, generous, warm-hearted man in the prime, bringing a leaven of colour and guts into the not-so-good lives of the Highbury boys and the Canonbury boys, and sometimes the Islington and Angel boys. Wherever the boys were, there was Mr Porteous; old Porty, always up to something, Porty was; make you—laughing, Porty could. Heard Porty's latest, boys?

The girls of Highbury, Canonbury, Islington and the Angel did not like old Porty at all, but seldom dared to tell their husbands as much. Porty only knew one way of spending money. Rent, doctor, shoes, school fees, food, light, heat . . . Porty never thought about money in connection with them. He was employed by a small firm which was trying to put a new brand of women's artificial silk underclothes on the market, having been given the job because, said his employers, he had just the convincing, jolly yet clean sales-talk which would get all the old girls who ran little haberdashery shops in the outer suburbs.

Old Porty, who was unmarried, was sometimes away for a week travelling, and sometimes at home doing the new suburbs like Mill Hill and Edgware; and the chief horror the Highbury girls had to cope with was never knowing which week he would be at home and able to pop in. Amy, like all the other girls whose boys were acquainted with old Porty, did not know whether he was at home this week; and suddenly dreaded that he would pop in and carry off her father before they could get away to the pictures. Her father sometimes called old Porty a filthy fellow, but he always seemed amused to see him.

She began to clear away very quickly, listening tensely for the bell or footsteps on the stairs, while her father lit a cigarette and changed his shoes.

Below in the rainy darkness Old Porty's car advanced cheerfully towards Highbury Walk.

Mrs Beeding glanced up from her knitting as it drew up outside the shop, got up without haste (there was plenty of time; he always fiddled with the car), and walked clumsily into the dark passage and quietly shut the door. Then she stood there, listening. Presently the Lees' bell rang. Mrs Beeding quickly opened the door and confronted Old Porty. He wore a very light tweed overcoat, a red scarf with horseshoes on it, and his hat on the back of his head.

'Hul*lo* there! It's all the same in the dark, as the nigger said to the nun!' roared Porty, peering at Mrs Beeding to see who she was and hoping she was her daughter Mona. 'Oh . . . Mrs Beeding. Evening! Beastly night, isn't it? Beg your pardon . . . didn't mean to bring you up to the door. Mr Lee in?'

'I was passing,' said Mrs Beeding. 'No. He's gone to the pictures with the little girl.' (Tim had mentioned earlier in the evening that he wanted to take Amy out when asking his landlady if she knew where Amy was.)

'Oh, well, never mind, never mind. Just popped in,' said Porty, and was going away again without a trace of disappointment (the world is full of boys), when voices and footsteps were heard coming down the stairs.

'Good night,' said Mrs Beeding, beginning to shut the door.

But it was too late.

'Hullo, Tiger!' roared Porty, as Tim and Amy came down into the hall. 'Just caught you, you old bu . . . sorry, ladies, that was a near thing, wasn't it! Ma here said you'd gone off to the pictures.'

'We're just on our way,' said Tim, rather disagreeably.

'I'll run you round, and we can drop in at the Chickens and have a quick one on the way. How's that? How's Amy tonight, eh?' And Porty gave her pigtail a spiteful wrench. He hated quiet, dull little girls of twelve. He did not mind them so much at about fourteen, especially if they were on the plump side.

'It's her birthday,' said Tim, glancing down at his daughter. Poor monkey, she looked pretty sick, though she was trying not to. 'But we've time for a quick one.'

'In you get.' Porty invitingly opened the door of the car, which smelled of stale tobacco smoke, and off they went.

'Just a quick one at the Chickens,' said Porty. 'Ju-u-u-u-ust a leetle quick one, eh, Tiger?'

'All right.'

Amy sat at the back of the car, trying not to look at Porty's wicked old face in the little mirror over his head. It was just visible in the dim light from the streets lamps; his greying eyebrows of long coarse hair and his cruel little eyes almost hidden in their deep sockets and his hooked nose and buttoned-in little mouth which twisted sideways when he laughed. His face was bright purply red.

He's my idea of an ogre, thought Amy. Not a giant; they have beards and you can imagine them being kind. Ogre. He just exactly fits the word.

She began to think what she would do when she got home, to make up for missing *Beau Geste*. I can put away the coin that the American boy gave me in my box, and look up Vine Falls on the Atlas and start another chapter of *The Wolf of Leningrad*. Yes, that's what I'll do.

They stopped outside The Hen and Chickens.

Twenty minutes later, while Mrs Beeding was locking up the shop for the night, she heard the side door open.

'Amy? Is that you?'

'Yes, Mrs Beeding.'

Amy came and stood in the doorway that led from the passage into the shop. Her pale little face was expressionless.

'Never mind, luv.' Mrs Beeding put a sheet of muslin over a tray of jam tarts. 'You and Mona go next week, when you get your pocket-money. Mona's going. It's Pola Negri in *Barbed Wire*.'

'Yes, that sounds lovely,' said Amy, politely.

'Didn't yer wait at all, luv?' Mrs Beeding pulled down the blind across the window.

'Oh, no. I knew he wouldn't come out till closing time.'

'Never you mind, luv. Have yer got a nice book to read?'

'Yes, thank you.'

'That's right. Good night, then, Amy.'

'Good night, Mrs Beeding, and thank you for the custard tarts. They were *lovely*.'

Mrs Beeding went slowly downstairs and Amy went slowly up. The house was full of the delicious smell of freshly baked bread; Mr Beeding was already at work in the bakehouse.

Back in the living-room, she re-lit the gas stove, drew the curtains more closely, pulled a chair up to the table and fetched a glass of water from the kitchen, then went into her own room to take off her hat and coat.

It was a small room, with one large window, covered by a faded purple curtain, overlooking large gardens with big trees. The floor had been painstakingly stained with permanganate of potash which was beginning to wear off and there was a blue rug beside the iron bedstead, a kitchen table for Amy's mirror, brush and comb, and a battered wardrobe, painted white, for her clothes. It was a shabby little room, but every object there looked as though the owner loved it; and the patchy yellow walls blazed with pictures, carefully cut out and pasted on sheets of white paper. There were pictures from advertisements, fashion plates, magazine covers and travel pamphlets, all widely differing in subject but all gorgeously coloured and exciting or beautiful. She had an affectionate, refreshing look at them while she changed her shoes. Then she took from the back of the wardrobe, from behind her school hat, a penny bottle of purple ink, a purple pen, and a brown exercise book. On the cover was neatly printed

THE WOLF OF LENINGRAD
A Thrilling Story of
The Russian Revolution

She carried these into the next room, arranged them on the table, and sat down in front of them. Then she sighed deeply, uncorked the ink, dipped the pen into it, and slowly began to write.

The room was very quiet. Sometimes the child stretched out her wrist as though to rest it, or took a sip of water from the glass. Her little hand moved slowly, tracing the characters as though she loved doing it.

Presently she said, without looking up and in a voice quite different from her usual one, deeper, slow and absorbed:

'Mother.'

She paused just long enough for someone sitting reading to look up and answer:

'What, my pet?'

'I've done the bit about Tamara rescuing Ivan. Would you like to hear?'

Again a pause, just long enough for someone to put down their book and say:

'Yes, please, darling. You read it to me.'

Then slowly, in the same deep absorbed voice, with her chin sunk in her hands and her gaze moving steadily over the page covered with neat purple writing, the child began to read aloud in the empty room.

2

Tim Lee, born late in their marriage to elderly parents, was the son of a don. His mother was a don's daughter, and all the family's friends were dons or appendages of dons, and a civilized, witty, intelligent, secure and privileged circle it was, very sure of its aims and of its position in the English picture.

Even when he was a little boy Tim found this life very dreary, and was not interested in the beautiful ancient colleges with their turf and their towers and their bells nor impressed by the wonderful old men, crusted with learning, about whom legends appeared in *The Times*.

Tim was too easily bored. That was the root of all his troubles and the anxiety he caused his family. He spent a great deal of his time asleep because he could never think what to do with himself when he was awake. He had no natural bent for any career and no ambition, and he was permanently discontented, for no reason that he could give. 'Christ! Is that all?' was Tim's attitude to life. 'Not bad while it lasted, but . . . is that all?'

The only pastime that did not bore him was gambling, and the only company he could endure for ten minutes was that of racing touts, raffish commercials, slavish bartenders, a waiter with a tip for a race, a barber who could tell a dirty story, or chorus boys out of a job. Shady people, living on the extreme edge of honesty and security, whose lack of responsibility fed the lack of it in him, who temporarily lifted the leaden clouds of his boredom. The petty shifts and dangers of their lives excited him, as though he were watching sharp-eyed, stinking little animals picking their way through a jungle. He knew that they were what he called filthy fellows, but he never felt that he must

25

renounce their company: the other sort of company bored him too much. The filthy fellows in their turn put up with him because he was handsome, amusing, unshockable and always had the price of a drink. His taste for low company distressed his family, who could not think where he got it from.

When he met Edie Kempe, daughter of a common old drunken estate agent in the town, at a party given by one of his low-class acquaintances, he fell in love with her more as a human being than as a woman. She carried a double charm for him: she was not a lady and it was impossible to imagine her being bored.

This thin dark pretty girl, neat and gay as a sailor, was extra-ordinarily popular with both men and women, not so much because she was kind (though she was certainly that) as because she cheered you up, people said, just to look at her. People felt that life, whoever else it got down, would never get Edie. She comforted people whom it *had* got down like the sight of a pretty picture or the sound of a cheerful tune.

Of course all the men she knew wanted to marry her (tempted by the prospect of having something to comfort them whenever they wanted comforting, which, as with most men, was pretty often) but Edie, in spite of the burden of her old father, did not want to settle down. Yet when Tim asked her to marry him the second time they met, without an instant's hesitation she said yes. He was twenty-four, and she nineteen, and it was the autumn of 1913.

They got married first and told Tim's people afterwards. Mr and Mrs Lee were naturally hurt by Tim's secrecy and wished that he had chosen a lady, but they were prepared to make the best of the situation, suggesting that the young people should take a small flat near them and that Tim, who had taken a Second in History, should try for a job in a good preparatory school outside the town, backed by his father's help.

But Tim refused, and Edie stood by him. They wanted to

leave the town, which they both disliked, and go to London. There was a scene in which Tim showed a frighteningly cold ill-temper, and then he got his way. His father gave him shares bringing in two hundred a year and warned him that if the money were not prudently used he would get no more, and the two young people went off.

Tim's parents were grieved: but they were also a little relieved. They, whose life was a web of responsibilities, had produced a son who was a monster of irresponsibility with a taste for shady company that bewildered them and a passion for games of chance that frightened them. He did not seem like a child of theirs at all. They had always been good friends, sufficient for one another, and now they drew even closer together. Three years after Tim's marriage they were killed in a climbing accident in Skye, and Tim came into a little more money, and felt some secret relief, in his turn, that a few more roots had snapped. He did not lie to himself about his feelings, and knew that he had never tried to like his parents. They did not speak his language.

In London he did a few months schoolmastering at a bad day school, helping his salary with slices from his capital. He had sold the shares, and he and Edie had good times running around in a cheap car, dancing in cheap places, and going to pits at theatres. They were both happy, Edie because she had a happy nature, and Tim because he was not bored and because Edie was there, and in London there were plenty of places to gamble.

In August, 1914, Tim rushed into the Army, delighted at the prospect of some excitement, and late in 1915, while he was in France, the tiny dark-haired Amy was born—and with her, Edie's sense of responsibility.

When Tim came home finally in 1916, with a convenient wound that would not let him go back, he found Edie changed. She was still unfussy, gay and casual about everything except Amy and her well-being, but *that* she took very seriously indeed.

She was not so unreasonable as to force Tim to buy a house or stick in a job if he was bored with it, but she took to making rows about his beloved gambling, saying that they needed the money to buy shoes and holidays and good fresh food for Amy.

Tim, who would have found this intolerably tiresome in any other woman, made excuses for Edie. He did not stop gambling, but he gave her as much money as he could possibly scrape up apart from his gambling, and as she made excuses for him, too, they were happy again.

Edie accepted the fact that Tim did not care much for Amy, whom he had never wanted. He found her an amusing little animal for five minutes, but he was not interested in her progress and if she cried he got furious. Edie did not resent this: she could give Amy enough love for both, she thought, and that was what she did.

As the little girl grew older, and the money that Tim earned by selling cars on commission, helping a friend run a night club, or an occasional bit of journalism, grew less and his savage boredom more easily roused, Edie became expert at whisking Amy out of his way and keeping her quietly employed with a book or her paper dolls . . . (Amy called them 'cut-outs') . . . and very clever at planning festivals and surprises on pennies. If anyone had asked Edie after ten years of marriage if she loved Tim, she would have answered 'Of course,' and meant it. She was a simple woman who took the ups and downs of life for granted and she had not a strain of bitterness in her nature. Tim was the lover of her youth, he had given her Amy whom she passionately loved, and they had stuck to each other without either of them thinking twice about another man or woman, for ten years. Had anyone asked Tim the same question about Edie he would have said, 'I suppose so. Yes, I think I must love her,' and as neither of them missed having possessions, friends or security so long as they could be together, with enough to eat, with Amy in good health to satisfy Edie, and Tim with an odd pound for his gambling, theirs may fairly be called a happy marriage.

Amy inherited her mother's loving nature and her power to get happiness out of little ordinary things, but she was not so happy, and shyer. Her smallness made her afraid of people and of the world that seemed so huge. She suffered from a lack of fats and starch like all the babies born in the war-years, and though she was healthy, she was not robust. Edie fed her carefully, but she never 'fleshed up' as Mrs Beeding called it, and she remained very small and rather plain, with her pale complexion, straight features and large light-brown eyes, and her pigtail of fine dark hair with a ripple in it. Her hair and her pearls of teeth were her only beauties.

Edie was not a solemn woman. She brought Amy up very simply, with as little fuss as she kept house in whatever three-roomed flat Tim chose to dump his family down. Always put things away after you, she told Amy; change your shoes when you come in from a walk, keep your neck wrapped up in cold weather, brush your hair and wash your face and clean your teeth every night, no matter how tired you are. Don't bolt your food. Be polite to old people. Be loving to little children and animals. Don't answer back, count ten instead. (Yes, I know I do, but I'm grown up. It's different for grown-ups.) Don't walk on the grass except in the summer, when it's dry. Try and change your underclothing twice a week. (One of the earliest pictures Amy remembered was her small knickers and petticoats, white flannel in winter, white cotton in summer, drying on the clothes-horse in front of the gas stove. Tim would dodge carefully round the horse three times, then snatch it up and carry it to a far corner, setting it down so violently that it quivered and a petticoat fell on the floor.)

Say your prayers every night, Edie told her little daughter. Our Father Which Art in Heaven, is the best one. It says everything you want, you see; asking God for your food, and to forgive you for being naughty, and saying you'll try to do what He wants you to, and asking Him to save you from all the bad, cruel things in the world. But Edie did not tell Amy what the bad, cruel things were because she herself was not very conscious of them. They were all about her, but though she knew that they were there, they could not frighten her or make her feel that life was dreadful.

But Amy was frightened. When she and Edie went shopping she held on very tightly to her mother's hand because the people were so big and bumped into her so hard. The sharp smell of fruit, the faint sick smell at the butcher's, the choking wood and paraffin smell in the ironmonger's, were all too strong for her and made her long to get outside the shops. The broad cruel wheels of the 'buses frightened her and the blunt snouts of motor-cars.

'There's nothing to be frightened of, pet.' Her mother's words went like a comforting song through her childhood. 'Mother's here. It's all right.'

Edie read her daughter stories about brave men who fought Indians or rescued people from wrecked ships or rode for help through mountain passes where lurked the cruel savages. 'Now *you* must be like that,' Edie would end cheerfully, slapping the book shut. 'He wasn't afraid, was he?'

'Wasn't he ever afraid, *once*, Mum? Not one teeny, teeny bit, no bigger than *that*?' A finger and thumb of doll-like smallness were held out, almost touching, while Amy gazed up earnestly into her mother's face. 'Not once. Not one teeny bit,' very firmly. 'Now you be like that too, lovey. God will always take care of you if only you aren't afraid, and it will all come right in the end. You'll see.'

So Amy grew up with Captain Scott and the boy riders of the Pony Express for her heroes, and later on Lindbergh and the first airmen to make solo flights across deserts and oceans; and the films she liked best were Westerns. She was not brought

up like a boy, for she played no games at school except a little
genteel netball and all her private pastimes, such as cutting out
paper figures or writing stories, were peaceful and quiet, but her
mind, partly because of its natural turn and partly because of
Edie's training, was very unlike the minds of other little girls of
her age and had a boy-like directness.

Just after Amy's eleventh birthday, when they had been at
Highbury eight months, Edie was sitting one day in the sitting-
room of the Highbury flat, letting down the hem of her daughter's
gym tunic and thinking about her. If only she can get over this
nerviness, being afraid of the traffic and all that, and Tim doesn't
chuck up his job with that old scream of a *Prize* and she can
stay on at school, she ought to be all right, bless her. She's
grown a lot this term, but she's no thinner than she was last,
and that's a good sign . . . now I suppose this ought to be finished
off with prussian binding . . . I'll just run round and get a bit.
Shan't fag to change my shoes, even if they do let water. Edie
slipped on her coat and hurried out into the rain in her house
shoes. She caught a cold that turned to influenza, and in a week
she was dead.

The grief that fell upon her husband and daughter was dreadful,
and the worst part of it was that they could not comfort each
other, because they had never loved each other; and now that
Edie, who loved both of them so much, had gone, they were
like two strangers, suffering the same misery under the same
roof, yet each quite alone.

At first Tim did try to be kinder and more affectionate to
Amy, because he knew Edie would have wanted him to, but it
was no use. He never had been any good with the kid and she
so got on his nerves, creeping about the place looking like a
tiny old woman, that he soon gave up and relapsed into his own
wretchedness. He had plenty to do keeping himself sober enough
to do his day's work without being sacked, and then getting
through the evenings somehow with the help of drinks and

gambling and Old Porty, and for the first few months after Edie's death he saw very little of his daughter. Slowly, very slowly, the ghastly wound made by death began to ache less unbearably. Then boredom and restlessness fell on him like twin demons; for not only had Edie been the only person he loved, but she had made life endurable for him; while she was there he had felt there was some point in the business of living. Now she had gone, there was none. He kept his job because they would have starved if he hadn't, and Edie wouldn't have wanted Amy to starve, and to starve would be even more boring than to drag on in the job. But he did not care if he lived or died. Many men say as much: he meant it.

A year after Edie's death, they were both beginning to get used to it. Amy's grief no longer offended her father's sensibility quite so violently, for she had learned to keep her feelings even more to herself than was natural to her as a reserved child; and Tim was discovering how to keep the nicest possible balance between drunkenness and sobriety, being never quite sober yet showing none of the signs of being drunk and thus having the best of both worlds.

She kept out of his way as much as she could. She had to get breakfast for them both, but he was usually out in the evenings and a good deal at week-ends with Old Porty and the rest of the boys, so it was easy for her to avoid him. He gave her thirty shillings a week for housekeeping, and thirty to Mrs Beeding for the rent, and kept three pounds for himself. Amy did the shopping after she came home from school, and the cooking, and kept the rooms tidy, and once a month Mrs Beeding scrubbed them over.

It was a regular, quiet, busy life. If only she had not missed her mother so dreadfully and had not been afraid of her father, Amy would have enjoyed it; and she did manage to enjoy school and sometimes going to the cinema, pasting up her pictures and slowly filling exercise books with long exciting stories.

Only there was no one to read them to, now. She went on reading them aloud, pretending that her mother was there listening, because often she got so interested that she forgot anyone was supposed to be there, but it always ended in the same way, with her head down on her arms in an agony of tears.

Tim knew that she wrote stories. He never asked her about them and she never spoke of them to him, but he was not so unobservant as to think his daughter a dull, stupid little thing because she was quiet; her school reports on all subjects, from Botany to Needlework, were rather surprisingly good. His attitude to her would have been the same had she been a beautiful, lively, glowing child. He did not like children; they bored him, and it was too much trouble to get to know his own. Poor monkey, was his tenderest thought of her; she doesn't have much of a life. But she seemed content enough. He knew she fretted for her mother, of course . . . Christ, so did he. There was nothing to be done about that. But she had her bits of things, and her school and that little horror Mona Beeding to run around with. It was a pity about her accent, and her thinness, but a man couldn't be expected to hold down a job nowadays and be a dry-nurse into the bargain, and she would have to take her chance, that was all.

3

A week after Robert Vorst and his mother and aunt got back from Europe, the family gave a party at their home just outside Vine Falls to celebrate the return.

The trees in front of the old white house were rosy and dark yellow, and some of the soft yet brilliant leaves lay about on the deep green grass. Sharlie Vorst, Bob's mother, had left them there because she thought they looked pretty, and Webster Vorst, Bob's father, did not mind them being there because that was not the kind of thing he noticed. The drive was crowded with cars. In a big room off the hall the radio was in full blast and some of the young people were dancing, and in a little closet half-hidden at the end of a passage and used as a store for over-shoes and the children's coasters, there was an improvised bar.

At five that morning when the big frosty stars were flashing down over the red maples, the cases of liquor had come up through the dim dewy woods on the shoulders of Webster Vorst and the handyman, Myron Blodgett, and below on the road outside Carr's gasoline station a car had driven quickly away.

It was neither dignified nor a good example to his young sons for a man of fifty-six, owner of three newspapers founded by his grandfather and left to him by his father, to carry his own hooch at dawn through the woods. Webster Vorst knew this. He also knew that as a good citizen and a public figure in Vine Falls he should not encourage the Carrs by buying liquor made in their illicit still. They were worthless people, who had drifted in the last two years from mere shiftlessness and debt to law-breaking, and it was the duty of Webster Vorst to condemn them in the columns of *The Vine Falls Inquirer*, *The Paul County Sentinel*, and *The Vinebridge Citizen* and to have nothing to do with them in his private life.

He knew this. But he did not feel it.

Neither he nor the other respectable citizens of Vine Falls could look on the Carrs as dangerous bootleggers; they were just the Carrs, one of the oldest families in Vine Falls, whose fortunes had steadily declined, while those of the Vorsts had as steadily risen, ever since Webster's grandfather had founded *The Sentinel*, *The Citizen* and *The Inquirer* way back in the eighteen-forties.

Now the Carrs kept a gasoline and hot-dog store at the foot of the hill behind the Vorst place, and were making money by 'alky-cooking' (illicit distilling). This was against the law. Everybody in Vine Falls knew it, but somehow it was not easy to take the attitude of stern, noble American citizens and hand the Carrs over to the Sheriff of the County (who would thus have lost his rake-off on the profits from the Carrs' still) and it certainly did not occur to Vine Falls to refuse to buy the liquor the Carrs made. The sympathies of Vine Falls were secretly with the Carrs, and with the hundreds of other hijackers and alky-cookers all over America who were light-heartedly risking death from the prohibition agents' guns so that honest red-blooded Americans might have a drink. Indeed, the whole United States, watching the battle in those golden years of the Coolidge Prosperity Era, felt itself back in the old cops-and-robbers game of its youth, and as the robbers stood for thrills and the defiance of a damfool law nobody wanted, public opinion towards the bootleggers was inclined to be indulgent.

It would be unsporting, as well as difficult and inconvenient, to take strong action against the Carrs.

Breaking the law was exciting, too. Respectable American business men could understand the kick the gangsters got out of it. Webster Vorst had delighted in that dawn journey through the hushed woods, the cold smell of the mist, the sudden shriek and flutter as a bird went up under his feet, making him feel eleven years old and a Redskin again! And every man who went off to a business convention with bottles of gin hidden in his grip, every woman who answered the whispered question through the speakeasy grille, felt the same excitement.

Most of the older people and the children were in the garden behind the house, where the warm sunlight of an Indian summer afternoon made it pleasant to eat and drink on the lawn under the shady trees. It was just half-past four, and everyone asked to the party had arrived. As well as Vorsts and Viners and their relations of all ages, there were friends from Vinebridge and nearby towns with their children, and old people who could remember the passing of the prairie-schooners through Vine Falls on their way to the Golden West fifty years ago; people who had seen the town's two oldest families founded and watched Vorsts and Viners growing up and marrying each other and starting families in their turn.

Charming faces these old people had, from which shone, as naturally as its scent floats from any woodsy bush, a dry and quiet humour. They liked to get hold of the children who were darting between the chatting groups and get them into corners, and ask them how they were getting on in school, and tartly accuse them, under a cool aged eye that was still able to quell any child living, of being 'a sight too smart nowadays to come in sometime and eat one of my cookies; yes y'are, you're real smart and grown-up, too smart for me nowadays.'

'Bob,' said Mrs Vorst to her younger son, who was leaning against an elm tree eating an ice. 'Where's all the rest of you . . . Stebby and Lou and Helen and Irene? They're not down at Carr's, are they?' suspiciously.

Bob jerked his fair head towards a beautiful child in a white organdie dress who was standing round the other side of the tree and listening, with her hands behind her back, to one of the woodsy old persons.

'Helen's right there with Miss Cordell. She's all right. I asked her if she would like to come with us and she said no, 'cause she was afraid she'd muss up her frock.'

He did not look at his mother, but carefully scooped up the last bit of ice cream.

'Where were you all going where Helen would muss up her frock?' probed his parent keenly. 'You haven't been down to Carrs', have you?'

He did not answer.

'Have you, Bob?' irritably. 'Are the others down there now?'

'Oh, Mother, we only went down for a minute to tell Francey she couldn't come to the party, honest we did. 'N I came back right away to get this ice, but they just stayed down there a little while, just to kind of talk to Francey. They'll be right back, they said so.'

'Now, Bob, you go down there this minute and tell them to come back here right away,' she commanded, putting her thin, pretty brown hand on his shoulder and moving him unwillingly across the lawn towards the wood that marked the end of the Vorst land. 'I told you this morning. I won't have you running round with Francey and Dan any more, and here you are disobeying me already. Now, understand once and for all, Robert, you are *not* to go down to Carrs' and play with Francey or talk to Dan. Do you understand me?'

'Yes, Mother, but——'

'Now just you promise.' She gave his shoulder a little shake, more like a push, and full of love, but she looked severely down into the grey eyes laughing up into her own.

'Oh, *Mom*! Gee, I don't want to. Must I?'

'Yes, you must, and don't say "gee!" Come on, now, promise. Yes, I said "promise". It's as important as that. Come along, now. Hurry up.'

'All right,' he said resignedly, and gabbled, 'I-promise-on-my-honour-as-an-American-I-won't-go-down-to-Carr's-or-play-with-Francey-Carr-again. Can I say "hullo" to Francey and Dan if I see them on the street, Mother?'

'Well . . . I suppose so. I don't want you to be rude or unkind, but——'

'Oh, Francey doesn't mind what a fellow says to her. Jonas and me told her she was a cheap skate the other day. "Francey," we told her, "you're a cheap skate".'

'Then that was very rude of you and Jonas and just what a couple of boys who were cheap skates themselves would say to a girl. Go on, now, run and tell the others to come right back.'

She paused at the edge of the wood that went downhill, and he paused as well, looking up into her dark face and the long languid brown eyes that made the brisk matrons of Vine Falls say of her: *Sharlie Vorst certainly has got that kind of elegant Southern look.* Even the shortness of the white chiffon dress fluttering just below her knees and her closely-shingled dark hair could not spoil the dignity which came to her from her deep femininity and her strain of Creole blood.

'Mother, is it because the Carrs are bootleggers you don't want me to talk to Francey and Dan? Everybody says they are.'

Mrs Vorst hesitated. Then she said gravely: 'Yes, it is. They're in with a bad crowd, Dad says, a dangerous crowd——'

'Gee!' said her son, with shining eyes.

('Don't say "gee!") And there's nothing exciting or brave about them, either. They're just . . .' she hesitated again—'. . . Rats, that's all. I know all you children are always playing gangsters and Feds, and you think it's mighty fine and thrilling, and Boone's always talking about that time he saw Capone and his thugs walk into the theatre in Chicago with guns under their arms and everybody scared stiff . . . but you don't understand. It isn't thrilling at all, it's breaking the law, and the Carrs and Capone are just rats. Remember that.' Her soft drawling voice made the words sound cool and bitter and true.

'Yes, Mother. Gosh, wouldn't I just like to pull in a gangster, though! Oh boy . . . oh boy . . . oh boy!' And he tore down the path into the woods, shouting over his shoulder, 'I'll be right back. You see!'

His mother walked back to her guests, thinking about him, and about the Carrs, and remembering the excited, half-admiring note in Boone's voice when he talked of Capone, and realizing that bootlegged liquor was at this moment being served to the young people as they danced. She was disturbed and rather apprehensive about the bar fixed up in the overshoes closet and those cases of rye coming up through the woods on her husband's shoulder; she sometimes had a frightened feeling that the good fun of breaking a stupid law might end in something that all America would not find good fun at all. A man must have his drink, of course. Her people came from Louisiana and had the easy Southern tradition of lavish drinking. But . . . already boot-legging had ceased to be good fun in Chicago and Toledo and Detroit and had become a terror. And why should terror stop at three cities, when there was all America for the bootlegger to plunder?

I wish Webster could get those Carrs run out of town, she thought, going up to old Miss Cordell and little Helen Viner.

At twelve years old Helen was the beauty of the Vorst-Viner younger set. Old Miss Cordell used to say the child's looks reminded her of Eva's in *Uncle Tom's Cabin*, and then she would prophesy, as St Clair's friend does in the story, '*By George, she'll make some hearts ache, one day!*' But so far Helen was neither coquettish nor vain, and her expression was even more beautiful than her face, with its pale skin and big dark blue eyes and dark red mouth. Her hair, the colour of a dead leaf, was short like that of all the other little girls that year in America, but it curled naturally and her mother had pushed it behind her tiny sensitive ears, making her look 'downright old-fashioned,' as Miss Cordell had just been telling her. She had perfect manners, and an odd attractive sense of humour, and wrote poetry about the woods, but quite the most surprising fact about Helen was that all her tough young cousins loved her tenderly and never felt even a passing desire to push her face in. Bob and she were particularly fond of one another.

Bob ran down the track through the woods until he came to a steep slope overlooking a clearing. At the far end was a shabby clapboard bungalow where hens scratched in the dust. It faced a road that ran through the woods and its walls were crowded with notices . . . HOT DOGS. GASOLINE. TOILETS. FREE AIR AND WATER.

There was a rail fence all round the clearing, but in one place it was broken, and a child could climb through.

In front of the wooden steps at the back of the bungalow three well-dressed children were standing round a fourth, a girl of thirteen with pale red hair, wearing a faded blue frock, who held up a black bottle. Bob slithered down the slope among the briars, not looking where he was going because he was watching the group in the yard.

'Come on!' taunted Francey Carr, pulling the cork out of the bottle. She held it up again. 'I dare you to!'

Slowly, in disapproving silence, the two girls shook their heads. The boy, who was about eight, piped up:

'I will, Francey Carr. I'll drink it. *I'm* not yellow. No, *sir*!'

'Stebby Viner,' roared Bob, but without heat, 'if you dare do any such thing I'll lam you. Come on, all of you. Mother says you're to come right home this minute.'

Startled, the three turned round, then obediently came towards the gap in the fence where Bob was now standing, looking amiably yet a little contemptuously at the girl in the blue dress.

'What you got there, Francey?' he inquired, giving his nine-year-old sister Lou a helping hand through the fence but not taking his eyes off Francey and her bottle.

'Sump'n good,' nodded Francey, her face screwed up and her eyes almost lost in scornful wrinkles. 'Want a drop?'

'I guess not. Don't want to be sick,' he said indifferently, turning away to follow Helen's little brother Stebby.

'Oh, you're yellow, Bob Vorst, that's what you are! 'Fraid cat!'

'No, I am not, so there,' he retorted, not looking round. 'Come on, all you kids, the ices have started.'

'I'm mad at you, Bob Vorst!' Francey flew down to the fence and hung over it, showing all her little white teeth in a grin of rage. 'I wouldn't come to your lousy party now if you went down on your knees an' asked me, I wouldn't. We got more fun down here. Dan's home, an' we——'

'Dan? Is he?' Bob turned round quickly as the four children began to climb the briar-covered slope towards the wood. 'Gee, I'd like to see him! Is he round there now?'

He started to run back towards the clearing, his face alight with excitement and pleasure, while Francey watched him, resting her chin on the black bottle, but suddenly he stopped, and turned back.

'Where you goin' now?' she shouted. 'Come on. Dan's inside. He'll like to see you again.'

He shook his head, turning to face her.

'No, I can't, Francey. 'N I can't tell you why. Gee, I'm sorry. I would've liked to see Dan again. You tell him . . . oh, *darn*! Never mind. Don't tell him anything or say you've seen me. I'm sorry about the party, too, Francey. I did ask Mother if you could come, 'cause you always used to come to our parties, but this time it's different, see?'

She nodded; then, still staring at him, lifted the black bottle to her lips.

'You watch me.' Her voice died away as she began to drink.

A trickle ran down her chin and she choked, but went on drinking.

'*Gee!*' shrieked Stebby, hopping with excitement half-way up the slope, while Irene and Lou halted and looked down at Francey with wide, disapproving, yet excited eyes. 'That's rye in that bottle, Bob . . . she said so! Oh boy . . . oh boy . . . will she be sick!'

'She's crazy.' Bob turned away and resumed the climb.

'There!' yelled Francey, lowering the bottle and staring up at them. 'Who said I wouldn't drink it? Now I'll fight the whole bunch of you.'

None of the four took any notice, for Francey was always trying to start a fight; she loved fighting. Only Stebby was slowly climbing backwards, never taking his eyes off her. Any minute now she would be sick.

'Comin' after berries tomorrow afternoon?' shouted Francey, leaning over the rail with swimming eyes and shaken by hiccoughs. (Gee, I *won't* be sick till they've gone, the lousy bunch, she swore to herself, leaning hard on the rail.)

'Nope.' Bob, the spokesman, did not look round. Now the four were almost at the top of the slope.

'Oh . . . why not?'

'Can't.'

'You mad at me, Bob Vorst?'

'Nope. I guess not. You haven't done anything to me, Francey Carr. But we can't come. Not any of us. Ever again. Get that?'

He turned round to shout this down to her, and the girls turned with him; Stebby had never ceased to climb backwards and watch her. She saw the four little figures standing against the crimson splendour of the fall woods, the girls in their light dresses with short bright hair, dark Stebby in white shirt and corduroy knickers, fair sturdy Bob in a blue shirt and tweed knickerbockers with one lock falling across his eyes.

'G'd-bye, Francey,' they called, waving. 'G'd-bye.' But Francey, leaning hard on the rail, felt too sick to answer and could only wave.

'Now she can't say we didn't say good-bye to her 'n start a fight,' explained Bob, as they went into the rustling, cool-smelling woods. 'Mother says we aren't ever to talk to her again, Irene and Lou . . . and that goes for you too, Stebby Viner, I guess Aunt Carol would say so, anyway. Understand?'

'Sure, if Mother says so,' murmured Irene, a pretty, conventional child of fourteen who was already more interested in styles and smuggled copies of *True Story* than in kids' games. 'But why, Bob? What's she done? We've always played with Francey ever since we were little.'

'Never you mind. You go read your old *Vogue*,' and Bob mincingly arranged an imaginary hat. 'Francey's a crazy girl and her folks are bad.'

'Sure. They're bootleggers,' said the nine-year-old Lou coolly, looking up at her brother with grey eyes like his own and shaking back the same lock of fair hair.

'You shut up. You're too little to know about bootleggers,' said Bob crushingly. 'Who told you, anyway?'

'Myron did. He said Dan got in a fight with the O'Banion gang when he was in Morgan.'

'Gosh, did he?' said Bob. '*Gee!* Why didn't he tell me?'

'"Cause you're too smarty. You don't think about anything but your old ball game, Myron says. But he told me,' ended Lou proudly. 'He always tells me everything.'

'Well, you oughtn't to listen, Miss Smarty yourself. Girls oughtn't to know about rats like the O'Banions. Gee, I'd've liked to see Dan, though! I wish I hadn't promised Mother. I haven't seen him for a year, not since he went to Morgan to get a job. We used to have good times shooting, remember? Oh . . . I guess it doesn't matter. Come on.'

He ground his knuckles expertly into the neck of Stebby,

who writhed himself free, and all four tore away along the track under the gorgeous canopy of the trees.

Francey hung on to the rail and presently, without being sick, she felt better. She continued to stare up at the woods where the children had vanished with a sullen look on her face. There was a faintly degenerate look about her large pale blue eyes and pale full mouth, and she seemed dirty and uncared-for in a dry, wind-tossed way. The children all thought her ugly and made fun of her dumbness and her limp red hair. All the good that had come to Francey from her original sound American stock was a beautiful body and her courage; she was afraid of nothing but her brother Dan.

Presently, from behind a tattered blind over a corner of the porch, a man's voice, low and young, called:

'Fran.'

'What?' she said, without moving.

'Come here.'

'Don't want to,' she said, half-looking round and tightening her clasp on the rail.

He said nothing. Presently, very slowly, she walked across to the porch and stood by the blind, looking down at the ground. All she could thus see of her brother was his foot in a tan shoe and a dark violet silk sock.

'If you drink that stuff again I'll knock your front teeth in,' he said in the same low voice, rustling the newspaper he held. 'If we're goin' to do what I said, you got to learn to do without that stuff. Understand?'

'Sure I do, Dan,' she said eagerly. 'I don't really like it. I was only showin' that lousy bunch——'

'I know . . . I know . . . but they ain't worth showin'. Remember what I said.'

'You used to like Bob.'

'Sure I did. But we were on'y kids then, an' he's soft. They're all soft. You and I gotta be hard, Fran. So you lay off them. Understand?'

'Bob said they aren't to go with me any more.'

'Well, isn't that what I'm tellin' ya? On'y I wished we'd got in first and told the lousy bastards they wasn't good enough for us before they told us, that's all. Shut up, will ya. I want to read this.'

The paper rustled again, and he was quiet. Presently she sat down on the porch step at his feet, picked up part of the paper that had slipped to the ground, and became absorbed in the pictures.

Up in the garden of the house most of the older guests were saying good-bye to Sharlie Vorst while the younger people were making plans to drive out to the nearest country club and dine there and dance.

Boone, the eldest Vorst boy, was a little drunk. He came quickly down the portico steps with his arm round Jeanette Waldron, a ripe beauty of nineteen from a nearby town, whose looks had that exotic touch sometimes found in American girls with Middle European emigrant blood and were carefully tended as those of a Manchu princess. Her rosy knees showed between her rolled stockings and yellow skirt.

'But we'll need to change,' she was protesting.

'We will not. No-one does nowadays. Come on. I need a drink.'

'You've had one.'

'Sure I have, but I want another.'

'All right . . . oh, there's your father! I must just kiss him good-bye!'

She ran up the steps to Webster Vorst, who stood laughing down at the young people, and stood on tiptoe and flung her arms round his neck.

'G'd-bye, darling!'

45

'Why . . . hey . . . it's little Jeanette! Not going, are you?' He returned her kiss quickly and held her away from him, looking down with a little embarrassment into her exquisite face.

'Boone wants to drive out somewhere and dance with the crowd.'

'On your way, then. I suppose we can expect you with the milk.'

'Sure!'

She gave him another hug, pressing her body against him, and ran down the steps and into the car.

'Do you have to do that?' said Boone, his handsome curly head lowered sulkily, when they had driven for a couple of miles in silence.

'Do what, sunshine?'

'Kiss Dad . . . like that . . . every time you see him?'

'I like him. He's got what you haven't.'

'Thanks. Why bother with me at all, then?'

'Oh, you're sweet sometimes, when I feel that way. Get going, will you? I'm thirsty.'

She settled back in her seat, arranged her leopard-skin coat, and carefully painted her mouth. She enjoyed kissing Boone's tall father, whose silver hair looked so distinguished above his hatchet Redskin face, and she enjoyed still more the look on the faces of Miss Cordell and all the other lousy old bluenoses, including that skinny bit of the Old South, Mrs Vorst, when she did it. It amused her and woke them up.

'Quite sure you've finished?' she asked sarcastically, as Boone lowered the flask from which he had been taking a long pull and handed it to her.

'Ah, don't be like that, Jeanette. Let's stop here and . . .'

He parked the car under the tall crimson maples rustling dryly in the evening wind, and they fell into one another's arms.

Sharlie Vorst stood beside her husband on the porch waving good-bye to the last of her guests and thinking how well the

46

party had gone off. But then her parties always went well, and had done so for twenty-five years. It was fun giving parties. She did hope that Webster's crazy notion about *The Sentinel*, *The Inquirer* and *The Citizen* having to be taken over by that New York syndicate quite soon if their circulations and the advertising did not improve *was* only a crazy notion. Of course, a lot of the old privately-owned newspapers had gone over into syndicate-control since the European war; and most every week she seemed to meet some writer or cartoonist or reporter who could no longer earn a living from his local paper because the syndicates were supplying all the necessary material from head offices in New York.

It was tough on local newspapermen, but then, everything had speeded up so since that War.

Of course, if the three papers were bought up by a syndicate, Webster would get a good price and his family would still be comfortable. But it was kind of nice, being married to the owner of those three old papers (here she slipped her hand through the owner's arm and pulled him slowly round so that they could walk back to the house together) and she certainly did hope that when Boone had finished college and went into the news-paper game his father would still be owning *The Sentinel*, *The Inquirer*, and *The Citizen*.

And thinking of Boone she said slowly in her soft drawl:

'Webster, I dislike that Jeanette Waldron. I don't think she's a nice little girl. I wish Boone wasn't so crazy about her.'

Mr Vorst looked a little embarrassed. For some time he had found it difficult to think of Jeanette as a wild but harmless and charming child, and the last thing he wanted was to discuss her with his wife. The handsome face looked more intelligent than it was: he was a rather stupid but honest man who loved his wife, his family, and his home, and disliked and feared the bold modern girl.

He said uneasily: 'Oh . . . there's no harm in her. All the boys and girls are wild nowadays; look at Frankwood's lot . . . out all night in their car and drinking like little fishes, but it doesn't seem to harm them. They're nice kids enough. It's the same everywhere since the War. It only seems odd to you and me, Sharlie, because we were brought up so differently . . .'

'I certainly was. Mamma'd have had the hide off me if I'd as much as asked might I smoke a cigarette.'

'Vine Falls is a long sight better than most places in that way. Our boys and girls are still straight. They like speeding and . . . and a little petting, but they're clean, Sharlie.'

'I don't think Jeanette is. I think she's a bad girl.'

'Oh, come! There's no harm in her. She's only crazy, like the rest. They'll all marry and settle down in a year or two, you'll see.'

'I hope Jeanette won't marry Boone.'

'You think of nothing, Sharlie, but who'll marry who. You were marrying Bob off to Helen the other day, and him not thirteen.'

Her face grew tender.

'That would be lovely. There's nothing I'd like better.'

'And for Lou to marry Stebby, I suppose?'

She laughed.

'They'd fight all day; they do now. Now, Webster, will you please go right along this minute and get Blodgett to clear up that disgraceful mess in the closet. I'm going up to take a shower.'

At the foot of the stairs she paused, her eye caught by the view through the open front door and enchanted for an instant by the evening sunlight on the motionless gold branches of the maples, and the glimpses of deep, cool blue sky between the red leaves. Her gaze moved over the five-pointed yellow and rosy ones scattered here and there on the soft green grass, and turned at last to the familiar roofs of the town, the spire of the Catholic church and the gleam of the river in the little valley below. This certainly is a good place to live, she thought contentedly, going up the stairs. It all went off very well this afternoon, and weren't the children just lovely! Everybody said so. She felt thankful that the three younger ones would not be thinking about petting and speeding and drinking for a year or two.

Singing in a low voice she went into the bathroom. As for the Carrs, hidden in their shabby bungalow down in the woods, she did not think about them at all.

4

Amy did not find the Anna Bonner School for Girls an appalling place full of nasal little rats. She enjoyed writing and cutting out paper figures more than she enjoyed school, but she liked school, too. She had no best friend, for she was not the kind of child that has a best friend, but there were three or four little girls with whom she usually walked round eating biscuits at Break and had mild little jokes with. They exchanged the gossip of school—so bright within its narrow frame—and said isn't-it-*ghastly* to one another about the homework.

Perhaps no other school in London would have made such a satisfactory refuge for a secretive little girl who was grieving passionately for her dead mother, for the Anna Bonner was a good place for dreamers. It was a private school of some ninety girls, founded in the 'eighties by a rich brewer's daughter who had been a pupil-teacher under the famous Frances Mary Buss, and was housed in a grey stone building in one of the quiet roads of Highbury not ten minutes walk from where Amy lived. It cannot be said that the Anna Bonner worked hard and played hard. Indeed, one ambitious and energetic member of the educational world had been known to refer to it as a nest of lazy hounds. But the Founder was still alive, a very old lady living at St Leonards-on-Sea, and although it was many years since she had retired from active headmistress-ship, the school was still her chief interest and she dealt very sharply with any attempts to pep it up. Miss Bonner had not been deeply influenced by Miss Buss's ideals, much as she had respected that pioneer, and she had her own ideas about the education of girls and what a girls' school should be. 'A cool frame for most seedlings, not a forcing house,' she was wont to say to her staff, for she was a devout gardener.

As a result of the Founder's influence, carried on by one of her great-nieces as headmistress, the Anna Bonner was an old-fashioned, pre-War type of school in which the best of the Victorian virtues were inculcated, and a well-balanced character, with proficiency in needlework and the domestic arts, was regarded as being of more use to the type of girl who attended there than the higher education and proficiency at games. The staff was contented if unambitious, and the girls had a quiet, pleasant place in which they could get through the time while waiting to grow up. No one at the Anna Bonner was *earnest*. While no one actually said to a girl who had muffed an exam: 'Never mind, dear, worse troubles at sea, and tea's nearly ready,' the words were implied in the slow-paced, unselfconscious atmosphere of the plain little school building. The daughters of prosperous tradesmen and managers of departments in big North London shops who went there always kept an affection for the old place; and most of them remembered what they had been taught about cooking and sewing and cutting out clothes. Miss Anna Bonner asked for nothing more ambitious.

In this mild little world Amy's intense grief for her mother was not suspected, and no one cared what her home life was like so long as her fees were paid regularly and she behaved like all the other little girls, which she did. Her work was so fault-lessly neat in its presentation that she was rather popular with the staff; otherwise, nothing but her pigtail distinguished her from the other seventy-nine pupils in the school.

Here she came five days out of the seven, moving quietly up and down the long bare corridors where budding branches or sprays of autumn leaves stood in the windows, changing with the season of the year against the white sky of Spring or the yellow sky of winter; or bent daily over her desk while an aeroplane droned above the school, taking no more notice of it than the schoolgirls of the 'eighties at the same desks had taken of the sound made by a passing hansom.

Once every six weeks or so she would ask her form mistress if she might have a new rough note-book.

'But, Amy, you've got through the last one very quickly, haven't you, dear? Let me see it.' (The Anna Bonner was one of the few schools left in London where the teachers called the girls 'dear'.)

Amy would silently hold out a note-book and quickly turn over the pages, full of her writing and calculations.

'Yes, it's quite full, isn't it! Very well, dear, ask Margery if you can have a new one.'

Then Amy would put away the used note-book in her desk, where it would stay until it came out in another six weeks to deceive her form mistress again; and carry home the new one to begin Volume Four of *The Wolf of Leningrad*. The school rough note-books were exactly the right size for lavish comfortable scribbling and there was always such a lot to be done with her shilling a week pocket money that she was pleased to get her writing-books for nothing.

This was not the only small deception she had taken to since her mother's death. Scarcely a day passed on which she did not tell a lie or deceive somebody by keeping silent when most girls would have spoken, but she deceived and lied so naturally that she never felt guilty about these attempts to keep bullies at bay, and idly inquisitive people out of her secret world. Since her mother's death she had bitterly learned that a child is not even safe if it keeps still, and quiet, and tries not to upset people. Her father and Old Porty, Dora Beeding and Mrs Beeding, and even Mona, her nearest approach to a best friend, were always picking on her about her accent or teasing her, trying to organize her spare time or worrying her to tell what she did in the evenings with the sitting-room door locked. Against all such intrusions into her secret life she had no weapons except deceit and lies, and naturally she used them.

By the time her mother had been dead a year, she was rapidly developing into a sly little girl.

But she was no longer such a coward as when her mother was alive: she knew that, and when she lay in bed at night in the dark, talking to her mother, she would tell her what brave thing she had done that day. Mother, I touched the wheel of a motor bus while I was waiting to cross. I waited in Sainsbury's for the butter and looked at the cut-up rabbits for ever so long and I didn't feel sick. Mother, you are pleased, aren't you? I do remember what you said about being brave. I'm not really afraid of anything now, except Dad when he's had a drop too much and Mrs Beeding reading *The Wolf of Leningrad*. I can't bear to think of anyone reading it except you. Please, please, God, let me dream about Mother. Amen.

On the evenings when she did not feel like writing, she would bring out the cardboard box in which she collected her pictures and sort them into two heaps, one for pasting up in her bedroom and one for cutting out, and spend the evening cutting out paper figures.

Sometimes she flew cut-outs out of her bedroom window on long pieces of cotton. It was exciting to murmur a story about some lovely girl from the cover of a fashion paper, as she fluttered near the branch of a tree, and when she was hopelessly tangled there to send her lover out on another piece of cotton to rescue her. He usually lost his life in the attempt, either getting torn in half when Amy tried to pull him free of the branch or else fluttering away on the night wind when the cotton snapped. Far, far over the dim gardens lit by the faint autumn moon he would sail, and Amy, leaning out of the window to watch his flight, would murmur the story to a close:

'*In a remote corner of the savage jungle, far from the civilizing influence of the white man, a lonely figure haunts the glades. None of the wondering cannibals know his name or his history. His leg is shackled with a huge rope. It is Buck Finch, who gave up his heritage as a white man for love. Will he ever return? Who knows . . . who knows?'*

Then she would draw her head in and shut the window. The room seemed very bright and cosy after the dimness and scudding silver clouds outside, and she felt hungry, so she would eat a slice of bread and treacle while turning over the contents of another box neatly labelled 'Curios.'

There was a sprig of white coral wrapped in a paper inscribed '*White* coral from Capri (Italy). Given to A. Lee, 12 Highbury Walk, Highbury, London, England, Europe, The World, Space, by Mr X, a friend of her father, T. Lee (Mr X's name is unfortunately forgotten as A. Lee was only eight years of age at the time the coral was given).' The box also contained a green jade heart labelled 'Jade heart from New Zealand. Bought for the sum of £2,000 (twopence) from a tray outside a second-hand shop in Holloway Road. The vendor told A. Lee that it came from New Zealand.'

And into this box she had put the coin given her by the American boy outside Kenwood House on her birthday, wrapped in a paper on which she had written:

'American coin given to A. Lee as a birthday present by Robert Somebody, an American boy from Vine Falls, Paul County, New Leicester, America, on the said A. Lee's twelfth birthday, October 31st, 1928.'

She was still not quite sure whether he had given it to her in mistake for a shilling or as a spiteful joke, and each time she unwrapped the paper to look at it, this doubt crept in and disturbed the tranquil pleasure of her collector's mood; but, remembering his face and the way he had looked at her and making allowances for the fact that boys always hated girls and thought they were soppy, he had seemed a kind boy, not the sort that would play a spiteful joke on a person, especially when he knew it was their birthday, and much nicer than the boys whom Amy, through Mona Beeding, occasionally had dealings with in Highbury.

That boy, Robert Somebody, had made her think of the brave boys her mother used to read to her about; the fourteen-year-old Pony Express rider who shot half a score of Indians in a dead end of the mountains before their arrows got him at last, whom the Redskins would not dishonour by scalping because he was so brave and his hair (they said) 'was like the rays of the sun'; and the fifteen-year-old Nelson on his Greenland voyage leaving the ship at night with one of his comrades to pursue a bear across the ice, which he attacked crying 'Do but let me get a blow at this devil with the butt end of my musket and we shall have him.'

Amy was sure that the Pony Express riders and the young Nelson must have looked like the American boy at Kenwood, and she often wondered about him. What was he doing at that particular moment, far away in America? Had he any brothers and sisters? She had found New Leicester and Paul County and Vine Falls on the big tattered old atlas which she used as a hunting ground for names of places in her stories, and now they were as real to her as the American boy himself. She wished that they could be friends. She had often wished this about boys in books, but never before about a real boy, because the Highbury boys had such a way of rushing out and bumping into her, bursting open her attaché case full of school books and sending them all over the pavement, that it was quite impossible to imagine being friends with them. But she was sure that if she had been friends with that American boy he would have been different. He would have taken her on exciting expeditions without once reminding her that she was a girl, and when she saved his life he would have thanked her in the proper way in a voice that trembled as he wrung her hand.

On the evenings when she did not feel like cutting out or writing, she would take one of the shabby old novels from the bookshelf and sit in front of the stove, dreaming over it rather than reading, for she knew all the books in her father's small library almost by heart. Most of the books had belonged to Tim as an undergraduate and had travelled round with him as his later fortunes rose and fell, getting some rough handling. But they were sturdy late Victorian editions that wore well enough to shame the cardboard backs of today; and their thick paper, good type, touch of gilding on the cover and charming end-papers, thrown in out of sheer grace, made any reader sensitive to books feel that here was a friend; a good story well dressed. Tim did not care for reading nowadays, but he had grown up with books like these, and their stories were part of that mental furniture which stays in a man's head through the steepest ups and downs. His own taste was for the minor classic, a type of book that has perhaps given more pure pleasure to more readers than any other kind, and as soon as Amy could read he had put her on to *The Cloister and the Hearth*, *A Gentleman of France*, *Tom Burke of 'Ours'*, *King Solomon's Mines* and many others.

But Amy also had her own library, and it was chiefly one of books about America.

The Wide, Wide World, given to her by her mother on her tenth birthday, had first fascinated her with its pictures of life in New England, its domestic details which were so different from those of England and yet so cosy-sounding. Ellen Montgomery had had biscuits and fried chicken for breakfast! And there was the mysterious incident of the birch-bark, when Miss Fortune (Amy hated Miss Fortune) dipped all Ellen's white socks into a brew made from it, and turned them grey. America sounded a lovely place; Amy longed to hear more about it. The people talked English. If you went there, you would not be frightened because they were foreigners, and yet they were different enough to be interesting. And Amy began to linger by second-hand bookstalls, hunting for stories about America. Presently she found *What Katy Did*, and the other Katy books; and then *Little Women and Good Wives*, and later on the Indians of Fenimore Cooper crept into her imagination, treacherous and brilliant as swamp snakes. And then she found *Uncle Tom's Cabin*, with the wild-voiced slaves of the South, and *Dred: a Tale of the Great Dismal Swamp* by the same author, and a wonderful book called *Down the Mississippi*, about some children and a little negro boy who were swept away in a flood down the mighty river on the roof of the cabin in which they lived. And she found *St Elmo*, with its wicked Southern hero and Edna, its lovely, learned heroine and the rich house bowered in magnolia flowers. She found *Daisy* and *Daisy in the Field*, and *Say and Seal*, with its shy saintly heroine, and leisurely blue rivers on whose shores the characters held clambakes. And last of all (but these belong not to America but to the world) on a misty November evening, on a stall of filthy and dog-eared books guarded by a shivering old man, she found a copy of *The Poems and Tales of Edgar Allan Poe*, and the magic circle was complete.

The volume was illustrated with blackish drawings taken from old wood blocks, and these, with the poems and tales, exercised upon her imagination a haunting spell, half horror, half fascination. After her mother's death, when she began trying to be brave, one of the tests she set herself was to read one of the Tales without putting her hand over the picture to hide it as she read. But gradually the stories and poems began to charm as well as to haunt her, and at length she came to love them, part of her pleasure coming from her self-taught power to look at the picture of The Pit and the Pendulum, or the Lady Ligeia's Burial, without fear (or with fear driven so deeply below the surface of her mind that she no longer knew it existed).

In all these tests of courage her only desire was to make herself the brave girl that her mother had wanted her to be. She herself did not care if she were brave or a coward. She never thought, 'It would be nicer and much more comfortable if I didn't mind things, like Mona'; she secretly despised Mona because the latter never noticed the cut-up rabbits, the strong smells and noises and brutal wheels that frightened herself. Had her mother not tried to make her brave, Amy would have accepted her own cowardice without a second thought, for she was as unselfconscious as it is possible for a female organism to be; and her pretences at being a cowboy, a spy, the young Nelson, went on without ever tapping the sealed wells of introspection.

When her mother had been dead for a year, an enormous space of time in a child's world, Amy's picture of her had become crystallized yet dim, and she could no longer think with certainty, 'Mother would have done this or that.' Thus it never occurred to her that her mother would have teased her wholesomely about this desperate effort to make herself brave. The last thing Edie had wanted was for her beloved little daughter to be solemn, and she had loved to make Amy's rare laughter ring out, to see her still, light brown eyes dance with amusement over some shared joke. She used to say that Amy had the nicest laugh she had ever heard, a fat deep sound that made anyone who heard it begin to laugh out of sheer infection, and all the funnier because it came out of such a serious little face.

But since Edie died no one could make Amy laugh like that. She giggled with her fellow biscuit-eaters at the Anna Bonner and with Mona Beeding but she never—literally never—laughed, and so lonely was she and so uninterested in her were all the people by whom she was surrounded that none of them ever noticed that they had in their midst a child of twelve who never laughed.

It would not be true to say that she was unhappy. Her life was full but sunless. The sun went out when her mother died, and she lived from that moment in the strange light (like that lying over the landscape before rain, magnifying trees and making distant objects seem near) of her mind's natural country. It was inhabited by heroic figures slightly larger than life-size, and of these the little American boy, whose real nature and background were so completely the opposite of Amy's own, was one. She thought of him, from time to time, as her *own* American, her own special and private representative of the United States of America, and as such he was dear to her as *The Wolf of Leningrad* and the young Nelson; and all the other dwellers in her private world.

One night just before Christmas Eve, Amy was leaning out of the Highbury sitting-room window to get a breath of fresh air, staring at the glittering lights sweeping upwards on the hills of Hampstead and Highgate and the roofs glistening with frost under the small violet moon. Her head was dutifully wrapped up in an old jersey that had belonged to her mother, because this was what her mother would have made her do. The air smelled of coldness and soot. Her hands, tucked in the rough jersey, felt warm against her cheeks. She was dreaming, not thinking about anything, only feeling how exciting was the scene spread before her.

Suddenly the side door of the house slammed and she looked down. Dora Beeding ran down the street with no hat on towards the public telephone box on the corner. Amy could hear the quick sound of her high heels on the pavement as she ran and once she slipped on the frost and only just saved herself from falling. She watched her jamming the pennies into the box, and impatiently waiting with the receiver at her ear, and saw her talking eagerly and nodding, inside the brightly-lit telephone box like someone on the stage. Then she came running back, and Amy heard the door slam.

A few minutes later a taxi came round the corner and stopped outside the house. The driver climbed out and rang the Beedings' bell, and when the door was opened he went in, leaving a yellow glow of light streaming across the frosty pavement.

Amy leaned a little further out at the sound of voices and saw a group of people come slowly out of the house supporting someone in their midst. Sentences floated up to her.

'All right, are you, Mum?'

'Yes, thank you, luv.'

'Oh, Mum! Your Stuff! Have you got it?'

'Ay, I have, Mona. You needn't shout at me.'

'Shan't be long now, mate,' said the taxi driver heartily, putting his arm round Mrs Beeding to help her into the cab. 'Orl right, are yer?'

'Sure you've got everything, Mum?' This was Mona again, hovering on the edge of the group and managing to convey to anyone who might be watching that she was just a bundle of nerves and all this was almost too much for her.

'Ay, I have, Mona. What d'yer think I been doin' with meself this last fortnight? Dozin' over them cinema papers o' yours?' roundly retorted Mrs Beeding from inside the taxi. 'Go on in now, Mona, do; you'll catch a cold and you know I can't stand you round me with the snivels. Go on in, now. Come on, Dora, do; yer Dad'll see to all that.'

Amy saw Dora's shining butter-yellow head vanish into the taxi, and watched while Mr Beeding gave some last instructions to the driver and got in beside his daughter and wife. Then the taxi drove off and Mona, having watched it out of sight, wandered disconsolately back to the house.

Oh, blow, now she'll come up here after me, thought Amy, reluctantly drawing in her head and shutting the window. She did not want Mona to know she had been looking at the moon and the lights; Mona always said such feeble things.

Sure enough, about fifteen minutes later, when she was sitting demurely by the stove reading *The Daily Express* (from which she gleaned a rich supply of information to make backgrounds for her stories), there came a tap at the door and Mona's voice called:

'Aime, are you there?' (Mona always shortened even unshortenable names; if she had known a Stella she would have called her Stel.)

'Yes,' Amy answered, not encouragingly.

'What're you doing?'

'Reading.'

'What?'

'*The Daily Express.*'

'Can I come in?'

'I suppose so, if you want to.'

On this gracious permission the door opened eagerly and Mona came in and perched on the table, swinging her fat legs in black stockings and gym shoes. She was a plump girl of thirteen in tunic and white blouse, with a stupid pink face and sausage curls of the same wonderful yellow as her sister's.

'Mum's been taken bad,' she began at once. 'Dora ran out an' got George on the phone an' he said he'd come right away. They've just gone off to the Royal Northern. Mum an' Dad an' Dora. Dora an' Dad'll just see her settled in an' come back, they said.'

Amy listened, sitting back in the armchair with her feet off the ground, looking politely at Mona. She did not say that she had watched Mrs Beeding's departure from the window.

'My heart, Aime, I didn't half feel awful when it started. I was in the scullery just rinsin' up a few crocks for Mum 'n case she didn't feel up to it termorrow before breakfast an'—my heart! I heard Dora say to her, "Mum, joo feel all right?" she said. Well, I thought I was goin' to faint. Honest, everything went black. I sort of swayed—you know. My heart! I thought, I know what *that* means.'

She paused for breath, extending a rather dirty hand decorated by a Woolworth ring upon her fat chest, and sighed.

'How soon will she be back?' asked Amy, wishing Mona would go away, for though she sometimes enjoyed a gossip with her, this was not one of her Mona evenings.

'No-body can say, that's what's so awful,' burst out Mona dramatically. 'George says Mrs Culver was three days with her Peggy, on'y of course Peggy was her first an' this'll be Mum's fifth. Course, the more you have the easier it is.' Then she clapped her hand over her mouth and glanced quickly at Amy, but the pale little face was turned towards the stove and Amy was miles away. Mrs Beeding's body was in the Royal Northern Hospital, but her will lay just as firmly upon her daughter as though she had been there in the room with the two girls, and Mona had been told more than once, very plainly, that she was not to say Anything Like That to little Amy, who was still a child. Anything Like That that's got to be said, I'll say, had promised Mrs Beeding. She had a good mother, Amy had, and I know she'd have liked me to keep an eye on her and so I will, while that father of hers keeps on my top flat. You don't want to go saying Anything to her, Mona; there's plenty of time.

And Mona, who was afraid of her big calm mother, did as she was told.

Amy, staring into the purring blue flame of the gas, had not heard a word about Mrs Culver with her Peggy because she was wondering how she could get Mona out of the room. She wanted some bread and treacle, but did not want to waste bread and treacle on Mona, who got more than enough to eat.

At that minute a taxi drew up outside and Mona slithered off the table, ran over to the window, and opened it.

'It's Dora,' she announced over her shoulder, leaning out into the cold moonlit air. 'Coo-eee! Dora, I'm up here with Aime!' she shouted, leaning far out.

Amy, leaning out beside her, saw Dora look up from her conversation with George the taxi-driver and wave them back impatiently.

'How's Mum, Dora?' shrieked Mona.

Dora shook her head violently at them, still motioning them to go in, said something to George that made him laugh, and ran over the frosted pavement into the house.

'Heart alive, I hope everything's going on as well as can be expected,' sighed Mona, drawing in from the window and pushing in one of the five Kirbigrips that held the stiff ridges of her hair.

'Come on, Aime, let's go on down an' hear the news. My heart, I wonder if I'd better sit up all night in case I'm wanted . . .'

They were hurrying downstairs, prudent Amy having first stayed to turn out the stove and the light.

'All night, Mona?' she said, skipping down behind Mona's heavy tread. 'Have you ever?'

'Heart alive, yes, when Mum had Arthur, Dora an' me never took our clothes off for two solid nights. Dora! Dora! You downstairs? How's Mum? Where's Dad?'

'Do shut up, Mona, you give anyone the sick,' said Dora sharply as they came down into the kitchen. She was combing her hair in front of the glass. 'Mum's going on quite all right and Dad's down at the bakehouse. Hullo, Aime. Come down to see the fun? You'd better have supper with us. Gosh!' settling a ripple of hair with a last vigorous pinch of her fingers, 'I'm hungry. Where're those kippers? Burned to a cinder, I 'spose, since Intelligence was looking after 'em. Where's Maurice?'

'Gone to the pictures. No, they aren't, so there, see, clever! 'Cos I turned the gas down soon's you went off,' said Mona triumphantly.

'Rightee-o. Pop the kettle on, will you, Aime, there's a dear. You stay and have supper with us, will you? You can eat Mum's kipper, she won't want it now, poor old Mum, and Dad says he doesn't want anything either. What a thing it is to be in love! Here, here, what's all this? What're you doing, young Artie? You pop off, back to bed, the sooner the quicker.'

Unnoticed by the busy females popping on kettles and taking kippers out of the oven, a small figure in pyjamas had crept in and was now sidling towards the table, gazing steadily at the lemon curd.

He stopped dead and looked up imploringly at his sister.

'Go on, hop it,' said Dora threateningly, towering over him on long thin legs in pink silk.

'Where's Mum?' he inquired, blinking.

'Gone for a soldier. What's the matter?' She knelt in front of him. 'What woke you up?'

'Young Mona.' Pointing accusingly and causing a shriek of 'Oh, I never!'

'I on'y looked in to see'f he was all right,' she added.

'Well, you've done it now and no error. Come on, fish-face, you sit next to Aime and she'll cut you a doorstep, won't you, Aime? That's right.'

She lifted her brother's lean little body on to a chair and gently worked his arms into the jersey he had wrapped round his shoulders.

'Will you have some lemon curd on it, Arthur?' murmured Amy, putting the bread and butter on his plate.

'NOT HALF!' yelled Arthur, bouncing up and down and banging with a spoon. 'Not half!'

'Now, now, that's enough,' said Dora crisply, setting down the brown teapot. 'Eat your doorstep and shut up. Here you are, Aime. With my blessing, and may it make you as happy as it has me. Mona, you don't want vinegar on that, you'll give yourself more spots than you've got already. All right, all right, it's your face, not mine. Gosh! I'm starved . . . clemmed, as Mum says.' She turned to Amy, her mouth full of kipper. 'I'd only just got in from Spanish when the balloon went up . . . not meaning Mum, of course!'

Mona shrieked with laughter, and after a struggle in which she looked down her long nose and tried to be shocked, Dora joined in. Amy giggled companionably, though not quite understanding what the joke was, and Arthur banged with his spoon. The big clean room rang with cheerful noise.

It was nice having supper with the Beedings in the kitchen, thought Amy, looking round at the familiar features of the room; the worn brown oilcloth and shiny green walls, the black range stacked with shining silver saucepans, the old gas stove about which Mrs Beeding was always complaining, and the dresser and draining-board that had been scrubbed until they were bleached white as driftwood. The two things Amy liked best in the kitchen were the red, black and white rag carpet in front of the range, its colours softened by Time and washing, and the red clock ticking loudly on the dresser; they made pretty colours in the clean, rather bare kitchen which was so tidy that, like Mrs Beeding, it was a bit frightening. But (also like Mrs Beeding) it was comforting.

The Beedings only used the kitchen for meals, never to sit in, for it became intolerably hot when baking was going on and as some of the stifling warmth lingered there after the bakehouse furnaces were cold, the kitchen was infested with black beetles. The range, an extravagant and temperamental set-piece, was never used except as a saucepan stand and as a Rowton House for the beetles, who occupied it in spite of the ceaseless war of aggression waged on them by Mrs Beeding. There was not a speck of dirt for them to enjoy, but there was the delicious fuggy warmth and grains of flour (all the Beedings except Mrs Beeding agreed that the beetles must live off the flour; what else was there for them to live off? But Mrs Beeding said they lived off their own nastiness) and so far no campaign had interrupted the perpetual ball-and-supper which the beetles enjoyed on the kitchen floor at nights.

Tonight everybody hurried to get supper finished and rush upstairs before the first slow, brown, misshapen form was sighted afar in some dim corner near the bakehouse passage.

It *is* a pity about the beetles; the kitchen's so nice, thought Amy, drinking her hot sweet tea and gazing slowly round the room over the cup. She felt soothed and sleepy and peaceful, and looked at the others sitting round the table as though they were people in a pleasant dream.

There was Dora, sitting with her elbows on the table and her usually sharp grey eyes gazing thoughtfully over the top of the cup she was nursing between her hands. She was thin and elegant, with the closest shingle and the shortest skirts in Highbury. Tonight she wore a green jumper suit, the waist well defined by a red belt over the hips, and a red choker necklace to match, high up on her throat. Under the table Amy knew that her legs stretched for what seemed to the little girl an immensely long way, covered in thinnest pink silk and ending in shoes of fawn leather. Two ends of yellow hair, thinned to a point, swept out on her cheeks. Her nose was too long and her lips too thin, but she had enormous dash and style, and was sharp as a needle. Boys were rather afraid of her, but she had a 'steady' whom she bullied and intended to marry, some day. She was ambitious and took her typist-ing seriously; she was learning Spanish because much of her firm's business was with Spain and Dora thought you never knew when a spot of Spanish might not come in handy.

Amy liked her, in spite of wishing that Dora would not sometimes try to boss her about and teach her to knit (the only occupation Amy really hated with all her heart). Dora was impatiently kind; more than once she had bestowed a lightning shilling on Amy and Mona and shooed them off to the pictures, and she had, in spite of her needle sharpness and bossy ways, the same comfortingly solid feeling about her that her mother had. It was not the comfort that Amy's own mother had given people, like a pretty picture or a cheerful tune; it was only the comfort of common-sense and decency, but to a child living Amy's life, any kind of comfort was worth having.

Then there was Mona . . . but Amy's sleepy gaze moved indifferently past Mona, whose face she did not enjoy looking at, and on to young Artie, pop-eyed with sleep, nodding his ginger head over the last of his doorstep. He was a pale little boy of five, spattered with gold freckles, who often had to be hauled out of a fight by his elder brother Maurice. Artie would fight about anything, even to defend the fair fame of Mona when some little boy or girl called her a bad name. He was all over scars of old battles and always rolling down his clothes to show them to shocked females and approving males. Amy thought Artie very brave, but found it difficult to be loving to him, as her mother had told her to be to little children, for love seemed to kind-of roll off him. So she compromised by being extra polite to him. He, unused to such formality and furiously embarrassed by it, never saw her without scowling and silently drawing back his fist as though preparing to punch her in the stomach, but his honour was apparently satisfied by the gesture, for it never developed beyond a gesture, and they got on amiably enough.

While they were finishing off with plum jam thickly spread on slabs of bread, Mr Beeding came in silently from the bakehouse, shutting the door of the passage behind him. His round face was pale as tallow and black hollows were scooped under his eyes, which were dull and moved slowly as though he were drugged.

He was a Welshman, and once could sing true and sweet as the deep notes of an organ, but that had been as a young man, before his trade had begun to kill him. He now had two men working under him and was making a good living; but he could not enjoy the money he earned, because the only night when fresh bread was not demanded by the residents of the crowded Highbury district was Saturday, and if he went out with Mrs Beeding and the younger ones to the pictures on Saturday evening he usually fell asleep in the peaceful dark, and disturbed people all round him with exhausted heavy snores. Usually he worked eleven hours a night, sometimes longer, in the stifling brick bakehouse with its inner lining of steel, stripped to the waist and wearing only a thin singlet, enduring the ravening thirst which he and his men must not quench with water because this might cause the dreaded 'baker's disease.' A man suffering from those sores on the skin, brought on by the action of water on chemicals used in the flour, is unemployable as a leper. And Mr Beeding was very fond of a drink; when he was not flung out asleep, motionless as a corpse on the snowy double bed in his wife's room, he was over in The Chickens having one with his neighbour Mr Flower or with some others of the boys. He had a nasty little cough, which the drink helped to soothe, and it also helped him to put up with his hernia. Mr Beeding endured the hernia, the cough, the thirst and the stifling hours spent in the bakehouse in order that the housewives of Highbury might have nice fresh bread in the morning. His wife never said a word about his work or his cough or what he spent at The Chickens, and none of the children mentioned it either. That was their life, and their father's; and all bakers had the same sort of life, anyway.

Mr Beeding smiled faintly but kindly at Amy and sat down at the head of the table.

'Tea, Dad?' asked Dora.

He nodded, and she gave him a cup which he drank thirstily.

'Yer won't forget the jug o' tea fer the men, will yer, Dora?'

'No, Dad. It's done,' jerking her head at a big blue enamel can in a corner.

He nodded. 'That's a good girl. Thank yer. Yer mother was just going ter see ter it when she came over bad.'

They ate in silence for a little while, only interrupted by a shriek from Mona who fancied she sighted a beetle under the range. There was the usual slight depression caused by the presence of Mr Beeding, looking like a corpse with his yellow-white face and drugged silence, and no one found much to say. Amy began to feel that she would be happier upstairs with *The Wolf of Leningrad*.

At last Mr Beeding got up, and stood for a moment swaying and muttering, '*For what we have received may God make us truly thankful for Jesus Christ's sake Amen*,' over the untidy remains of supper. Then he picked up the jug of cold tea (the only liquid the men were allowed to touch while at work) and went back to the bakehouse.

When they were all filing upstairs to the Lounge, having stacked the washing-up, Amy slipped past Dora as the latter slowly mounted with Artie in her arms, muttering, 'Good night, Dora. Thanks ever so for having me to supper,' and ran up the dark stairs to her own kingdom.

'Aime!' came a faint anguished howl from below. 'Aren't you coming to play Fox and Geese? *Aime!*'

'Oh, let the kid alone, can't you? You know what she is,' came Dora's voice sharply; then she heard the Lounge door shut.

All night there were unusual sounds in the house, such as might be caused by people making themselves tea because they had convinced themselves they were unable to sleep for gnawing anxiety and also wanted something to tell their schoolfellows about the next day; once Amy awoke when the front door slammed heavily in the small hours.

And the next morning, while she was cooking the bacon for breakfast and Tim was shaving and swearing over the scullery sink, Mona rushed up to announce hysterically that Mrs Beeding had produced a girl weighing seven pounds eight ounces, a perfect little angel with red hair. Born at half-past three that morning.

'Dolores,' said Mona confidently. 'That's what I've got a *feeling* Mum'll call that baby. After Dolores Costello. You see.'

The child, however, was christened Marie Noreen and never called anything by all the Beedings but 'Baby'.

5

One week-end in April there was a spell (the word is exactly right for the enormous drowsy bubble of sweet air that enclosed all England) of warm weather. Amy was glad to shut up her desk on Friday afternoon, and walk slowly home through the streets where the green leaves were unfurling on garden hedges and trees almost as she watched. There were enormous baskets at the street corners, even in that poor neighbourhood, in which daffodils, narcissus, tulips, wallflowers, freesias and hyacinths were glowing like coloured stars. The air was so warm that people loitered as though it were already summer, under the sunny blue sky where white clouds tinted with gold slowly, slowly glided. There was a feeling everywhere as though something lovely were about to happen.

The ancient brown bricks of the houses in Highbury Fields were turned to rich dark gold, and delicate tree-shadows fell across the paths at the feet of old men and women, who had crept out to enjoy the good sunshine, lifting their worn faces with closed eyes to the light. There was a great blowing of bubbles and eating of crumbly biscuits among that year's crop of babies, moored in perambulators under the trees with their tender scalps sternly exposed to the newly-fashionable rays. Amy looked among them for the Beeding Baby, but she was, as usual, moored to her own select length of railing. Yorkshire was afraid of her Catching Something Up the Fields.

As she turned the corner she saw the shabby perambulator that had served Artie and Mona before him tied to the railings by the side door, with Baby's red curls shining out of a mass of

70

shawls, and Artie himself in sullen attendance, lounging on a piece of carpet spread on the steps.

'Hullo, Artie,' said Amy, putting down her attaché case and bending over to say 'Giddy-giddy-giddy-giddy,' very quickly to Baby. This was the only thing she ever said to her, and she had learned that from Mona. Baby took no notice. She was sucking the end of the leather strap that fastened her in and her chin was all brown.

''Lo, Aime.' Artie drew back his fist and scowled as usual, but he spoke without rancour.

'Ought she to suck that, do you think, Artie?' said Amy doubtfully, leaning on the pram and gently rocking it. Baby looked so absolutely drunk with satisfaction that even in Amy's unmaternal heart a faint alarm sounded. Could so much sheer rapture be good for anyone?

'She likes it, 'n it stops her yellin',' said Artie indifferently. His gaze was not on Baby at all, but fixed upon some boys of his own age playing down in the Fields. Amy's eyes followed his.

'I'll mind her, Artie, if you want to go down the Fields and play with Johnny.'

'Mum said I was to mind her.' Artie darted a glance of pure loathing at Baby.

'She wouldn't mind me minding her. You go on. I like sitting here, truly I do.'

Much Artie cared whether she liked it or not. He shot off without another word or glance, and Amy sat down on the piece of carpet and continued to rock the pram gently to and fro, staring with wide-open eyes, almost golden in that light, at a tree across the road. Baby went on blissfully sucking.

As Tim Lee came round the corner, his glance was caught by the shabby little picture, and he thought disgustedly, 'Brats. . .' Highbury was full of them, a noisy reminder of the sort of life that other human beings found so absorbing . . . there was an

unattractive thin chip of a child on his own doorstep, in the gym
tunic that was a uniform for the girls of these parts, skinny legs
in wrinkled stockings, a scrap of faded bloomers showing, a grubby
white beret on the side of her head. About as useful and beautiful
as frog-spawn, these brats were, and with just about as much
individuality, thought Tim.

The child turned, and he recognized his own daughter.

The shock was so great that he had nothing to say for a
minute. He stopped in front of the pram, looking down at her
in silence, and when at last he answered the 'Hullo, Da—Father,'
she gave him, peering up at him with eyes half-shut against the
sunset, it was in a gentler tone than she had ever heard from
him.

'You shouldn't sit out here, you know, Amy.'

'All right, Father. But'—the expression on his face gave her
courage to go on— 'I was only minding Baby for Artie. Why
mustn't I?'

'Well . . .' He turned away and stared at the groups slowly
strolling across the paths under the greening trees; a tall man
who wore a shabby well-bred suit with the proper casual air,
whose greying gilt hair caught the light under a hat at the right
unostentatious angle. He had been going to answer, 'Because I'm
a gentleman and your grandparents on my side were gentle
people too, and so were all our people, as far back as we can
trace the family.' But what was the use? The words sounded
pompous and absurd even in his own mind, here in the midst
of a spring evening's crowds in Highbury Fields.

He forgot Amy for a minute, as he stared into the past,
remembering his own carefully-guarded childhood in the privileged air of the ancient University town, with all the riches of
culture and tradition slowly opening before his growing mind,
supported by the sense of order and responsibility with which
his parents had been so particular to imbrue his background. He
did not regret that he had thrown culture, tradition, responsibility

and order away. He had done what he wanted to do: chosen Edie and the filthy fellows. I regret nothing, he told himself, staring unseeingly at the figures strolling in the golden haze. But he could not ignore the contrast between his daughter's childhood and his own. What would Edie, who had never let Amy play in the streets, have said about the picture he had seen as he turned the corner just now? What kind of a woman would Amy grow up into, with this background and one of Nature's filthy fellows for a father?

Amy kept quiet; she regretted asking her question and hoped that if she said nothing more he would go away.

But at last he said, not looking at her, 'Come up and help me get some things into a bag, will you, there's a good monkey. I've got tomorrow morning free, and I'm going off with Old Porty for the week-end.'

Amy glanced uncertainly at her charge, but fortunately at that minute Mona came flying up on her way home from school and fell rapturously upon Baby, muttering, 'giddy-giddy-giddy-giddy,' so quickly and quietly that only Baby, who took absolutely no notice, could hear what she was saying. Baby was smiling, unheeded, up at Tim.

Suddenly Mona bounced away from the pram as though stung.

'Heart alive, Aime Lee, don't let her suck that! It's enough to kill the poor little mite!'

'Artie said it stops her crying.'

'Artie's barmy. Here, lovey, givey Mona. Narky-narky strap. Bad for Baby.' She knew better than to angle for the strap but twitched it out of Baby's hand and dropped it over the side of the pram. Baby, stunned, stared up at her sister in silence.

''N her poor little chin all filthy dirty! You supposed to be minding her, Aime Lee?'

'I just said I would while Artie went down the Fields.' In fact she had offered to mind Baby because from the door-step she could obtain a new and interesting view of a cut-out named

Mabel Purdey who was hopelessly tangled in the lower branches of a tree over the road.

'You're a nice one to mind a kiddy, you are, I don't think—letting her poison herself!'

'Come along, Amy, will you.' Tim went impatiently into the house. At the same instant Baby burst into a roar of utter despair.

'Is she all right?' Amy lingered an instant, looking at Baby's large crimson face.

''Course she is, you sloppy ha'porth, on'y she doesn't like it 'cos your Dad's gone indoors. She likes him. We was only saying so tea-time yesterday, all of us.'

'Well I don't know why she does, Mona. Because he never takes any notice of her. I don't believe he even knows what her name is.'

'Oh, babies are funny that way. They just like people or they don't. Now she hates Artie.'

'I know. He hates her, too.'

'He's potty. She's a sweet little honey-bunch, aren't you—giddy-giddy-giddy-giddy.'

Seeing that Mona would now be responsible, Amy went upstairs to help her father.

He threw the clothes to her from his room, and she neatly caught and fitted them into his once-handsome, shabby old suitcase. There was an unfamiliar holiday feeling in the big bare room full of westering light.

'Where are you going, Dad?'

'The sea somewhere. Cornwall, probably. Ought to be rather good.'

'The paper said this morning the fine weather was going to last.'

'Oh, it did, did it? And what paper was that?'

'*The Daily Express.*'

'That rag!'

Tim threw across a ball of clean socks. 'There-is-only-one-newspaper-and-that-is-*The-Times* . . . only I won't manage a shilling a week for my news. What were you doing, reading that tripe-sheet?'

'I always do.'

'Why, in God's name?'

'It's interesting. Mrs Beeding has it, and she lets me have it after she's done with it.'

'(*Int*eresting, not int*er*esting, Amy.) What interests you in it?'

'(*Int*'resting.) Oh . . . about Russia. I like reading about the Kulaks.' (Though Amy knew Kulaks were a kind of farmer, she could not help thinking of them as an ogre with long teeth, which added a peculiar interest to their doings.)

'So they keep you well up on modern Europe at the Anna Bonner, do they? There, that's the lot.'

'Will you have tea before you go? There's a kipper.'

'No, thanks. Porty'll be here any minute . . .'

A horn sounded persistently below.

'. . . there he is, the old devil. Well——' He turned at the door for a minute, suitcase in hand, and surveyed her as she stood by the table, her arms folded in an elderly way over her chest, her big light eyes looking steadily at him. 'Thanks for helping me. You're a good monkey. Here——' He felt in his pocket and a big silver coin flew glittering towards her. 'Buy yourself *The Times*. You and I haven't much in common but I can't have my only daughter reading *The Daily Express*.'

She caught the coin. It was a half-crown.

'Oh, Da—*Father*! Thanks *ever* so!'

'That's all right. Good-bye. I'll be back on Monday evening but you can get me at the office on Monday morning if you want me.'

'I don't expect there'll be anything. Good-bye, and thanks *awfully* for this.'

She held up the half-crown in the sunlight, her little face

smiling with pleasure, and that was the picture of her he carried away as he ran down the stairs.

Old Porty, fearfully gay in a new light overcoat, was just climbing into the car as Tim came out.

'There you are, cock,' bellowed Porty. 'I nearly forgot to post me Littlewood's.' He nodded towards the pillar-box on the corner. 'That would have been a nice start, that would—get half-way to God-knows-wheres-it and find I hadn't posted me Littlewood's.'

'I can't imagine why you bother with that stuff.' Tim was packing himself into the car. 'Where's the kick in it, anyway? Dog-racing is the game for me. No time to get bored; over in a flash.'

'There isn't any kick; it's skill, not luck. That's what I like, my boy; gives you a chance to use your brains.'

'Brains my—never-mind. Do you want me to take the map now or when we get out of London a bit?'

'Later on'll do; I'll tell you. Are you right? Off we go, then, and Christ help the Cornish girls.'

The car moved away and was soon lost in the traffic.

Left alone, Amy went over to the window and leaned her elbows on the sill, dreamily looking at the tree-tops covered with new little yellow leaves, and breathing in the sweet air. It was nice to be alone, and to think that she would have a whole two days to do as she liked in without her father at home. She thought about him a little as she leaned there, the sunlight warm on her face and the half-crown safely held in her hand. He had been worse lately, there was no doubt about that. In the last three weeks she had lain awake in the dark night after night, trembling with fear, while he stumbled about getting himself off to bed after an evening with Old Porty and the boys. He had never hit her nor even sworn at her when he was like that, but just the sight of him frightened her; the stupid look in his eyes and his thick careful speech; while the noises he made blundering about alarmed her even more because she could not see just how bad he was. And last week he had gambled away the rent, and Amy had had to explain to Mrs Beeding and ask her if she would be so kind as to wait until this week for the money. Mrs Beeding had said yes, but she made it plain that she was disgusted with Amy's father, and although Amy shared her feelings, this made her feel uncomfortable and ashamed. It had only happened once before, the week of Amy's birthday. Amy had hoped very much that it would never happen again; but it had. It was awful to be in debt: her mother had always told her that.

He had also begun to grumble when he handed over the weekly thirty shillings he gave her for their food, saying that it was a great deal of money; and when he was in to meals he ate less and less. Half-way through the meal he would push his plate away half-full, and light a cigarette and sit in silence, his fingers spread over his forehead, with bent head. He was getting thin; Mrs Beeding had commented on it to Amy. His daughter, patiently searching her mind for a possible explanation of his behaviour during the past three weeks, suddenly remembered that her mother used to laugh and say, 'Oh, Tim's always worse in the spring.'

Satisfied, she nodded to herself and put it down to the spring. When the weather was more settled, perhaps her father would be—as settled as he ever was.

She continued to lean on the window-sill and plan her week-end.

This evening after supper (a fried egg and two bananas and Ka-Ola) she would wash her weekly pair of bloomers, vest, stockings, and two white blouses. Put them in a bowl all night, ready to hang them out in the garden tomorrow. Then wash her hair. Sit by the stove and dry it and read *Tom Sawyer*. Go to bed. Tomorrow she would spend the morning hunting for American books on the secondhand bookstalls in the Charing Cross Road, eat her lunch in the little Gardens tucked away at the side of Whitefield's Tabernacle in Tottenham Court Road and in the afternoon go to the British Museum and Collect Material for 'Pharoah's Curse: A Tale of Ancient Egypt.'

On Sunday she would start the story.

It would be a very nice week-end—if only Mona didn't come poking.

Fortunately Mona had been asked to spend the two days with some cousins at Edmonton, so she didn't come poking and Amy was able to do exactly what she had planned to do . . . a privilege which many prosperous grown-up people during that fine week-end might have envied her. The clothes and hair washing proceeded calmly and with method. If the clothes were not as snowy as they might have been, if some soap lingered in the hair after washing, that was because the washer had not much strength in her wrists and also because she was planning the bit where Amenophis drugs Rameses with a wheat-cake in the first chapter. Amy did, as best she could, what her mother had told her and taught her to do. She had no one to come behind her and snatch the blouse from the water with a vigorous: 'That isn't half clean yet, childie! Look—all round the collar'; no one to give a final rinse of lemon juice to her hair. Her standard of grooming, like her standard in ethics, had unconsciously declined since her mother's death, just as had Tim's appetite and his conviction that life mattered.

The British Museum is at its most enjoyable on a blazing hot day, when the visitor can step out of the sunny courtyard into the coolness under the portico, where water trickles out of the silver lions' mouths and even the pigeons running about the mighty bases of the columns are a cool purple grey. Inside, past the pleasant noise of the doors as they continually swing open and shut, there are refreshing spaces of clean stone floor, the great height of sombre walls ending in the dimness of the roof where quiet echoes float about, and, above all, the flat oddly welcoming countenances of two animals seated on either side of the great stone staircase. They are intended for lions, but on the base of their pedestals stand out clearly the words 'Amaravati Tope,' so that any frequent visitor to the British Museum cannot possibly think of the two by any other name.

Amy loved the Amaravati Tope. She always went up to them first of all on her visits to the Museum, and stood in front first of one and then the other, staring up at them and thinking—not where they came from or how old they must be or who made them—but simply how nice they were; and it would be more than interesting to know what the carvers of the Amaravati Tope would have thought about this reaction of Amy's to their work.

All that sunny afternoon she moved slowly round the Egyptian Rooms, staring at necklaces, combs, and chairs so that she could furnish, on paper, a house in the Thebes of three thousand years ago. She had a penny notebook in which she scribbled descriptions, hiding it away whenever she drew near an attendant or when some benevolent grown-up, attracted by her smallness, her pigtail and the notebook, peered kindly over her shoulder to see what she was doing.

'It's for school. They like us to take an interest,' she said politely more than once to a kindly questioner, and then, as they turned away smiling at the pretty little incident, she made a hideous lightning face at their back.

And at the end of the afternoon she came away from this stone building, filled with beautiful worn stone faces and shapes, feeling dreamy and calm. The presence of stone has a peculiarly soothing touch upon human senses, tranquillizing as the names of granite, marble, porphyry, and slate. It is the least obtrusive of backgrounds; no substance so well displays the fleeting beauty of flowers, nor does such justice to a haunting echo, nor looks so steadily into the face of Time. It is not only because it lasts well that men have always built their temples and tombs of stone.

Going home on the bus to the Holloway Arcade, Amy thought dreamily: I had a lovely time. I got a lot of Material, and I did enjoy my tea with the bun and butter with all those professory-looking men in the tea place and I saw the dear Amaravati Tope. It was all *lovely*. Oh—Mother! I'd forgotten! I forgot for a whole afternoon!

It was the calming presence of stone that had soothed her grief to sleep.

In the evening after supper she copied out the rough notes she had made at the museum into a fat book labelled 'Material,' and went to bed early. Sometimes she woke up frightened on the nights that her father was away, and lay listening to the faint sounds the old house made in its sleep, trying not to think about the Lady Ligeia, trying not to look at the dark shape of the wardrobe against the pallor of the wall, calling frantically in her mind, 'Mother! Mother! I'm frightened—I can't help it,' and then feeling new terror lest something—a shade, a white shape like her mother, should appear.

But on both the nights of this week-end she slept peacefully, awakening slowly and happily in the little quiet room to see all the rich colours of her pictures glowing in the sunlight. Sunday passed pleasantly between spells of ironing and writing *The Mummy's Curse*, which was Beginning to Run, as Amy always said to herself when she had a writing fit on. Her stories never stuck, but sometimes she enjoyed writing them more than she did at other times. When the pen flew and her hand ached, when there was nothing real in the world except the white paper before her and the flying tip of the nib, and the picture in her mind that she was describing turned so quickly into words that she could no longer tell at what instant the figures in it became marks on the paper—then the story was Beginning to Run, and unfortunate is the writer who has never tasted such a moment.

The Beedings were used to her ways and left her in peace except for an occasional friendly shriek up the stairs, explaining her taste for solitude to one another by saying that Aime was a great reader, for none of them knew that she was also a great writer.

She went back to school on Monday morning with some of the week-end's dreamy calm lingering in her mind. She always liked getting back to school on Mondays. It was still sunny weather and the class-rooms were full of chestnut and palm branches in bud.

Second hour was History for Amy's form on Monday mornings, and they were in Room 6 answering Miss Seager's amiable questions about the Star Chamber when the door opened and the head of Miss Lathom, the headmistress, looked inquiringly round the room.

Miss Seager stopped with a piece of chalk in mid-air and in her turn gazed inquiringly at Miss Lathom, who, evidently having found the person she wanted among the fifteen pairs of clear eyes fixed upon her, went up to the form mistress and spoke quietly to her for a minute or two.

Miss Seager was nodding—'Of course. Yes, of course, Miss Lathom. Yes, certainly.'

Miss Lathom went out of the room.

Miss Seager put down the chalk on her desk.

'Amy, Miss Lathom would like to see you in her room for a minute, dear,' she said gently, leaning forward a little and smiling at the child. 'Run along. Jean, then, do you know?'

Amy, not alarmed because her conscience was clear and she liked Miss Lathom, went out of the room, quietly shutting the door behind her. It was probably about Botany next term.

The headmistress's room was close to Room 6. She tapped at the door, listened for Miss Lathom's clear 'Come in,' then opened the door and entered.

Miss Lathom was sitting at her desk, where a bowl of fresh primroses stood in the sunlight pouring through the window. She looked up as Amy came in, and took off her glasses.

'There you are, Amy. Come here, dear,' she said and then, as the little girl crossed the carpet and came to a halt opposite her desk, she did a surprising thing. She put out her thin arm in its grey tweed sleeve, and gently drew Amy within its circle until she was resting against her knee, looking down with surprised but unalarmed eyes into Miss Lathom's lined, pleasant face.

'Now, dear,' the headmistress went on in the same subdued voice, meeting Amy's gaze steadily with her own, 'can you be a brave girl?'

Amy's inside gave a sickening movement. But her large light eyes still rested steadily on Miss Lathom's pitying face. She nodded. Her mouth had gone dry.

'Because you must, Amy.' Miss Lathom paused for an instant. 'It's about your father, my dear little girl——' The arm tightened. 'He has been in a car accident. The police have just telephoned. I'm afraid it's very bad news indeed, Amy.'

Amy's lips moved. After a second she whispered:

'Miss Lathom, is he dead?'

Miss Lathom nodded, and gently tightened her clasp until Amy's cheek rested in silence against her shoulder.

6

On a fine afternoon two days later the funeral procession set out from Highbury. The two cars, followed by a third which was none other than that of Mr Porteous and driven by that prince of good fellows himself, went slowly past the interested gaze of a few women on the pavement until it reached the end of the Walk and then moved forward at a brisker pace along the Holloway Road to Highgate Cemetery. Edie's grave was there and Tim would be buried beside her.

'That coffin hasn't many flowers, has it?' remarked more than one onlooker. There were only four wreaths for Tim; a cross made of daffodils from the Beedings, an anchor of laurel leaves with a very large card attached—'From E. Talbot Porteous, with Deepest Sympathy,' a beautiful sheaf of narcissus and white tulips from the staff of *The Prize*, and a circle of rich wallflowers (Miss Seager's suggestion; 'unusual, and not so *dreadfully* funerally-looking as most wreaths, girls') from Amy's form at the Anna Bonner.

Amy's own small bunch of freesias was buried under Porty's laurels. The flowers did not make much of a show, spread out forlornly along the coffin.

In the second car sat Amy, almost hidden by the bulk of Mrs Beeding, who had bought her a black coat and hat at Jones Brothers of Holloway that morning, taking it for granted that as the only living relative her father had in the world, she would of course go to his funeral. Dora protested in vain that kids never did, and it was a damned shame to drag the poor little devil along like that, and enough to upset her for weeks even worse than she was already, and even Mr Beeding put in a word against it. But Mrs Beeding seldom listened to what Mr Beeding had to say and she stood firm; she had a very strongly developed sense of what was demanded by the human relationships, and she would sweep aside convention, even inclination, without hesitation in order that proper respect and duty might be paid to an aged aunt, to some worthy cousin four times removed. There was that time she got up against the doctor's orders a week after having Artie and went to Uncle Barker's funeral; that just showed you what she was. So Amy went, looking like a little white-faced doll in her new black. She did not much mind going, except that she was frightened of seeing the grave because it would make her think of *The Lady Ligeia's Entombment*, and so she had decided to shut her eyes while the actual burying was going on; no one would notice.

She had cried so much in the last two days that her head felt empty and light. She was so dreadfully lonely! She peeped out of the window as the car moved along the Holloway Road, staring at the crowds hurrying past in the spring sunshine. So many people, in so many cities all over the huge world! and not one of them belonged to her or would know who you meant if you said, 'Amy Lee.' For the first time in her life she wondered what was going to become of her.

But then she glanced sideways at Mrs Beeding's stout person, looking grave yet somehow not dismal in the black coat and hat bought for the funeral of Uncle Barker, and she felt a little better.

Mrs Beeding had been so kind. She had come round to the school at once to fetch Amy home, and after a little talk with Miss Lathom (they had seemed to like each other, Amy had thought afterwards, though she had been crying too miserably to be aware of this at the time) she had asked one of the maids to telephone for a taxi because Amy felt too upset to walk. And all the afternoon she had sat beside Amy in her little bedroom, giving her sips of still lemonade to drink and putting a wet handkerchief on her forehead because she had given herself a headache with all that crying. Amy had gone to sleep that night in Mrs Beeding's bed (poor Mr Beeding having been banished to a sofa in the Lounge) with Baby slumbering in a crib at the foot, and her hand held fast in Mrs Beeding's work-roughened one.

Mrs Beeding had certainly made things better, and she was comforting without slopping over you and trying to nose out what you were thinking about like Mona or snapping cheerfully at you and trying to make you forget all about it like Dora. But although the Beeding men had been very kind as well, with Artie (prompted by Maurice) offering Amy a suck off his Halfpenny Wonder and Maurice himself inviting her to accompany him to the pictures next Saturday afternoon and Mr Beeding baking her a special tiny loaf with A on it surrounded by a curly twist—none of these comforting things really got inside her mind where the frightening lonely feeling was. She thanked them all in a whisper, and just for a minute felt a little better, but the feeling always came back again.

After the funeral was over, and Amy had slowly opened her eyes, stinging because she had screwed them up so tightly in order not to see the coffin sink into the grave, they walked slowly back to the car. The flowers arranged on the bare mound of earth trembled in the mild wind and the sunlight made their petals look transparent. Old Porty came glumly up to Amy and Mrs Beeding, touching his hat with a despairing sort of flourish, and walked beside them in silence.

Porty was not directly to blame for Tim's death. It was not his car that had been crashed into by a lorry whose driver, half-dazed for want of sleep, had been trying to deliver a load on time. Tim and Porty had picked up one or two of the boys on the way back from Cornwall and Tim had come back in a boy's car; it was this that had been destroyed and its unfortunate driver, as well as Tim, instantly killed. But Tim would never have gone to Cornwall and his death had it not been for Old Porty, and Mrs Beeding, in the glance she gave Old Porty, amply conveyed as much.

'Well, well. Poor old Tiger.' Old Porty compressed his lips and shook his head and looked quite frighteningly like a vulture. 'I can't believe it—can't realize the poor old bu—poor old chap's gone. Why, only the other night he was showing us all how to shift it at the local in one of those godforsaken little holes we stopped at on the way back—had us all in fits. Roaring, we were, simply holding on to the mantelpiece. And now he's gone.' Porty shook his head and glanced at Mrs Beeding, who was marching along with her fair-skinned face severe under the Uncle Barker hat.

'Ay, it's very sad,' observed Mrs Beeding, barely parting her lips and then shutting them up once more.

'And how's Amy, eh?' Porty bent to peer at the little girl in black walking quietly at Mrs Beeding's side. 'Poor little girl. Ah, Tiger often talked to me about you, Amy.'

She glanced up at his cruel purple face, dark like an ogre's against the pure blue sky, and gave him a steady look from under the brim of her hat. Her eyes were red, but washed wonderfully clear by weeping.

'I'm all right, thank you, Mr Porteous.'

'That's right.' Porty gave her black-ribboned pigtail a subdued yet jovial tug. 'That's a real little sport. Always be a sport, little girl. Yer father was—poor old Tiger. One of the best. Ah, well, wherever he is now, he's at rest, poor old bu—poor old chap. Yes, well, I suppose I must be toddling. So long, Amy. So long, Mrs B. I won't say good-bye, I'm often round this way and I'll pop in and see you some time, eh?'

'Aye. I expect you will,' said Mrs Beeding. Amy stared at the ground.

Bloody women, thought Old Porty turning aside to begin preliminary fiddlings with his car (which like most of the things always had some minor ailment troubling it). Sour-faced b——s. Gawping at me as if the whole business was my fault. I can't help it. Gave me a—nasty turn; I shan't forget it in a hurry. Two hours till they open . . . Christ, what a country!

With a vague wave of his hand to the Beedings and Amy he drove quickly away. One of the Boys had gone; the Boys, whose business it was to make one another forget unpleasant facts like duty and death. Sons of the cup and the lyre, priests of pleasure, leagued in a vague resentment against women—what business had one of the Boys to go and die suddenly, letting in the draught on all the rest? Already in Old Porty's mind Tim was 'Chap I used to know in advertising. Came to a sticky end . . . hit a lorry one night.' With this epitaph Porty buried his friend.

While the Beedings were speaking to the driver of their car, a middle-aged gentleman in a dark blue overcoat came briskly towards them. He had already been noticed by them as he stood in the group at the graveside, and Dora and Mona were wondering who he could be. A handsomish car parked near their own seemed to be his, for he unlocked it before he came over and addressed Mrs Beeding.

'Good-afternoon,' he said pleasantly, taking off his hat and holding it while he spoke. 'My name is Ramage. I'm representing *The Prize*. Is this the little girl—his daughter?'

He bent a little, just as Old Porty had, to look into Amy's face, and she slowly lifted her gaze from the ground and met the friendly look on a reddish, kindly countenance with observant eyes.

'Ay, this is Amy.' Mrs Beeding knew a gentleman when she met one but was not permitted by Yorkshire to address him as 'sir.'

'I want to tell you, my dear,' continued Mr Ramage, 'how very sorry we all are on the paper, and how much your father will be missed.'

'Very kind of you, I'm sure,' responded Mrs Beeding. 'There,

Amy,' for she was anxious that her charge should show pretty manners. 'Isn't that kind?'

'Thank you,' murmured Amy, giving Mr Ramage the clear look she had given Old Porty, but with a difference.

'And what are you going to do now, Amy?' pursued Mr Ramage, collecting her name from Mrs Beeding's speech and making easy use of it to increase the friendliness of his own. 'Have you any relatives or friends to take care of you?'

He spoke almost lightly, so as not to distress her and perhaps make her cry, yet his question held real interest and concern. Because of her appalling black outfit and the fact that she should, of course, never have been allowed to attend the funeral at all, Mr Ramage was attracted by Amy. It was a shocking sight, a child at a funeral, and Mr Ramage, a father of daughters, liked the look of this child. He was perhaps the first stranger in her life to do so. He stood smiling down upon her, waiting for the answer that she suddenly found herself too lonely and miserable to give.

'Oh yes, she's goin' to stay with us.' Mrs Beeding at length answered for her, pulling Amy's hand within her arm. 'We'll take good care of her; that'll be all right, won't it, luv?'

Amy nodded, and Mr Ramage, pleased by the warmth of that 'luv,' felt a little easier about her.

Yet not altogether easy. She was quite plainly porcelain to the Beedings' clay, and Mr Ramage knew that porcelain, especially the natural porcelain that does not get its fine glaze from money and culture, can crack and chip with painful ease when bumping alongside earthenware pots. Also, Mrs Beeding's little mouth was very firm indeed.

'You see,' Mrs Beeding went on in a lower tone, looking steadily at him, 'Mr Lee's left his Insurance Policy for her all paid up, an' by the time the funeral's paid for (me and Mr Beeding's seein' to that, just for the time being) she'll have about two hundred and seventy pounds, the Company said. I went down to see them yesterday afternoon. So that'll keep her going at school for another three years easy, and when she leaves there'll still be a bit over to start her learnin' dressmakin' or somethin'.'

'I'm very relieved to hear that,' Mr Ramage answered in the same lowered tone. He looked down curiously at the top of the future dressmaker's doleful black straw hat; he could just see the tip of a creamy nose and a tiny but firm chin. Poor scrap. Mr Ramage thought of his own two healthy girls at a boarding school in Eastbourne and reflected, not for the first time in his life, that the world was an uncertain and frightening place. If he, a successful man, found it so, what must it seem to Amy Lee?

But there, she had two hundred and seventy pounds and Mrs Beeding. She was better off than some. He said a friendly good-afternoon to Mrs Beeding, shook hands with Amy and said, 'Good-bye, Amy. I hope very much that everything turns out well for you,' and drove away in his car to Muswell Hill, where he lived (for Mr Ramage had reached that point of grandeur in business life at which a person does not dream of returning to the office when an afternoon engagement has kept him out later than three o'clock).

He drove away; and in a week he had almost forgotten the little Lee girl. Almost, but not quite; somewhere at the back of his mind lingered her demure name and secret little face.

'That's a real nice man, Dora,' commented Mrs Beeding, settling herself comfortably as their car moved off. 'A gentleman, that was. Aye, I shan't half be glad to get these shoes off me, they're fair punishing my feet.'

'Mr Porteous didn't know where to put his face, Mum,' said Dora. 'He'd never say so, the old monkey, but he feels bad about it, I'm sure. Notice him sucking up to Aime?'

'He told me I'd got gorgeous hair,' giggled Mona, twining a red finger in and out of the sausages. 'I do think he's *awful*.'

'He's a wicked man and God will punish him for it one o' these days,' stated her mother without heat. 'And you're a silly girl to be pleased with his lies. Now you stop messing about with your hair, Mona, and sit quiet; everybody can see us sitting up here and it don't do to jig about.'

'Oh, I do hope Baby's all right,' sighed Mona, wisely turning the conversation. 'She don't like Mrs Flower much, does she, Dora?'

'Baby's all right, Mona. Mrs Flower'll look after her. You just be quiet, now, will you. Amy, luv, I expect yer want yer tea. You had no dinner an' you'll be clemmed.'

'Yes, I do rather, Mrs Beeding, please.'

'Aye, so do I. Well, we'll soon be home.'

They were all tired with the emotions and excitements of the day, and leant back and let the remainder of the drive pass in a not unpleasant languour. When grief is not so personal as to be agonizing, and duty has been done, and our spirits have been awed and calmed by a brushing acquaintance with death, there is a subdued pleasure in taking up the routine of daily life once more; it is as if we had been shown, for an instant by a lightning flash, the dearness of the simple things we must one day leave for ever.

When the car had put them down outside the shop and driven away, and they had taken off their outdoor clothes and reclaimed Baby from pretty little Mrs Flower, and tea was being got ready in the kitchen, there was a feeling of relief in the air that gave a fresh cheerfulness to everyone except Amy. Dora had asked for leave from the office, Mona had stayed away from school, Mrs Beeding had entrusted the shop to Mr Beeding and Baby to Mrs Flower, all in order that Amy might have their support at her father's funeral; but now that it was over they could not pretend to any personal grief over Mr Lee. Mrs Beeding, indeed, was so relieved to find that Amy had a little bit of money and could now be brought up proper and made into a good decent girl with a trade at her fingers' ends, that she found herself feeling quite glad that Tim was dead. Mrs

Beeding had already had a little talk with Amy, and arranged to open an account for her at Barclays on the corner of the High Street where Mr Beeding banked the takings from the shop. And Amy would pay Mrs Beeding twelve and sixpence a week for her keep, and Mrs Beeding had found time to slip round and see Miss Lathom at the Anna Bonner and inform her that Amy would stay on at school until she was fifteen, her fees being paid regular at the beginning of every term. Everything, in fact, was arranged for Amy and all she had to do now was to get out of her mopey ways and stop fretting.

Amy sat at tea that afternoon for the first time as a member of the family, with Dora on one side and the red-haired Maurice on the other. All round her was the chatter of cheerful voices, the clink of spoons and clash of china, the passing of full or empty cups down the table, demands for 'more paste, please,' 'pass the bread, will you, Dora,' and the smell of hot tea and fresh dough cake. Mrs Beeding sat at one end, pouring out competently for everybody yet getting her own meal as well, and Mr Beeding had managed to wake himself up in time for tea for once, and sat at the other, keeping an eye on Baby and supplying her with fingers of bread to sop in her milk-and-tea; he was very fond of her and spent much of what leisure he got with her. All down the table the yellow or carroty heads of the Beedings bobbed busily as they ate and drank and talked to each other, and the two dark heads of Amy and Mr Beeding looked oddly out of place among so many fair ones. It was a lively scene in the big clean kitchen, with Baby's cries and clumsy little movements making everyone pause now and then to exclaim admiringly at her and bless her little heart; the dough cake was rich and light, the tea strong and sweet, and the paste savoury. There was laughter and fun and plenty for everyone. Family life at its best.

Yet Amy sat there crumbling cake, with the room dancing

through shimmering tears, only longing to get up and say, 'Thank you very much for asking me to tea, Mrs Beeding. I think I'd better be going now,' and escape upstairs to the quiet, deserted rooms at the top of the house where the golden light of evening poured through the closed windows. She had had enough of the Beedings. For nine hours she had never been out of the company of some sort of Beeding, and as her natural air was solitude, she was beginning to feel desperate with the need to escape. And she was just beginning to understand, as she sat there at tea in the middle of the Beedings, that she would never be able to escape again.

At first she was unconsciously glad to be with them because they were comforting and she was too miserable to think much about her secret world, but now her thoughts kept returning to *The Mummy's Curse* and the Pony Express riders; she wondered if the cut-out Mabel Purdey had survived last night's high wind, and if the little American boy's father was alive and if he was a nice father. In short, her thoughts were beginning to get back to normal, as people's thoughts do after a funeral, but Amy's returned from a daze of grief to find their owner in a foreign world.

The Beedings have got me now, she thought, and I'll never be able to get away. It will be *awful*. If I say can I go upstairs to the flat for a bit they'll say 'What for?' And Mona'll want to come too. And where can I write *The Mummy's Curse* without them seeing and wanting to read it? And Mrs Beeding'll never let me fly cut-outs out of the lounge window. And where will I sleep? If I have to sleep with Mona I *swear* I'll kill myself, I'll keep on buying ether for a toothache and save it up until I've got a whole jug full and then drink it. And where will I keep all my things? Oh, it's going to be *dreadful*. What *shall* I do?

As the situation unfolded itself, getting worse every second, her tears welled warmly out and rolled down her face, but no one took any notice except Artie, who observed, quirking his fingers at her:

'Cry baby cry, stick yer finger in yer eye.'

'You shut your fat face,' growled Maurice, and under the table he pushed his big dirty khaki handkerchief into Amy's lap. Artie, crimson with embarrassment both at the length of his own speech and the public rebuke from his admired elder brother, buried his face in his teacup.

Amy muttered her thanks and wiped the tears away with the stale-smelling handkerchief. A lump ached in her throat, but she fought it down somehow, fiercely remembering her mother's voice telling her to be brave. And then, exactly like a door quickly opening, she thought of Buck Finch among the savages, the Pony Express rider surrounded by Indians, all the heroes of her secret world who had faced danger against horrible odds—and she ran straight through the open door and suddenly felt better.

Now I must be cool and wary . . . the words came into her mind. She looked coolly and warily round the table at the Beedings, met Mrs Beeding's glance, and smiled politely.

'Feeling better now you've had yer tea, luv?'

'Yes, thank you, Mrs Beeding.'

'That's right.'

I shall just have to work to keep all my things together, that's all, she decided, finishing up her dough cake with a new relish. It'll be simply awful, but I must make a plan like Nelson did with his battles and stick to it. If only they'll all get used to me and leave me alone I can manage somehow.

Her first impulse after tea had been to creep upstairs when nobody was looking, but she realized that if they got used to seeing her about like one of the family they would be less likely to notice when she disappeared, so she offered instead to help Mona wash up; and when they had finished and hung the sopping teacloth to dry on the wall nearest the bakehouse, she accompanied Mona upstairs to the Lounge.

The agent who had showed Mr Beeding over the house fifteen years ago had called the back parlour overlooking the garden the Lounge, presumably because its french windows opened into a small conservatory built by a former tenant, and the name had stuck. It was a large room. The wallpaper was covered with small blue and green objects shaped like tongues and little orange balls on a mud ground. There was a suite covered in grey cut-velvet, a shabby brown carpet, and lace curtains stiff and white as a waterfall across the french windows. The Beedings did all their sitting, sewing, reading, listening-in and entertaining here, yet the Lounge never looked anything but cold and stiff. The only nice part about the Lounge, to Amy, was the conservatory, where Mrs Beeding harboured pots of cherry pie and mignonette and one or two aspidistra, whose leaves she kept glossy with polishings of salad oil; there were two old deck chairs in there where Mr Beeding liked to sit on fine Sunday mornings and read *The Sunday Express*, and the place smelt faintly earthy and warm. That was because the bakehouse immediately below it kept it at greenhouse temperature six nights out of the seven.

Amy sat down on a chair near the door and opened one of Mona's cinema papers; Mrs Beeding put on her spectacles and took up some knitting for Baby, who was playing on the rug at her feet, while Mr Beeding hurried back to the shop to let Jack off to get his tea. Dora went upstairs, Artie rushed off to the Fields with Maurice. Only Mona was left, a bored and ever-present peril to the occupied, lounging round the room, picking up things and dropping them again, putting on the headphones and taking them off, interrupting Baby's game, saying at intervals she wished she hadn't finished her knitting.

'Then go out and buy some more and start a new bit, do, Mona,' said her mother firmly at last, looking up over her spectacles. 'Take sixpence out o' my purse an' go on, now, at once. You're more worry than a blowfly over the meat, goin' on like that.'

Mona decided that she would. 'Coming, Aime?' She stopped by the door and caught hold of her friend's pigtail. 'Coo! Isn't your hair thick! I wonder you don't get spots on your face. Coming?'

Amy's control snapped. She jerked her head violently away and sprang up, her imploring eyes turned on Mrs Beeding.

Mrs Beeding did not fail her.

'Go on, now, Mona. Amy doesn't feel like going out just now. You run on; I've got to take the shop in a few minutes and I want you to mind Baby.'

Mona went, and Mrs Beeding continued, her gaze fixed steadily on her knitting:

'Would you like to get a book for yourself from upstairs, luv? There's not much to read down here. I'll be packin' all your stuff up in a day or two an' we'll have to think what's to be done with it, but it'll stand over just for a while.'

'Oh . . . yes . . . thank you, Mrs Beeding!' gasped Amy, and not even waiting to ask the all-important question about where she was to sleep, she darted away.

Half-way up the stairs to the top (what a long time it seemed since she had been there!) she met Dora going into her room with some clean sheets over her arm, looking rather irritable.

'Hullo!' Amy muttered, flying past but greeting her on the principle that all Beedings were suspicious and must be hailed every time one was sighted in order not to make them more so.

'Hullo, where are you off to like a fire-escape?'

'Only to get a book.'

'Well, I hope when you're old and grey you won't say I've never done anything for you; I'm late for Spanish now, but I'm making up your bed before I go. Hope to heaven you don't snore, that's all.'

Amy stopped dead.

'*Oh!* Oh, Dora, am I going to sleep with you?'

'Yes. There's plenty of room for us both, Mum says. There is, too, really; you can bring all your muck down and stick it over in one corner and I'll have mine in another, and woe betide you, Aime Lee, if you go spilling rubbish all over my area, that's all. Dad and Jack moved your bed down this afternoon while we . . . while we were all out. Only no pictures messing up the walls in *my* room, thank you. I never saw such a sight as you've made of the small-top-back in all my life, the Royal Academy isn't in it. Good thing you haven't pasted 'em on, that's all, or Mum would have had something to say.'

She went in and shut the door.

So she was to sleep with Dora! Well, that wasn't so bad, thought Amy, going on up the stairs. Anything was better than sharing Mona's room, and never getting a second to herself. Dora was often bossy and sharp, but she had so many things to interest her—the office, her Spanish classes, her cycling at week-ends, her boy-friend—that she was always busy and therefore less likely to interest herself in Amy's doings. And her room was large and pleasant, immediately under Amy's bedroom in the flat, and therefore overlooking the same quiet old gardens with big trees. And she had said that Amy could have a corner for her things! Amy gave a little skip as she opened the sitting-room door

But as she opened it, and stood on the threshold looking in at the familiar objects already coated with two days' dust—the table marked with hot plate stains, the picture of Victorian ladies skating in a yellow sunset, the sturdy backs of her American books on their shelf, the well-known flood of light coming in at the dusty windows with all London spread out like a ghostly painting behind the golden splendour—such a rush of agonized longing for her mother swept her that she staggered and half-fell to the floor, exactly as though she had been struck. Resting her weight on one hand, with her head bowed, she gently pushed the door shut with her foot; and then slid to her full length on the floor, her eyes pillowed on her arm. She lay there for half an hour, quite still, until Mona's blundering entrance (without the courtesy, now, of a preliminary knock) brought her scrambling to her feet.

7

There was no one to object to the Beedings taking possession of Amy and her two hundred and seventy pounds. Only four persons outside the family circle were at all interested in her— Miss Lathom, Mr Ramage, the gentleman-at-the-insurance, and Old Porty, and of these four Old Porty and Mr Ramage soon lost what slight concern they had, while Miss Lathom and the gentleman-at-the-insurance were both won over by Mrs Beeding's common-sense, and the kindness and honesty that shone from her every word.

She said frankly to both of them that Amy's twelve and sixpence a week would be a help; but she also said that Amy was a nice good little girl whom she liked and for whom she wanted to do her best. Both Miss Lathom and the gentleman-at-the-insurance were intelligent people, and they were more convinced by the moderate tone of Mrs Beeding's statements than they would have been had she vowed that it wasn't the money but the poor little mite had no mother and might end up on the streets unless Mrs Beeding rescued her and took that mother's place. After the formalities were concluded which handed over the money to Amy under Mrs Beeding's trusteeship, the gentleman-at-the-insurance felt easy in his mind about its proper administration and dismissed the matter to the care of his files. Miss Lathom, for her part, felt that as Amy would be under her eye for the next three years she would be able to see at once if the child showed signs of being neglected or unhappy. But she did not assume that Amy would be either. She had not only taken a fancy to Mrs Beeding; she knew her type and liked it, and was sure that the Lee child would be safe in her care.

Both Miss Lathom and the-gentleman-at-the-insurance returned to their routine affairs, once Tim Lee's funeral was over, with that comfortable feeling we experience when we have seen a fellow creature adequately provided for and realize that we need worry about them no longer.

Mrs Beeding told Amy more than once that it was a Blessing and a Mercy that her Dad had kept up the payments of his insurance, for he had not a penny of any other money put away. It was Edie who had made Tim take out the policy as soon as Amy was born, Edie who had simply taken the money from him whenever he had any and posted off the premiums regularly, and it was Edie's memory that had kept him faithful for a year after her death to this one piece of prudence. Thanks to her mother, Amy was not a pauper nor an object for charity. The policy and receipts were found in Tim's small suitcase together with the certificate of his marriage to Edie and that of Amy's birth, and some yellow snapshots of young people laughing before the War (the last time any one had really sound reasons for laughing in a snapshot) and some of Amy's grandparents outside the house covered with ivy and built in the reign of George II in which Tim had been born.

Yorkshire was a little impressed by these relics, for the Georgian house was handsome and Amy's grandparents looked an imposing pair, but Mrs Beeding did not let her charge see that she was impressed nor did she alter her manner by one note from its calm, complacent, yet comforting tone. Like everyone else under Mrs Beeding's roof and within her circle, Amy would be managed, gentry or no gentry. Her money would be scrupulously laid out for her, she would be properly fed, clothed, warned against Life and coaxed in time out of her mopey bookworm ways. In return, Mrs Beeding wanted that Amy should be a clean, neat, self-supporting decent girl, the sort that her dead grandparents who had lived in that fine house need not look down from wherever-they-were and feel ashamed of. It did not occur to Mrs Beeding that old Mr and Mrs Lee might have wanted something other for Amy than this perfect parlourmaid character, for her ideas about the gentry were hazy; the only clear notion she had of gentry was that it demanded, and usually got, proper behaviour. As for the gentry that romped brightly all over the Sunday papers, Mrs Beeding looked upon *that* gentry as a sort of warning circus, a Horrible Example to the Virtuous but also a relish with the Virtuous's tea. She did not connect it at all with Amy's grandparents, in which she showed a wisdom beyond her actual knowledge.

She was fond of Amy and there could not be too many children in the house for Mrs Beeding, who liked nothing better than to sit at the head of a table crammed with food and faces. Amy was just one more face to make full and shiny with hotpot and dough cake and apple-pudding. Nor was Mrs Beeding completely insensitive to Amy's nature and tastes. She had no intention of trying to make the little girl different all at once. She knew, of course, that Amy liked being alone with a nice book, and she saw no harm in that, provided it did not happen too often and make her mopier still. She frequently sent Mona off with a flea in her ear when the latter was worrying Amy to come out on a boy-hunt in the Fields or sit and knit on the side doorstep, telling her daughter to leave the child alone while she was quiet. For a week after Tim's funeral Amy was able to escape for a little while every evening up to the flat and read or dream (she did not dare to write, for fear of interruption and consequent discovery) and she was just beginning to resettle herself into her secret world and recover a little from the shock of her father's death—when Mrs Beeding sent her heart into her gym shoes one evening at tea by announcing:

'We're going to pack oop yer bits tomorrow afternoon, Amy, luv. Mrs Martin comes in on Monday and I've got to clean the place.'

'Where will they go, Mrs Beeding?' inquired Amy faintly but

politely. They were alone in the kitchen except for Mr Beeding and Baby.

'In yer old bedroom, luv. Mrs Martin and her daughter don't want the small-top-back, she says, because they haven't enoof stoof to make it look nice, so we're goin' to put yer bits in there an' lock it oop until yer leave school and we can decide what's ter be done with 'em.'

'I should rather like some of the books kept out, please, Mrs Beeding.'

'Please yerself, luv. You take what yer want, an' p'raps Dora'll let you keep 'em in her room. There'll be plenty o' room for all yer bits in the small-top-back now yer bed's gone downstairs.'

'What's Mrs Martin like, Mrs Beeding?' inquired Amy after a pause.

'An old cow,' struck in Mr Beeding unexpectedly, handing Baby a tremendous burnt crust in his excitement. 'Bad-tempered old cow, that's what.'

'Now, David, no language, please,' warned his wife. ('Don't give her that, luv, it's burnt').

'She's bedridden, poor old soul. The daughter works in Walton, Hassell and Port's, down the High Street. I told her I can't wait on her moother, she'll have to do for herself.'

'Hope she does, and quick,' Mr Beeding said, tickling Baby's white fat neck. Baby threw back her head, her brilliant blue eyes half-shut, and exploded with gurgles, then imperiously dashed her crust to the floor and looked hopefully at her father.

'Pick it oop for her, David, luv.'

'You're a grown man's work, straight you are,' observed Mr Beeding, smiling lovingly at his daughter before he stooped to grovel among the wet crusts, splashes of tea, and cake crumbs under her chair.

'Are the Martins nice, Mrs Beeding?' Amy was wondering if she could get to know the Martins and sometimes go into the sitting-room at night to see the starry lights, the little wormlike golden trains and marching streets of lamps spread up the hillside like an exciting map that moved.

'She's an old maid. Keeps herself to herself. A bit fussy, Dora says. She knows 'em more than I do, really. They heard about us through Dora.'

'Both cows,' said Mr Beeding, passing his cup and sucking his dark moustache. 'Another cup, Marie, please.'

''Ow,' repeated Baby, looking from one to the other with a bewitching smile. They all laughed, Amy's thin little giggle joining with the rest.

But she escaped upstairs directly after tea to the flat and spent an agitated half-hour choosing books and stacking up her treasures ready to take down to Dora's bedroom tomorrow afternoon. She had carried her stories to school in her suitcase on the first day she went back after her father's death for fear the Beedings might poke about and discover them, and they had been there in her desk ever since. She was fretting about them because she had not had a chance to write a line of *The Mummy's Curse* ever since the Beedings had swallowed her up. Her head was full of the story, Beginning to Run in her mind, but there was never a minute that she dared snatch to write. She had a desperate fear of the Beedings finding out and reading the story. Even had they been kind and full of admiration she would have hated them knowing about her stories. They were kind, the Beedings, but they would not understand.

As for her furniture, one day, when she was grown-up and had a job, she could take all the things out again and furnish her own room with them. Meanwhile, it made her very miserable to think of all the things shut away in that little room; it was like losing friends. Her mother had cut out on the table, slept in the divan bed, sat in the armchair. Still, it might be worse. The things were not going to be sold. One day she would have them back.

But her dreams about the future were vague. The idea of next Sunday was as remote as that of her eighteenth birthday, and far less real than any event in *The Mummy's Curse*, and her sense of money was completely that of a child. Half-a-crown was a fortune, but her mind could not take in the fact of two hundred and seventy pounds in her name in the bank. She knew that she would not have to live on charity and she was glad, but only because Mona was always sneering at the Edmonton girl cousins to whom their local doctor's wife sometimes gave old frocks of her own daughters', saying that it was awful to live on charity and she, Mona, would sooner die. Apparently charity was something dreadful, thought Amy. Oh, well, I'm all right. Mrs Beeding said so. But it never occurred to her to demand a separate bedroom for her twelve-and-sixpence a week nor to take on the airs of a lodger and insist on just a shred of privacy. She let herself be swallowed. Once inside the Beeding whale, however, little Jonah was very active in preserving her secret world.

On the Monday morning after the flat had been cleared out ready for the Martins to occupy, Miss Lathom was surprised to hear a soft knock on the door of her room, during the eleven o'clock Break.

'Come in!' she called, lifting her eyes with a sigh from an American woman's lowbrow paper which she was enjoying with her Horlicks and digestive biscuit. Which of the younger members of the staff was having a conscience over nothing *now*? Naylor, probably. Oh, dear.

But the person who came in immediately was the Lee child, carrying a parcel wrapped in brown paper and tied with string.

'Amy, my dear, what do you want? You haven't an appointment, you know. You ought not to be here. What is it?' Miss Lathom's tone was kind but brisk. Even the death of a father must not make a headmistress get-at-able whenever someone in Upper IV felt like seeing her.

'Miss Lathom, please, can I speak to you a minute? It's urgent.'
So was Amy's tone; though quiet, as usual.

'Very well, just this once. What is it?'

'Miss Lathom——' She came over and stood by the Head's
chair (and Miss Lathom had the strength of mind not to slide
the lowbrow magazine under some half-term reports) 'you're
the only person I can tell.'

'All right. What's it all about?' rather drily. She was guarding
herself from a possible emotional explosion; little girls of nearly
thirteen were uncanny fishes.

'Well, you see, in this parcel I have some private things: I
don't want anyone to see them. Please will you take care of
them for me and lock them up in your desk and never, never
let anyone see them, Miss Lathom?'

The Headmistress was completely taken aback and felt a little
ashamed of herself and more than a little moved. She was also
impressed in a curious way by Amy's manner. The child might
have been speaking without self-consciousness or fear to someone
of her own age. Miss Lathom said kindly:

'Of course I will. Give it to me.' She took the parcel, unlocked
a drawer in her desk, and fitted the books comfortably into it.
Amy watched the parcel, not Miss Lathom, in silence while this
was being done.

'There. It'll be quite safe there.' Miss Lathom straightened
herself and looked at the child. At that moment a thousand
pounds would not have tempted her to ask what was in that
parcel, though she was so interested by this sudden sidelight on
the little Lee child that she longed to know.

'Thanks most awfully, Miss Lathom.' But as Amy lingered,
quite as aware as Miss Lathom that something more ought to
be said to round off the incident, a sudden glow of happiness
warmed her. Her stories were safe! The Beedings could never
find out now! Miss Lathom, looking at her curiously, saw her
face turn pale pink and her eyes suddenly shine. She leaned

forward and said confidentially, her voice full of the writer's pride:

'Miss Lathom, they're stories.'

'Are they?' said Miss Lathom, calmly and in a low tone, very conscious that a door had been suddenly opened to her. She stood on the threshold, afraid of saying something that would cause it to shut.

'Yes. A lot of them.'

'Oh. Then I suppose you've been writing them ever since you were quite small?' Miss Lathom went on in the same quiet soothing tone.

'Oh, yes. Ever since I could write properly—when I was about six, I mean. And before that I used to make them up to myself. I'm writing one now called *The Mummy's Curse*. It's about Ancient Egypt. At least——' She looked disturbed, and hesitated, 'I *was* writing it, but now I'm afraid I shall have to leave it for a long time. Three years nearly. It's awful, Miss Lathom. It was just Beginning to Run in my mind, and now I've got to leave it.'

'Why is that?'

'Well, Miss Lathom, there isn't anywhere to write at home, now that I live with the Beedings. You see, they're awfully kind but I don't want them to see the stories because they wouldn't understand.'

'They might laugh, do you mean?'

'Oh, no. The stories aren't *funny*, Miss Lathom, they're exciting. I just mean the Beedings wouldn't understand. There's no place I can have to write in at home, now.' Her voice was low and worried and she stared right into the Head's eyes with her own bright brown ones, clear as water and like water full of secrets.

Miss Lathom made a sudden decision.

'Amy,' she said, unable to resist putting her suggestion in the form of a question so that she might have the joy of hearing the child cry, '*Oh, yes, please!*' 'Would you like to have the old exam room to write in, after school in the afternoons sometimes?'

'Oh, yes, *please*, Miss Lathom!' cried Amy, in a deep, excited voice that was startling. 'Oh, I *would*! Thank you very, very much, Miss Lathom! It *is* kind of you!' Her face had flushed deeper pink and her eyes sparkled with delight. Miss Lathom looked at her, smiling, experiencing a pleasure almost as strong.

'Well, then, you shall. You'll be quite safe there. I've got the only key, and no one ever goes in except to clean it twice a term so you won't be disturbed. I'll give you the key,' she turned to her desk, 'and you can keep your stories in there too, so that you won't have to worry me every time you want them,' turning to smile at her.

'Miss Lathom, I promise faithfully on my sacred honour I'll never worry you,' said Amy solemnly, 'and I won't ever tell a single living soul either, Miss Lathom.'

'No, don't, Amy, because it isn't at all an . . . orthodox . . . thing to do, you know, and if the other chil . . . girls knew about it there might be all sorts of tiresome fusses. Besides, you want to have it all to yourself, don't you? That's the whole point.'

'Oh, *yes*, Miss Lathom!'

'All right, then. Run along now. Break's nearly over . . . wait a minute. You'd better put your stories away first, hadn't you? Yes. Hurry now, dear, there goes the bell.'

She handed the parcel to Amy, who darted across the room to a door on the far side, and fitted the key in the lock, bending over with the books clutched to her chest and her pigtail flopping forward. Then, just before she ran into the room, she turned and gave the headmistress a sweet and triumphant smile.

Good gracious! thought Miss Lathom, staring at her through the open door of the old exam room, when all her secrets come out into her face instead of hiding behind it the child's enchanting! Then she said:

'That will do, now, Amy. Run along. You can come and write tomorrow afternoon after school.'

'Yes. Thanks *awfully*, Miss Lathom, it *is* kind of you.

Miss Lathom——' she turned again at the door, 'I will dedicate *The Mummy's Curse* to you.'

'Thank you, Amy. I should like that very much,' answered Miss Lathom.

The door closed.

Now that's the first time since Great-aunt Anna put me in charge here that I've done anything that might be described as imprudent, mused Miss Lathom, sitting down and stirring the cold Horlicks.

Still, the circumstances are unusual. She's an orphan. Great-aunt Anna always had a soft spot for orphans! And she's unusual, too, and possibly gifted. I may be nursing a genius! But even if her stories are rubbish they obviously mean more than anything in the world to her, funny little packet, and she hasn't much else.

Suppose she overhears me having Naylor up on the carpet, or soft-soaping a Parent?

She won't. She isn't the sort to eavesdrop, and anyhow she'll be too absorbed in *The Mummy's Curse* to hear anything.

Oh, I feel sure it will be all right.

Smiling, she drank her Horlicks and turned to the pile of half-term reports.

Amy flew downstairs and joined her Form just as it marched into Room 6 for Scripture.

'Enter Piggy, flushed and breathless,' muttered the Form wit. 'Where've you been? We waited simply years for you by the sundial. Honestly, Piggy, you are *feeble*.'

'So are you feeble. My suspender burst and it took ages. Do you know your feeble text? I don't. I feebly didn't look at it until this morning.'

The old exam room was a small chamber containing a row of desks at which pupils had formerly sat for the simple entrance examination admitting them to the Anna Bonner. Earlier still, in the 'eighties, it had been furnished with a sofa and a shawl, and here the Founder had been wont to refresh herself with fifteen minutes' nap every day after lunch, and heaven aid anyone who woke her out of it upon any pretext whatever. Now the room was disused, partly because it was situated in a dark little cul-de-sac next to the Headmistress's room and that made a bad impression upon visiting parents, and partly because it had no means of being heated, the builders of the 'eighties having light-heartedly omitted to provide it with a chimney because it was so small. It was entered by the door in the cul-de-sac; the door in Miss Lathom's room was never used.

It was a sunless little apartment with one narrow window of red, yellow and blue glass overlooking the School garden, but it was clean and pleasantly quiet, and here during the next three years Amy spent her happiest hours. Sometimes the autumn moon crept into the sky while she was writing there in the late afternoon, when the school building was empty save for a few pupils taking music or typewriting in remote rooms; and she would look up, pen resting against her lip, and stare into that solemn silver face. Sometimes on spring afternoons, when the rosy reflection of sunset fell on the worn grey floor-boards and tinted the crayon portrait of the Founder near the door, and her wrist ached from writing, she would go over to the window and gaze through the narrow panes of red or blue glass at the familiar garden thus transformed into a sinister landscape under a lowering sky. No one ever chanced on her desk-full of stories or discovered that she wrote there.

In this room *The Mummy's Curse* was finished, and Amy proudly showed the dedication to the Headmistress:

To Miss Lathom, M.A.
with
The Author's Silent Gratitude

'I put "silent" because of course I can't ever tell anyone how kind you are to let me have the old exam room, Miss Lathom,' explained Amy.

She did not explain that she had laboriously covered all the exercise books with cretonne in the fond hope that her head-mistress would not recognize them as School property; and Miss Lathom turned a blind eye on that fact, which confronted her as soon as Amy presented the book.

Any desire that Miss Lathom may have had to read *The Mummy's Curse* disappeared when she glanced at its opening lines. They seemed to her disappointingly bald, without Style, Originality or Sensitiveness to Beauty. They were made up of short words in short sentences, describing the desert at noon and two men sitting below the newly carved Sphinx waiting for a third, whose name was not given. Miss Lathom's thoughts returned more than once during the day to that picture. She found herself wondering who they were waiting for, and why. But there was nothing unusual in that: of course one always wanted to know what happened in a story. It was just a story, that was all. That was the impression Miss Lathom received of *The Mummy's Curse*, and as she had more than enough duties with which to fill her days without wasting time on reading rubbish, she was glad that she had not asked if she might read it.

Amy had no intention of letting her read it; she whisked it away at once and never mentioned it again, and the next day she had begun *The Hero of the Desert* which was about Colonel Lawrence, and had almost forgotten *The Mummy's Curse*, as writers do forget their earlier works.

And so for the next two years the months glided past while she lived her two lives, the bustling ordinary life with the Beedings and the secret one with her stories in the old exam room at school. She adjusted herself to the balance in time, as she had adjusted herself to life alone with her father. She missed flying cut-outs from the window at night and having the evenings alone to dream over her American books and the back numbers of *The Prize* that Tim had brought home every week; but she soon got used to sitting in the brightly-lit Lounge with any of the Beedings who happened to be at home, taking her turn with the wireless earphones, gossiping with Mona about the stars in her cinema magazines, sometimes neatly darning her stockings or putting a patch in her bloomers.

The Beeding home life was constructive as well as active, and when they were at home all were occupied; Mona was the only one who knew the meaning of boredom. Had they lived in the eighteen-eighties instead of the nineteen-thirties Mr Beeding would have read aloud to them while they worked. Their only fault as a family was their inability to imagine a human being who might sometimes wish to be alone; and in this they were not unique.

As for the sharing of Dora's bedroom, Amy found it more than bearable; it was pleasant. Beside her bed, which stood in an alcove, she had a table with a roomy drawer where she kept her Curios, the box of cut-outs and other small treasures. Her American books were kept on the table with her brush and comb and her handkerchief case made of pink satin embroidered with bright violets and 'A' in yellow, a birthday gift from Mona which Amy much admired.

Dora was so neat, quick-moving and quiet that it was like sharing a room with a needle or a pin. She did not snore, or scatter powder, or dream, but lay thin and silent in her bed all night and awoke punctually at seven o'clock every morning to wash herself in cold water and dress with amazing speed inside the shelter of her pyjamas, which she dodged on and off and peeled up and down in the most complicated manner imaginable to prevent the world from getting the smallest peep at her naked self. Amy performed the same contortions, but slower, inside a narrow nightgown with long sleeves and a high neck; and while they dressed they shot muffled comments at each other about the look of the weather.

As each was absorbed in her own affairs and not very interested in the other and each was tidy and reserved, they made
satisfactory stablemates. And when Amy awoke trembling from
a bad dream as she somtimes did, it was comforting to lie awake
in the dark and slowly realize that Dora was there, quietly
asleep in the narrow bed on the other side of the room.

She still missed her mother painfully, and it terrified her to
think about the two bodies, lying inside the earth together on
Highgate Hill. She knew that *they*, their real selves, were with
God in Heaven; yet somehow this picture was not so real as the
picture of two bodies inside the cold earth. She thought of them
on wild nights when the rare snow whirled over London and
the wind screamed high overhead in the darkness. How strange
and awful it was to put people into a hole in the earth, *people
one had known*. Her mother, whose warm hand she could feel
now, clasping her own!

She sprang up and dashed across the room to the wireless, to
sit by Mrs Beeding, anything to drive that thought away!

But as the months passed, the memory of her father and
mother slowly sank deep, deep into the clear dark water of her
unconscious memory, to lie on the floor of that mysterious ocean
and trouble the upper regions only occasionally. *The Hero of
the Desert* was finished and *The House with a Secret* begun. That
was finished in its turn and so was *The Mysterious Barge*, which was
about smuggling in Essex; and all these stories were hidden away
in the desks of the old exam room. Amy never showed any more
of them to Miss Lathom, who was much occupied during Amy's
last year at school with the long illness and death in the Summer
Term of her great-aunt, the almost legendary Founder; and Miss
Lathom did not ask her more than once or twice, 'how are the
stories going?' She was a little disappointed in the Lee child; she
had seemed to promise interesting developments, but none had
come. It was only a lonely child's passion for scribbling; common
enough, if not common at the Anna Bonner. Miss Lathom, like

111

everyone else, soon took Amy for granted. That was exactly what Amy wanted.

During her two years with the Beedings her height and weight increased satisfactorily as a result of Mrs Beeding's cooking, and insistence upon walks in the Fields or Up Highgate as opposed to mopeyness. Her nerves improved: she learned to take buses, smells, and cut-up rabbits more or less for granted. Edie would have been pleased. She was lonelier than ever, but she was more or less used to that, too, and never consciously thought about it. Her loneliness and lack of someone to love only found expression in dark unchildish moods of depression. Then she dreamed that the crowds in the streets could not see her, because they were all hurrying past her on their way back to happy homes. She dreamed she stood in front of them screaming: 'I'm Amy Lee! Look, I'm Amy Lee!' but nobody saw her or stopped, and she awoke crying heartbrokenly in the dark bedroom. 'Do shut up, Aime; you're dreaming,' Dora would mutter crossly, turning over, and after a while Amy would fall asleep again.

But these dreams did not come often; and as a whole her life was tranquil. The months slipped away, and presently three years had passed since the little American boy had given her the coin on her birthday at Kenwood House.

8

When he was sixteen Bob Vorst suddenly made up his mind that he would be a doctor.

His father and mother were pleased, for Boone was causing them much grief and worry at the time and they naturally turned to the younger son for comfort. It was fine that he should have made up his mind for himself so young, and a doctor's career was a splendid life-work. As well as helping one's fellow men, it was possible to make a fortune.

On a late summer morning during the Great Depression, he said casually at breakfast:

'I'm going to be a doctor.'

'Well, well, that's fine,' said his father sarcastically and affectionately, looking up from his paper (it was *The Sentinel*, which had not yet followed *The Inquirer* and *The Citizen* into the maw of the New York syndicate). 'Now *you're* all fixed up, anyway. And when did you make up your mind?'

'Yesterday.' Bob was not irritated; he was slowly stoking himself with food which he chewed steadily with his beautiful widely-spaced teeth. His day at the High was a heavy one, crammed with hard exercise and with studies which he did not find easy, and he could not get through it on the toast and orange juice which was enough for his sister Irene, sitting opposite him and slowly sipping with her rounded arms resting on the table.

'And why was that?' went on Mr Vorst.

'Oh . . . I don't know. I thought it'd be interesting work and a fellow'd get around.' Bob looked at his father lazily, still eating. His grey eyes gave no secrets away, but his mother, eating toast and sipping her own orange juice at the other end of the table, looked at him and thought: He was down in the Polak quarter in Morgan the other day again, I wonder if he saw something down there that made him want to be a doctor? I don't like him going down there, I'm scared he'll catch something in that dirty place.

'Well, it certainly is interesting work but it's hard work, too,' she remarked. 'Look at Doc Roberts. He's only as old as Dad but he looks seventy, and he never gets a chance to go out anywhere or see his folks or eat a meal in comfort, he's everlastingly hopping up to answer a call. He'll kill himself one of these days.'

'But he must like it or he wouldn't have stuck it for thirty years, right here on Main,' said Bob.

'Ah, but you won't do that, Bob. You'll get ahead, get out into the world, go places, be a great surgeon, perhaps,' teased his father.

'Make a fortune,' said his mother, smiling at him.

'Swell chance anybody's got of making a fortune nowadays,' said Lou, who had grown into a fresh little girl of thirteen with a cool manner and a mind of her own.

Everybody groaned, and Irene began to chant: 'Prosperity-is-just-around-the-corner . . . around-the-corner . . .' until the others joined in and there was uproar.

An Englishman looking at the delightful faces of these three American children, would have at once noticed their openness. They looked blown clean, as though pure winds were always sweeping over their eyes, clear as water, and their high cheekbones dropping Indian-straight to their generous mouths. They looked younger than English boys and girls of the same age, young as the Archtype of Youth, and their very clothes had a flying, casual appearance that suggested swift movement over great spaces of country.

Impossible to picture a tightly-buttoned-up young American!

The life they led had given them this look. None of them had ever felt the soft, mournful, mysterious hands of the ancient Past reaching out from buildings five hundred years old; rising from fields where the plough turns up a green Roman coin in the purple earth, subduing the mind with wonder. When they thought of forests, these rolled in their fancy from the dark pines of Vermont to the giant redwoods of California two thousand miles away; and when they thought of the sea they saw the mighty waves of Cape Race and the indolent ripples lapping the smallest bayou of Florida; and because they could drive along splendid roads for a thousand miles before they reached the coast, and because they lived in a county the size of Yorkshire that was only part of a state the size of half England, they had never known what it was to feel crowded.

Also, for two generations these young people and their cousins the Viners had enjoyed such a good time that young English people of moderate fortune can hardly imagine just how good it was. There were always plenty of them to do things together in a gay familiar crowd, because both Viners and Vorsts had a tradition of large families and lived up to it; and the three newspapers had earned money steadily for the Vorsts for three generations, just as their two hardware stores had earned it for the Viners, and if neither family was rich judged by American standards, by both English and American standards they were comfortable, which is better. There was always something going on; a dance, a picnic, somebody's birthday, a wedding, a chris-tening, a shower for the latest bride, movie-parties and drives out to the country club to dance on Saturday evenings; and the two families, as the aristocracy of the little town, lived in one another's pockets and enjoyed together every pleasure that their social position could give.

Some trace of this happiness and liberty had passed into their young faces, giving them the look which in England is found only in the faces of children in country families who have grown up with horses and dogs. But in these American faces there was also a faint exciting look of the Indian. It was so faint that sometimes it was not there, and it was never more than a hint, a shadow, but behind it waved the woods of Virginia and the tomahawk glittered. It was stronger in Bob's face than in Irene's or Lou's, because his cheekbones were the highest of the three.

'Come on, Lou. Pay up.' Irene handed her the moneybox into which everybody who mentioned the Depression had to put a dime. At the end of the week the box was emptied and the money given to charity.

'I'll pay up, but I think it's crazy,' said Lou, paying up. Her pocket money had just been raised to half a dollar a week and every cent was precious. 'What good can a few dimes do among all those millions of people out of work and broke?'

'Every little helps and I like you children to think of others sometimes. Besides, it's only a joke, just a little fun,' soothed Mrs Vorst.

'Will you be just an ordinary doctor, Bob, like Doc Martin, or will you be a specialist?' asked Lou, changing the subject.

Lou did not like most jokes. This was not because she had no humour, but because her own ironical taste in jokes made her think the other kind silly. She very seldom teased her brothers and sister and did not laugh when they did, but she had chuckling fits over dry and rather malicious anecdotes about local unworthies relayed to her by Myron (who still told her 'everything' as he used to when she was nine) and with one or two favoured girls at her school. And sometimes, when she could get Bob to herself, away from those great boys with their everlasting ball game, he and she had jokes together, her kind of joke, which Bob understood perfectly when he bothered to. Lou loved Bob. She thought him crazy, the way he believed everybody was swell and a great guy (she and Myron knew better!) but that only made her love him the more. And he was so strong, and kind, and always giving her dimes when she was broke, and not shutting her up when she began to tell him about things that interested her. Bob was the loveliest person in the world.

'I guess I'll just be an ordinary doctor,' he answered her, going a little red as the attention of the breakfast table turned on him. 'Like Doc Martin.'

'What . . . and stay down on Main for thirty years dosing kids for the bellyache and all the old cats for rheumatics? Ambitious, aren't you?' drawled Irene.

'Oh, he won't be like that after he's qualified,' said his father confidently. 'He'll be ambitious enough then. That won't be for another seven years, and by that time the country'll be clear of the Depression and forging ahead again . . . it can't last (all right, Sharlie, here's your dime) . . . and there'll be plenty of opportunities again for young men . . . if he still wants to be a doctor. Last month he wanted to be an ace flyer, I seem to remember.'

Bob grinned but said nothing. He carefully poured syrup on a waffle.

'Well, it's the least crazy thing any of you have wanted to be up to now, and I'm glad one of you is sensible,' said Mrs Vorst. 'I think it's a fine life work, and your Uncle Lewis'll be pleased, too. You might go down South later on and room with them while you're qualifying . . . for a while, anyway.' Her brother Lewis was a doctor in Louisiana.

'Well, there's plenty of time to talk about it later, when he's graduated.' Mr Vorst got up from the table. 'Ready, son?'

Bob drank up a great bowl of coffee, wiped his mouth, waved to his mother, pulled Lou's forelock and dashed after his father, who would drop him at the High on his way to the offices of *The Sentinel*. Irene and Lou walked down the hill a little later under the lilacs looking over rail-fences, past the pleasant houses set back from the wide road, and calling for their cousin Helen, who also attended the High, on their way.

When they had all gone, Mrs Vorst picked up the paper (not *The Sentinel*: *The Sentinel* did not have such good Women's

Features as the syndicated paper) and went over to a comfortable chair by the window, but although she sat down and turned at once to the article on *Summer Luncheons* she did not begin to read. Instead she stared out of the window and thought about Boone.

Jeanette's family had moved to Chicago six months ago, and Boone, with his father's help, had got a job on a Chicago paper as a reporter so that he could be near her. He was drinking hard, and in debt, and not making good at his job. She would not marry him and she would not let him go. She had been engaged to him once and broken the engagement to engage herself to his best friend, and had broken that as well. Boone ran around with her hard-boiled, hard-drinking, hard-playing set, wretched as a dog in disgrace with its master, spoiling his own life and boring her and amusing her friends, while his mother and father were grieved and angered to the depth of their hearts. Sometimes, when he had hidden his torturing jealousy and let an evening pass without asking her to marry him, Jeanette told him that he was sweet.

'I wish she'd die, I do. She's just bad,' thought Sharlie Vorst, swishing the sheets of the newspaper together and getting up with a desperate movement. All the others are lovely, and doing so well (dear Bob, with his funny old notion of being a doctor! But I'm glad about that, I really am). Irene so pretty and all set to marry in a year or two, and Lou so clever with her dress-designing . . . we'd all be so happy, I'm sure, if it weren't for that old Depression and Boone.

She folded the paper and went to see the hired girl about lunch.

There had been a vague plan that in the evening Helen and Bob should play tennis with Irene and her latest young man, so about six o'clock Helen, in white and carrying her racquet, strolled up the drive of the Vorst home, wondering why no one seemed to be about. When she found all the big cool lower rooms empty, she went round the drive to the lawn back of the house, sat down under the big elm where she had listened so prettily to old Miss Cordell's chatter at the Vorsts' homecoming party nearly four years ago, and stared dreamily round the garden while she waited for someone to turn up. She was just sixteen; only last week her parents had given a big party for her birthday.

How many thousands of times it has been written or recalled with a smiling sigh: Yes . . . she was the prettiest girl in the village . . . in the town . . . for miles around . . . we were all in love with her! It must be one of the oldest sentences in the world, and is so full of poetry that it is not possible to imagine a world in which those words could not strike an answering note from the human heart. One day, long years ahead, they would be said of Helen Viner, but they would be followed by a thought which does not often follow the sigh given to the memory of a Beauty: *she was a darling*. Already in the hearts of her friends at school, of her own people, and of everyone who knew her in Vine Falls, her legend was growing, and she was loved as only those are loved who are good as well as beautiful.

At sixteen she could have lived the life that most sub-debs (and many older women) dream of, for college boys lay about in heaps at her feet and she never had to buy her own candy or movie tickets or flowers; she did not know what it was to get through a dance without at least six cut-ins, and could choose her escort for every free evening weeks ahead. It was this kind of popularity that had spoiled Jeanette Waldron and was fast spoiling Irene Vorst. Because they had had to make themselves just a bit cuter than Nature had meant them to be, they felt so relieved when the popularity came that they rushed at it and got drunk on it. All the women's supplements told girls to Play Up to Your Type when once you had found out what your type was, and the Irenes and Jeanettes feverishly played up, but Helen never troubled to be anybody but herself, and in spite of this, was adored.

This made other sub-debs who did not know her feel bitter, at first. Well, I throw in my hand. Hell, what's the use? was the sub-deb's first thought on meeting Helen. And strangely enough, when after a little while they realized that Helen was not a sly, deep beau-and-date poacher but a serious and artistic student of the Drama who was far more interested in that than in grabbing every man in sight, the other sub-debs were not comforted. To have all that beauty and to use it was human; to have it and not use it was divine, and therefore maddening. If she had not been such a lovely person they would have hated her.

She lived nearly as full a life at sixteen as some Englishwomen do at forty, for she enjoyed the exercising of her own gifts as much as she enjoyed dancing and parties. She designed some of her own clothes and made them expertly, she painted a little and wrote (the Prologue to the Vine Falls Pageant held last summer was by Helen) and sometimes had poems about Nature in *The Sentinel*, *The Inquirer* and *The Citizen*, and once even in a literary quarterly published in Virginia.

It was hoped by her father and mother, her uncle and aunt Vorst and all her other relations, that she would marry her cousin Bob. They had grown up almost next door to one another, and had enjoyed berry-parties, coasting parties, picnics and dances and skating together since they could walk. Nothing could be more suitable in a few years than their marriage.

Vorsts and Viners had been marrying one another for the past sixty years. It was a tradition. Naturally, as the Viner girls grew up, they began to look with distaste upon their Vorst boy cousins, swearing to themselves and to a few chosen friends that nothing, nothing in earth or heaven could persuade them to even think for one instant of marrying that dumb, crazy creature, while the boys did not think about it at all. But what with dancing together in the moonlight in summer, and going skating together in winter, and riding in the glorious fall woods, and going on camping parties together in the spring . . . somehow the Vorst girl and the Viner boy would find that they had quite a crush on each other, sweetened by common memories, and before they knew where they were they had discovered that it would be delightful, as well as in the family tradition, to marry.

But Helen had not yet become aware that all her grown-up relations wanted her to marry Bob. She often thought seriously about marriage, but only to vow to herself that she did not want to marry for years and years, probably not until she was twenty-seven. She wanted her life to go on as it was now (but with an increasing knowledge of the Drama) for as long a time as her imagination could dream of. She was happy.

She lay back in the long chair staring dreamily at the leaves above her head . . . shade on shade of fresh transparent green, with not the faintest wind to move them, but birds were restless up there, orioles and robins going to and fro with straw for nests, darting between the still leaves and showering fresh chirrups over the quiet evening air. It would be lovely to live up there among the clean branches and cool leaves and to look down on the white hyacinths from above. They would look like eighteenth-century wigs.

'Hullo there!'

She looked down, and saw Bob coming over the lawn pulling off his white sweater.

'Hullo! Where's everybody?'

'Walked out on us. Irene thought she'd rather dance, so of course her pet Parlour-Pink said so would he, and they've gone over to Roselands.'

He leaned both arms on a garden chair, looking down at her.

'Want to play?'

'We may as well, don't you think, now we're all changed?'

'I'd like to. Gosh, Helen, can you imagine . . . Irene's probably going to marry that wet stick.'

'He's a Red, too, isn't he?'

'He's a Pink. Hasn't got the guts to be a Red.'

121

They were strolling across to the tennis court.

'Does she really like him?' She pulled off her white wool coat and bent to tighten her shoe-strings, looking up at him interestedly. He was winding up the net and frowning over it.

'I guess so. She's funny that way. He gives me a pain. Gosh, Helen, this net's awful. Myron ought to see to it.'

'Haven't you played much this season?'

'Nope. Been too busy. So have you, I guess. I don't seem to have seen you in weeks. How's everything?'

'Oh, all right. I went in to Morgan last night to see the Eva le Gallienne show.'

'That must have been a big thrill,' he said, grinning at her with a touch of irony like Lou's. Helen had a crush on Eva le Gallienne.

'Oh, Bob, it was *wonderful!*'

'I'm sorry I missed it. Looky, will you take this side, 'cause the sun's on the other and I'm better than you, so that'll be a handicap for me.'

'You are not better than me,' she smiled, going over to the other side of the court. She suddenly felt so happy that little wings seemed fluttering and dancing all over her body, and she threw her racquet up in the air and caught it again.

'We'll see. You take first ball.'

She did, and served a double fault. Bob had suddenly grown serious; he did not like fooling at tennis, and she forgot her happiness and gave all her attention to the game.

Nevertheless, he beat her 6–1, 6–2, and when they at last stopped playing, he was inclined to be patronizing as he helped her into the white coat.

'You did very well, Helen.'

'Thanks,' she retorted.

'No, honest, I mean it. You've got a good service but you need practice. I wish I weren't so busy, I'd coach you.' They were strolling back to the house, which still seemed deserted. It was about half-past seven.

'That's kind of you but I'm pretty busy, too.'

'All right, don't get mad. I only meant that you *are* good, only you need lots of practice and, of course, I'd always beat you because I'm so much stronger than you.'

'Are you?' They were making for the kitchen, where the ice-box was.

'Of course I am. Couldn't I always beat you in a fight when we were kids?'

'Only because I used to hate getting all mussed up and you always rolled me in the dirt.'

'Gosh, doesn't it seem queer? I wouldn't do it now.' And he gave a droll look at her fresh white dress and unruffled hair.

'You'd better not try,' she said without coquetry, just coolly putting him at grubby-boy's arm's length; and perched herself on the table.

'I could, though.' Bob was a little irritated, and came over to her holding out a brown bulging arm above a rolled white shirt. 'That's muscle. Feel.'

'No, thanks. It looks kind of alarming,' she said firmly, and they both laughed.

'Well . . . what'll we eat?' He turned away to the ice-box. 'I guess supper won't be for hours yet. You don't have to get back, do you, Helen?'

'I said I'd be back about half-after eight; Jonas is coming over to see Stebby.'

'Oh yeah? I guess he is. He just adores Stebby. Smoked turkey . . . have some?'

He sat down in an old hickory rocker with a scrapwork cushion, that seemed more suited to its setting than the chromium faucets, ice-box and other up-to-date appointments of the old kitchen. This was the property of Myron, who preferred it to the Seats Scientifically Planned to Give Perfect Support with Complete Comfort provided for the maids. 'Give my bottom enough room and it'll look after its own support and comfort,' pronounced Myron.

Helen, whose appetite was not large, nibbled the turkey and studied her cousin. It was a long time . . . mercy! it must be a year! since she and Bob had raided the ice-box together on an evening like this when everybody had been out and he and she had come back from a swim at Roselands. Since then there had been so much to do; so many boys asking her for dates and being a darned nuisance, so much to learn about World Drama, so much writing, and studying, and social life at College, that although she had seen her cousins two or three times every week she had not once been alone with Bob. But she had often thought about him. Why (she was staring at him as this thought struck her, and at once looked quickly away) he had been in her mind more often than any of her beaux! Not that Bob was a beau, of course. He was just Bob, and had none of a beau's annoying yet flattering habits. He isn't anybody's beau, he's too young to be, she thought. But he's going to be darned attractive.

Bob had grown so much in the last few years that he was now noticeable in any group of his own age by his height and big frame. He wore his Swedish-fair hair rather long and never would do anything about the lock that fell over his forehead when he moved his head quickly. He looked lazy and sweet-tempered and tough. He seldom got angry, and when he did it was over something no-one thought would have angered him. When angry, he hit as hard as he could, knocked teeth out, and was not sorry afterwards. He had just a dash of unselfconscious charm, like a trace of coffee in pure milk, that was not enough to make him rotten when he grew older but quite enough to make girls already a little dreamy about him. He was quietly pleased with himself, laughed a good deal because he found life as amusing as it was good, and was popular wherever he went.

Mercy! Am I getting a crush on Bob, thought Helen in sudden panic, frowning down at her shoes while struggling with a desire

124

to go on looking at her cousin (just as she did at Eva le Gallienne!). Bob—and Eva le Gallienne! She must be crazy! She swung her feet and smiled with relief.

'What's funny?' He looked across at her amiably, ready to laugh too.

'Nothing. Just a crazy notion. Bob, are you going to be a doctor? Do tell me about it. When did you get the idea?'

'Well, the way things get around with you girls!' he said disgustedly. 'I only said something about it this morning at breakfast when they were talking about what Lou would do when she'd graduated, and now I suppose she's been shooting off her big mouth about it to you.'

'She only said you told Uncle Webster you wanted to be one. Bob, where'd you study? I think it's lovely, honestly I do. I'm not laughing at you,' she ended kindly.

'There's nothing to laugh at, anyway,' he growled. 'I guess I'd go to the Owen Vallance Medical School in Morgan. That's a good hospital, too; Doc Roberts says so.'

'Yes, it is; Eleanor Boadman's brother goes there and she says it is, too.'

'Then it must be swell, of course,' he interrupted with cubbish sarcasm, and began to whistle *The Star-Spangled Banner*.

'Where'd you practise?'

'Right here, I guess.'

'Here in Vine Falls?'

'What's wrong with it?'

'It's . . . well, it's so *small*.'

'Folks get sick here the same as they do anywhere else, don't they?'

'Yes, of course, they do, smarty. But what I meant was, you won't have much scope, will you?'

'I'll get all the scope I can manage.'

'But don't you want to get on, Bob, be famous, and have a splendid career?'

'No one can have careers since the Depression.'

'Well, prosperity'll come back. Everybody says so. Besides, you might *want* a career, even if you couldn't have it.'

'Well, I don't. Too much trouble.'

His cousin stared at him. This very un-American statement really shocked her; it sounded more like the things Englishmen said in books. Then she remembered that Aunt Sharlie, of course, was a Southerner, and the South, even nowadays, was naturally, shamefully, unprogressive. Bob must inherit his peculiar streak of laziness from his mother.

'You're not a bit like Boone, are you?' she said curiously. 'He's crazy to get on and make a fortune.'

'Swell chance he's got, hasn't he, tagging around after that little . . . after Jeanette all the time.'

'Well, he does *want* to, anyway . . . and so do I! Not the money so much, but to be famous . . . oh, Bob!' She pressed her slender long fingers on the edge of the table leaning eagerly forward, her lovely face flushing. 'Sometimes I feel I just can't wait until I'm through High, and can go on to Cedars and really start my work! I feel I want to go out on the top of a mountain and . . . and shout out loud, and tell everybody how wonderful the Drama is, and about all the wonderful things men of genius have written and . . . and how it's all linked up with religion and everything——'

She stopped, gave him her lovely smile, and shook her head as if her feelings were too much for her.

He was looking at her curiously.

'Helen, you're very pretty. Doesn't everybody tell you so?'

She nodded tranquilly.

'Yes, they do. But that's just luck, Bob, like your being . . . being tall, and not a skinny little katydid like Stebby. It isn't a credit to me to be pretty, like it will be if I get on and study hard and become famous.'

'But don't you like it?' he persisted. 'Gosh, you're as pretty as

Mary Astor and your face is kind of good, too. Only I never noticed it till now, somehow.'

'Oh, I like it, of course,' she answered simply, 'because I get plenty of dates, and girls always like that, and candy, and I get bunched most every day by somebody. Any girl would like it. But I'm kind of used to it, too. Ever since I was little, you see, people've been saying how pretty I was, just the same way that they say a child's like its mother or father, and so I take it for granted.'

'And how about all these stags who bunch you and call you up and ask for dates? Who's your special?' He was teasing her now, and his voice, his manner, made him seem much older than she was.

'I haven't got one,' she drawled sweetly, looking slowly away from him.

'Quite sure?'

She nodded, still looking away from him, and unable to speak because of the strange, bewildering feeling that was making her feel both happy and sad, and the sudden beating of her heart.

'Maybe I'll be your special one day.'

He spoke very quietly, without taking his eyes off her averted face. There was a little silence, then she said in the same sweet slow drawl, still not looking at him, almost in a whisper:

'Maybe you will.'

Then the front door slammed, and a moment later Myron came in carrying two chickens. He glanced at Bob sitting in his chair, raised his eyebrows, muttered 'Evenin',' to Helen, opened the ice-box, stowed away the chickens and slammed it shut.

'Where's Dad?' asked Bob.

'Hain't seen him,' retorted Myron, as though accused of a crime. 'Git up out of my chair, Bob, I want to sit down.'

'You're welcome.' Bob stood up, and Helen slid off the table. 'Where's Mother?'

'Be in any minute now and Lou too.'

'How do you know?'

'Saw the Ford on the Square outside Frankwoods.'

'What time's supper?'

'Half-after eight.'

'Gosh, Myron, you ought to take a look at the tennis net some time, it's falling to pieces.'

'Hevn't time.'

'Boloney. You haven't got so much to do now we've got this new girl.'

'She won't stay the week out.'

'How do you know?'

'Said so.'

'Oh, well . . . Helen, I guess I'll walk down with you.'

'That's sweet of you, Bob, but I'll be all right. I'd rather have a . . . a little walk by myself, if you don't mind,' she said gracefully, giving him her charming college-social smile.

'Oh, well, of course, if you want to make up a poem or something, I won't intrude,' he said, looking a little bewildered.

'No, it's all right. G'd-night, and thanks a million for the tennis.'

The kitchen door softly shut, and she had gone.

'You been tryin' to kiss her?' demanded Myron.

'No, I have not, and it's like your blasted cheek to ask,' said Bob in a low voice but furiously.

'No harm if you hev.' Myron gave a sudden loud cackle which did not disturb his face. 'I should hev, at your age.'

Bob muttered something and strode out of the room.

9

He went across the lawn of bleached grass now pink in the afterglow, and down towards the woods, walking quickly with hands in his pockets and staring at the ground and only once glancing up when a flight of black duck went over on their way to the marshes. He thought he would go down to Carr's, and have a cigarette and a drink before supper.

He had taken to doing this lately. The old ban on the Carr place had lapsed since the young Viners and Vorsts had ceased to be children, for it was taken for granted that the squalid noisy place would have no appeal for them when they had so many pleasanter places to go to, and this was how the situation had worked itself out with all the children . . . except Bob.

Carr's still had a fascination for him because of the atmosphere of secrecy and excitement in that shabby ordinary old frame house. He liked to sit on a stool smoking, and slowly sipping the rye that Francey brought out from some hidden cupboard and drawling wisecracks at her while she baked the fruit pies. He would sit quietly when a car stopped outside, watching the men who walked in as noiselessly and casually as shadows, jerked their heads at Francey, and went upstairs at her nod. He never asked any questions and Francey never talked. He knew what they were up to at Carr's, and the secret—though it was an open one—excited him. He came away from the place with his head ringing, not with drink, but with a confused thrilling pleasure. Everything seemed to move quicker, he got more of a kick out of everything, after he had been down to Carr's.

He kept his visits a secret from everyone.

The evening was lovely, calm as a dream and steeped in

gorgeous colour. It made him feel disturbed and vaguely unhappy, just as Helen's face had made him feel when he said to her, 'Maybe I'll be your special one day.'

He did not know, now, why he had said that, for he certainly did not want to tangle himself up with any skirt (girl, not skirt . . . skirt wasn't a nice way to speak of his cousin, anyhow) for years yet. Girls had a dreadful effect on a man. They got him soft. Look at Boone and Jeanette. Look at that sap Jonas over Helen. Their minds were never on their game. Yet he did not like the idea of anyone else being Helen's special. It made him mad. She was so beautiful! The unfamiliar word slipped into his mind and he said it under his breath as he went down into the dim green twilight of the woods. Beautiful . . . it was kind of pretty, just the sound of the word. For no reason, he sighed.

Then, slowly, there rose all about him, from dewy leaves and moss and rainsoaked trunks of young trees, the smell of the woods, making him remember nutting picnics years ago when he was a kid, games of cops and robbers with Boone and Jonas, days spent shooting out in the deep woods with Dan Carr, and his spirits rose.

Oh, shucks, I don't want to be Helen's special or any other skirt's, he thought, beginning to whistle. Guess I must have been crazy. I upset her, too, going on like that sap Jonas. Her own cousin! If she couldn't stick by me being sensible and keeping off that line, who could she stick by? I guess I won't ever say anything more about it and then she'll forget.

He scrambled down the briar-covered slope, his eyes fixed on the gap in the fence. There it was, just as it had always been (Carrs never mended anything), a break in the white rails glimmering through the dusk. His heart beating with the old excitement, he slipped through into the yard.

When he entered the front room of the bungalow, which had been turned into a coffee-room and had a long window overlooking the front porch, Francey was eating her supper alone behind the bar with a steaming cup of coffee in front of her and a hot-dog in one hand, reading a tabloid. Mrs Carr, a thin woman with dyed hair and a red, permanently angry face was just going out of the room, and nodded at him, but did not stop or speak.

''Lo, Francey.'

''Lo yourself. Whadda you waunt?'

'The usual.'

'Awright. Jus' let me finish this.'

She screwed up her eyes as she always did when eating anything good and crammed her mouth with sausage. Bob went round behind the bar and leant beside her, twisting his head to see what she was reading. Standing so, his cheek was very close to her red hair and his shoulder pressed her round bare arm. It was a pleasant feeling, and he moved closer. She twitched herself away. He put his arm clumsily round her waist, still reading, and held her so firmly that she finished her hot-dog and drained the coffee without trying to get free.

'Jeez, that's pretty hot!' he observed at last, turning the paper over. 'I wonder they get away with it. Where'd you get it? Have you been into Morgan today?'

'You're late tonight, big boy.' Francey, still in the circle of his arm, slid the paper over to her side and folded it up. 'Been playing tennis, haven't you?'

'Uh-huh.'

'Who with?'

'My cousin.'

'Which one? Dolly Daydreams?'

He said nothing but twisted her wrist quickly and cruelly behind her back and held it there while she squealed 'Lay off, you lousy bastard!'

'You lay off, then.' He shook her.

'Awright. But you started it, you big stiff, third-degreeing me like some lousy great bull.' She was whimpering.

131

'Oh, all right, all right,' he said disgustedly. 'Here, get me a packet of Luckies, will you, and the drink, I haven't got long.'

'Awright.'

She turned away, rubbing her wrist, and groped in a wall cupboard at the back of the bar. 'Say,' she went on, 'I saw *her* . . . your cousin—you know, Helen, goin' into Frankwoods today. Has she got class! Oh boy! Honest, if I had her looks I wouldn't waste my time in this place, no I wouldn't, I'd go to Hollywood and try for the movies. She's got a regla film-face. Honest, everybody says so.'

He did not answer, for he was thinking about something else. Holding his glass up to the light, he said:

'Francey.'

'What?'

'Francey, don't think I'm trying to make you say anything you don't want to. You know me, don't you? I wouldn't ever tell about anything you didn't want anyone to know about, but . . . how's Dan?'

'Awright. Getting along fine.'

She was busy polishing a glass.

'No, Francey, listen. I mean, what's he doing nowadays? I heard he was running a speakeasy in Morgan.'

'Who said so?'

'Myron.'

'Well, he ain't now.'

'Oh. Where is he, then? Francey, do tell. I won't say a word, honest I won't. I'm not trying to *make* you tell. Only when I was coming down here tonight I was thinking how much I'd like to see him again. That's all.'

'Well, you can't. He ain't visitin' around much nowadays,' she said over her shoulder.

There was a pause. Then, in the silence, they heard a door slowly swing back with a long creak, as though someone standing at the top of the stairs, listening, had let it slip from their hand.

Bob and Francey stayed quite still, staring up the dark stairs at the back of the room. Then——

'Bob?' called a man's voice, low and young, yet penetrating. 'That you? Like to come up a minute, kid?'

Bob glanced at Francey, silently questioning, his eyes blazing with excitement. She nodded, and he went noiselessly across to the stairs and up them two at a time.

Francey stayed where she was, idly looking over the tabloid. In the last few years she had grown taller and plumper and learned how to paint her face expertly with cosmetics from the five-and-ten, and had shaved her brows and drawn herself a new long elegant pair with an eyebrow pencil. She looked quite twenty and very embraceable, for her body was perfect, but she had not lost that faintly debased look of good stock gone to seed. Skirts were getting longer that year, but she wore her blue and white gingham up to her knees and her limp carrot-gold hair was bound with a bit of the same cotton; it never would take an elegant perm like that of other girls.

Voices came from upstairs and once a burst of laughter, Bob's and her brother's. She liked to hear that, and she was glad Dan had called Bob upstairs because now Bob would see how Dan had got on, and pr'aps Bob would tell that lousy bunch up the hill.

They never came near her nowadays. Bob was the only one who stopped to speak to her if he saw her downtown. She saw them riding round in their folks' cars or going off to Roselands to swim or in the best seats at the movies, the girls always dressed in the newest styles and the boys so nice and polite with them and never looking at other girls, and it made her mad. She was as good as they were, her folks had been here since the war, too, and just because the Vorsts and Viners had got on and the Carrs hadn't, that bunch up the hill stuck it on so you'd think they'd crack sumpin'.

Bob was the only one who was worth a dime.

Dan felt like that about them, too. He always had. When he was a kid he used to hate them having more money than he had, and the way they looked at you sometimes, kind of as if you were funny but they'd never tell you why. He used to like taking Bob shooting, but only because he said he could get Bob away from that bunch if he wanted to, and show him how to be a tough guy, a regular fellow, not soft. Dan hated soft guys.

Then she thought of Dan and his mob and felt better. They were showing that Vorst crowd and all the other Honest Johns where they got off, yes sir. That bunch and the other Honest Johns had to pay money to guys like Dan, or Dan and his mob and all the other mobs made hell for them. It was Dan and the other mobsmen were sitting pretty now, not the Honest Johns, so what call had that lousy bunch up the hill to be so pleased with themselves? And everybody knew Bob's old man had lost a packet when the market crashed.

Upstairs, the long whine of the creaking door sounded again. Glancing up from her paper, Francey saw two shadows on the wall at the top of the stairs, Bob's and a man's.

'So long, kid.' The shadows clasped hands.

'G'd-bye, Dan. Thanks for having me up. I'm mighty glad to have seen you again.'

'That goes for me, too, kid. Don't forget, if you're ever down my way. So long.'

The door creaked, and the light vanished, and Bob ran down the stairs.

'Well, whadja think of him?' demanded Francey eagerly, looking up from Dan's tabloid and smiling excitedly. 'Hardly've known him, would ja?'

'Gee, he has got on, hasn't he?' Bob was flushed with excitement and his eyes sparkled. He drained his glass and put it down. 'Francey, do you know what he was doing up there, with all the boys shooting craps in the same room? Reading!'

'Sure, he reads a lot. He ain't like those hoodlums 'at never look at anything but the tabloids 'n the funnies,' she said proudly. 'He reads books. He buys 'em, too. He tried to make me, but nothin' doin'. It takes me all my time to follow the styles 'n fix my hair . . . but he's crazy about books.'

'It was a Life of Napoleon,' said Bob impressively.

'Kind of a wop, was he?'

'Not exactly' (he looked at her as he used to when they were kids, as though she were kind of funny), 'he was Corsican (Corsica's an island way off Italy), and he was a corporal in the French army. He made himself Emperor of France and conquered most all of Europe.'

'What happened to him?'

'Oh, the British beat him at Waterloo.'

'Sounds kinda historical. Did he make a pile, too?'

'He didn't care about money. He wanted power and glory, and all that sort of thing.'

'Well, that's like Dan, too, on'y he waunts to make a pile as well. He knows how to spend it, too. Lookit!'

She proudly held out her wrist, where a tiny jewelled watch glittered.

'It set him back fifty bucks. He said so.'

'Gee!' Bob picked up her wrist and admired. 'You didn't have that on before I went upstairs?'

'No, 'cause I was afraid you'd see it and start third-degreein' me about who gave it to me. Isn't it pretty?' She moved her freckled wrist this way and that, making the diamonds flash.

'It's ever so pretty. Gee, Francey, he's swell, isn't he?'

'Sure he is.'

'And I'm glad . . . you know . . . Francey, he's never been mixed up in any bad shooting? I asked him what it felt like to kill somebody and he laughed and said he never had killed anybody, he'd been lucky. He's just in the racket for the kick of it. He says he gets a hell of a kick out of making money that way, same as a guy does out of selling cars or anything.'

'Sure.' Her back was towards him as she put the bottle of rye away and he could not see the grin on her face.

'He says he gets such a hell of a kick out of it he can't quit.' She said nothing.

'He says if I'm ever in Detroit, I'm to go in to *The Ecstasy Club* and the place is mine. Gee, I'd love to go down there some time, Francey!'

'It certainly is a jawbreakin' name,' she said, cautiously trying 'ecstasy' over under her breath. 'Kind of a Mexican name, maybe?'

Bob was staring at the floor. He said suddenly in a low voice:

'Of course, people do get shot, don't they?'

'Sure they do . . . if they get in the way.'

'He says the first time he has to shoot to kill he'll quit.'

'Yeah,' she said, yawning. 'Guess you'll be late for supper, won't you?' glancing at the flashing watch. She liked fighting boys and kissing boys, not listening to boys.

'Guess I will, too. So long, redhead.'

'Ah, gwan!' cried Francey, pleased at this return to a level she understood. 'I'll fight you any day! So long!'

He went down the porch steps and out into the warm still air, whistling. It was nearly dark, but his eyes were trained by long days in the woods, and he saw a darker mass in a thicket across the road. A powerful car was parked there: Dan's. He went over to it and put his hand on the bonnet. It was cold and slippery with dew. A faint thrill, chilly and intoxicating, raced down his back. This must be the one Dan took the boys in when they were on a job . . .

Crash! The black-powder bomb struck the shop, and everything slid into ruin. Men ran out shouting, and this long black car, this, that he was touching now, dwindled away down the road . . .

What sort of a kick must Dan get out of it if he, Bob, got a kick like this from just touching the car?

He was ravenously hungry. He climbed the familiar hill in

the swiftly-coming darkness and went through the wood where two owls were calling. Gee, it was good to have seen Dan again! What'd Jonas and the rest of the bunch say if they knew he'd been talking to Dan Carr? It was most as good as talking to Lindbergh or Al Capone . . . well, maybe not quite as good as talking to Lindbergh, but pretty nearly.

But he would never tell Jonas and the bunch, because Dan trusted him not to. He hadn't said, 'Don't talk, kid,' but Bob knew that was what his smile and handshake had meant. Dan was a wise guy; the police had nothing definite pinned on him, but he didn't want anyone to know he'd been visiting his home town and his folks, and as Bob crossed the lawn towards the house he swore to himself that he would never tell.

He yawned. It had been a long day, and his head was swimming deliciously with drink and a feeling of secrecy and danger, while pictures flashed in his excited brain . . . the black car parked in the bushes, Dan's face smiling down at him, the crap-shooters glancing up startled as he came to the door and then going on with their game at a nod from Dan . . . Helen's face, so beautiful, looking away from him . . . and the doctor's hands, moving over the ribs of that woman who had been knocked down in the Polak quarter in Morgan, as though they were alive on their own and knew exactly what to do . . . and the doctor's face, kind of listening, as if his hands were telling him what they were finding out . . . and the crowd all round, so quiet, watching . . . that had been wonderful. That had made him suddenly know that he wanted to be a doctor, too.

He yawned again. The house was lit up. Supper would be ready, and was he hungry! But confused and excited and hungry as he was, he remembered to unwrap and put into his mouth a piece of a gum sworn to remove, without possibility of failure, all traces of alcohol and tobacco from the breath of the most hardened addict in the United States.

10

It was the last day of the summer term at the Anna Bonner, and Amy's last day at school. The sunny corridors echoed with cockneyish young voices crying:

'Mind you write to me, Sylvia!'

'Ooo! . . . here's Miss Seager! Come and say good-bye to her with me, Molly, be an angel.'

'Miss Naylor, *please* will you sign this?'

Amy was sitting on the bench outside the Headmistress's room waiting her turn to say good-bye to her. Muriel Wilcox was in there now, probably having one last long jaw about her maths, poor sop. When Muriel came out it would be Amy's turn.

Nursed carefully on Amy's knee was a large brown paper parcel. It was her stories, which had trebled their number in three years and were now so bulky that she was seriously worried about what to do with them. She had collected them yesterday from the old exam room and made them into this parcel and it had spent the previous night in her form-room cupboard, for she was Monitor this term, and as such was the only person allowed to go there. After today there would be no more hiding places at the Anna Bonner and if she took the parcel home the Beedings would be almost sure to ask what it was; for as she got older, they seemed to get nosier.

In three months she would be fifteen. She sat with the sunlight falling warmly on her lifted face and stared dreamily out of the window at the sky. In three years she had, of course, grown taller but she was still noticeably small among girls of her own age and still very slender. Mrs Beeding frequently expressed the opinion that Aime would not grow much more.

Aime was going to be just as high as my heart, said Mr Beeding (he was, without much encouragement and for some reason best known to himself, fond of Aime). The pigtail was still there. Her skin had improved, the last trace of sallowness had gone and it was creamy, showing off her eyes. But though she looked much healthier she was not the kind of girl that people watch in trams and buses, for her face had the same guarded secret look it had worn as a child and there was no warmth in her expression. Still, light, cool, limpid as water, yet wary— those were the words that would have gone through the mind of someone trying to describe her.

Her love of her secret world, her love of being alone, had grown in the past two years to a passion. Day by day she cared less for people and more for imaginary pictures so strong that they were more like feelings or dreams than ideas inside her head. She felt only a passive affection for the Beedings. Indeed, she did not feel active affection for anyone living; she only loved the memory of her mother, while for the dream-people in her mind she felt such a strong interest and concern that it could have been described as love.

Both feelings were secret and deep and she never talked of them to anyone nor thought about them; they were just *there*, like her pigtail, and she took them for granted, as indeed, she took all her feelings. Though she sometimes identified herself with someone in one of her stories she never thought about herself in her daily life. If she was lonely, she did not know it. The dream-images in her mind absorbed her interests and affections with dangerous ease, as anyone who has ever lived with such phantoms will immediately recall their power to do. *Empty, vast and cold were the halls of the Snow Queen. They were all lighted up by the vivid light of the aurora* . . .

The door of the Headmistress's room opened and Muriel Wilcox came out giggling.

'Hullo, Piggy. I say, you're leaving too, aren't you?'

Amy nodded.

'What're you going to do?'

'I don't know yet. What're you?'

'Pitmans. Isn't it ghastly.' She turned her eyes up and her mouth down.

'Amy? Come along, dear.' Miss Lathom's voice was a little sharp. She had not only been left the School in her great-aunt's will, but also a very large house at St Leonard's, bursting with useless but beloved personal possessions of Miss Bonner's which the Will forbade her to sell or give away. She foresaw quite five years' work at sorting and packing, to be fitted into the midst of all her other activities. Also, the last day of term was quite trying enough without people making it worse by wasting her time.

Amy scurried in as quickly as she could for the weight of her parcel.

'Well, now, Amy—good gracious, what *have* you got there?'

'It's my stories, Miss Lathom. You see——'

'You must have wasted a lot of time in the last three years, child, if that's all stories, and it explains your eye-strain, of course. I expect you know that Mrs Beeding has been to see me and we talked over what you're going to do?'

'Yes, Miss Lathom. Please, Miss Lathom——'

'Just a moment, Amy (put it down on that chair, you make my arm ache to look at you). Now, Mrs Beeding told you, I suppose, that I don't think your eyes are strong enough to stand the close work in dressmaking. And it's no use your getting into a firm as an apprentice and wasting two or three years if your eyes aren't going to let you take up the work later on, is it? Do pay attention. Never mind your stories, now.' For Amy's gaze was wandering.

'No, Miss Lathom. Miss Lathom, I suppose you couldn't possibly let me go on keeping my stories in the old exam room?'

'No, I could not, Amy. It's quite out of the question when once you've left school.'

'Miss Lathom, when I've got a job I could pay you a sort of rent for them. Half a crown a week. It could go to the Missionary Society.'

Miss Lathom shook her head, but not severely. Amy's expression grew secret, and still. She stared at the Headmistress in silence.

'My dear,' Miss Lathom put out her hand and pulled the girl gently towards her until Amy stood in the circle of her arm, as she had stood three years ago when Miss Lathom had told her of her father's death. 'I expect you will think I'm very hard, but I am only telling you for your own good. You really must try to be a little more practical. You're not really in the least interested in what you're going to do when you leave school, are you?'

There was a pause. Amy tried to lie, but for some reason—perhaps because she associated the face looking gravely into her own with kindness when she had felt unbearably desolate—she could not. She shook her head.

'I knew it,' announced Miss Lathom. 'You just want to be left alone to scribble, isn't that it?'

Another nod.

'You don't care about anything in the world except that bundle of—that bundle on the chair, do you?'

A shake, this time.

'Well, it won't do,' vigorously. 'We all have our dreams (I wanted to be a pianist, once) but we can't all have them come true.'

'Some people can,' said Amy mildly. 'Kipling wrote a poem about that. It's called, *The Dreamer Whose Dreams Came True*. It's my favourite poem,' she added, colour coming into her face. 'It says:

> *Down with the drawbridge and let him through!*
> *The Dreamer whose dreams came true.*

Do you know it, Miss Lathom?'

'Yes. It's a bad poem.' Miss Lathom's temper was gone. She removed her arm.

'It's my favourite,' repeated Amy dreamily, glancing down at her parcel.

'Well, to get back to your affairs. You had better try for some kind of a job in which you'll have time to write as well. I suppose you do want to be a writer?'

'I am a writer,' opening her eyes in surprise.

'When you are grown up, I *meant*,' explained Miss Lathom, glancing at her watch. Amy considered.

'I don't know, Miss Lathom. I never thought about it. Mrs Beeding said last night she's going to write a letter to that man, Mr Ramage; you know, who was at Dad's funeral. He's on *The Prize*, where Dad was. It's a boys' paper. Mrs Beeding's going to ask him if there might be a job there for me.'

'Why on earth didn't you say so before, Amy? You really are tiresome. It's a good idea. (Mrs Beeding is a very sensible woman as well as a very kind one, and I hope you appreciate her as you should.) But what sort of opening would there be there for a girl? Of course, I know *The Prize*, and so did Miss Bonner; her brothers and mine used to take it in.'

'Well, Dad always said they had such a bother with their office boys, they were always sacking them. He said they had six while he was there. So Dora Beeding (she's twenty-three, she's Mrs Beeding's eldest), Dora thought perhaps they might like to have an office girl, instead. Dora only thought of it last night, or I'd have told you before, Miss Lathom.'

'And that might lead to your getting some writing job on the paper later on—I see. Have you told Mrs Beeding about your stories?'

'Oh, no, Miss Lathom!'

'I think you're silly not to, Amy. She would probably be very interested.'

Amy said nothing.

'Well . . . that settles you,' sighed Miss Lathom, again glancing at her watch. She was hungry. 'Mrs Beeding's going to try to get you on to *The Prize*. Do you like the idea, yourself? Of course, you're very young to be leaving at all, but in your circumstances I think it's the wisest thing . . . how do you feel about it all?'

'I don't mind, Miss Lathom.'

'Wouldn't you like to have a story in *The Prize* one day, Amy?' demanded Miss Lathom. (Like most adults, she enjoyed seeing the young enthuse.)

'I couldn't, not if I was an office girl.'

'Why ever not?'

'They won't let you have a story in the paper if you're on the staff. Dad said they had to do that, because everyone was always trying to get stories into the paper because they thought it was so easy. All the office boys used to try. It was an awful nuisance, Dad said. That was why they were always being sacked.'

Miss Lathom laughed.

'Oh, well, that rather spoils your chances, doesn't it?'

'Oh, I don't mind. The stories in *The Prize* aren't very exciting. Mine are much better.'

'I rejoice to hear it,' said Miss Lathom drily, recalling that bald paragraph about the two men waiting by the desert tomb and thinking; Poor little cocksure sprat. The worse they do anything, the surer they are. Haven't I seen it again and again! She said rather severely, 'I hope you won't develop into a conceited girl, Amy; there's nothing so putting-off. Well,' she stood up and held out both her hands, 'good-bye, my dear. Be sure to let me know how you get on, I shall be interested. And you'll be coming back to Old Girls next term, won't you?'

'Yes, Miss Lathom. Thank you very much. Yes, I will.' Amy passively let her slim cool hands be shaken, then picked up her parcel and made for the door. On the threshold she paused and made one of her surprising exit-speeches.

'Miss Lathom,' giving the Headmistress the lovely excited smile that she had given her once before, 'thanks most awfully for letting me write in the old exam room.' She paused. A sentence came into her head and she added, without realizing what she was saying, '*One day I'll be the dreamer whose dreams came true, and then you'll be glad.*'

The door shut.

Amy flew downstairs to the cloakroom to say good-bye to the special five with whom she had eaten biscuits and giggled for three and a half years. None of them were leaving; they were all staying on until they were sixteen and they were all sorry for Amy but too polite to say so. They knew that she had no parents and hardly any money and had been adopted by a baker's wife and, nasal little cockney rats though they were, their farewells to her were as delicate as they were full of affection.

She managed to get her parcel away unopened by saying it contained old copies of the School Mag.: for Mrs Beeding, who would make paper spills from them with which to light the Beeding gases and fires. A tactful silence greeted this statement, and no more was said about the parcel. When she left Jean, Hilda, Mavis, Iris and Peggy at the corner of Baalbec Road and turned into the Fields alone; she was thinking only of how to get her parcel into the house unopened.

She managed in the end by taking it unflusteredly to Mrs Beeding, who was cooking, and telling her that it was school books and asking might she put it for the time being up in the small-top-back? Mrs Beeding, her mind not on the parcel, said yes, she might, and Amy rushed upstairs and hid it away before Mrs Beeding could change her mind. She dared not linger and dream in the big-top-front, though it was for the time being empty; old Mrs Martin had found the stairs too much for her and she and her daughter had left.

Amy came slowly downstairs again, feeling easier in her mind. For the time being her stories were safe.

That evening her family helped Mrs Beeding to write the letter to Mr Ramage. They all gathered in the Lounge after supper, except Mr Beeding, who was upstairs snatching an hour or two's sleep after several quick ones at The Hen and Chickens to nerve him up for the night's baking, and Artie and Baby (now a fine girl of two and a half), who had been put to bed. The windows were open wide to catch what little freshness there was in Highbury at the end of a summer day, and Mrs Beeding sat squarely at a small table with a penny bottle of ink, a packet of shiny notepaper and envelopes, a penholder with a new and very fine nib and a sheet of fresh pink blotting paper spread before her.

She and Amy were the only two people there who did not look as if they had just come back from a holiday. Dora's long nose was skinned by a cycling holiday in Wales, Mona was brick-red from a fortnight in Camp with the Junior Staff of Fletcher Brothers, Ladies' Outfitters and General Stores, of Islington, where she now worked; and Maurice was all over freckles like a cheerful orchid, after a week in Southsea with a friend from the motor-cycle shop where he was employed. All three were larger, more self-confident, less afraid of their mother than they had been three years ago. Mona and Maurice's weekly pay envelopes had done that for them (*Mum hasn't a penny except what Dad gives her, but Maurice and me, we're earning two pound ten a week between us*) and Dora had recently been given a rise of five shillings a week and promoted to taking letters in Spanish, which had considerably increased her ambition and self-respect.

Maurice looked much the same, only sturdier; but Mona was now a regular vision of love with red nails, cherry lipstick, no eyebrows to speak of, a tight blue jumper and a little black skirt, while the yellow sausages were arranged in a switchback perm which looked exactly like a wig.

Dora, whose style had grown quieter with the five-shilling rise and the Spanish dictation, and was beginning to run to tailored costumes and plain silk blouses, loudly told her sister that her appearance gave her, Dora, the sick. She often silently handed her a penny, which turned out upon questioning to be intended for an individual vaguely referred to by Dora as The Old Guy, but was known by everybody to be no less a person than Mona herself. Mona was interested in nothing in earth or heaven but boys and their opinion of her looks. If she could get a whistle or a 'There's a bird!' from a boy on her way to work she was happy for the rest of the day.

Amy sat on the sofa beside Mona, looking young and thin by contrast, and Maurice lay on the floor studying some literature from Littlewood's.

Mrs Beeding glanced across at Dora, who was lying back in her chair wearing nothing but a clean old overall, pink cami-knickers, and flattened red slippers. Mrs Beeding disapproved of this costume and also of the cigarette that was Dora's fourth since she had got home, but in spite of cigarette and costume, she looked so thin, serious, and proper that her mother could feel only confidence and pride in her.

'Dora, do I begin "Dear Sir," or "Dear Mister Ramage?"'

'Oh, Mum, you don't wanter be so ordinary!' burst in Mona, bouncing up and down on the sofa with the wig shifting in time to her bounces. 'You wanter write something with person-ality in it—something that'll make him remember your letter, like. You wanter start off with a bang—something like "I won't waste your time if I knew I couldn't be of use to you"—some-thing snappy like that, see?'

'Mona, you're nowt but a silly date. He'd never bother to read to the end of it. He'd think I was soft. "Dear sir," shall I put then, Dora?'

'I'd put "Dear Mr Ramage," then he'll see at once you know his name and he'll look to see who you are—at the end of the letter—and then he'll remember seeing you at the funeral.'

'Ay, that's it.' Mrs Beeding bent over the paper and slowly wrote.

'Don't forget to tell him she's got long hair,' put in Maurice, not looking up.

'An' then what'll I say, Dora? "Please excuse me for troubling you?"'

'That'll do. Sounds a bit soapy but anything to get our Aime started as a world's worker. Remind him that you met at Mr Lee's funeral (sounds nice and sociable, I must say), then go on to say does he remember Mr Lee's little girl, and—oh, go on, Mum! You can do it all right if everybody stops telling you how.'

'I bet you he never even bothers to read it,' insisted Mona, earnestly. 'Why, joo you know how many letters Fletchers get a week askin' for jobs in the Junior *alone*? Two or three hundred. They do, straight. They don't trouble to read them through; Miss Wallis, she just files them. 'Tisn't likely anyone's going to bother reading one letter out of hundreds of them unless it's got personality.'

'They don't worry about personality on *The Prize*. *The Prize* was started before personality was thought of,' yawned Dora. 'Now shut up everybody, and let Mum get on, do.'

All this time Amy had sat in silence, wearing a red and white checked cotton frock from a shop in the Holloway Road where dozens more hung outside on a rail, with her thin creamy arms and legs bare and her feet in blue slippers as squashed as Dora's; staring at a fine geranium that Mrs Beeding was nursing to perfection in the conservatory—and wondering whether there would be a private place in which she might manage to write if she got a job on *The Prize*.

It was too hot for anyone to want to talk much, so after the first burst of advice Mrs Beeding was allowed to get on by

147

herself and finally produced a letter which said so exactly what she meant it to say that not one word in her clear unaffected hand was crossed out.

This was the letter that reached the offices of *The Prize* next morning:

DEAR MR RAMAGE,

Please excuse me for troubling you. We met at Mr Lee's funeral two and a half years ago and I am wondering if you have forgotten his little girl Amy, you spoke to her then. She is now nearly sixteen and has just left the Anna Bonner School for Girls, Highbury, where they speak highly of her work. She is a good girl in every way. I am wondering if you might be in need of a tidy quiet hard-working girl in your office to run errands and talk on the telephone. If you are I should be very pleased if you would let me bring Amy to see you one morning, any time you like.

Yours truly,

M. BEEDING.

Mr Ramage, advertising manager of *The Prize*, was attracted by this letter. He read it through twice; then took it downstairs to a door on the floor below, on which he tapped, and was told by a sleepy, irritable male voice to 'Come in.'

In a room which resembled with its cream-painted panelling and faded but rich Turkey carpet the writing room in a women's club, a large blond elderly gentleman in an old yet beautiful blue suit was leaning back in a swivel chair before a very large desk and staring crossly out of the window at another window not twelve feet away on the other side of the road. Rosemary Lane by St Paul's, where the offices of *The Prize* have been since its foundation in 1860, is one of the narrowest thoroughfares in the network of streets lying directly about the Cathedral.

The blond gentleman looked up as Mr Ramage came in and gloomily blew his upper lip, which was festooned with a large yellow moustache.

'Hullo,' he said despondently. 'I say, have you heard about this Gossey business? Little beast. Danesford was at me the moment I put my nose round the door this morning.'

'Yes, I heard last night, he caught me just as I was going out,' said Mr Ramage soothingly. 'It's a confounded nuisance.'

'It's all the worse because for three months he's seemed *all right*,' cried the blond gentleman bitterly. 'Whenever I was in here I used to watch him like Hawkshaw himself, Ramage, I assure you I did. I can't make out how the little monstrosity managed to get his piece of rubbish written, he must have locked himself in the lavatory for hours on end, I simply can't explain it in any other way, and neither can Danesford.'

'What's it called?' inquired Mr Ramage.

'*The Horror at Marsh Grange*,' retorted Lord Welwoodham. 'What else would it be called?'

Mr Ramage nodded.

'Can't we keep him on until after the Double Number?' he suggested. 'Poor Grace was grumbling to me last night about having all the stuff to collect for that and find a new office-boy at the same time.'

Lord Welwoodham shook his head.

'Out of the question now. I blew him up and packed him off this morning as soon as I got here.'

'Did he weep?'

'Not he, the little scut. He told me the paper was going to pot for lack of new blood. It happens to be true, but none of us can help if it Henty, Ballantyne, Weyman, Haggard and Herbert Strang are most of them dead and haven't dropped their mantles on anyone else, can we? And I will see every contributor to this paper in the hot place, Ramage, and all the readers too, before I will lower the standard of boys' fiction which we have maintained since 1860. If I can't get the right sort of new blood I will go on printing copies of the old. What I will *not* do,' declared Lord Welwoodham, getting up and staring at the wastepaper basket, 'is to print work by writers who think that because a boy *is* a boy he must necessarily be an ass who will swallow any rubbish they care to sling at him because they need money to feed themselves while they are writing master-pieces for adults . . . Do you want to see me Ramage? I shan't be in again this week.'

'Well, this comes in rather pat,' said Mr Ramage, handing him Mrs Beeding's letter, 'in the circumstances.'

Lord Welwoodham read it frowning and blowing on the moustache.

'A girl, eh?' he said, putting it down on his desk. 'Well, heaven knows she couldn't be worse than the boys. Lee's daughter. What's she like? Like him at all?'

'Oh, not in the least,' said Mr Ramage decidedly. 'Small and dark, very neat and polite. None of that rather . . . no, she isn't at all like he was.'

'This woman writes a good hand. Good letter, too. Who is she?'

'She's the baker's wife who adopted the little girl, Lord Welwoodham. I told you at the time, I think.'

'Oh, yes, of course, I recall it perfectly; you thought she seemed a very capable sort. Managed everything, including dragging little whats-her-name along to the funeral; of course, I remember now. Well . . .' he glanced irritably at his large bowler hat which lay with a glossy yellow silver-knobbed walking stick on a table in a corner, 'have her down and let Danesford see her and if he and Grace think she'll do, we'll have her. Doesn't giggle, won't stink us out with scent, will she? D'you think she's grown into a dangerous beauty in three years?'

Mr Ramage laughed and told Lord Welwoodham that he should be very surprised indeed if she had; he remembered her as being not unpleasing to look at, but anything rather than striking.

'Good, good,' said the owner and editor absently, pulling on his dirty gloves of beautiful tough hogskin. 'All right, have her down tomorrow if you like. Just tell Danesford and Grace about it, will you, there's a dear good fellow, I must run. Shan't be in again this week, I'm going into the country.' He nodded to Mr Ramage; and walked loosely away down the corridor, shooting out his long legs in front of him in the striking walk that the prewar cartoonists had enjoyed, and swinging his stick.

Mr Ramage went through another door in the editor's room into the general office, where Miss Grace, the editor's secretary, and Mr Danesford, the sub-editor, sat at their respective desks, and explained the situation to them, making it plain beyond any possible doubt that it was expressly at Lord Welwoodham's wish that Amy Lee was coming down to the office for an interview. For Mr Danesford and Miss Grace were more than a little set in their ways and inclined to be suspicious of a new idea, and an office girl, instead of an office boy, on *The Prize* was a very new idea indeed.

But the wishes of Lord Welwoodham, that shabby, grumbling, ageing man whose dignity could be suddenly as natural and impressive as that of a hundred-year-old tree, were law to Miss Grace and Mr Danesford; and that same afternoon Miss Grace wrote the briefest possible note saying that Mr Danesford the sub-editor would see Miss Lee at eleven o'clock (Miss Grace disdained to add '*sharp*') on the following morning.

11

The arrival of this letter by the last post on Tuesday night threw everyone in the household at Highbury into a state of great excitement, with the exception of Baby, who was cutting her final tooth, and Amy herself, who was looking forward to seeing St Paul's Cathedral, which she had never visited, but was otherwise unmoved.

When the doors of Barclay's bank on the corner opened on Wednesday morning the first person to march in was Mrs Beeding accompanied by Amy, and she drew out three pounds.

'Ay, it seems an awful lot o' money, Amy,' she observed, putting the notes safely in her bag, 'but if ye're going after a job ye've got to look decent. Yer heard what Dora said, an' that silly kite Mona too; nothin' puts a boss off like a dirty untidy girl.' Here Mrs Beeding leaped upon a passing bus, dragging Amy with her, and booked two pennies to Jones Bros. of Holloway.

Exactly at a quarter-past ten they emerged from Jones Bros. of Holloway with Amy transformed, and set out on their journey to Saint Paul's Underground Station which, so Dora had instructed them, was exactly opposite Rosemary Lane. 'And mind you don't miss the lane, because it's only about as big as a bee's knee and you might easily, if Aime got star-gazing and you were trying to dodge traffic,' concluded Dora.

But when they came out of Saint Paul's Station, blinking in the brilliant sunlight with Amy holding rather tightly on to Mrs Beeding's plump arm, they looked across the road as they stood on the edge of the pavement and saw Rosemary Lane at once. It was the narrowest little passageway imaginable, whose old houses seemed to be leaning slightly towards one another because they were so close together, their windows like dusty old eyes 'playing owls' as children do, and a ray of sunlight striking dramatically aslant their walls. A flower-shop stood just under a beam of sunlight and a long sheaf of flowers outside looked exactly as though it were made of blue stained glass. And far above the little lane, soaring in the sunlight, was a tall white tower; and even farther above that—like a colossal dark blue mussel shell that hid half of heaven and dwarfed the hurrying people and the red 'buses and the shaking lorries and dusty vans—loomed the mighty dome of the Cathedral, its golden cross shining against the pale blue sky of summer.

'There it is,' remarked Mrs Beeding, pointing across at Rosemary Lane. 'Old-fashioned sort of a place.'

Amy said nothing. She so seldom went anywhere away from Highbury except Up Highgate, that she found the roar and confusion of Cheapside terrifying. She had learned in the past three years not to mind the Highbury trams and 'buses and crowds, but this crowd and traffic was quite different. None of the people here carried shopping baskets or pushed perambulators full of grubby woolly babies, as they slowly glanced in shop windows; all these people were hurrying forward with their chins a little stuck out and their arms swinging smartly. They were like the Hurrying People in the dream she sometimes had, who could not see her even when she stood in front of them screaming out her name. She shut her eyes, holding tightly to Mrs Beeding's arm.

'All right, are yer, luv?' asked Mrs Beeding, glancing down at her a little anxiously. She looked right smart, today, Aime did, a real little business girl, and Mrs Beeding did hope that she was not going to spoil her chances by being sick.

'Yes, thank you, Mrs Beeding,' in a very low voice.

'Come on, then, luv!'

A policeman was now holding up the lorries, vans and cars,

and Mrs Beeding and Amy hurried across the road with all the people.

Once they were walking down Rosemary Lane, Amy felt much better. It was so narrow and small, and the noise of Cheapside seemed abruptly shut off and far away, as though a curtain had been drawn. Suddenly a sweet tinkling noise broke on the air, with a delicious sensation of coolness in that stuffy little alley, and Amy squeezed Mrs Beeding's arm and pointed to a shop window filled with Hindu bracelets, slippers from Japan, tiny carved ivory figures and lengths of closely-embroidered purple and crimson silk.

'Look, Mrs Beeding. Wind-bells. Aren't they pretty? The Chinese hang them outside their houses.'

'I wonder they don't get stolen,' marvelled Mrs Beeding, looking at the slender strips of glass painted with flowers moving gently in the breeze. 'They're ever so pretty.'

'The Chinese are very honest, Mrs Beeding. All over the East they're known and respected for their honesty,' reproved Amy, and was going on to relate a story which had much taken her fancy about a Chinese merchant who hired a motor launch at enormous expense to himself in which to dash after an American vessel and pay the captain a dollar he owed him—when Mrs Beeding announced, 'Here we are, luv,' and stopped in front of a little shop whose window was full of books, with a large notice outside, 'BARGAINS IN BIBLES.'

Above this window hung a signboard on which was painted a scene very familiar to Amy—a boy going up some steps to take a casket from a man with a beard, the setting sun in the background (or perhaps it was the rising sun: Amy had always wondered about that). It was the cover design of *The Prize*, and on the windows above it was written in gold letters the name of the paper.

They went in at a side door and up a dark but clean old stairway until they came to a door with *The Prize: Enquiries.*

Please Knock, on it, but before they could knock, someone came quickly down the stairs from the next landing and they looked up and there was Mr Ramage.

'Good morning, Mrs Beeding. Good morning, Amy. I'm only here to wish you good luck. I passed your letter on to Lord Welwoodham (that's the editor), and he asked Mr Danesford to see you. Luckily for you we do happen to want a boy . . . Lord Welwoodham sacked one yesterday for trying to get a story he'd written printed in the paper . . . I hope, Amy, that *you* don't write?' suddenly turning a sharp yet amused look on her.

'Oh, no, Mr Ramage,' said Mrs Beeding, rather shocked, and Amy shook her head.

'Well, I mustn't keep you.' And he nodded and smiled at the door. 'Good luck.'

'Thank you very kindly, Mr Ramage. Amy, say thank you to Mr Ramage.'

'Thank you very much, Mr Ramage,' repeated Amy, almost in a whisper, lifting her eyes to his. She looked dazed and frightened. Not too good, thought Mr Ramage. He went upstairs quickly, and Mrs Beeding knocked at the door. After a pause a female voice called (in a cool, absorbed sort of tone as though it was busy reading an important document and had momentarily glanced up from its task to wonder who that could *possibly* be at the door):

'Come een!'

They pushed open the door and went in.

In a small light room with two desks, a very smart lady of about forty-three was seated in front of a typewriter, reading a sheet of figures. She was dressed in a grey skirt of finely striped cloth and a pink silk blouse fastened at the neck by a gold brooch with 'L' on it in seed pearls. A little above the brooch came a triangular piece of white silk edged with snow-white lace, then came a section of exceedingly skinny chest, then a turquoise cross, and finally a gold chain from which the cross depended. Above the cross was a skinny neck, and ultimately a face chiefly remarkable for two very deep lines running down on either side of a mouth that descended at the corners. A careful layer of pinkish-purple powder covered the face. Two flat round grey eyes, behind pink-rimmed glasses, glanced coldly across at Amy and Mrs Beeding for an instant; then the lady absently waved a dry chalky hand with two rings at two empty chairs.

'Mr Danesford will see you in a minute. Sit down, will you?'

They sat down. The lady went on studying the sheet of figures, an old-fashioned clock with a noticeably white face ticked slowly high on the wall, and one shaft of sun-light burned its way steadily across the bound volumes of *The Prize* lining the shelves on three sides of the room. In a far corner was a door marked *Editor: Private*. Amy stared out of the window and felt sick. She wished she had never left school, never let Mrs Beeding write the letter to Mr Ramage, never come after the job. She suddenly discovered that she hated and feared strangers. She did not care much for the people she knew, but at least she was used to them and could get on with her own affairs without noticing them or them noticing her. But strangers—there was no telling what strangers would do next! She sat there with her hands feeling light and chilly, her mouth dry and her heart beating hard.

Suddenly, as though a door had opened, she *saw* herself talking easily and without fear to the unknown Mr Danesford in the next room, seeing him as no more than a blur rather like Mr Ramage, and, just as it had on the occasion when she had seen herself speaking to the American boy at Kenwood and when she had seen herself asking Miss Lathom to take care of her stories, the fear vanished as she ran through that open door in her mind, and escaped. And just as she looked quickly up, the dazed expression no longer in her eyes, a bell rang somewhere and the smart lady slowly got up from her desk, observing:

'Mr Danesford will see you now,' and went across to the door marked *Editor: Private*.

Amy followed her without one glance at poor Mrs Beeding. She was not in the least afraid now. She was Lawrence surrounded by Turks, Lindbergh alone over the Atlantic. I must be cool and wary and betray nothing. Bluff wins.

Miss Grace (this was the lady in the pink blouse) marched into the Editor's room and sat down, and Amy followed her, with the dismayed and un-Lindberghlike reflection, 'Oh, lord, is she going to be here too?' For she had taken a dislike to the Vision.

But the next instant she was no longer aware of anyone but Mr Danesford.

She never forgot her first sight of Mr Danesford, and never quite conquered the awe of him which sank into her spirit as he slowly rose from behind the desk at which he sat, resting his outspread fingers upon it and looking steadily at her from under thick overhanging eyebrows. He was an unusually tall man, wide-shouldered yet gaunt in build, with something actorish, blue-chinned and bloodhoundish in his heavy features and skin suffused with a dark flush. Black hair receded from his high shiny brow and was carefully brushed over the back of his head, from neatness rather than vanity, for it was thick as a boy's. He was dressed in a shabby frock-coat, grey striped trousers, wing collar and broad black stock caught by a black pearl pin. He had a strangely youthful look, yet it was impossible to mistake his age for anything but sixty; he seemed one of those men who might wake any morning to find themselves old. When he addressed himself to Amy, still steadily regarding her, his deep, measured voice seemed to match his face and huge-boned body.

'So you are Miss Lee,' he said.

'Yes,' said Miss Grace, busily pulling up the snow-white lace frill and at the same time refreshing herself by a peep down her own neck (a ritual that it was as well Miss Grace performed from time to time, as it was most unlikely that her neck would ever be peeped down by anyone else). 'The other one's waiting outside.'

'Oh, yes.' Mr Danesford glanced at Miss Grace, then slowly sat down again. Amy, Lindbergh forgotten, was too frightened by his size, face and voice to utter a word.

'Well, Miss Lee. I understand that you were at the Anna Bonner School for Girls in Highbury.'

'Yes. She's just left,' said Miss Grace, adjusting the turquoise cross and repinning the seed pearl 'L.'

'Are you used to the telephone?'

Miss Grace, faced at last by a question that she could not answer, looked at Amy and said sharply, 'Well? Are you used to the telephone?'

Amy shook her head.

'She's not used to it,' said Miss Grace to Mr Danesford triumphantly, pushing in a hairpin.

'But I could learn.' Amy found her voice, though it sounded hoarse and queer. 'I mean, I could learn.'

Mr Danesford nodded. All this time he had never taken his eyes off her. They were large blue bloodshot eyes with red rims, mournful and dignified and severe like some old dog's.

'Have you a specimen of your handwriting, Miss Lee?'

'Pardon?' whispered Amy, moistening her lips, though she had heard perfectly.

'Your writing. Writing. Write something,' snapped Miss Grace, getting up irritably in the act of re-fastening a gold curb bracelet and rummaging about on the desk. 'Here. Write your name and address and the date. That'll do.' She pushed a fountain pen and scribbling block at Amy.

Amy took it; and the familiar friendly feeling of a pen between her fingers encouraged her. At least she could write! Obediently she bent over the block, holding it on her knee, and wrote. While she did so they both studied her.

They saw a thin girl in a dark red dress with white collar

and cuffs, black shoes with high heels, light silk stockings that were a little too big for her thin legs. A severe black straw hat decorated with a little cockade of red ribbon sat firmly on her head and her pigtail was neatly finished by a black satin bow. All her clothes were modern as the lorries rumbling down Cheapside, yet she had an old-fashioned air that matched (both Miss Grace and Mr Danesford were honest enough to admit this to themselves, though reluctantly) the premises and policy of *The Prize*. She was simply not of the same world as the ambitious Gossey and the rest of his tribe.

They had both been prepared to dismiss her as hopeless at the first glance but found themselves, in dutifulness to Lord Welwoodham, unable to do so. Also, when once they had accepted the idea of having an office girl instead of an office boy at *The Prize*, all kinds of advantages in the plan suggested themselves. Girls were neater, politer, more punctual, less rebellious, more contented, quieter, less ambitious, than boys. They did not feel it their duty to smoke, drink, swear and fight—at least, not in their mid-teens. They often enjoyed their work. They could be paid less. Oh, they had many advantages over boys. And Miss Lee (if she came, though, she would, of course, be addressed as Amy; 'Miss Lee' was absurd at her age) seemed the sort of girl who would do as she was told (if she doesn't I'll know the reason why, thought Miss Grace, pulling down her blouse) and her appearance was undoubtedly satisfactory; clean and neat yet smart. That is, Mr Danesford thought it was smart but Miss Grace only thought it was clean and neat. No more than it should be, too.

Amy looked up and timidly handed the paper to Miss Grace who surveyed it and passed it with an inscrutable face to Mr Danesford.

'Yes. Yes. You write a plain hand, I see,' said he, putting it down on the desk beside him. He added, 'Readable. How old are you, Miss Lee?'

'I'll be sixteen on the 31st of October,' she answered, a little more confidently, looking across at him with large bright brown eyes.

'And this is your first application for a post?'

'Oh, yes.'

'I suppose that if I wrote to the Headmistress of your school she would be able to give me some idea of your capabilities—whether you are quick, and neat in your work, and—er—polite, and so on?'

'Oh, yes. She said she would. It's Miss Lathom. Miss M. Lathom, B.A.'

'Well, I will do so, Miss Lee, and then I will write to you again in a few days and let you know what I have decided. I think we must leave the matter there.'

He stood up and so did Miss Grace, fastening a button on her cuff, so Amy stood up as well. But before she could move to the door:

'In the matter of salary, Miss Lee,' added Mr Danesford, 'we pay our office boys twenty shillings a week. You would receive the same amount—if we decide you are to come, that is.' He paused. 'Suppose we did decide that you were to come, when could you begin your duties?'

'As soon as you wanted me to,' retorted Lindbergh firmly, considering and dismissing in an instant the idea of hesitating and hinting that she had another job in view.

'I see. Well, you will hear from us. Good morning.'

'Good morning. Thank you very much for seeing me, Mr Danesford,' said Amy, surprising both her audience and herself by her pat use of his name. (Not so quiet as she looks, I'd better make sure she doesn't want to write, thought Miss Grace, shepherding her out of the room. That was how Gossey and Brabbage and Hooter and Wamwick started—very quiet, and then suddenly had a lot to say for themselves. I'll sound *her* at once.)

Mrs Beeding's anxious face, one large question, greeted them as they came back into the other room but the words 'Did yer get it, luv?' died upon her lips as she met Miss Grace's cold stare.

'Mr Danesford's going to write to Miss Lathom about me, Mrs Beeding, and then let me know whether I've got it,' said Amy at once, ignoring Miss Grace and her stares.

'Ay, is he? Well, that's better than a poke in the eye, luv, isn't it?' said Mrs Beeding, disappointed that no immediately favourable decision had been reached but relieved that Amy had not been rejected outright. 'Well, I s'pose we better be getting along home. Good morning,' to Miss Grace, 'thank you kindly.'

Miss Grace took absolutely no notice, being apparently absorbed in reading some shorthand notes, until they got to the door. Then she looked up and said in a quiet tone:

'Amy?'

'Yes?' whispered Amy, very frightened by this sudden and unexpected use of her Christian name, which made her feel as though Miss Grace were God and knew everything (an effect upon which Miss Grace had counted).

'Do you know why Gossey (Gossey was the last office boy here) was dismissed?' pursued Miss Grace in the same low expressionless voice.

Amy shook her head. Mrs Beeding's lips formed the sentence, 'Fer not lickin' someone's boot polish.'

'He was dismissed for wasting office time in writing a rubbishy story, on office paper, in office hours, and then having the impudence to try and sell the story to the paper,' said Miss Grace. 'Another boy, called Hooter, was dismissed for the same reason. So was a boy named Brabbage. Also a boy named Wamwick. If you come here, and if you ever write a story, like those boys did, on office paper, in office time, and then try to sell your rubbish to the paper, you will be dismissed too. Without a reference. So remember, Amy.'

'Yes,' whispered Amy. 'Thank you. Good morning.'

They went out.

Going down the stairs Mrs Beeding said, 'If I had a face like that I'd pawn it and lose the ticket. Never you mind, luv. She mayn't like you, silly old date, but she means to have you, I'm sure.'

'I don't,' answered Amy. 'Mind, I mean.'

'What was th' chap like?'

'Mrs Beeding, he was the most frightening person I've ever seen in all my life,' answered Amy solemnly. 'He made my hands go all cold, truly he did.'

'They're a rum lot down there, I will say; the freaks at the World's Fair aren't in it with them. Come on, luv, let's get home an' have a bit o' dinner an' we'll feel better.'

As soon as the sound of their retreating steps had died away down the stairs, Mr Danesford came through into the office where Miss Grace was, and sat down at his own desk. Miss Grace glanced across at him and he at her.

'Well? What did you think of her?' They spoke together.

'I was impressed rather favourably, on the whole,' admitted Mr Danesford. 'Much more so than I expected to be, I must confess. What did you feel about it?'

'A bit too good to be true, *I* thought,' said Miss Grace, who had not thought anything of the kind but who intended to be in the position of one who had never been deceived for one moment just in case Amy did something awful later on. 'All the same, one can read her writing and she looks neat. And with the Double Number coming on and everything . . . Of course, I don't care for girls myself, so I may be prejudiced, I'm quite ready to admit that I'm a man's woman, and always have been.'

Mr Danesford said nothing. He never did when Miss Grace made this confession, which she did about seventy-four times a year.

'But I really haven't anything against her, apart from that,' ended Miss Grace with an indulgent giggle. 'And I certainly should be glad if I could give my mind to the Double Number without having to worry about getting a new boy.'

'Yes. That would certainly be an advantage. Well, I will write to Lord Welwoodham this morning and as soon as I hear from him, I will write to—Miss Lathom?—yes, that was the name . . . Lathom. And if her reply is satisfactory, perhaps you will be good enough to write to the girl—to Miss Lee—offering her the post.'

'Not offering. Saying she's got it. Begin as you mean to go on,' said Miss Grace crisply, running the carriage of her typewriter along with a whirr and bang.

The result of this discussion was a postcard from the editor saying, 'Pray do as you like. Every confidence. W.'; and on Friday morning the Beedings crowding round Amy, cheering and slapping her on the back because she had got the job.

12

Lord Welwoodham had inherited *The Prize* from his father, who founded it. In the 'sixties, when there were few papers for young people, it had been by far the most successful of all the boys' journals; with an imposing list of contributors which included some of the famous artists of the period, as well as all the best-known writers of stories for boys and occasionally the name of a literary giant who did not usually write for boys, but who was pleased to send his slighter work to such a well-written, well-known and well-bred paper as *The Prize*. From the 'sixties to just before the Great War *The Prize* had also earned a pleasantly solid income for its proprietor; it was not large, of course, but it was large enough to make the present Lord Welwoodham sigh when he compared it with what *The Prize* had earned for him in the years immediately after the Great War.

The former Lord Welwoodham had cared much more about *The Prize*'s tradition than about the money it brought him; its high standard in boys' stories, its articles on technical subjects written clearly by first-class experts, its reticent yet sincere patriotic and religious references, the simplicity of its ideals.

He loved to think of his paper going into thousands of homes all over England on the first day of every month, and of young grubby hands impatiently turning the pages to get to the more important of the two serials; of little sisters waiting meekly until George or Willy had finished with it; of sixpences hoarded in money boxes on the schoolroom mantelpiece or saved with unbelievable self-control from the maw of the school's tuck-shop; of big brothers on vacation from their university saying carelessly, 'Hullo, is that the old *Prize*? Is there a "Barty" story?

Good heavens, I thought that chap Antrobus must be dead years ago'; of governesses glancing indulgently through its pages at the end of the evening when the last gaping sock had been darned and placed on the neat pile by the work-basket; of the bound volumes filling shelves in many a vicarage dining-room and many a nursery bookshelf in London and provincial towns. He never imagined *The Prize* in children's hospitals or in Boys' Clubs in the slums, because he was a delightful, happy old man who did not think about the sufferings of people without enough money, but *The Prize* often found its way to such places and brought as much pleasure to poor children as it did to rich ones. In its pages goodness was rewarded and wickedness was punished, and it was made to seem passionately important that a boy should be brave, truthful and kind. Any child, rich or poor, young or old, enjoys a story with those values; and as the stories in *The Prize* were also simple and exciting, thousands upon thousands of children in England did enjoy them, for the fifty-four years before the Great War.

It was the Great War and Lord Northcliffe between them that ended this desirable state of affairs; Lord Northcliffe by tapping a reading public whose appetite for excitement was the stronger because it had not the money with which to buy security and security's quieter pleasures, and the Great War because it taught millions of such people to question values which their parents had taken for granted as they took the sunrise. *The Prize* soon found itself struggling in competition with boys' papers whose wildly sensational stories were neither stiffened by accurate knowledge nor made convincing by a touch of imagination, in which the heroes were almost indistinguishable from the villains and the cautious prophecies of scientists, reported luridly in the press, were distorted to provide the plots.

Of course, *The Prize* steadily lost ground. The public for which it had catered was grown up or dead, and its children were more sophisticated and lived at three times the pace their parents had.

The Editor and staff began, about 1925, to have the most discouraging and frightening feeling that can creep over a paper or a man . . . that of being too old and slow for the hurrying world on every side. Lord Welwoodham was obstinate, too; and he would not change the paper's policy. A group of kind friends had approached him with the suggestion that he should form a limited company with himself as chairman, or amalgamate with some more prosperous paper. They would, they promised, put money into the paper and pep it up. It was a fine old paper with a fine old name; but it must move with the times.

'*The Times* doesn't,' pointed out Lord Welwoodham. 'Doesn't move with the times, if I make myself clear. When *The Times* does, *The Prize* will.' He added despondently that he would see everyone frying in the hot place before he pepped up *The Prize*.

His friends went away rather offended and waited for the paper to go smash. Every year it earned a little less and the staff (never a large one) was reduced a little more, until it really was a skeleton staff, consisting only of two travellers covering London and the provinces, two space-sellers under Mr Ramage (Tim had not been replaced), Mr Ramage himself, Mr Danesford the sub-editor, Miss Grace the secretary, Lord Welwoodham as Editor, and an office boy, usually coming or going.

But in spite of the depressing feeling that any week might be its last, that Lord Welwoodham might die and his nephew and heir (a simply ravishing young man who decorated people's interiors) might do the paper up with a new cover by Rex Whistler and a series of articles on how to make amusing wax flowers, *The Prize* was a pleasant paper to be on. This group of middle-aged people working on two floors of the little old house in Rosemary Lane had the sense to know that it was safe—while the backwater lasted—in a comfortable Victorian backwater; and as (like most of us nowadays) they placed security above ambition, they took pains to keep it safe so far as they could. No one intrigued, backbit, or jockeyed for place. Miss Grace, the only woman on the staff, might be disagreeable but she did not run down Mr Danesford. Mr Danesford might be gloomy but he did not bully Miss Grace, and neither of them carried on the war which the Editorial usually carries on with the Advertising. Their spirits may have been subdued by St Paul's Cathedral, most of whose face stared severely in at them through the window of their room. It would take more impudence than either of them possessed to get up a backbiting with *that* staring in at you.

The staff had all been there for years, too; that made the situation easy for everyone. They knew each other's ways; they made allowances, and thought tolerantly when so-and-so was touchy—'It's the east wind, he never could stand it,' or 'His wife's been cutting up rough about him having his holiday in July, her sister won't be able to go with them as usual.' They were not exactly matey; a sober cheerfulness best describes their attitude, but they certainly made *The Prize* a pleasant place in which to work.

Nevertheless . . . from Lord Welwoodham down to the just-dismissed Gossey, there was not one of them who did not know that the destruction of their backwater was only a question of time.

The stories in *The Prize* were written by men who had made a lifetime's work of writing stories for boys. Old Antrobus, author of the Barty stories that had been running for thirty years and were still the best thing in the paper, was the only contributor of fiction to *The Prize* who had made a name by writing novels for adults. The Barty yarns were only a sideline of his. They were very funny; even after thirty years they were still funny, with dry, rather sophisticated plots worked out in absurd literary language that boys loved. Barty was a creation: Lord Welwoodham often thought despondently about the gap that would be left at old Antrobus's death. He was over seventy and could not last for ever . . . but perhaps *The Prize* would go first, the last 'Barty' story sinking gallantly with it like some old captain who preferred to die with his ship. If Antrobus went first, Lord Welwoodham knew of no writer who could replace him. Mr Wodehouse was the obvious choice, but his prices were far, far above what *The Prize* could possibly afford, as befits the prices of a writer of genius whose work has been fully appreciated in his lifetime.

But apart from old Antrobus, living under layers of comfort in his house in Regent's Park and fatly enjoying his life though kingdoms crumbled, there were no writers with imagination working regularly nowadays for *The Prize*. Lord Welwoodham often mused upon the writers who were working regularly for it, and had come to the conclusion that what ailed their work was exactly the fact that they had gone on writing for boys long after their first freshness had withered and they should have been writing for men. To write for boys (mused Lord Welwoodham) a writer needed something of a boy's own simple yet mysterious picture of the world. But nowadays there seemed hardly any writers with that outlook. Everyone is so damned clever, thought Lord Welwoodham despondently, recalling a volume of short stories which he had picked up in a friend's house and which had made him feel that the author was uttering a series of sharp yelps—Ow! I can't bear it! It's awful. Ow! Take it away! Ooh!—'it' being Life.

It was his half-expressed dissatisfaction with the contents of *The Prize* that made him drop so severely upon the literary office boys. What! Did the very office boys feel that the stories were so bad that they could write better ones? It was the last straw; and Lord Welwoodham made the rule about no contributions from the Staff on pain of instant dismissal. They could always hawk their pieces of vileness round to the other boys' papers, he pointed out, and there they had quite a good chance of being taken. In fact, he had a theory that they often *were* taken; the stories in *The Prize*'s rivals all read as though they were written by Hooter, Brabbage, Wamwick and Gossey in collaboration.

And until writers became less damned clever or until he found a new writer with the fresh mysterious picture of the world in his head that a boy carries, there was nothing to be done about the stories in the dear old *Prize* that he loved so well.

On the first Monday that Amy walked up Rosemary Lane to begin her duties she had a disagreeable experience. She was hurrying along with her quick light step, her suitcase and her pigtail swinging and her shadow running beside her in the clear morning sunlight, when she became aware that she was being followed. Or rather, accompanied, for the person whose shadow mingled with her own on the pavement was walking at her side and only very slightly behind her, and mincing along on the tips of his toes in a manner that was plainly an imitation of her own gait, while she could only conclude that a large ball of newspaper which distended the front of his tightly-buttoned jacket was intended to represent her chest (a libel, for it was not fat).

As she glanced at him, unable for the moment to believe what she saw, he contorted his face in a hideous grimace, squinted, stuck out his tongue further than it seemed possible for a tongue to shoot, and began in a high squeaking voice:

'Yes, Miss Grace. Ay'll goo at wence, Miss Grace. Wez thet the phoone? Are you thee-ar? Shall ay lee out fresh blottin'-paper, *old Daddy-Bloodyhound-Great-Danesford*' (this in a voice thick with bitter spite). 'What about a little bit 'er sugar fer the bird? *Gar!*'

He made a lightning swoop as though to pick up something at her feet and viciously nipped her calf.

'Shut up!' blazed Amy, swinging at him with the suitcase but missing.

'*You* shut up—half-inching my job!' he cried. '*You* ain't fourteen yet, you look 'alf-starved, you do. You wait till my Mum gets 'old o' you, she won't half give you something, she won't, comin' sneakin' in and sucking up to old Bloody Great Danesford'—he was running beside her as he talked, to the vast entertainment and amusement of the people hurrying through the lane—'I'll make it 'ot for you, so you just watch out, Cissy, see?'

Amy began to run. Oh! if the lock of her suitcase only held! She had a tasty little lunch packed by Mrs Beeding in there and an exercise book containing two chapters of *The Great White Rajah's Servant*.

The boy began to run too. He was a large roughish boy of about sixteen with patched boots and oily hair that stuck up in quiffs on his forehead.

'Look here,' panted Amy, glancing from side to side as they drew near the offices of *The Prize* and hoping that Mr Danesford and Miss Grace would not see her in this humiliating situation, 'if you'll go away, I'll give you——'

But her bribe was never offered, for at that moment a large hand came out and gripped the boy by the scruff of the neck and a pair of grubby hogskin gloves struck him a stinging box first on one ear, then the other.

'There, you dirty boy,' severely observed an elderly gentleman in a shabby but beautiful dark blue suit. 'Go away, be off, do you hear?' And he shook him again.

'She 'alf-inched my job!' cried the boy, struggling.

'Bosh. You lost it yourself for breaking office rules. I've spoken to Mr Newton on *Thrilling Tales of Space*, about you; go home and clean yourself, you very dirty boy, and see him this afternoon. If you worry Miss Lee again I'll tell your mother.'

'All right, my lord. Thanks.' Gossey dusted himself down and ran off, without another look at Amy but singing loudly:

> *'Skinny Lee*
> *Caught a flea——.'*

'Go on, go on upstairs, Miss Lee, what's your name, Amy, isn't it,' said the tall gentleman, absently shepherding her in front of him with a thick stick of yellow wood topped by a worn silver knob and flapping at her with the gloves. 'I'm the editor, Lord Welwoodham, and I always like tea when I'm early. I suppose you can make tea?'

'Oh, yes. Mrs Beeding taught me,' she answered confidently, going ahead of him up the stairs, her blood warmed by danger and her eyes sparkling with the fun of being rescued. Suddenly she paused and turned round, waiting for him to draw level with her. When he did so:

'Please don't mind me asking,' she said very politely, 'but what do I call you? "My lord," like Gossey did?'

'You call me Lord Welwoodham when it's impossible to avoid doing so; otherwise you call me "you." I shall call you "you," too, except when I can't help it and then I shall call you "Miss Lee." I like the tea very weak with one lump of sugar. Bring it in the minute it's ready, there's a dear good fell— a good girl, will you?' And he went into his office and shut the door.

'What were you doing, Amy, to annoy Gossey like that?' inquired Miss Grace, gliding out from a recess near the window where she had been hanging up a tasteful black silk coat with kilted frills on it wherever the designer could get them, and revealing herself in a bright navy blue silk dress with bunches of flowers all over it and a georgette modesty vest on which was pinned a brooch made like three white enamel daisies in a row, and a necklace of pink crystal beads and pearls, and golden hoop earrings, and three pink carnations pinned on her shoulder by a single silver bar with an aquamarine sparking in it.

'Good morning, Miss Grace. He was pinching my leg and Lord Welwoodham hit him with his gloves,' replied Amy.

Miss Grace made a faint sound of disgust at the scene of riot thus conjured, and hauled up the modesty vest.

'But you must have said something, Amy or done something to annoy him. Gossey used to be a quiet, respectable lad.'

'No, Miss Grace. He just said I'd taken his job and then he pinched me. Miss Grace, Lord Welwoodham wants his tea. Where is everything, please?'

'Look in the cupboard,' replied Miss Grace, repressively, pointing with one finger while adjusting the carnations with the other hand, and so the day began.

Amy's duties were light and not too dull. She had to answer the telephone, put the rejected manuscripts into the stamped addressed envelopes which had accompanied them to *The Prize*, and enter their titles and authors' names in a book, together with the dates of their arrival and return, see that the two desks of her seniors were kept tidy, make the tea at eleven o'clock and again at a quarter-past four, tend the fire in winter and the little electric fan in summer (Lord Welwoodham liked himself and all his staff to be comfortable while at work); and once a month or so, on Press Day, to go round the corner to Paternoster Court, where the printers had their works, to fetch an important proof without which *The Prize* could not go to press.

The printers, Messrs Hobday, had messengers known to the staff of *The Prize* as Hobday Boys whom they sent round with proofs of the stories and articles as they were set up in print; and as Press Day drew near this stream of boys swelled until they were arriving every half-hour or so with matter to be corrected, and sent off again by the next boy. But on the final day, though the flood of Hobday Boys roared in full spate, it never roared full enough for Lord Welwoodham, who was always poking his head round the door and fretfully asking had not the proof of such-and-such come yet? Where the devil was the Hobday Boy, and would Amy mind running round and fetching it at once?

Though the Hobday Boy had usually left by another way when she arrived at Paternoster Court, Amy much enjoyed these dashes through the narrow alleys and yards of old brown bricks and plaster black with age; where the spirit of the Cathedral could be felt, even when its bulk was hidden, by the sudden noise of bells and a sensation as of some enormous presence brooding in the sky. And then as she turned a corner she would come upon it again—that vast slope of the soft dark blue of a mussel shell and with something of the same exquisite curve—the Dome.

She soon became at home in the office—as much, that is, as she was at home anywhere in the real world—and liked being there. Of course she would sooner have been at home in the big-top-front, writing, or in the old exam room at the Anna Bonner, writing, but she liked getting away from the Beedings for nine hours or so every day and enjoyed the journey to and from the City, which she found exciting because she was not yet old enough to find it exhausting. She enjoyed going into the Cathedral three or four times a week in her lunch hour or on her way home, and wandering slowly round it looking at the pictures and statues, particularly *The Light of the World* by Holman Hunt. She would stand for minutes at a time gazing up at the sad patient face of Jesus waiting in the twilit orchard, where stars are tangled in the branches of the trees and apples lie scattered in the grass so deeply green by the light of the lantern, where withered meadowsweet and rich brambles grow against the cottage door, and beside these familiar flowers are the stars and moon of Heaven on the lantern in Jesus's hand, throwing up rainbow lights on the white robe.

Next to this picture, which she loved because it told a story and had gorgeous colours, she liked the grave of an old man who was squashing a lot of guns and cannons under his tombstone as though he had energetically used them as a mere ladder to climb a little nearer to Heaven. Amy had never seen such a sensible and businesslike tombstone, and it was cheerful, too, in a queer way. She never tired of looking at it. For some reason it comforted her, in the same way that Mrs Beeding did, and helped her to think more calmly about her father and mother lying inside the earth of Highgate Hill. After all, Heaven was true: and that old man's monument, impatiently crushing the instruments of his earthly fame, seemed somehow, for Amy at least, to make it truer.

She soon felt at home in St Paul's, which is, indeed, not a gloomy and a solemn place but so gloriously beautiful that it sounds, as one looks up into the Dome, like a colossal shout of praise to God. No one makes any attempt to keep it solemn; guides take visitors round, old ladies pray in corners, men hammer the walls and cheerfully shift benches about with a prolonged thundering echo, office boys nip round and out again, cap in hand, and quiet girls sit and eat their lunch out of paper bags. No noise nor lunch-eating can spoil the solemn yet soaring feeling given to the spirit by those walls of palest pink stone touched here and there with airy gilding, and the wreaths of darker rosy stone on the roof. It is comforting just to stand, and stare and stare, and to know that men once lived whose feeling about God expressed itself thus.

Now that Amy had fewer chances to get to the British Museum, the old man lying on his cannons and *The Light of the World* rather took the place in her affections of the Amaravati Tope. St Paul's was useful to her in many ways; it not only provided her with a beautiful refuge from the roaring streets and a place where she ate her sandwiches on wet days, but a good deal of *The Great White Rajah's Servant* was written there, with a three and sixpenny fountain pen purchased by Amy out of her first week's salary on a very small scribbling block. She first politely approached a verger and said that she wrote every week to a cousin in Australia who was very interested in churches as he was going to be a curate, and would it matter if she took down some notes about the Cathedral sometimes to send to him? The verger, after a rather lengthy study of her neat person and inquiring face, said that he supposed it would be all right, and she settled down with a light heart to start Chapter Five.

She had not been at the office a day before she decided that it would be quite impossible to write *there*. Miss Grace watched her closely all the time without seeming to, and often she would look up from her seat at the table by the door to find Mr Danesford's bloodshot, melancholy eyes fixed immovably upon her in a long, terrifying stare. Even Lord Welwoodham had said to her more than once 'Not writing a story, are you, Miss Lee? No, no, that would never do.' And Mr Ramage had said when she thanked him for telling Lord Welwoodham about her, 'Well, you're quite safe so long as you don't try to write for *The Prize!*'

The fact was (though she was not the person to realize it) they found her a completely satisfactory office girl and were anxious not to lose her. She was so neat, polite, intelligent and efficient that they all found it hard to realize that she was poor Lee's daughter. She seemed to belong to a lower caste, to the world of respectable small shopkeepers, with her touch of anxious politeness and her faint cockney accent—though that, Lord Welwoodham had noticed with some amusement, was fading. It must be unconscious mimicry, he decided, for I'll swear she never thinks about the difference between my accent and her own (of poor Miss Grace's accent Lord Welwoodham had the same opinion that he had of Amy's, but Mr Danesford's voice had such a rich, deep, sad colour to its tones that not even Lord Welwoodham thought about accents in connection with *him*, any more than one thinks of them in connection with a bloodhound's bay). That cockney whine and her haberdashery-respectability must be the mother, I suppose, thought Lord Welwoodham. Poor Lee. Caught young.

For Lord Welwoodham, like his father before him, was a charming chap but a chap so shut in by his caste that he knew little about human nature outside it.

175

But although they all in their different ways approved of her, Mr Danesford never unbent towards her, never bayed a single stately joke at her nor praised her when she did right, but only gloomily instructed her day by day in her tiny yet necessary duties, and she continued to be, if not exactly frightened, very much in awe of him.

13

On a snowy night four years later, the house in Vine Falls was echoing to music. The family was in the living-room amusing itself, the older members with bridge and the younger ones with talking against the noise of the radio, while at the piano sat Bob, vamping a soft accompaniment to the tunes coming over the air and doing it very well.

Strangers were always surprised to learn that he could play the piano, for medical students usually prefer the hotter instruments, but his family had been used ever since he was a little boy to hearing the piano singing under his big hands; at first uncertainly in stiff little traditional pieces given him by his music mistress (a cousin of that same old Miss Cordell present at the home-coming garden party) and later, as he grew older, with easy casual sweetness. He read music slowly yet accurately, but was happier when finding the prettiest way through the newest tune by ear, or playing an air thirty years old to please his mother. The piano and boxing were his chief recreations in his first year at the Owen Vallance Medical School; he had an old Bosendorfer in his rooms at Morgan, where he lived during term, and made himself temporarily unpopular with his fellow boarders by playing it after midnight as a rest from his text-books.

At a few months over twenty he was a very large young man indeed, with what Lou called 'the swellest figure around.' But he was a little too thin, because he was just entering (without anyone knowing it, least of all himself) upon that second adolescence which many young men pass through between twenty and twenty-five, when they get mysterious skin-troubles, cannot decide on a career, tire easily, are unconsciously cruel and moody with their young women, and finally emerge not much the worse (if they are lucky) into maturity.

Bob, who was only at the beginning of these trials, had no regular young woman with whom to be cruel and moody, though he squired dozens of girls (he usually picked them small and dark) from Vine Falls and Morgan and Alva to the movies and dances, and kissed them good-night with ardour but without much personal interest. It was always he who said cheerfully on these occasions, 'Well, I suppose we'd better be getting along now.' But the gentleness and strength that went with his nice manners and unconventional good looks made him irresistible to most girls, and he often came home feeling puzzled and vaguely guilty from an evening that had begun pleasantly enough, but had ended—heaven knew why, he didn't—in temper or tears.

The tempo of his nature, like that of a piece of music, was slow. Like some music it was also deep and sweet, but it could not be forced, and it was the despair of the quickly-fired, aware girls who were his contemporaries; they felt the depth and sweetness in him but could not, so to speak, get at it. And if they tried to comfort themselves by thinking scornfully, 'He's only a kid,' the thought rang singularly false inside their heads (where there was usually ample room for it to ring) for he certainly had none of the crudeness and freshness of a kid; his gentle easy manner covered a calm self-assurance.

This confidence grew out of a natural happiness, that nothing—so far—had shattered. He had grown to young manhood in a happy prosperous American home, sheltered by a father and mother who loved one another and loved their children; it would have been strange had he not been happy.

And only one, of all the girls he danced with, kissed, and took to the movies, knew that he was romantic, that he could not fall in love with love as most young men do, but must find the one girl.

Helen was sitting on the couch beside Irene, talking over plans for the Christmas vacation which was only a few days old. Bob had gone before dinner to fetch her through the snowstorm from her home, which was only a quarter of a mile or so down the hill, and brought her up hanging on to his arm, their laughing faces wet with snow, her eyelashes sticking out in wet points above her wind-rosed cheeks. He steered her along the sidewalk, in the raccoon coat and warm ski-ing trousers she had put on as the only sensible wear in such weather. They were breathless and shouting with laughter, the snow stinging their faces.

'Look at that crazy pair,' said Helen's mother, pleased, leaning back in the car as it left the walkers behind on the short climb up to the Vorst home. 'They don't care so long as they're together.'

Mr Viner, a slim man whose little dark Imperial beard gave him a foreign air, smiled and nodded and both felt a glow of comfort, a strong sense of the solidity of their family traditions all round them, as they drove on through the gale.

Helen had been happy, hanging on to Bob's arm and drawing her breath in gasps against the force of the wind, and loving the pure smell of the driving snow. She knew that this—the feel of Bob's warm firm arm, the sound of his laughing voice coming down to her above the wind, the knowledge that they were alone together, fighting the storm side by side—was happiness. She knew that when she was an old woman, whatever happened between Bob and herself, she would remember such moments with the deepest tenderness that her heart had ever known.

But this evening she was also in a mood of natural girlish confidence, hopeful and gay. Bob had been struck almost into shyness, for a moment, at the first sight of her! And when he got his breath back he had said, still staring, 'Hullo, Helen,' and forgotten to give her his usual cousinly kiss.

Helen, who knew everything about how young men fell in love, thought that these were hopeful signs.

Perhaps . . . this very evening . . . he would . . . say something.

She *was* his special now—at least, in one way. He wrote to no other girl, she knew, as he wrote to her; short letters, but letting her know what he was thinking and feeling. He wrote in short stiff sentences that were nevertheless exciting to her because she knew him so well and could give each word its proper weight and shade of meaning as though she were translating from a foreign tongue.

She often wondered if he translated her letters in the same way? But there was not so much need for him to, for she wrote him everything (save only one thing) that she was thinking and feeling, and—and a man's mind didn't work the same way as a girl's, anyway, and Bob was more reserved than she was and could not express his feelings so easily: men often couldn't. He was younger in many ways, too, than she. Yet in some ways he made her feel the younger, and she loved that, because she was so sensible that she was always treated by her crowd at college as adviser-in-chief—a rôle which can become unsatisfying.

She was so happy in the special course of Drama study that she was taking at Cedars, a women's college in the next state, her life was so crowded with delightful activities and and friends, that she felt hardly a shadow of pain about her caring for Bob. She did not call her feeling for him 'love,' she thought of it as 'caring', and no doubts about the future had crept into her heart. Sometimes, when their visits home had not coincided, and she had not seen him in months, she felt faintly alarmed at the strength of her longing to see him again. But as soon as they met she felt quite easy once more; they were so happy together in the old familiar places they had known since they were in rompers, and it seemed unbelievable that she should have so longed to see Bob again—that long-legged creature with the lock of hair he never would wear decently short, who only a few years ago had held a place in her heart a long way below Eva le Gallienne!

Ah, but now there was no question (this always frightened her when she admitted it to herself) about who came first with her! She was an unusually loving daughter in that casual post-Jazz Age, a tender elder sister to the conceited and skinny Stebby now working his way with unexpected intelligence through High, a loyal friend, and a soul dedicated to whatever demands the Drama might make—but Bob came first. He was the 'you' in a dozen or so poems hidden in a locked desk that would never be shown to a dearest friend, much less to an editor. He was her standard of comparison for all her luckless young men, who did not so much come off badly as never get a look in at all. He grew through her whole life like the root, stem and branches of a big gentle tree; and as she sat tonight in her pale yellow dress, moving her shoulders gently in time to Bob's playing and smiling at Irene as they discussed what they would wear to the Frankwoods party on Thursday, she was in exactly the same plight as the Princess in the fairy story. Dowered with beauty, goodness, riches, but . . . *she shall prick her finger on a spinning wheel*. The wound was already there, and she in the magic sleep blinding her to all faces but one.

'Oh!' Irene suddenly interrupted herself. 'I knew I had something to tell you! Francey Carr's left Frankwoods and nobody knows where she's gone!'

'She's gone to Morgan. Dan got her a job,' observed Lou, looking up from the latest Kathleen Norris.

'How do you know?' demanded Irene.

'How does she ever know anything?' Bob glanced across the glossy surface of the piano and smiled, nodding his fair head as if he liked the sound of his own playing and the pretty picture made by the group of girls near the fire. 'Myron told her, of course.'

'Is that so, Lou?'

Lou nodded, not looking up.

'Oh, well—I'm glad if she's fixed up.' Irene looked a little embarrassed and lit another cigarette. She had grown into a pretty, smart and completely ordinary girl, and was more than a little jealous of Lou, who at nearly sixteen wore her plain summer ginghams and tough fall coats with the casual but unmistakable air that means a girl is going to be not merely a follower of styles but a setter of them. This was as it should be, for Lou planned to be a dress-designer. She was plain and slender with a good figure, a good skin, and a small but manageable head of fair hair. Irene, who was to be married in the spring to Jesson, the Parlour-Pink, often felt vaguely dissatisfied with her own conventionally smart appearance.

'She was working on the stocking-counter at Frankwoods, you know,' Irene went on.

'I didn't know,' said Helen. 'Bob never told me the last time he wrote—somewhere 'round Independence Day, that would have been.'

'Well!' Bob struck a tremendous chord, causing the table of elderly bridge-players at the far end of the room to look up, and his Aunt Carol Viner to say mildly, 'Bob, please! I'm trying to concentrate!'

'I get such a heap of time to write you or anyone else a Sunday supplement about the old home town, don't I? Besides, I didn't think a nice girl like you would want to hear about a cheap skate like Francey.'

They smiled at one another across the room, and Bob struck two soft chords.

If ever I fall for anyone I hope I'll be cagier about it than Helen is, thought Lou, turning over three pages of the Kathleen Norris. *Anybody can see how she is about Bob.* Suspecting a story from Irene's embarrassed tone, she smoothly went on:

'Why are you glad she's fixed up?'

'Oh—it wasn't anything, only I was in Frankwoods on Monday

to get some gloves and Francey got so darned fresh with me I reported her.'

Helen said nothing. The shrill little voice jarred on her, with its fashionable use of slang and she did not like the picture of Irene, bright ornament of the Junior League, patronizing poor stupid Francey Carr.

Bob looked across at his sister and observed:

'Well, that was sweet of you.'

'Well, I know it sounds kind of mean, Helen, but honestly, it was for her own good——'

'And not to get a bit of your own back, why *no*!'

Bob struck another tremendous chord.

'Well, I didn't say anything for a while, because I knew how she always used to try and start a fight when we were kids—remember, Helen?—but at last she got me so mad, and Mrs Boadman——'

'Attaboy!' And Bob struck up *The Star-Spangled Banner* in hideous contrast with the radio, causing the bridge-players to jump and look up irritably, while his father called:

'Bob! Please!'

The three girls laughed; it was an old family joke whose origin was lost in the Vorst-Viner past that Bob always whistled this tune whenever Mrs Boadman's name came up.

'Mrs Boadman happened to be there getting stockings for Elenor, and she whispered to me that if I didn't report Francey someone else would, and not so nicely, either——'

'So you went right ahead and did it nicely?' said Lou, shutting her book and looking at her sister with her head on one side.

'Yes, I did. I said, "I'm afraid I shall have to report you——"'

'And what did Francey say?'

'Oh, she didn't say a thing, she was throwing the stockings around and just burning up—you know how she always does. But after I'd reported her, what do you think she had the neck to say?'

'Irene Vorst, you're *lousy!*' said Lou promptly, and they all laughed.

'Lou dear, I don't like to hear you talk like that, it's ugly,' called her mother absently from the other end of the room.

'It's all right, Aunt Sharlie, she was only quoting,' said Helen. 'Well, then what happened?'

'Yes, that's just what she did say, and you should have seen Mrs Boadman and everybody's faces! And when I went in yesterday there was a new girl on the stockings, and they told me Francey'd gone.'

'Fired, do you mean?' Bob's voice was suddenly stern and he looked quickly across at his sister.

'Gosh, no! She just walked out, the girl said.'

'Well, it's no thanks to you if she wasn't fired.' Bob got up from the piano and came across to the girls and sat down on the sofa between Irene and Helen with his arms behind his head. 'It was a low-down thing to do.'

'She asked for it!' cried Irene indignantly.

'Maybe she did, but you ought to have taken no notice. You know Francey's about as dumb as anyone could be. Besides, she's jealous of you girls—always has been.'

Helen nodded. 'Yes—I always used to notice when we were kids how she looked when she saw us at the movies, and I used to feel sorry for her.'

'Well, I wasn't,' said Irene hardly. 'I always thought she was just a cheap skate and I do now. But Bob always had a kind of crush on her, hadn't he, Lou—Helen? You remember?'

'Yes, and he went dancing with her last summer,' said Lou composedly.

'How do you know?' demanded Bob, surprised. 'You can't have seen us, she used to meet me at a place in Morgan.'

'I didn't see you, smarty, but Myron's got a friend who knows someone in a band in Morgan and this bandman told Myron's friend he'd seen you and the friend told Myron and Myron told me.'

'All right, all right, I give up.' Bob put his head in his hands. 'You win.'

'Oh, well, if Dan's got her a job, that's swell,' concluded Irene, taking another cigarette. Lou casually took one as well, but on her mother's voice calling in the same absent tone:

'No, Lou dear. Not until you're eighteen,' she put it back with a grin.

A few years ago, Mrs Vorst would not so easily have been able to stop a young daughter from smoking, for social opinion would have been on the daughter's side. But the collapse of the Coolidge Prosperity Era, and the Depression that followed, had helped a natural reaction to set in against the licence and bad manners of the Jazz Age, and Bob and Irene and Lou, Helen and Stebby, had grown up into a world in which 'hard-boiled' was no longer the highest word of praise for an American girl. The knee-length skirts and close shingle of the 1920's seemed like an amusing dream to Helen and Irene in their long graceful evening frocks balanced by clusters of soft curls; and Helen, like a number of her friends, did not smoke. Because everyone took girls smoking for granted, it would never have, for these twenty-year-olds, the daring appeal as of a broken *tabu* that it had for their elder sisters who were now nearing the thirties. If Irene talked cheap slang, drank whenever she could get drink, and smoked hard it was because she liked doing those things, not because she saw herself—as Jeanette Waldron had—as a smasher of blue-nosed Victorian traditions. Nevertheless, the Jazz Age had branded its followers for life. Jeanette and Boone, who had been married for two years, were just finding this out.

'What kind of a job is it, Lou?' asked Helen.

'Myron doesn't know. He said he was down at the station yesterday meeting his cousin who had come out for the day—he's staying in Alva, the cousin is—and he saw Davy Sawyer. (He's one of the porters.) And Davy said Francey had taken a ticket to Morgan and she told Franklin Meyer (he's the man in the ticket office) that Dan had got her a job there. But she wouldn't say what kind of a job. Franklin and Davy both kidded her along, Myron said, and tried to make her tell, but she wouldn't.'

'You're as good as *The Citizen* and *The Inquirer* and *The Sentinel* all rolled into one, isn't she?' Bob indulgently kicked Lou's slim knee and grinned at the other two. 'I wish I could remember my biology half as well as you do, all that blah about Myron's cousin. *I* didn't even know Myron *had* a cousin. What colour's his hair?'

'He's bald,' she said instantly. 'His name's Peter Pawley and he lives in Westwater, Maine, and he's down in Alva on a business trip selling a sort of little comb and brush in one—very handy, Myron says it is, only he wouldn't let his cousin come up here because he might try to sell it to all of us . . .'

By this time the laughter was so loud, less at what Lou was saying than at her expression, that the bridge-players had to call out for silence once more. When they had comparatively got it, Bob asked:

'Is Dan in Chicago, do you know?'

'Francey wouldn't tell. They did try to make her, but she wouldn't.'

'He must be quite a big shot by now,' said Bob thoughtfully, taking a cigarette. 'I haven't seen him since we had an evening together at his joint in Detroit, when I was down there the fall before last.'

'The Ecstasy Club,' murmured Lou.

'That was it. But it's not there now; it was raided and closed, and I haven't seen Francey in months, so I've no idea where he is. I'd like to see him again, he was an original sort of guy. Do you know' (to Helen) 'I remember one evening I was down at Carr's when he was there, and he was reading a life of Napoleon, just sitting there reading, in a room full of the boys shooting craps!'

'Vanity,' she said calmly. 'Liking to be different. One of the most marked characteristics of the criminal type.'

> 'Philo Vance
> Wants a kick in the pants'

he quoted. 'Dan isn't a criminal type. He's in the racketeering game because he gets a kick out of it. He isn't a killer.'

'How do you know?'

'I know Dan. He wouldn't kill. He's kind of cool and thinks it's all a bit funny.'

'That's just the sort that does kill,' she said.

'Oh, you know all about it, Sister Lombroso, don't you? Dan's all right. He sends a packet home to his mother and father every now and then, Francey says.'

'To keep them from talking,' said Helen.

'You win, then,' Bob said amiably, getting up. 'Dance?'

As she came towards him, the sight of her lovely faintly-smiling face made him think of another girl's face, the one he sometimes dreamed about. Last night he had seen it again, floating beside him in blue water; surrounded by waving fine black hair. They were swimming together naked, and the sun was very hot, and he was delightfully, completely happy. Crazy dream. The craziest part of it was that girl's face. It was real; he would know it again. Sometimes he did not dream about it for months, and forgot it, but it always came back again and he was always pleased to see it—a dear little face, not exactly pretty, yet cute.

The radio was playing a languid and despairing tune that made one long to slide away slowly, slowly across the shining floor. Bob put his arm round Helen and they moved away together, but before they had got a couple of steps the door opened abruptly and Myron put his head round, saying:

'Here's Boone.'

187

Everyone looked up with exclamations as Boone came in quickly, brushing snow off himself, and looking round with eyes that glittered in his dissipated young face.

'Why Boone! It's lovely to see you.'

'However did you make it? We only just did, and that was three hours ago!'

'Boone, where's Jeanette?'

The last question, his mother's, cut quietly across the laughing babel, and he turned to answer it.

'Gone. She's left me.'

'*Gone*?' echoed everybody, and Lou got up noiselessly from beside the fire and joined the group, staring up at her brother's wild miserable face.

'What—gone for good, do you mean?' stammered Irene. Now there would be a scandal just before her spring wedding, the expense of a divorce, trouble and family conferences, her mother in tears, and everybody shooting off their mouths about nothing but Jeanette—Jeanette! The hell with her—I always did hate her, thought Irene.

'Gone with Dietz,' he said shortly. 'Give me a drink, will you?' (Bob went over to the cocktail cabinet and got some brandy. Jeanette! The little——! Walking out on Boone, after all these years!)

'The usual note,' went on Boone, swallowing the brandy. 'Left on the radio. It just said——'

His face puckered, and he bit his trembling lips savagely, then controlled his voice.

'. . . just said he'd got more of what she wanted in every way than I had, so she's gone with him.'

'Sit down, son.' Mr Vorst's kind handsome face was very red. He gently pushed Boone towards a chair, but Boone shook his head impatiently and turned to his mother.

'You see I couldn't make enough, Mother, that was the trouble. She wanted such a hell of a lot.'

'I know, son. Sit down and try to relax a little.' She put her arm around his shaking shoulders, and glancing up met Lou's interested stare.

'Lou dear, go right up to bed this minute,' she said quietly. 'Helen, take her up, will you, and Bob, will you go along to the kitchen and get Myron to fix something for Boone to eat.'

Helen put her arm round Lou and the three young people went quickly out of the room.

'There wasn't anything to eat at home, except something that had turned sour in the ice-box—she'd left the door open—and the bed wasn't made—the girl hadn't turned up, so I thought you wouldn't mind if I stayed here,' said Boone. 'Irene, please go away, will you? I want to talk to Mother and Dad, and I know you always hated her and I don't want you to hear,' and he hid his face in his hands.

Irene opened her mouth indignantly, but on receiving four determined jerks of the head from the elders, went meekly to the door, murmuring, 'I guess I'll call up Elenor,' and shut it quietly behind her.

When Helen had seen Lou into her room and lingered there for five minutes, wisely indulging her with a grown-up discussion of the disaster, she went downstairs into the kitchen. She felt so unhappy about poor Boone's wretched bloated face and his tears that she longed to work off her feelings by helping in some way—even by toasting sandwiches. But at the back of her mind was a feeling of amazement: how *could* anyone hurt another human being like that? A human being who loved you, who was working hard to give you everything you wanted! Jeanette's the cheap skate, not poor Francey, she thought, as she opened the kitchen door.

Bob was fussing in a drawer, looking grim, and said nothing for a minute. She sat down in Myron's old chair and kept quiet.

'Where in hell's the can-opener?' he burst out at last. 'That fool Myron is *out*—can you beat it—on a night like this?'

'He always goes to the movies on Monday,' she reminded him, getting up. 'He had his hat on when he looked round the door. Let me look.'

When she had found the can-opener she silently handed it to him.

'Oh . . . thanks. He'd better have soup, hadn't he, Helen?'

'Yes . . . and bacon sandwiches. Let me make them—I'd love to. You do the soup.'

They were busy for a little while in silence, then he said:

'Dietz is a New Yorker.'

'Yes. He produced the Morgan Little Theatre Club show this fall.'

'Of course she only took Boone because all the men in her crowd were sick of her. He was the only one who'd stuck by her.'

'I know. Switch on the griller, will you? Thanks.'

'Helen, isn't it horrible?' he burst out again, standing looking helplessly at her with the can-opener in one hand and the soup in the other. 'He was so happy—remember? And everything was going to be swell, once they were married.'

'None of us thought so.'

'Well, everybody knows she's a so-and-so. It's her crowd that's done this—parties every night and always half canned. Nobody can do that sort of thing and hold down a job. Poor old Boone. He ought to have socked her one on the wedding night. I would.'

Helen laughed, but she felt frighteningly desolate. How fragile and fairylike was her happiness! It was borne almost entirely on the wide shoulders of the young man at the other side of the kitchen table. If only she and Bob had been engaged to be married, and could have comforted each other in this miserable business by holding each other close and swearing that their love should be different, should last until they died!

It's got much worse this vac, she thought unhappily, putting

190

the bacon under the griller. I guess if he doesn't say something definite before we go back to college I'd better try and stop feeling like this, because it can't do me any good, I'm sure. I've been silly and let it get a hold on me, and now if he doesn't say anything, what'll I do? But how was I to know? I've felt like this for so long I suppose I kind of didn't notice it. But I notice it now, all right, all right.

'You know,' said Bob, putting the saucepan on the stove. 'If ever I married anyone——'

Her heart suddenly beat fast.

'. . . I'd never let that sort of thing happen to me. Would you?'

'I'd certainly try not to,' she answered faintly.

'You see' (he was stirring the soup), 'I'd make so darned sure I'd got the right one and that she was the right one for me that it *couldn't* happen.'

'Yes.'

'If I wasn't sure, I wouldn't marry anyone.'

She said nothing but attended steadily to the bacon.

'Helen?' Surprised by her silence, he came round and peered into her face. 'Is anything—what's the matter?'

'It's all right,' she said at once, lifting her eyes, dark and blue as the sea in his dream, and smiling. They gleamed with tears. 'I'm all upset about poor Boone, that's all. He looked . . . so lost. It's all right, Bob. I'm not really crying. Give me my bag, will you, it's over there.'

He got the bag, then came and stood beside her and gently patted her shoulder while she wiped her eyes with a fresh little handkerchief. Presently she found herself being given a gentle kiss or two, which she returned with an exquisite feeling of happiness and peace—but without hope.

'If anyone ever hurt you,' said Bob softly but intensely, tightening his arm round her waist, 'I'd *lam* him!'

She had to laugh. She tucked her handkerchief away and stood upright, still in the circle of his arm, put her hands on his shoulders, and looked up calmly into the beloved face gazing down concernedly at her own.

'Thank you, dear.'

'Sure? Do you feel better now?'

'Quite better. It wasn't anything much. Look, shall we take these in? They're ready.'

14

Like a murderer who cannot keep away from the spot where he did it, Old Porty always drove past Number 5 Highbury Walk whenever he happened to be in the neighbourhood, tooting on his horn and looking up at the windows of the bakery to see if Amy or Mona happened to be looking out of the window. Mrs Beeding always reported these transits of the comet to the girls, as a soothing reminder to Amy that even after four years have passed there is no peace for a guilty conscience, and as a warning to Mona that he was on the prowl and might ask her to go out with him (not that Mona took it as a warning, for she would have gone out with Nero had he been alive and willing).

Amy always fearfully hoped that she would never have to talk to Old Porty again. He was so mixed up with memories of her father's death that the very thought of him frightened her, and whenever Mrs Beeding announced that he had been tooting and peering past, she hurried home along the Walk looking down at the pavement and praying that she would not be hailed by his rich port-type voice.

One warm evening towards the end of the summer when she was nearly nineteen, the worst happened. Porty had been in transit only yesterday, and she was hurrying home as fast as she could without looking up, thinking that the coolest place this evening would be the pictures and that she might slip off there after supper, when a loud tooting and bawling broke out just at her elbow and she became aware that a car had drawn in to the pavement and was moving along at her side.

Horrified, she looked up, and there was Porty.

'Hullo, Amy!' roared Porty; then, observing her alarmed expression, he softened the port-type tones to a kind of damson-wine effect and put his head on one side as though he were addressing a six weeks' old puppy, 'How are you getting along after all this long time, eh? Still in the same office? Haven't grown much, have you? Going to be a pocket-Venus, eh? How's Ma—how's Mrs Beeding and Mona and Dora? All right, are they? Haven't seen any of you fer ages.'

She reluctantly moved over to the car and stood beside it, staring at him with the polite expression that gave nothing away and that used to annoy him when she was a child. He had aged a good deal in the last few years and the purplish hands linked on the steering wheel were veined like an old man's.

'We're all quite all right, thank you, Mr Porteous,' she said politely.

'Oh, come off it, Amy! Yer very stiff all of a sudden, aren't yer? "Mister Porteous"! It always used to be Porty in the old days.'

Liar, thought Amy, staring at the toes of her shoes and saying nothing.

'I haven't seen you for months, little girl,' went on Porty, lowering his voice confidentially and bending towards her, 'not to talk to alone, I mean. Are you in a hurry? How about a cuppa tea? I can run you round to the A.B.C. in a minute. Come on, be matey.'

Amy hesitated, looking doubtfully at him.

Among the simple statements with which Mrs Beeding enlightened her foster-daughter she had included a truly vehement tocsin about Old Porty. 'As soon as look at you, and Dora says the same,' had concluded Mrs Beeding. Amy had put most of this out of her mind, partly because she had not found it interesting and partly because she had a vague impression, acquired from Mona, that It's Disgustin', and one did not think about Disgustin' subjects. But now, as she stood looking at Old Porty, Mrs Beeding's tocsin sounded faintly in her mind.

Yet there seemed, somehow, to be the widest and most fantastic gap possible between Mrs Beeding's warnings and the actual, purple Old Porty, sitting there. Why, he used to talk to Mother! thought Amy. He's a person who knew darling, darling Mother. It was—no, it was not possible to foresee such goings-on as Mrs Beeding had prophesied. Her imagination yawned, and turned peaceably away from the fence. And as it happened, it was quite right.

And then suddenly she found she was no longer afraid of Old Porty, and imagined herself saying, 'Thank you. I should like to.' Her eyes seemed to grow larger and brighter.

'Come on!' he coaxed, encouraged by her expression, hospitably opening the car's door.

'Thank you. I should like to,' said Amy, and got in beside him.

'That's the style!' he exclaimed gaily, turning on the port-type voice again and sending the car rattling down the Walk towards the High Street. It was a horrid little car, smelling of hot petrol and stale tobacco and Porty's beery breath, and the back seats were piled with boxes containing samples of the ladies' underwear in which Porty travelled. There were pink silk knicks with a blue lovebird on either leg, and pale green nighties with the bosom made of beige lace. The collective noun for these garments was Undies (a word which ought, were proper control exercised in such matters, to be publicly banned by the B.B.C., the Bishops and the senior Universities and the use of it forbidden on pain of the instant liquidation of the user). But Amy had thought them very pretty when Porty used to bring them up to show them to her mother and try to sell them to her, and now bought similar ones whenever her small stock needed replenishing at Jones Bros. in Holloway or (supporting home industry, so to speak) at Fletcher and Sons where Mona was still employed. I'm really growing up, she thought, pleased, as the car turned into the High Street. That's (meaning Old Porty) one more thing I'm not afraid of.

They stopped outside the A.B.C., and Amy waited while Porty parked the car just round the corner. Then he put a moist warm hand under her bare elbow and they went into the teashop, which smelled pleasantly of hot tea and toast.

'There's an empty one!' cried Porty excitedly, and they steered their way to it and sat down opposite one another.

'There we are. All nice and cosy, eh, Amy?' He stretched out his legs under the table, kicked her ankle, and said, 'Oh, sorry, Amy! Did I hurt you?'

'Oh, no, thank you, Mr Porteous.'

'Call me Porty, do, Amy.'

'Porty,' she repeated obediently, staring round the A.B.C. and thinking it would be a good place to make two spies meet in a story, because everyone was so busy trying to signal a waitress or eating or talking that they were not noticing what anyone else was doing.

'Now, what'll you have, Amy? Have anything you like, little girl. This is my treat, yer know. Azza mattera fact,' he lowered his voice embarrassedly and bent forward, staring at her with his bright fierce little eyes in their deep caverns overhung by the long white hairs of his eyebrows, 'I've been wanting to give yer a little treat for a long time, Amy. Justa show there wasn't any ill-feeling between us. About yer Dad, I mean.'

'Oh.' She nodded, as embarrassed as he, and not knowing what to say.

'Yer know, Amy, there was never any question about me and yer Dad being tiddley or anything like that,' Porty went on, while his eyes wandered fiercely round the room in search of a waitress. 'We were both cold sober. Believe me, I haven't been on the road driving me own bother-and-fuss for twenty years without knowing anyone who tries to drive when he's had one over the eight's a b.f. The other poor devil wasn't tiddley either, nor the poor b—— (beg pardon) of a lorry driver either, he was jus' half-asleep in his seat, thass all . . . what I'm trying to say is, Amy, it was just cruel bad luck and no one's fault, see? Cruel bad luck.' He pressed his thin lips together and stared down at the glass top of the table. 'And so sudden! Cripes, there wasn't time to hold on tight fer the shock before he was inter 'im. Like *that*!' He drove his fist hard against his open palm, then glanced fretfully round the room and jerked his head at a waitress, who nodded but did not come. The place was full of people having a snack before going along to the first house at the pictures, and all the girls were busy.

'She'll be along in a minute. Not in a hurry, are yer, Amy?'

'Oh, no, Porty.' It was exceedingly queer to be sitting here in the big steamy teashop with the late afternoon sunlight pouring through the windows, and Old Porty the ogre, the lurking shadow of her childhood that had ruined so many jaunts to the pictures, sitting opposite her!

'Did yer get the insurance all right, girlie?'

'Oh yes, thank you. Mrs Beeding put it into the bank for me.'

'Ah, she's got her head screwed on the right way, but I'm glad she don't handle *my* Friday packet! About run through it by now I expect, haventcher?'

'Mrs Beeding says I've got about seventy pounds left. You see, I haven't had to spend much of it at a time, because I've had my salary from the office; they started me at a pound a week and then last year Lord Welwoodham (that's the Editor) gave me a five-bob rise and this year he gave me another five bob (a week, I mean). That's very good, isn't it.'

Porty nodded, and not superciliously; he too, thought it good, for he knew the post-war world of employment and the hideous struggle to find jobs and keep them, and the scandals of over-and-under paying.

'And he says I'm a sort of editorial assistant now, not an office girl any more. But of course,' she ended, looking a little sobered at the thought, 'Miss Grace and Mr Danesford (she's the secretary and he's the sub-editor)—*they* still call me the office girl. I don't think they liked me getting the rises, either.'

'Jealous,' nodded Old Porty. 'Don't tell me. *I* know.'

'So I have a good lot left for myself, you see, 'cos I only have to give Mrs Beeding twelve and six a week and I never draw out any money from the bank unless I want something in a hurry or like when we went to Bracing Bay this year.'

'Ah, Bracing Bay—that's the place! Best air in Europe, my doctor says; yer can smell it the minute yer put yer nose out of the train—MISS!!' roared Porty, half rising from his seat, and a waitress came over to their table.

'Now, Amy, whattlya have? Have something solid, the damage is on me.'

'Oh—fruit salad and cream, please.'

'That isn't much. Have something solid. How about fish cakes and tomater sauce? Salmon mayernaise? Egg on chips? Yer can have yer fruit salad and cream afterwards, yer know,' he added. 'I want yer to have everything yer want because of—you know. Now go on, Amy, choose.'

It ended in her having fish cakes with tomato sauce, and him having two eggs on a double portion of chips, with a roll and butter each and a pot of tea for two; and presently they were eating together as amicably as two old friends. Amy poured out the tea and dropped in Porty's three lumps for him, and then they were quiet for a little while, taking the edge off their hunger and gazing rather glassily but peacefully about them while they ate.

People are always writing sniffy bits about teashops. Of course, they don't mention names because they are afraid of libel actions, but they go on for pages about the damp steamy atmosphere and the flat feet of the waitresses and the tea drips on the tables and the miserable faces of the customers and the tasteless food, and any reader who doesn't skip that bit knows where they mean. In fact, teashops are perfect caverns of romance for people with eyes in their heads rather than bees in their bonnets; and heaven knows there are thousands of worse places where a person might sit in the late afternoon, adding more and more water to the ever-weakening tea in the pot and smoking while talking, and listening to an unexacting friend. But be warned, and never take an orchid to such places; orchids spoil the atmosphere by wishing they were in Assisi or at Gunter's and the tea-y smell upsets them and they notice smears and drips and can't find a thing on the menu to eat. Never again.

Amy and Old Porty had their faults, but neither of them was an orchid, so they enjoyed their high tea very much. Presently, as she was carefully dipping the last fragment of fish cake into the last tiny pool of tomato sauce, Amy said, looking intently at her plate:

'Mr Porteous, I want to ask your advice about something.'

'Ask away. I'll tell you anything you like—if only you'll call me Porty,' he replied, with a sudden gleam of interest deep down in the eye caverns. 'You just think of me as though I was yer Dad and say anything yer like to me. I'm a good many years older than you are, little girl, and I know this wicked old world; I know the words *and* the music, I read the book *and* seen the pictures, and anything there is to know about certain subjects you can bet your last brass farthing I know it,' and he bent towards her, trying to look sympathetic and wise.

'Well, said Amy, taking a sip of tea, 'suppose you knew somebody who wanted to get a letter from somebody and didn't want anyone at their home—the first somebody's home, I mean—to know about it. What would that person do? The one who wanted to receive the letter, I mean?'

'What would they do?' repeated Porty, looking a little dazed and also a little disappointed. 'How do you mean, do, little girlie? Say it again slowly.'

'Well . . . suppose you wrote to me.'

He nodded, frowning with the effort of concentration.

'And I didn't want Mrs Beeding to know.'

He nodded again.

'Well, where could you send the letter?'

Light, glorious as the alpine dawn, broke over Porty.

'Ah—ha! *Now* I rumble yer! One of yer boys wants to write to you, and yer don't want Mrs Beeding to find out! Is that it?'

She nodded, her big clear brown eyes looking steadily at him across the brim of the cup she was holding to her lips.

'Well, there I *can* help you, of course—but you're a naughty little girl, you know, a very naughty little girl! and I ought really to smack yer beatyem instead of tipping you the wink like this—but I'm not going to smack yer beatyem, I'm going to help yer, little girl, because yer Dad was my pal. And we're pals, too, aren't we, Amy? Say, "Porty, we're pals".'

'Porty, we're pals,' she repeated, looking demurely at him and thinking how ugly he was.

'That's right. Well now, about what yer asked me. Yer've come to just the right person, sermatterofact, because I get all my letters sent this way when I'm on the road, have done for years. Well, you find your nearest Branch Post Office. That means a proper office, not one in a shop, see? And tell them you're a visitor in London or haven't got a permanent address, and so you want to have your letters sent there for a bit, see? You'll have to show them a letter addressed to you, or your Post Office Savings Book to show them you're who you make out to be. Then you just tell your boy to write to you care o' that Post Office, and they'll mind it for you till you call for it. It'll be safe as the ruddy Bank of England.' Porty drained his tea and slapped down the cup. 'And nobody'll be a penny the wiser. There! How's that, umpire?'

'Thank you very much, Porty. I'll tell him.'

'Who is it, Amy? Tell Old Porty all about it,' leaning across the table again and gazing at her with his head on one side. 'Do yer love him very much?'

Her instinct was to reply in Dora-ese, 'Oh, he'll pass in a crowd with a shove,' but she saw that this would not do at all and substituted for it a single nod, with her long eyelashes modestly lowered.

Porty sighed. 'And what's his name, lucky young beggar? Ah, Amy, I wish I had a lovely young girl to care about me.'

'Michael. Michael Danesford,' she answered. 'He's Mr Danesford's son. The one in the office, you know, the sub-editor. You see, he can't write to me at the office because his father's there all day. It's very awkward. It all started about a month ago,' Amy went on, leaning forward in her chair with her eyes, very bright, fixed upon the sympathetic face of Porty. 'He came in one day to see his father, and Mr Danesford happened to have gone out on business for Lord Welwoodham and I was there alone.'

'Were you and all!' exclaimed Porty, still sympathetic but unable to resist the temptation. 'What a chance! Well, did he kiss you on the spot?'

'Oh, no. Not then. You see, his father came back and we had to stop talking to each other and pretend nothing had happened, but he told me he had fallen in love with me and said he wanted to see me again, but he was going to Italy for the rest of his holiday and then of course he would have to go back to college——'

'Oh. Still at college, is he? Well, I've never had a college education meself and can't say I've ever felt the want of it, but I daresay it's very nice if you've got the money. And what's he like? Handsome?'

'Oh, yes! Tall and fair, with grey eyes and lovely broad shoulders,' she answered at once. This was her idea of manly beauty and always had been, like a picture in her mind.

Something in this remark appeared to amuse Old Porty very

much, for he laughed a good deal to himself, shaking his own shoulders and also his bald head and glancing furtively round the room as though wishing he could see someone with whom to share the joke.

'And what's he want to do about it? Marry yer?' he demanded at last.

Amy nodded. 'Some day,' she said demurely.

'Well, it all sounds very romantic but you take my advice, girlie, and watch your step,' said Porty, suddenly cross, looking disagreeably at the slender girl sitting opposite him in her white cotton frock patterned with red flowers.

She had taken off her hat, and the coils of fine dark hair at either side of her head made her look a little different from all the other girls in the teashop with their curls, but she was not pretty. Her forehead was too high to suit that style of hairdressing and her face lacked warmth and expression. It was like a thin delicate mask modelled while the original was asleep; and it seemed to have lost its childish look without gaining the indescribable bloom, the bud-like colour and dew, that comes with normal youth. She was not weazened, for her skin was clear and fine as ivory, but she might well have been a woman of thirty who had lived a quiet, sad life. Everyone in her small circle, except the Beeding girls, said she was such a nice, quiet, reliable girl, so sensible for her age, none of this disgusting paint and powder and waved hair business, just the sort of good old-fashioned girl that men, alas, never look at because, the beasts, they prefer *something else*. But Mona and Dora always swore that old Aime was a dark horse. Why they did so, whether their conviction was based upon some action of Amy's that did not quite square with the general idea of her character or whether they simply felt it, with the simple power of judging its contemporaries which youth possesses, they never said. But whenever some old trout trotted out the stock remarks about Aime, Mona and Dora said meaningly,

'Don't you be too sure, Auntie—or Granny—or Mrs Todbottle—Aime's a bit of a dark horse.'

'Oh, I will,' the dark horse now assured Porty earnestly. 'I'll be ever so careful. And thank you very much for your advice and for my tea, I have enjoyed it so much—Porty.'

'That's all right. Glad to have been of any use,' said Porty, still crossly but obviously a little soothed. 'Didn't mean ter say anything against yer boy, but it never does a girl any harm to be on the look-out, yer know.'

Amy nodded.

'And I know yer Dad wouldn't like yer to get up to anything like that because he was a gentleman, poor old Tiger, good luck to him wherever he is, and if he's looking down on us now he'll know I'm on'y saying what I did say to yer for the best, Amy.'

'Yes, Porty,' she said, looking at him solemnly.

'Well. There we are then,' concluded Porty, looking round fretfully once more for a waitress. 'I wish I could do a bit more for yer, Amy. If I had a place where yer could meet yer boy, I'd let yer have the run of it, and no questions asked. I know I can trust two clean, decent kids not to get up to anything their mothers wouldn't like,' giving her a severe look. 'But I haven't, so I can't.'

'Where do you live, Porty?'

'Murray's Hotel, King's Cross,' said Porty, fumbling in his pocket. 'Been there for ten years now. It's not at all a bad little place, really, and they don't do you as badly as some. Oh, I'm part of the fittings there now; got me own table, and my waiter's always got a word for me when I get back after a trip. I like that, yer know. Makes it more like home. There's a tip fer you, girlie, if ever you're landed in a strange town, you make for the hotel nearest the station. It's pretty sure to be good because all the commercials drop in there straight off the train and they won't put up with—MISS!!'

A waitress came unhurriedly across and made out their bill, which Porty magnificently paid.

'Now where can I drop you, Amy?' he inquired when they were once more standing by the car.

'Oh, I'll be all right, it's no distance home,' she said. She added hastily, on observing a black cloud rush across his jovial front (these princes of good fellows were certainly tricky to deal with; you never knew when they would fly into a tigerish fury over absolutely nothing at all). 'And besides, I'm rather afraid of Mona seeing us and being, well, a bit jealous.'

'Would she, the little devil! I must smack her beatyem some time for that!' cried Porty, enchanted, his good temper quite restored. 'Oh well, if you're sure you'll be all right. Good-bye, Amy, and many thanks for the pleasure of your company, my dear.' He took her hand and squeezed it. 'We must meet again soon, eh?'

'Yes, please, Porty. I'd like to.'

'That's the ticket. And don't forget what I said. *Ro*-mance is all very well, but you keep your eyes skinned! Cheery-bye!'

And Porty drove away, waving without looking round, into the traffic of the High Street.

Amy walked quickly away, wiping her hand hard against her dress. She was not afraid of him any more, but he was very stupid and horrid and she hated his jokes and the way he flew into rages and had to be soothed down and managed, exactly like the Beeding baby at home, except that Baby was pretty and funny and Porty was neither. Oh, well, she had got the information she wanted and that was all that mattered. She walked quickly homewards, not noticing, as she usually did, the pavements, patterned with the dust of a rainless August, the burnt brown leaves lying in the gutters, the exhausted pale faces of bus and tram conductors with their shirts open at the neck, the quivering filthy-smelling haze of hot petrol that hung above the jammed, shaking traffic. She walked quickly homewards with a dream. Mr Antrobus was responsible for the dream. If she had not gone to his house that morning, it would never have entered her head.

Exactly a week ago she had been sitting at her table in the outer office putting manuscripts into their envelopes ready to be returned, when Mr Danesford came out of the Editor's room where he had been speaking to Lord Welwoodham and said:

'Lord Welwoodham wants you to go to Mr Antrobus's house and fetch some copy. If you go at once you will be back in time for Miss Grace to go out at one.'

He seldom used her name in addressing her, and always gave his instructions in this dry clear style without details or explanations.

Pleased at the prospect of a break in the morning's routine, and also a little excited at the thought of seeing the famous Mr Antrobus's house, Amy put on her hat while bending over the address book (unaltered since 1909) to make quite sure of his house's number—73 Regent's Gate, Regent's Park. She went over and stood by Mr Danesford's desk to receive final instructions.

Miss Grace had neither looked up from her work nor commented upon Mr Danesford's announcement, for she made a point of never intruding upon his side of the work unless it was strictly necessary, a piece of almost inhuman self-control which may have prevented the development of backslappery in the Outer Office but which also undoubtedly helped to preserve its peace.

Miss Grace was employed at this moment in typing some letters which Lord Welwoodham had just dictated. She looked no older than when Amy had first seen her nearly three years ago, for she was covering that great stretch of life when a person's looks do not alter, unless blasted by illness or sorrow, between maturity and the beginning of old age. But she was more tastefully dressed than ever in a coat and skirt of pink linen, a white ruffled blouse embroidered with gay bunches of flowers, a necklace of small foreign seeds decorated with coloured spots and strung on a gilt chain, and a large brooch of glittering mixed jewels, and pearl earrings. Most of her salary was spent on her clothes, for her circumstances as the only daughter of a successful retired game and poultry merchant were comfortable. Her father and mother, two plump old people who pottered cheerfully about the garden of a large Victorian house in Hendon, often wondered to each other how they could have produced such a piece of efficiency, decorum and elegance as their daughter. She made them feel sub-human. Nevertheless, Mrs Grace most frequently referred to her daughter in her absence as 'Poor Lena,' while old Mr Grace had a habit of pausing on his way through the hall to the garden with a pot in one hand and a dibber in the other, and contemplating his child as she stood drawing on her gloves ready to depart for the office in some glorious new outfit, and observing in a low tone with a shake of his head:

'It's no use, my girl. *You'll never get one.*'

This prophecy annoyed Miss Grace very much, for as it happened she was not trying to Get One. She dressed to please herself and to feel nice, and that is why most women do dress, despite the winsome old theory that they dress to attract men and to annoy other women.

'"Here is sixpence for your fare," said Mr Danesford to Amy. "Mr Antrobus's copy has been lost in the post and he has had to rewrite it and his secretary is ill. You will be back by one." He turned to the galley-proofs of "How to Make a Model Seaplane," on his desk.

The large white houses round Regent's Park looked shut up and listless in the brassy sunlight of late summer, and massive trees like banks of dark cloud hung on the horizon across the withered lawns of the Park. Men lay there in shirtsleeves with newspapers over their faces and the London County Council school children were camped with prams and babies and bottles of lemonade under the dusty trees. A strange heavy sound rolled out in the distance where the Mappin terraces showed grey against the sky; the lions in the Zoo felt end-of-seasonish and bored.

But once Amy had pushed open the green door in the high wall surrounding Number 73, and carefully shut it behind her, the sad, end-of-summer feeling fled completely. Here was a green square of lawn freshened by a circular spray that made a cool hissing noise, and the beds surrounding it on three sides were crammed, their very earth was utterly hidden, by the gorgeous staring faces of every imaginable kind of dahlia in every produce-able shade of red, yellow, purple, crimson, magenta pink, and white. The old brick wall behind them was bare and perfectly displayed their glory. Amy stopped dead and stared, and slowly a smile of pure pleasure crept over her face. She did not notice beautiful things much as a rule, her fancy being too alert for the exciting, the dramatic, the strange, but this was as if someone had burst into a bugle call right in her face, and she just had to stop and listen.

The house was tall, and newly painted dazzling white. The curtains were of frilled white net and the copper door-knocker was made like the torso of a merman, and matched the copper bands on the black tubs on either side the green front door. These tubs were covered with the curled green-white heads of the monster Chinese chrysanthemums which are sold in the flower shops of Wigmore Street for half-a-crown apiece. The doorstep was washed with pale green hearthstone and at one side of the door glittered a long band of mirror coolly reflecting the green door and part of the blossoms in the tub. Amy slowly advanced, her whole person experiencing a completely unfamiliar feeling as though it were expanding like a flower-stem in water or cold hands held to the warmth of a fire. For the first time in her life she was surrounded by beauty and order, produced to perfection by wealth and by the exercise of an unconventional but completely self-confident taste. The taste just happened to match her own, which was stirring in its youthful sleep, and she was dazzled, moved and satisfied all in one delightful moment.

A fat little man in a blue and white striped jacket opened the door and asked her crossly in a foreign voice what she wanted.

'Mr Antrobus is expecting me; I'm from *The Prize*,' she answered, composedly. Her errand was a perfectly proper one, and she was determined to get inside the house, for over the man's shoulder she could see that it looked just as exciting as the outside.

He nodded, and was standing aside to let her come into the hall when a shout, uttered in what can only be described as a kind of powerful squeak, came from upstairs:

'Come up, will you? I'm not quite ready.'

The man nodded and smiled at her and went away quickly down the hall towards a faint and delicious smell of cooking, and Amy went on alone.

The stairs were carpeted with what looked like velvet, the red of plum juice, and all up one side were the most exciting pictures imaginable, which she longed to stop and stare at. There was 'Derby Day' (she knew that because of a visit she had once made to the Tate Gallery) and one of a boat with a white figure in it going across water to a tall island crowned with dark trees, and one of a bulky, horned monster brooding over the roofs of a town, and another of a city in flames with a strange frozen sea in the distance—oh! she tried to take them all in at once as she hurried up the stairs to the landing, across which a door stood half open.

She went over to it, and knocked.

'Come in and sit down, will you,' absently said the same voice. 'There's the *New Yorker* on the sofa and a box of peppermint creams. Shan't be long.'

She went obediently to the sofa, which was covered in shiny

pink stuff with shells on it, and opened the *New Yorker* and put a sweet into her mouth, but of course she did not look at the paper, she only held it up and pretended to look at it while she stared round the room. It had not much furniture except the sofa she was sitting on and a large desk between the french windows. Here Mr Antrobus was sitting with his back to her. The room was tidy except for papers bursting out of the desk and scattered on the red carpet; all along the top of the desk were photographs of young people and children in modernist frames. The pale green walls were adorned by only one picture, in which a naked lady floated on the sea in a shell while two others waited to wrap her in a cloak. Amy admired this very much, and studied it for some time. But indeed, she admired all of this red, pink and pale green room, and felt that she would like to write her stories in just such a retreat with its pleasant view over the park.

'Do you smoke? There are cigarettes in that green box on the mantelpiece,' suddenly said the writer, still without turning round, his hand moving steadily over the paper.

'No, thank you, I don't,' she answered, just stopping herself in time from saying, 'They make a nasty taste in my mouth,' by remembering how she herself hated being interrupted when she was writing.

After this he wrote steadily for a little while and she intently studied his broad back, covered by a blue suit rather like Lord Welwoodham's, and his hair, which was a brighter brown than most men's because it had no oil on it, but very thin and fluffy. Fancy him going on writing Barty for all those years, she thought. He must seem like an absolutely real person to him by this time. But she did not think *fancy him going on having ideas for the Barty stories all those years*, because she herself had so many ideas that it never occurred to her other people might run short of them.

'Ah!' suddenly exclaimed Mr Antrobus, so loudly that he made her jump. 'There!' And he put a bit of green blotting paper over the sheet and she watched his short white hands thump and smooth it firmly. '*There* we are. Sorry to have kept you waiting.' And he turned round in his chair and smiled at her, fixing her steadily with the brightest and clearest blue-grey eyes she had ever seen, set off by a forehead high and white as her own, above which the brown hair stood up in a silly little fluffle. Between this undignified hair and small weak mouth set in a too-heavy chin there was the superb beak of a Roman nose matching the splendid brow and slow-moving, bright, observant eyes. But the face on the whole was a face whose features contradicted one another, and though Amy could not put the point clearly in her own mind, she dimly felt that Mr Antrobus's character did not hold all his features together and unify them. He's a muddly sort of a man, she thought, politely returning his steady look.

'You put it in the envelope. Here you are.' He gave her the manuscript and watched her while she deftly put it away. 'Tell Lord Welwoodham how sorry I am there's been this bother.' While he was saying this in his rather pettish, high voice he was taking in every detail of her face and dress, sitting sideways with one white hand hanging over the edge of the table. As she carefully licked the envelope, he said abruptly:

'Do *you* read Barty?'

'Oh yes!' She looked up and smiled. 'Every month.'

'And do you enjoy it?'

'Oh yes, *very* much.' But as she spoke she remembered feeling that Barty wasn't exciting enough for her.

'What other books—stories—do you read?'

Amy hesitated. Instinct warned her that here was a mind-poker; and she did not at all like having her mind poked into. She said enthusiastically:

'*Thrilling Tales of Space* I read, quite often, and all the *Tarzan* books.'

'Not love stories? No, you're not old enough to enjoy, those yet, are you? What are you, sixteen? Have a peppermint—oh, they're on the couch. Do have one,' and he gave her such a wonderfully friendly, warm, affectionate smile, as though there were a secret between them, that she suddenly felt happy, and thought: He *is* nice! Nevertheless, she still had a faint feeling warning her not to tell him the truth about anything—except her age, there was no harm in that.

'Thank you very much. I'm nineteen in October.' She put a sweet in her mouth.

'Are you! You look about sixteen. Well, you're quite old enough to like love stories, then. Do you read *Peg's Paper?*'

'Not very often. The girls are all such sops.'

M͞r Antrobus laughed. 'Have you any brothers?'

'No,' she answered.

'And no boy of your own that you're—walking out—with?'

'I haven't got a boy friend,' she retorted rather tartly, recalling sundry boring yet embarrassing comments from the Beedings on this subject.

'No boy friend. I see.' Mr Antrobus looked pleased, as though someone had given him a present, as indeed, someone had. For the next time he sketched a typist in a novel she would say she had a boy friend, not that she walked out with someone. For Mr Antrobus, who was over seventy, had reached that stage in his career as a writer when he was too busy, too popular, too dignified, too well-known and too lazy to go and sit behind *The Evening News* in Lyons Corner House and listen to typists for himself. As a young man he had been as passionately and burningly devoted to his art as any young man to a mistress. Now they were still together, but they had had forty children and were used to one another's ways; that was all, but it was not the same thing as it had been forty years ago.

A faint sadness came over the writer's mind as he dimly realized the change, and to banish it he glanced round the rich, peaceful colours of the room, then said abruptly:

'Do you like this room?'

'Oh *yes*! It's lovely!' she answered earnestly, pleased to be able to speak truthfully at last to Mr Antrobus, who was so nice. 'And the garden's lovely, too, and that little sea-man on the front door and all those pictures up the stairs! I've never *seen* anything so lovely, except the inside of St Paul's.'

Mr Antrobus let out a joyous crow, and slapped his knee. The perfect story for his speech this evening at the Anglo-American Literary Society's Annual Dinner! It would be crowded with all his literary friends, who said, 'George is a darling, and has heaps of taste and it's all bad. That house of his——!'

'I didn't think there *could* be a house like this, Mr Antrobus,' she went on, her face pink, her eyes shining. 'Only in a book, I mean——' then stopped, alarmed lest the mind-poker should notice that her speech implied that she read other works than *Tarzan* and *Thrilling Tales of Space*.

But she need not have worried. Mr Antrobus had caught fire from her enthusiasm, the shade of sadness had passed, he was himself again, and proud with good reason of the career that he and his mistress-gift had made between them.

'Yes, you know,' he said excitedly, leaning towards her with his little, deeply-lined white hands hanging between his knees, '*I love* this house, it's got all the things in it I've loved best ever since I was a boy, and longed for, even the red carpet on the stairs—did you notice it?' (She nodded eagerly.) 'And "Derby Day" . . . I was very poor when I was young, you know, young No-Boy-and-No-Brothers. My father was an assistant in a big shoe shop in Colchester and my brothers and I went to a National School and my mother washed and mended and slaved for us like a navvy's wife—only it was worse for us, because we dam' well had to keep up some sort of an appearance. (My father wore a collar and tie at work, you see.) My head was always full of stories and people, people, people, all struggling and bursting to get out. It was like having a circus inside me; I couldn't get the people out fast enough, the clowns joking, and the exquisite fairy on her black horse, and the great-eyed Punchinello watching her, shaken with coughing, and the ring-master in his trousers that were too tight, and the captive lions snarling——' He broke off, and was silent for a moment, staring down at the carpet; then held up the middle finger of his right hand.

'Do you see that?'

She came closer, bending forward curiously, and saw that the finger carried a little round raised corn of yellow-white skin, on the top joint at the left, just below the fingernail.

'That's the mark of my trade. That's where the pen presses,' said George Antrobus. And Amy pulled her glove a little tighter over her own right middle finger, which carried a smaller but identical mark.

'It's the most delightful trade in the world, you know, young No-Boy-and-No-Brothers,' he went on. 'If you're my kind of writer. It's pain and grief to some of us, of course, but not to me. Never to me. I don't know what it means to have to hunt for ideas. Even now, after forty years of steady work, they come faster than I can get them down. That's pretty wonderful, isn't it? It's a gift, of course; just a gift like gorgeous red hair or a singing voice; you can only use it properly or abuse it. If you use it properly you've every right to be proud of what you've done with it, but not of the gift itself. Go down on your knees fasting and thank Whatever you believe in for the gift itself.'

He was silent for a moment, staring at the floor, while Amy watched him, enthralled. He was saying things that she seemed to have known ever since she could remember, but could not put into words. And he was like her about his writing, too! He had so many ideas that he did not know which one to do first! He loved doing it! He wrote with a pen, not with a typewriter! Oh, he *was* nice, Mr Antrobus! She was so glad that Mr Danesford had sent her; there would be all kinds of lovely things to think over when she was in bed that night.

'And when I was a spotty yob in a greasy suit I used to plan this house, furnished with all the pictures and colours I loved—bright rich colours that I never saw in the hideous little houses of our friends in Colchester because they show the dirt and it costs money to keep them clean. (I *hate* mud colour,' said Mr Antrobus violently, 'there isn't one shred of mud colour in this house from attic to cellar). Then, I sold my first short story to *Anderson's Weekly*, and they paid me ten guineas for it, and I knew, when I opened that envelope and that cheque fell out on to the brown serge tablecloth in our front parlour, that everything was going to be all right and I'd never have to worry about money again.'

'Ten *guineas*!' exclaimed Amy. 'For one story, Mr Antrobus?' (The amounts paid to *The Prize* contributors were very properly kept a secret from the editorial-assistant, and in any case they were not often so much as ten guineas.)

'Yes. For one story,' he nodded smiling. 'Does that seem a lot to you?'

'Yes,' she answered dreamily, but she was really thinking that it must have been even nicer than the money to see his name for the first time in print—'by George Antrobus.'

'What was it called, Mr Antrobus?'

'*A Butterfly's Revenge*. It was about a silly little wife who poisoned her husband.'

She nodded politely. Wives . . . husbands . . . that did not sound exciting. But perhaps his other books were better.

'My gift's been wonderfully faithful to me,' he went on, looking at the trade-mark on his finger. 'I only hope I've been as faithful in my turn. I just tell stories, you know, that's all,' he added, suddenly looking up at her with an expression, sly, humble and innocent all at once. 'Just stories. Oh, I'm no stylist; don't pretend to be. No time for it. The people all want to come out—open the door! No time to polish the key and oil the lock.'

'What's a stylist?' inquired Amy.

'It's a man who lets the matter get in the way of the manner

. . . (damn, I meant the other way round; that comes of trying to be epigrammatic). No . . . a stylist is a man who cares more about *how* he says a thing than about *what* he says. Is that clear to you, No-Boys?'

She nodded. Which am I? she was thinking.

'It's stories, you know, that everybody wants,' confided Mr Antrobus, bending a little towards her and lowering his voice as though imparting a secret. 'Just stories. Bless their hearts, if you can tell stories they'll come round you like the pigeons in Trafalgar Square, and pay your bills for you, and write you letters correcting your grammar and spelling, and educate your children for you, *and* keep your memory green (with luck) when you've been dead twenty years. Bless their hearts. So if you can tell stories, No-Boys,' concluded Mr Antrobus, turning again to his desk, 'your fortune's made. Now you have one more peppermint cream, and here,' he felt in his pocket, 'is five shillings for a taxi because I've kept you talking to me and it's a quarter to one. Good-bye.'

She took the money and the sweet, said prettily, 'Good-bye, thank you very much, Mr Antrobus' (which he received with a wave of his unoccupied hand but did not turn round) and hurried away. On the landing she stood aside to let a slender lady of about sixty, elegantly dressed in a frock of blue and grey silk stripes which matched her white hair glinting with a blue rinse, come slowly up the stairs. The lady, whose face wore an amused, patient expression, glanced at her and said kindly:

'Did you get the copy, my dear? And did my husband give you your taxi-fare?' And as Amy nodded, murmuring, 'Yes, thank you,' she smiled and went slowly up the next flight.

Amy enjoyed hailing the taxi and riding in grandeur through the wide squares and crescents and the narrow canyon of Fleet Street back to *The Prize*, but she would have enjoyed it far more if her head had not been so full of what Mr Antrobus had said about writing. If you can tell stories . . . it's stories, you know, that everybody wants . . .

She paid the driver off and ran lightly upstairs and tapped on the private door of Lord Welwoodham's office, for she had been told to take the copy straight to him.

When he had opened it and glanced over it in a satisfied way he said casually:

'Well, how did you get on with Mr Antrobus?'

'Oh, he was *very* nice,' she said, smiling. 'He gave me some peppermint creams and paid for me to have a taxi back because——'

'"If you can tell stories, your fortune's made," eh?' quoted Lord Welwoodham absently, still skimming through the Barty story. 'And did you hear about the circus going on inside his head, and about the cheque fluttering on to the brown serge tablecloth in our front parlour, and about thanking Whatever you worship for the gift itself? Yes, I can see by your face,' glancing up at her despondently, 'that you did. So, to his downfall did Gossey. It was Mr Antrobus who started Gossey on his career; and he would have started a good many more people if they had been asses enough to take him seriously. Now don't *you* be led astray, as Gossey was, and try to make your fortune out of *The Prize*, will you, Miss Lee?'

'Oh no, I won't,' she said, rather faintly, and got out of the room as quickly as she could.

Mr Danesford had already departed to the old-fashioned Italian restaurant where he had lunched every day for the last forty years; and Miss Grace was putting the final irresistible tilt to a pale blue hat with daisy buds adorning its crown when Amy entered the outer office. One glance at her face, which still faintly reflected her inward excitement, and Miss Grace observed (the elders on *The Prize* never lost an opportunity, even after four years without one sign of literary ambition on her part, of warning their office-girl against having any):

'I suppose Mr Antrobus talked a lot to you about his writing, Amy? He used to talk to Gossey, too, whenever the poor lad went up there to fetch copy. He only talks like that to people when he knows they can't write, you know. So I hope you won't go getting ideas into your head. Because it would only be a waste of time. You know the rule here.'

'Yes, Miss Grace.'

Miss Grace went out.

When she had gone, Amy lavishly licked her forefinger, tiptoed over to Miss Grace's chair, and touched the seat. This insulting ceremony, known to her as Putting Spit, somewhat relieved her feelings.

15

A few days later Lord Welwoodham was sitting in his office reading through the morning's batch of manuscripts, already weeded by Mr Danesford. He was trying to concentrate upon his task a mind still bemused with the colours, smells and sounds of the New Forest, where his family place was, and where he had passed the week-end. He could still see, more clearly than the manuscripts on his desk, the solemn blue-green of the pines and their rough rosy trunks, the thin emerald moss fostered by the damp wind on oak boles, the long hollow rides ending in a square of silver daylight down which his horse had cantered so surely, loving the fresh smell of woods in the early morning and eager to go fast. On the edge of the Forest near Bucklers Hard he owned a large Victorian-Gothic palace; difficult to run and expensive to keep up, to the satisfaction of his enemies (he was not a mild man and had more than a few) and the despair of his friends. But he and Lady Georgina were contented there. Lady Georgina, an elegant old lady whose religion was music, had never liked marriage but did like old Gus Welwoodham and as they both loved the place, they had made a go of their forty-five years together.

As well as being full of New Forest smells and colours, Lord Welwoodham's head was buzzing with a long list of autumn plants and winter plants and fertilizers to be ordered on behalf of Lady Welwoodham. He would *not* make a list ('Georgy, you know I never make a list') for he prided himself at seventy-two, upon his memory; but relaxed and sleepy with fresh air and exercise as he was, he found it difficult to concentrate upon the manuscripts before him and also remember what he must presently order from Whiteleys.

But he was soothed as well as relaxed, and disposed to deal mildly with the usual rubbish spread before him. Even *The Stratosphere Scouts!* did not make him more than mutter, 'Bosh, what bosh.' He skimmed *The Horror at Hurley Dene!* without comment, and likewise *The Prehistoric Circus!* which was about two jolly Neanderthal boys named Ug and Mug who tamed a diplodocus and charged their parents two flints a head to watch it do tricks. There was an article on how to keep racing pigeons which he put aside to discuss with Mr Danesford; and then the last of the batch—a story called, *The River Boy*, by A. Lowndes, neatly typed (but to do them justice all the contributions were that) in a green cover.

The simple title caught Lord Welwoodham's attention because it had no exclamation point. He opened the story in the middle, and read a few lines. He read a few more lines, then suddenly pushed all the other manuscripts on the desk aside, so that some of them fell on the floor, put *The River Boy* on the space thus cleared, leaned forward with his chin on one fist, and quickly—as though he were afraid the thing were going to vanish before his eyes—turned back to the beginning and began to read.

. . . Of course, it is impossible for the thousands of readers who love *The River Boy* to imagine the first time anyone ever read the first of the stories. There it lay on Lord Welwoodham's desk, the fresh-mined, yet unminted gold of what was to become a beloved minor classic—the commas and semicolons still in a molten state, as it were, the final sheen not yet on the surface, for here and there a sentence was pencilled through or a word neatly printed (not written) above a correction. Yet that first reader, the old man sitting absorbed at his desk in the offices of *The Prize* on that sunny autumn morning shared something with the latest scrubby little prep school boy who got *The River Boy* from an aunt last Christmas: delight.

But just as it is useless to try and convey in words the freshness of woods in the early morning, so it is useless to try and convey in words the spell exercised by a writer of genius; and therefore no attempt shall be made to tell those who have not read *The River Boy* what it is like, beyond saying that Lord Welwoodham had found, at long last, his writer who looked at the world with the simple yet mysterious vision of a boy.

He read it three times before he looked up from the page and gently, almost reverently, shut the folder. 'That's good,' he muttered, staring down at it. 'By George, that's a fine story. What a plot! with a beginning, a middle—and I'm damned if it hasn't got an end as well! I must . . . here, where's Danesford——'

He got up and went quickly across to the outer office.

'Danesford,' he called, standing at the open door with the manuscript in his hand. 'Can you come in a minute? I've got something quite extraordinarily good here I'd like you to look at.'

'Is that *The River Boy*?' inquired Mr Danesford in his deep baying voice, loping into the inner office while his editor held the door open for him. 'I only glanced at the beginning, but I thought you'd better see it; it looked promising, I thought, very promising.'

'It's a beauty,' said Lord Welwoodham; he added absently without looking at his editorial assistant, 'Miss Lee, will you be so good as to make my tea, please,' and shut the inner office door.

Miss Lee, with very pink cheeks and very cold hands which found difficulty in striking matches, put the kettle on.

'We are out of biscuits,' observed Miss Grace without looking up from her work. 'I reminded you yesterday. At lunch-time, you may remember,' continued Miss Grace in a voice laden with the doubly voluptuous pleasure of ticking somebody off and regretting lost opportunities. 'I said to you, if you remember, "Amy, don't whatever you do forget the biscuits".'

'I know, Miss Grace. I'm awfully sorry.' Amy spoke in a muffled voice because she was kneeling in front of the cupboard getting out the cups and saucers.

'You had better slip out now while the kettle is coming to the boil and get Sixpennyworth of Mixed,' pursued Miss Grace.

Amy said nothing but continued to clank about with the crockery. She was a long time over it, so long that only when Miss Grace remarked again:

'Hurry up, Amy, the kettle is nearly boiling,' did she jam on her hat, snatch sixpence out of the Petty Cash, and march out of the room with a furious face.

Didn't want to go. Lazy. Miss Grace, continuing unmovedly with her typing, knew quite well what had been going on. Do her good. Never does a girl any harm to break her will. Now *why* didn't she want to go, just at this minute? She's usually only too pleased to go out in office hours. Queer. More in this than meets the eye. Shall keep both mine open. Miss Grace continued to type.

When Amy got back breathless with the biscuits Mr Danesford had come out of Lord Welwoodham's room and was standing by Miss Grace's desk, outlining a letter.

'. . . we like his story and would like to use it and will pay him ten guineas for it.'

Miss Grace glanced up at Mr Danesford. Mr Danesford met the surprised glance of her flat grey eyes with his own sad brown ones and nodded portentously.

'Lord Welwoodham is very much impressed with this story,' confided Mr Danesford. 'He considers we have found an important new writer for boys—if he can keep it up, of course.' Miss Grace nodded tolerantly. In her experience they seldom could keep it up.

'. . . and if he has any more work, say a story between forty and fifty thousand words that we could use as a serial, we should be very pleased to consider it. Oh—and if he is in the City at all during this week Lord Welwoodham would be glad if he could make it convenient to call here to discuss the possibility of regular contributions for us. That,' concluded Mr Danesford, 'is all.'

'A. Lowndes, c/o. Hampstead High Street Post Office, N.W.3' read back Miss Grace. 'Postal address, eh? Rather unusual, isn't it?'

'Lord Welwoodham thinks he may be an unmarried naval or military man on leave, without a permanent address, or possibly someone whose work makes it necessary for him to travel about a good deal and therefore has no fixed abode,' said Mr Danesford, his gloomy voice giving a blasted heath, fleeing-from-justice colour to the picture.

'I suppose it *is* a "he"?' said Miss Grace idly—idly, that is, for Miss Grace. She never spoke *quite* idly, though often she dropped sharp remarks more by instinct than by reason.

Mr Danesford actually gave a short baying laugh, but otherwise he did not trouble to reply. As though Lord Welwoodham would accept a story for *The Prize* written by a female! The only female who had ever been thus honoured was Charlotte M. Yonge; even E. Nesbit had been considered too fanciful and feminine for *The Prize*.

Now just as Mr Danesford gave his laugh Miss Grace happened to dart a glance across at Amy, who was absorbed in pouring out Lord Welwoodham's tea. Miss Grace did not glance at Amy for any reason except the fact that she was always darting glances at the young and subordinate just to see that they were behaving themselves, but in this case her dart was rewarded, for Amy was not behaving herself; she was steadily pouring Lord Welwoodham's tea over the cup and into the saucer and on to the table, with a crimson face and eyes that actually glittered with excitement.

'Amy! The tea! What are you doing!' cried Miss Grace in a warning but low tone, for Lord Welwoodham must not hear female screams coming from the other office. 'Get the Cloth—the Cloth, quickly, and wipe it up!'

222

Amy got the Cloth, which had lived over the cloakroom basin almost as long as Mr Danesford had washed his hands there, and mopped up the tea and carried the cup into Lord Welwoodham, but not before Miss Grace, studying her shaking hands, flushed cheeks and feverishly shining eyes, had jumped to a wild, an amazing, yet not an utterly impossible suspicion, and had resolved to put her suspicion to the proof.

That evening she was going to play badminton with a friend who lived in Hampstead, and this friend's bedroom happened to command a view of no less a place than the Hampstead High Street Post Office. Miss Grace remembered this well, for many a time while powdering her long mauve nose at her friend's dressing-table she had absently observed out of the corner of her eye the postman making the six-thirty collection from the High Street box.

It will all fit in perfectly, thought Miss Grace. I can be there easily by a quarter to six if I leave early and I think I will; yes, I will certainly leave early, on purpose, and wait at the window (having Explained to Joan) until . . . anything should happen. I may be wrong. I hope (she didn't) that I am. But at least it can do no harm to Watch.

As soon as Miss Grace had admitted her wild suspicion to her mind, she began to behave as though it were true; for towards lunch-time when Amy was gathering the letters from the wire tray to take to the post, Miss Grace slid a dry chalky hand over her shoulder and abstracted two—one to Mr Antrobus with his monthly cheque and the other addressed to A. Lowndes, Esq., announcing:

'These are important, Amy: I myself will post these,' and took them out with her to lunch. She wanted to be sure of the Lowndes letter arriving at Hampstead by six o'clock.

Amy went out to lunch at one; and sat for an hour in St Paul's picking bits off a twopenny ham-roll and staring at the Whispering Gallery. Sometimes she smiled to herself, and sometimes she looked very frightened and sometimes she looked quite bewildered, as though she had not the least idea what she was going to do next. By two o'clock she was back in the office, industriously filing letters while Lord Welwoodham talked on the telephone with the door open to somebody named Squire whom Amy knew to be a friend of his; telling him what a first-rate story he had got hold of for the next number of *The Prize* and asking him if he, Squire, had ever heard of A. Lowndes? But apparently Squire had not. In the pause immediately before tea Miss Grace daintily picked up *The River Boy* from Mr Danesford's desk and skimmed its pages while Amy, busy with the tea kettle, covertly watched her. Presently Miss Grace put it down again, observing to Mr Danesford:

'Rather far-fetched, don't you think?'

'Lord Welwoodham does not think so,' bayed Mr Danesford reprovingly. 'I myself have not read it.'

Miss Grace sharply asked Amy was the kettle boiling yet?

Miss Grace's friend was very pleased to see Miss Grace, and at once conducted her to the bedroom, and while Miss Grace was taking off her dove-grey hat with two red roses on its brim she told her friend what she suspected, and asked if she might watch out of the bedroom window for half an hour or so? You can be getting on with supper, suggested Miss Grace. The friend, who was large and red and cheerful and worked in a Government office, said that of course she could and added admiringly, 'You little devil, Lena. Nobody can put anything over on you, can they?'

'What is it? What are you girls gossiping about in there?' called the friend's old mother from the next room. She was in bed with an Attack and had not had much fun lately. 'Nothing wrong at Lena's office, I hope?' she added eagerly.

'Couldn't Mother watch with you?' suggested the friend scripturally.

Miss Grace said of course, it would be company for her, so

the old mother hobbled in between the two of them and was put at the window in a chair wrapped round with a blanket and nearly wrecked the proceeding by having the Attack again with excitement.

'Been stealing something, has she, the wicked thing?' demanded the friend's mother. 'Ah, trust Lena to catch her out. I wonder she dared to do it with Lena in the office. Much, was it? Poor, is she? What does she want more money for, eh? Paint and powder and all this hair-dressing. *I* know. Eh?'

The friend said good-naturedly: 'No, Mother. It isn't stealing. Now just keep quiet, there's a dear, and Lena will tell you all about it afterwards, won't you, Lena?'

Miss Grace, looking steadily through the cream net curtains, said nothing but nodded.

For a while nothing exciting happened. People went into the post office and came out pressing stamps on letters and posted them. A lady bought a bunch of crimson dahlias from the flower man outside the furnishing-and-decorating shop on the corner. Miss Grace watched steadily, her fingers clutching the curtain.

Suddenly her clutch tightened and she gave a little gasp. Someone whom she knew was crossing the road from the tube-station, and they went into the post office.

'Is that her?—Show me?—Which is it? That one in the red and white? Why, she's quite young!' cried the friend's old mother, bending eagerly forward and peering through the curtains.

'Old enough to know better,' pronounced Miss Grace solemnly, letting the curtain fall as the figure, having been inside for some moments, reappeared at the post office door carrying a letter and insolently swinging its hat. 'Well—this evening you've seen a girl who will very shortly be in want of a job, Mrs Naseby.'

'Fancy, Lena! Do tell me all about it? What's she been up to?' And so Miss Grace told.

★

The next morning when Amy got to the office she found Miss Grace already there. This was unusual. When Miss Grace took absolutely no notice of her 'Good morning, Miss Grace,' but continued to rub Glymiel jelly into her hands in awful silence, Amy began to feel frightened. When Mr Danesford arrived, carrying the light macintosh which never left him throughout the summer and hung up his dark soft hat and put his umbrella in the stand and Miss Grace said levelly: 'Can I speak to you for a moment?' and they retired to the window and spoke earnestly together for several minutes without once glancing in her direction, she was more frightened still, and when, at last, at a quarter to ten and after nearly half an hour of agonizing suspense on Amy's part, Lord Welwoodham arrived swinging a new pair of hogskin gloves that were getting dirty nicely and Miss Grace said sepulchrally, 'Lord Welwoodham, may I speak to you for a moment, please?' and Lord Welwoodham said, 'Of course, Miss Grace. Come in, won't you?' and held the door open for her— then did the full force of terror fall upon Amy, and she sat at the table by the door shaking from head to foot.

Only once did she glance across at Mr Danesford, and it happened to be at the precise moment that he was bending upon her such an awesome gaze—so mournful, severe, disillusioned and at the same time suspicious—that she started as though he had hit her, and returned to her task of entering up the morning's manuscripts in a state of even greater terror than before.

Miss Grace was with Lord Welwoodham what seemed to Amy about eight hours, but in fact it was ten minutes. At the end of that time the door opened and Lord Welwoodham, looking agitated and cross, put his head round it. 'Danesford, can you spare a minute?' he demanded without a glance at Amy, and Mr Danesford hastened across to him. The door of the inner office shut. Amy was alone with St Paul's staring in through the window, the loudly ticking clock, and her conscience.

In spite of her terror she could not help feeling triumphant because Lord Welwoodham liked the story so much. She did not like him particularly as a person, but she was excited and pleased because he was—her first reader. He was the only person who had read a story of hers since her mother died, and although of course she, Amy, knew her stories were exciting and good, it was nice to have someone else think so too.

Oh, do buck up! she inwardly implored her three judges, glancing at the firmly-shut door. What on earth are they going to do to me?

Then she jumped nearly out of her skin. The door was opening. Out came Miss Grace, out came Mr Danesford, looking as glum and severe as though they had been to a funeral. Lord Welwoodham glanced across at her and held the door open, saying gravely:

'Come in a moment, will you please, Miss Lee?'

She got up and went over to him. The other two had seated themselves at their desks and were beginning on their morning's work, with never a glance at the accused, and she felt a sudden flare of hatred for the pair of them—soppy, miserable old pigs! But not a trace of it showed in her face as she quietly shut the door of the inner office after her, and turned to face the Editor. Her eyes had the old, still, polite expression, wary and secretive, that she had made them wear as a mask ever since she was a child.

'Sit down, won't you, Miss Lee,' he said, pointing to the chair opposite his own. She sat down on the edge of it, facing him with the light on her young, thin face and brilliant child's eyes, the unbecoming plaits of dark hair clamped against her delicate temples, her square rather ugly little hands clenched in the lap of the red and white dress, her small body very upright . . . and looked politely at Lord Welwoodham, waiting for him to speak. For almost the first time in her life she was in a serious situation and was not pretending to be a hero surrounded by enemies.

This was because the situation concerned her previous writing, her stories, the only things she cared about in the real world, and therefore the situation was, for once, completely real to her. The little door in her mind would not open, there was no escape. She sat there with thudding heart and dry mouth, staring politely, with eyes now a little glassy, at Lord Welwoodham.

'Miss Lee,' he began gravely, 'Miss Grace has made a serious accusation against you, and I want you to tell me if it's true. It appears that she—er—saw you go into Hampstead High Street Post Office yesterday evening and come out with a letter. She suggests that it was the letter written by myself earlier in the day to the writer signing himself A. Lowndes, who submitted a story called *The River Boy*, which we accepted. She suggests, in fact,' went on Lord Welwoodham, dropping his smart horn-rimmed oval glasses and fumbling irritably for them, 'that you—er—*wrote The River Boy*. Did you?'

Amy swallowed.

'That's right. I did,' she said faintly, her thin young voice almost inaudible.

Lord Welwoodham stared, and put on the horn rims again. He tried to look severe but it was no use; an expression of the liveliest interest, curiosity and something like wonder had come into his faded blue eyes, and no pretended severity could banish it, even when he said firmly:

'Then I consider that you have behaved very badly, Miss Lee, quite disgracefully, after the—the confidence and trust that this paper has always reposed in you, especially as you have always been—er—perfectly aware—er—you wrote it entirely yourself, did you, without help of any kind, no-one gave you the plot or anything of—anything of that sort?' he suddenly demanded, vigorously polishing the horn rims and staring at her.

'Oh, no!' she said, a little louder this time. 'Nobody helped me at all.' And she went on (for quite suddenly she had stopped feeling afraid, and knew that he was not angry with her, and that everything would be all right in the end, just as her mother used to say it would be if only she was a brave girl and asked God to help her). 'What a funny idea—anyone helping me write a story!'

'Have you written others, then?' Still polishing and staring.

'Oh, yes!' she said, and even smiled a little, cautiously, 'lots of them! Only no-one knows about it at home, you see, because——' She hesitated.

'They might not understand?'

'Yes. My old headmistress at school knew about them. She was awfully kind. She let me write in the old exam room. But she was the only one who knew.'

'Did she read any of your work?'

Amy shook her head.

'Why not? Didn't you think them good enough to show her?'

'Oh, no! It wasn't that. I just didn't want anyone to read them except me——' She stopped, and the still, guarded look came over her face.

'What made you send in *The River Boy* to *The Prize*, in that case, Miss Lee?'

'Oh, that was Mr Antrobus!' she explained quickly, smiling broadly now. 'When I went to his house the other day it was all so pretty, I'd never seen anything so pretty in all my life and then he talked to me, you know——'

'About the circus. Yes, I know,' he nodded.

'And how all the people were shut up inside his head and trying to come out, and I thought "That's just like me; only me head's full of stories, not people," and then he said everybody wanted stories and if you could tell stories your fortune was made. And that made me want to have people reading *my* stories, too——'

'You didn't only do it to get money, then?' he demanded.

'Oh, well, I did think it would be nice to have three guineas, of course, but what I really wanted,' her voice deepened, grew strangely warmer in tone, 'was to see my name on a story, you know. *By Amy Lee.* That was what I really wanted. And to think of people reading it—lovely! So that was why I had it typed round the corner at Hilditch's and fixed up to have it sent back to the Hampstead Post Office if *The Prize* didn't like it, because I knew it wouldn't have a chance, of course, if I sent it in with my own name on it——' her voice faltered, died away as she suddenly realized that she was relating a crime, not a success-story, and she stared at him in dismay.

Lord Welwoodham was silent for a moment. Then he said: 'Miss Lee, I like your story very much, and I want to use it in the next number. I am very annoyed with you, of course, for having sent it in under a false name—wait a moment.' He held up his hand, checking her eager attempt to speak. 'But I quite see that in the circumstances you could not do anything else. The whole situation is very unusual—er—most unusual and peculiar. Now, are you willing for us to use the story, Miss Lee, at a fee of ten guineas, as I suggested?'

'Oh, yes, please, Lord Welwoodham! Only isn't ten guineas rather a lot of money?'

(It must here be noted that this was the first, and the last, time that Amy ever suggested she was being overpaid.)

'The story is worth about four times that amount by modern rates of payment,' he answered rather curtly, 'but in fairness to the financial state of this paper I cannot offer you more. Er . . . about your name . . . you want your full name to appear, I presume. You would not prefer to use only your initial—"by A. Lee"?' There was a hint of hope in his voice, but Amy soon sat on that.

'Oh, yes, please,' she replied decidedly. 'By Amy Lee. In quite large type.'

'Very well.' Lord Welwoodham made a note. 'And now that we have settled that, Miss Lee, I have to break it to you that I must enforce the rule usual in these cases and insist upon your leaving. But,' he added hastily, as her lips parted in dismay (would she be out of work for ten months like Maurice Beeding?), 'there is no need for you to leave immediately. I propose to give you a year's notice. That will give you time to look for another post, will it not?'

'Oh, yes. Thank you very much,' she murmured, feeling grateful but also a little dazed.

'And now I should like to discuss with you the possibility of writing regularly for us. Something in the nature of a series, perhaps . . . or a serial. But perhaps,' glancing at her keenly, 'you have no more ideas?'

'Oh, yes I have!' confidently smiling at him. 'I've got a beauty, another one about *The River Boy*. I was going to start it tonight. Would you like to see it when it's done?'

'Very much indeed,' replied Lord Welwoodham, staring at his editorial assistant, if possible, even more intently than before. 'About how long, pray, do you think it will take you to finish it?'

'Oh, about a week. You see, I haven't got a place to be properly alone in at home, so I have to write whenever I get the chance—in my lunch-time and in the tube going home (if I get a seat, of course) and so it takes me rather a long time.'

'I see,' he said. 'And that was how *The River Boy* was written?'

But when she nodded, and added with an uncontrollable giggle that most of *The River Boy* had been written in St Paul's Cathedral, he shook his head a little as though he quite gave it up. And if she had been looking at him at that moment, instead of dreamily staring out of the window at the dark old house opposite, she would have seen his lips shape the word 'Wonderful!' But all he said, a little severely, was:

'Now, Miss Lee, we have been able to come to what I hope will be a satisfactory arrangement, at least for the next year. You will continue to work here at your present salary, and I will pay you ten guineas for every story of yours that we print in *The Prize*. Is that clear, and does the arrangement satisfy you?'

'Oh, yes. Thank you very much,' she said, smiling with happiness.

'You are quite sure? It is only fair to tell you that if you took this story elsewhere you would get much more money for it. I am telling you this because other people—agents and editors and so forth—will very soon be on your track, trying to get you to write for other papers, and I want to know exactly how *The Prize* stands with you. Would you agree, Miss Lee, to write only for *The Prize*, say, for the next year?'

Amy made a faint effort to weigh this proposal and to be very businesslike and wide-awake and smart, but it was no use. Her eye caught someone moving mysteriously behind the curtained window opposite, and off she went into a dreamy state that lasted nearly a minute, while Lord Welwoodham silently studied her, amused and interested by her lack of nervousness, her simplicity, her general oddity, which was now (since his attention had been drawn to her) so striking.

'Well, Miss Lee?' he inquired at last.

'Oh, yes.' Her gaze moved from the window, came to rest tranquilly on his face. 'Yes, I would agree. I won't write for anyone but *The Prize* for a year. Then if I get another job I can try somewhere else with my stories.'

'Exactly. Well, that is very satisfactory. I will draw up a simple contract that we can both sign, shall I?'

'Yes, please.' She knew what a contract was: Mr Danesford and Miss Grace sometimes discussed Mr Antrobus's contract with *The Prize*. It made her feel delightfully important and grown-up to think of having one.

He stood up, leaning both hands on his desk.

'That is all, I think, isn't it, Miss Lee? Is there anything else?'

'Only . . . Lord Welwoodham, I was wondering if I might write here? In my spare time, I mean?'

'Certainly. You want to fit in your writing whenever you have a slack hour in the office, is that it?'

She nodded.

'By all means. Can you—er—you don't find that the presence of other people disturbs you when you're writing, then?'

'Oh, no. I don't notice them, unless they start chinwag—talking, I mean.'

The reference to Other People reminded them both of the two in the next room, whence came the muffled tap of Miss Grace's typewriter, the distant baying of Mr Danesford pursuing some tardy Hobday Boy down the telephone; and they both seemed suddenly to return to the world of everyday. Amy's usual secretive look eclipsed the brightness of pleasure and excitement in her face and Lord Welwoodham coughed and aimlessly moved a glass paperweight along his desk.

'Well, I think that's all, Miss Lee.' He glanced at the clock. 'Nearly eleven! I suggest that we both get on with some work.'

'Yes. Thank you.'

They smiled at one another with a lingering reflection of the friendly excitement that had linked them a moment since, then, as quietly as she had done any morning during the past four years, Amy went out.

Left alone, Lord Welwoodham felt so pleased that he had to get up and go over to the window, out of which he stared unseeingly for a minute, humming a little tune to express his sense of energy and excitement. She was a discovery! There was no doubt at all about that. He had been reading boys' stories since the 'nineties, and the only other stories that had given him the same sensation of delighted surprise and expectation were the youthful stories of George Antrobus and Marjorie Bowen's *Viper of Milan*. Amy Lee's way of writing was remarkable for clearness, richness and a peculiar sensation of *speed*. *The River Boy* raced; he could not remember another story in which the words were so completely the perfect vehicle for the action. And she had the same startling originality of plot as Antrobus, the same shapeliness in form that left the reader first awakened, then

233

eagerly following, then completely satisfied by the climax. Above all there was the sense as of a strong personality laying a hand on the reader's shoulder and saying—*Listen . . . I will tell you a story . . .* possessed by a born story-teller.

If only the next one is as good! thought Lord Welwoodham, flapping irritably with the hogskin gloves at a blue-bottle that had blown in from Rosemary Lane—I hope she won't be long over it—it's delightful to think of the dear old *Prize* printing a first-rate writer again—we haven't done that since we did the first Barty story and Antrobus, of course, was fairly well established by then. But nobody's heard of her! She's only nineteen! She's completely unknown! This is the first thing she's ever had printed!

Really, if she can keep it up, we ought to have a very interesting and stimulating year. Ought to do the circulation a bit of good, too. I will eat my gloves if even the present generation doesn't like *The River Boy*. And it would film, too. Lots of possibilities ahead. Gottim! Lord Welwoodham felled the fly to the earth and sat down again in a mood of complete satisfaction.

There was an exceedingly sour and heated atmosphere in the outer office as though someone had been boiling the vinegar, but nothing was said to Amy about her crime, and by lunchtime she had realized with surprised relief that nothing was going to be said. Miss Grace was cool to her, Mr Danesford forbidding and aloof, but they were always that. Nothing was said during the afternoon, either, and by tea-time she knew with amazed and slightly malicious delight that Lord Welwoodham had taken her under his wing, had told those two about her stories and what he was going to do about sacking her, and warned them not to start nag-bagging at her. It was amazing, too good to be true, and yet it was true. All that afternoon while she deftly whisked manuscripts about, answered the telephone, made and handed the tea, she was revelling in the fact—the delightful, plain-as-daylight fact, that those two older people had been told her stories were good, and that they must leave her alone! There was triumph in the very curve of her wrist as she slid Miss Grace's cup on to her desk. She flitted about like an annoying fairy. Miss Grace banged the typewriter keys very hard, Mr Danesford spread terror and desolation among the Hobday Boys, and thus worked off their very justifiable indignation.

That evening just before six o'clock Lord Welwoodham and Mr Ramage were standing by the window in the editor's office, staring down into the narrow lane and gossiping. Mr Ramage had just been hearing about Amy and *The River Boy*, exclaiming, 'How extraordinary!' 'Remarkable!' throughout the narrative, his reddish face alight with pleasure and interest and a sensibility—as the father of two daughters—almost tender. Lord Welwoodham had brought out *The River Boy* and Mr Ramage had glanced at it and commented, and it was just after the editor had locked the manuscript away, while they were still discussing its admirable qualities, that Mr Ramage glanced down into the street and observed:

'There she is.'

They both watched Amy as she hurried down Rosemary Lane, already half in twilight because of its narrowness but filled with the reflection of a misty golden autumn sunset. She was late this evening; her talk with the editor had thrown her behindhand with her day's work and she had stayed on to finish it; and now she was hurrying home, moving lightly in and out of the pedestrians in the lane, looking like any other little junior typist on her way back to high tea and the second house at the pictures with her boy, except that she was dowdier than most.

Lord Welwoodham watched her out of sight with some complacency; there went the boys' writer of the half-century, pledged to write only for *The Prize* during the coming year. But the thoughts of Mr Ramage were touched with wistfulness and curiosity.

'There goes young Dickens,' he murmured, half to himself, staring down after the slender disappearing figure, 'stumbling home after a day's torture in the blacking factory with his head crammed to bursting with grotesques. And young Keats, hurrying off to forget the smell of drugs and the weight of the pestle in the summer fields—and young Kipling climbing into the gharry, too tired to sleep after putting *The Pioneer* to bed. Lucky young devils all! I'd give something to know what's going on in her head at this moment, eh, Lord Welwoodham?'

'Yes—yes. It must all seem very exciting to her; she's a funny little thing, quite—unworldly is the only word I can think of— apart from her gift.'

'Wait till she finds she can earn a lot of money,' said Mr Ramage rather sadly. 'That will soon cure her unworldliness.'

'I hope not, but I fear so,' replied Lord Welwoodham, gathering up the yellow stick and the hogskin gloves in readiness to go home. 'Still, money is very pleasant, you know, Ramage, very desirable. No harm in money, so long as it is harmlessly earned. Eh? Don't trouble much about the stuff myself but then my tastes are simple, thank God, and I've always been able to gratify them and have a little over. That makes all the difference.'

You said it, thought Mr Ramage somewhat coarsely, with a passing pang of impatient envy. Aristocrats! Between even the best of them and the ordinary salary-packet slave, how great a gulf lies fixed!

Homeward through the tired, hurrying crowds went Amy, just as she used to in that old dream of her childhood when the flock of hastening blank-faced strangers would not stop or notice her although she screamed her name at them and implored them with outflung arms. But this evening was quite different from all the others on which she had hurried home during the past four years because everything looked so amazingly exciting. The buses were such a brilliant blazing red and the petrol vapour that hung above them such a lustrous blue, the twisted copper leaves on the plane trees were so strange that she nearly got knocked down by a lorry as she stared up at them, the smoky yellow sunset far down between the tall buildings of offices and banks was so wonderfully far away and peaceful (*it's like that over the forests of Poland, where the bison are*). The faces of the people on a level with her own in the stifling tube, under the glaring lights, were brimming with secrets and strangeness under their tired pallor. She devoured each one, stamping features, colour, expression, into her mind, thinking of a name for that woman, imagining that man's house. Her heart beat heavily and she shut her eyes. Slow spirals of purple, green and bronze at once unrolled over a pale brown field, making the word 'India' ring slowly through her mind. She opened her eyes again, and saw the pale faces full of secrets, the brilliance of the silver-violet lights, the dark wall of the tunnel rushing by.

I'm awfully tired tonight. It's lovely about my story. Miss Lathom'll be pleased, I must tell her. It's Old Girls next Saturday, I can tell her then.

And suddenly, just as the train ran into Caledonian Road Station, there exploded in her mind like a fountain of silver stars—

> *Down with the drawbridge and let him through—*
> *The dreamer whose dreams came true!*

That's my favourite poem, and fancy, I'd almost forgotten it. After supper if Dora's out I'll start the new *River Boy* story.

The train moved on into the tunnel, and once again, exactly as though the sea had flung up a wave and drenched her with spray sparkling in the sunlight of a secret land, the poem broke over her—making her shiver and her eyes fill suddenly with tears—

> *Down with the drawbridge and let him through—*
> *The dreamer whose dreams came true!*

237

PART TWO

PART TWO

16

The old road to Alva was a rutted track bordered by willow trees. On either side of it uncultivated fields rolled away to the mountains. The road was hardly used since the Depression hit Alva some years ago; in the winter it got blocked with snow and in the rainy weather it stood under water, and no-one cared except the few farmers who used it to send their vegetables and milk into Alva, and the pupils of the Jabez Culver Infant School, which provided education for the children in this lonely district. The children knew the old road well. They went bumping down it to school in the family Ford, or loitered home along it on the fall afternoons, picking golden rod and asters.

The air smelled wonderfully sweet on a spring night three years later, and the old road was beautiful in the moonlight.

Miss Ridgeway, of the Jabez Culver Infant School, was very busy about nine o'clock that evening. The curtains had just fallen on the last Tableau of the series given by the School at the End of Term Party, and the parents were still clapping and cheering. In this tableau Sally Best, aged seven, had appeared as *Liberty* in a white robe, a silver cardboard halo and a gold cardboard torch, bestowing a gold casket labelled *Prosperity* on Joe Murphy as *The American Worker* (wearing a boiler-suit and a white shirt), while Marguerite Frost, aged nine, stood on the one side impersonating *Culture* (pink robe, wreath of bay leaves from the Frost backyard), and Ruth Pittson, aged eight, stood on the other as *Progress* (blue robe, crown of golden stars) with a fat finger pointing unsteadily at a portable radio. The three little girls and the boy stood quite still, at first, against the background of the

241

Stars and Stripes but as the fathers and mothers burst into murmurs and applause, the younger children began to wobble and bite their lips in their attempts not to laugh, and only *The American Worker* stood still as a statue. When the curtains swung back for the third time to display the tableau, Sally Best piped:

'Say, Miss Ridgeway, can Joe take *Prosperity* now? My arms is aching awful!'

—and the curtain came down for the last time amid a shout of delighted laughter from the parents.

'Joe, Sally, get your things off quickly and pack them away and wait for me in the hall, I won't be long.' Miss Ridgeway dropped her hand for a second on the shoulder of *The American Worker* as the children moved off the stage. Miss Ridgeway had leanings to the Left which the Depression had not lessened, and Joe's dress and character had been her contribution to the tableaux planned by her sister. 'Then I'll run you home, both of you.'

A few minutes later the boy and the little girl came out into the hall, where Miss Ridgeway stood with her sister saying good-night to the parents as they slowly streamed out of the schoolhouse, and receiving their congratulations.

'Gee, I'm hungry!' Sally did a little hop, her bright dark eyes darting about among the crowd.

Joe felt in his pocket and silently handed her two peanuts.

'Gosh, Joe Murphy, I hate peanuts!'

'Be hungry, then,' said Joe indifferently, but he shelled them for her and soon she was nibbling them, while Joe, huddled into his shabby old coat, stared at the crowd and exchanged waves and grins with his friends.

He was too old at twelve years to attend the school any longer, and now went to the Vine Falls High, but he had been so popular while at the Jabez Culver that Miss Ridgeway and all the children had decided to invite him to be in the Tableaux. He was perhaps the most popular boy in the neighbourhood; a spry, fresh, good-tempered kid, often in mischief but never in mischief of the wrong kind, intelligent and full of energy as yet undirected, the kind of boy for whom all the neighbours vaguely predict great things when he is grown up. His home was poor, for his father was a truck driver only in occasional work and his mother was delicate and could not work as hard as she wanted to, but the family was liked and respected by their neighbours south of the tracks in Vine Falls, and everybody in town knew Joe's tow-coloured head and small twinkling blue eyes. His parents were not at the Party, because his father was away on a night trucking job and his mother was in bed with a three-days-old baby. Sally Best was also alone at the party; her father and mother were two gay young people who found parenthood a tie, and had parked her on a grandmother who was too old to gad about at nights, even to admire Sally in a Tableau. But Miss Ridgeway was going to drive both children home: they would be quite safe with Miss Ridgeway.

Children were clustered in the hall, hooded and scarfed like elves, their round excited little faces suddenly yawning as they were picked up by Dad or big brother and suddenly discovered that they were sleepy. It was awful late! Most half-after nine! Gosh, there was the old moon up in the sky! One or two of the younger ones looked solemn; wasn't there something about witches riding in the sky on Hallowe'en? Oh, Miss Ridgeway said there weren't any old witches and it wasn't Hallowe'en. So that was all right.

'That sure was a swell party, Miss Ridgeway!'

'Didn't Ruthie look cute!'

'Thanks for a lovely party, Miss Ridgeway!'

'G'd-night!'

'G'd-night!'

Slowly the crowd thinned, and one by one the cars got away, with everyone calling out laughing good-byes, until only Miss Ridgeway's little car stood outside the school in the moonlight.

'Get in, will you, Joe, and help Sally? I won't be a moment,' called Miss Ridgeway, busy in the hall.

'Sure.' And Joe advanced on Sally, who was hopping on and off the doorstep. 'C'm on, kid. I'll lift you in.'

'I don't want you to lift me, Joe Murphy. I kin get in by myself.'

'Awright. Maybe you'd like to open the door as well, Sally Best, and put in the gasolene and drive the car right home?'

'I could too, Joe Murphy, so you leave me alone.' And Sally walked with dignity to the car, Joe sauntering after her, grinning. She was only a pint-size number, but such a fresh little thing with her Shirley Temple airs and her black fringe and her big brown eyes!

'Want me to open the door?'

'Well, Joe Murphy, are you dumb! How kin I get in if you don't?'

Joe opened the door, picked her up, swung her into the back seat with a flash of white frills, and climbed in beside her.

'Gosh, Joe Murphy, be careful, liftin' a lady up like that!'

'You ain't a lady, you're a rat,' said Joe coldly, suddenly bored with her airs. 'Eat those an' shut up.' He gave her three more peanuts, and they settled down to wait for Miss Ridgeway.

Earlier that evening, Bob turned his car away from Morgan and set out on the road for Vine Falls. He usually went home for week-ends, and this week-end he particularly wanted to be at home because Helen would be there, and he had not seen her for some time. Their vacations had coincided, but their plans had not: she had been south to visit relations, he had been north to visit friends, and he had been so busy this last year that he had not written to her so often as he used.

But he wanted to see her again, and the thought of seeing her gave a lift to his spirit and made him whistle softly as he sent the car along Sixteenth Street and into Mailey Avenue, where the pretty houses and unfenced gardens gave way to open lots and the country began.

Swell night, he thought. I'll go home by the old road, it's a short cut. More than one girl looked interestedly at the big fair young man driving the big car, for Bob in his early twenties had an air of natural happiness that attracted girls, sometimes against their will.

The last few years had been difficult ones for the Vorsts; Mr Vorst had been forced to sell the last of the three newspapers to the Syndicate and had also lost large sums on the stock market. Irene had married Jesson, the Parlour-Pink, and gone to live at Cape Cod, which was a long way from Vine Falls, and Boone had married again, a clever, hard newspaperwoman some years older than himself, and was living in New York; they seldom saw him. Only Lou and Bob were left at home. Mrs Vorst would not have minded the scattering of her family, which was inevitable as they grew up, if she had felt sure that both her married children were happy. But Boone had been too embittered by Jeanette to make a success of a second marriage, and Irene refused to have children and was disappointed in her husband because he could not make a fortune. The days when the family had been so happy, in the golden Coolidge Prosperity Era, seemed like a dream, and Mrs Vorst sometimes found the house on the hill very lonely.

Bob was the only one who did not seem to mind the change of fortune. He was not ashamed of owning an 'old' car, though Myron suffered acutely and was always pointing out that everybody in town had a new car every six months and adding that Prosperity was likely to stay just around the corner while folks didn't spend. Bob gave up his expensive flat in Morgan without a murmur and went into cheaper rooms; he did not complain when his father (who felt it far more than he did) broke it to him that his allowance for the year would only cover fees and lodging, and could not be stretched to take in subscriptions to expensive college clubs. He seemed to have a spring of happiness in himself that could not be dried up. His father was relieved

245

that he took the economies without complaint, but he was also a little contemptuous and surprised. The boy didn't seem to want to cut a dash at all! It wasn't natural. Why, at his age . . . ! Irene said cuttingly that Bob was just a small town hick and always had been, with no drive and no push. Even Lou, trying to make the best of life in Vine Falls and put behind her the delightful vision of two years at an art school in New York, admitted that Bob had her guessing. The family finally decided that he was so crazy about his work that he did not mind what else he gave up so long as he could keep that.

They did not suspect that Vine Falls had produced one of the rarest specimens the modern world can show: a complete human being.

Miss Ridgeway came briskly over to the car and smiled at Joe and Sally.

'All set?'

'Sure, Miss Ridgeway!'

'Let's go, then.'

She climbed into the driver's seat and slammed the door. The moonlit road was empty. Very faint and faraway across the fields sounded the melancholy tolling of the night mail.

Miss Ridgeway started the engine, and the car moved off.

As soon as Bob left the town behind he let the car go fast. One or two cars flashed by him and the lamps began to string past in a golden chain. A low roar filled the air, and he smiled faintly as the speed increased. The cool, sweet-smelling air rushed past his face and he softly hummed an old song:

> *I'm one o' those rarin-to-go galoots*
> *That aim to die in my high top boots . . .*

while the needle moved on to seventy.

At the new Vinebridge road he slowed and turned down a narrower one bordered with elms, leading to the old Alva-Vine Falls road. He drove carelessly, for this part of the country was very lonely, with no lights, no houses, nothing but miles of rough fields, grey-green in the moonlight, stretching away to the hills. A real estate board, offering magnificent frontage for stores and homes on the main road, suddenly looked over a dark hedge. The lettering was faded: the board had been there two years. This district would have developed if Alva had developed; but Alva was dead, killed by the slump in real estate. Bob's eyes were half-shut, he drove in a dream.

Once he passed a car drawn up to the side of the road with two motionless figures in it pressed close together. He drove on with a new turn to his thoughts. He had never been in love. Since Boone's divorce he had had a horror of girls like Jeanette, who were beautiful but cruel; and in every girl he met he saw cruelty, the desire to boss and to hurt, under the soft skin and behind the clear eyes. Suppose he gave in to his longing to love, and loved one of those girls? Sooner or later she would hurt him, and he would be spoiled for life as Boone was spoiled.

If he could find a girl who was brave yet tender, like Jo in Lou's old favourite, *Little Women*! That was the kind of girl he wanted, but American girls, lovely and grand as they were, were not like Jo—and would they laugh at the idea! He laughed a little to himself, as the car sped along the lonely road, at the thought of the expression on certain young faces in Morgan if he announced that his ideal girl was Jo in *Little Women*!

A girl who did not want a man to give up everything for her, a girl who would do as she was told (Ah! what would the Morgan faces say to *that*?), a girl who was 'tender and true' as the old song said . . .

There was Helen, now; beautiful, clever and good, as nearly perfect as a girl could be. She was like a third sister to him and

247

he loved her dearly, but imagine having to live up to Helen! It would take all a poor guy's time to be worthy of her, it would be like having to house the Hope Diamond, one could never relax.

It was lucky that he and Helen had never felt that way about each other. They would never have suited.

The car went down into the warm air under some thick trees.

English girls were supposed to give in to their men much more than American girls did. But English girls were also supposed to be cold, and that would never do for him. Two of his friends had married English girls; and were mighty happy. They were rather surprised, because they could not get used to having their wives do what they were told, but they were certainly happy; that could be seen in their faces.

Oh, well, there was plenty of time, and meanwhile he was happy enough himself. And he began to whistle softly as the car came out into the moonlight once more.

Miss Ridgeway drove at her usual careful thirty-five miles an hour, keeping her eyes fixed on the moonlit road. Sally was sleepy and dozed in her corner, but Joe sang:

> *California, here I come*
> *Right back where I started from!*

and presently Sally's little piping voice joined in. Miss Ridgeway smiled, not taking her steady eyes off the pale road moving towards her. Ten years of teaching had not cured her of loving children.

Joe broke off to say:

'Miss Ridgeway, I'm goin' to teach the baby to pitch as soon as he's old enough.'

'Why, Joe Murphy, you'll have to wait ever so long before he's old enough to pitch, won't he, Miss Ridgeway?' said Sally scornfully. 'Babies is so small, they can't walk or pitch or do anything, can they, Miss Ridgeway?'

'I guess he could start in to pitch a soft ball when he was three, couldn't he, Miss Ridgeway?'

'Maybe, Joe.'

'And it would keep him out of Mom's way a bit if I was to take him out pitching every day after school, wouldn't it?'

'It certainly would.'

'Gee, but I'd hafta take him some place where the gang wouldn't see us!' he muttered presently. 'They sure would rib me if they was to catch me taking a baby out pitching!'

'C'm on, let's sing some more,' interrupted Sally, and Joe's clear voice, not yet broken, and her fairylike but self-conscious treble broke again into

California, here I come!

as the car drew near the first of the old bridges.

Bob put on the brakes abruptly. A girl in a white coat stood on a steep bank, looking down at him and making the hitch-hiker's signal. She wore no hat on her thick curls and looked pretty, standing up there in the moonlight.

'Hullo?' he called 'Want a ride?'

'Whaddya think?' She slipped unsteadily down the bank with her white shoes close together. 'My date never turned up, and—why, Bob Vorst! Of all things!' She held out her hands, the red fingernails black in the moonlight, and Bob took them, laughing too, and pulled her up on the running board. It was Francey Carr.

'Well, well, well. Small world, isn't it!' He opened the door and she got in beside him. 'How come you're out here? Who was your date?'

'Oh——' She glanced round in an oddly cautious way at the

silent moonlit road and the deserted fields. 'I was only kiddin'; I hadn't got a date. I was waiting for Dan.'

Bob nodded, looking steadily at her under the lock of hair fallen over his forehead.

'So he's around, is he?'

'Sure. He got into a hot patch, so he's lying low for a while.'

'He's got plenty of nerve. Where is he?'

'I don't know, Bob. Honest, I don't. Somewhere up in the mountains. He don't tell me nothin', and I don't ask. I don't waunt to know too much, in case the bulls pick me up and third degree me.'

'How are you doing, Francey?'

'Oh, I'm all right. I'm in a beauty-parlour in Morgan. Liselle's, on Ninth Avenue. I room with another girl on John Foster Street. Sure I'm all right. I get plenty of dates, and good money and everything, and Dan sends me a little present every now an' then. But I ain't mixed up with his gang, Bob. They get me scared. Gee, I wish he'd get out of it.'

'Not married?'

'Jeeze, no! There's a guy, he's sales representative for Sweetbriar Toothpaste in Morgan, wants me to get engaged to be married, but I don't know, I make good money an' I'm kinda used to having a good time now, I don't waunta settle down.'

She smiled at him, her little white face and large eyes looking like a doll's in the faint moonlight. She had learned how to move and how to stand still since they had last danced together, and her perfect body, clothed in a fresh dress of thick white silk, gave off a faint perfume. He suddenly kissed the hollow of her throat, keeping his mouth against it for a moment.

'Fresh, aren't you,' murmured Francey. 'Gee, I wish Dan would show up.'

'How long have you been waiting?'

'Most an hour. My room-mate gave me a lift out here; she's got a car.'

'Well, let's go. He's probably been detained,' said Bob smiling, but he glanced away at the wooded hills, dark and silent. There were deserted farmhouses and cabins up there that would make safe hideouts for an army of gangsters. 'How about a little drink at Roselands?' He gave her a cigarette and lit it for her.

'Suits me.'

'Come closer, will you.'

She moved against his side, and he started the car.

'Make her go, Bob. I like to go fast.'

'Me too.'

A few minutes later, when they were out of sight, another car, long and black, came out of the woods on the hills above and took the rough track down to the old road.

'California, here I come!'

sang the children, excited by the movement of the little car through the moonlit night.

'Open wide those Golden Gates!'

chanted Sally, kicking her heels against the seat.

The long black car reached the foot of the hill and slowed its pace, and the man who was driving looked about him.

'She ain't here, Silk,' he said at last.

'All right. Get on down the road. Maybe she's further on,' said a low voice from inside the car.

'Ain't you gointa wait? Maybe she's late.'

'Get on, will you.'

The driver, a thick-set man in a light raincoat and hat pulled over his eyes, sent the car along the road taken by Bob and Francey some minutes before.

★

251

Willow trees, road and grey fields rushed past. Francey leant towards Bob and he twisted his lips to meet hers, keeping his eyes on the road flying ahead. He was intoxicated with the cold sweetness of the wind rushing past, the silver sky wheeling overhead, the soft hot pressure of Francey's mouth.

'Gee, Bob, what're we making?'

'Can't see. Like it?'

'Sure!'

'Sit tight, children. We're coming to another bumpy bridge,' said Miss Ridgeway. She could see the lights of another car, moving very fast, rushing towards them between the trees some distance away, and she slackened her own car's pace.

'Open wide those Golden Gates!'

sang the children, and the bridge came in sight.

And then Ann Ridgeway screamed and jammed on her brakes, twisting the wheel violently to the left, but it was too late. A big car leapt roaring round the sharp curve of the road, struck the little car sideways on, and knocked it through the rotten rails of the bridge into the river bed below. Miss Ridgeway heard a dreadful little scream behind her, and then something hit her head and everything went out.

After the hideous confused crash of collision there was a silence, in which nothing moved but the white figure of Francey as she clutched at Bob, who was lying over the wheel with blood pouring from his nose. Their car had run half-way up a bank.

'Bob! Bob!' whispered Francey. 'Are you dead? Oh God, it was a kid—I saw her. She fell out . . . Bob . . . say something.'

He never moved. Down in the little valley below the broken

bridge someone was crying loudly and moaning. And then the long black car swept round the corner, with the pale faces of two men staring out. It stopped, and both men got out and ran across.

'Oh God, it was a kid . . . I saw her . . .' screamed Francey, turning on them. One of the men saw Bob, and drew in a quick breath, and began to curse.

'He's dead! Can't you do something?' shrieked Francey.

'C'm on.' He seized her arm and dragged her out of the car. 'We've got to get out of this. We don't want to be here when the police come . . .'

'He's dead!' She looked back at Bob as the two men half led, half dragged her across the road.

'Sure. And he can't talk,' the other man muttered, flinging open the door of the car. Then Francey opened her mouth to scream again, but a hand was smacked down over it and she was forced inside. The driver scrambled into the seat and the car fled away, dwindling down the moonlit road until it was only a flying black dot.

When Ann Ridgeway slowly opened her eyes, she stared into the white blood-smeared face of a young man who was sobbing. He was staring down at her, and gently, cautiously, with sobs shaking his body, he was moving her hands with the movements a doctor uses to restore a human being to consciousness.

'Where are the children?' she whispered very slowly, staring up at him.

He gulped, and looked away from her to a place a little distant. She raised herself on her elbow, groaning, and peered where he was looking.

'Are they dead?' she whispered.

Two bundles, one with a white thing over its head, lay side by side on the grass.

'The boy's alive. He's unconscious. I think his eye has gone,' he said in a slow hoarse voice. 'The little girl——'

He suddenly put his face into his hands and sobbed behind them, saying something she could not hear.

17

Helen went to her bedroom window for a moment to look out at the snow. It had come in the night, thick and deep, loading the budding branches and filling the world with the strange silver light that is like no other, and no one all over Vine Falls could talk of anything else that day. For spring was well advanced, the orchards were in blossom, and here was the snow, killing and destroying like a wicked, beautiful army! It was strange to see it lying under the light of a spring evening and to hear the children shouting and running past with their coasters, as they did in January.

She had come upstairs to change her frock for the Boadmans' cocktail party, and had just gathered up her fur jacket when the still, silver light coming through the window had attracted her, and she moved slowly across and looked out. The trees with their delicate load, the blue light, and one star shaking above the darkening roofs, were so beautiful that they were unbearable. She could still see Bob's face as it had been when he left the court yesterday, coming slowly down the steps between an angry crowd. That was all she could see, and because of the look that had been on his face, beauty was not to be borne.

The telephone bell rang while she was standing there, and then her mother's voice called up the stairs:

'Helen! It's for you.'

Mrs Viner was standing at the door of the parlour, with the large blue eyes that were so like her daughter's looking troubled and frightened, and as Helen went past her she said:

'It's Bob, dear. He sounds pretty bad.'

'Shut the door, will you, Mother,' said Helen over her shoulder as she picked up the receiver; and from the corner of her eye she saw her mother very gently do as she was asked, the door slowly closing on her pretty, disturbed face under the pile of high curls that even older women were wearing that year. Dear Mother . . . thought Helen . . . so kind and lovely . . . and then she forgot everything but the sound of Bob's voice.

'Helen?'

It was his voice, of course, it must be, but so low and hoarse and so exhausted that she hardly knew it.

'Bob? This is Helen.'

'Listen, Helen. Can you drive me out to Black Lake Inn?'

'Of course. Where'll I pick you up? Are you at home?'

'I'll be on the corner of Culver and Sycamore in fifteen minutes.'

'I'll be there.'

She hung up, and went to the door, calling, 'Mother!'

'Helen, what is it? He sounds so bad! Is he coming up here?' Mrs Viner came through from the kitchen where she had been giving the Polish daily girl instructions about the evening meal, and followed her daughter upstairs. She was dressed for the Boadmans' party, all but the little Edwardian black hat with pale blue feather wings which she now put on, looking anxiously at her daughter while Helen was pulling on her fur jacket and tying its hood under her chin.

'He wants me to meet him downtown and drive him out to Black Lake. Mother, tell Mrs Boadman something for me, will you? Think up some excuse.'

'Oh, I'll say you've taken Bob for a drive, he was feeling pretty bad after yesterday——'

'Please don't tell her I'm with Bob or say anything about Bob, *please*, Mother.' Helen's usually low voice, one of her charms, was almost shrill as she turned at the door. 'You know how she talks. She was in court yesterday, taking it all in, looking so cruel

. . . she's a case for psycho-analysis if ever anybody was! I just can't bear to have her knowing how bad Bob feels . . . you think up something for me, Mother.'

'Of course, darling. Helen!' (calling after her), 'When'll you be back? Those people are coming in after supper——'

'Oh, I don't *know*!' The faint exasperated cry was drowned in the slamming of the front door.

Five minutes later she was driving down the avenue under the fairylike trees laden with buds and snow. The strange weather had given everybody a little shock of surprise, almost of pleasure, because it was unexpected enough to shake everybody out of their everyday feelings and to awaken their sense of wonder, and as a result everybody moved more briskly, and eyes were bright and voices quicker and more crisp. The town might have had a piece of good news in which everybody could share, instead of having seen thousands of pounds worth of fruit blossom killed in a few hours. The snow and the damage to the crops and everything . . . that'll give people something to talk about, and maybe they won't think so much about Bob, thought Helen.

It's a good thing it's the beginning of the vacation. Bob'll be able to get away, and when he comes back next month, maybe people will have forgotten . . .

Maybe they will.

It was all perfectly straightforward. The jury weren't out more than ten minutes.

Everybody could see how broken up Bob was, even after he was acquitted. Everybody was so sorry. Amalie Cordell was crying . . .

But I do wish Uncle Webster hadn't hired Schroeder for the defence. He's got such a bad reputation for cases of this kind.

That's what made the crowd so angry.

'Lucky not to go to the chair!'

'Dirty mobsman's lawyer!'

257

I'll never forget those women screaming when he came down the steps, so slowly. And the look on his face. Darling. I can't do anything to help you.

Oh, what's the use of lying? There *was* something queer about the jury. They looked . . . frightened.

Oh, well, what does it matter? He was acquitted, wasn't he? What does it matter *how* it was done, so long as he was acquitted, and won't have to go to prison? I won't think about it.

But why did he look like that? Why did he look . . . ashamed? I've never seen Bob look like that before. It was horrible.

Uncle Webster kept on saying *It'll be all right*. He was worried sick until he'd talked to Schroeder, and then he kept saying *Everything's going to be fine*. And Lou wouldn't say a word. She looked so queer when she came out of court, relieved yet kind of ashamed, too.

There *was* something queer about it.

It was darned clever of Schroeder to dig up those two on a petting party in their car. It gave us the case.

If they really *did* see the crash . . .

If Miss Ridgeway really was on the wrong side of the road . . .

If . . . if . . .? What does it matter? He's safe. He was acquitted. Five hundred dollars, and he mustn't drive a car in the State for a year . . . but he was acquitted, wasn't he?

I won't think about it.

Everybody was so glad we won. Everybody loves Bob. I suppose it ought to be a comfort to me that I'm not the only one.

I suppose I'll go on feeling like this all my life.

But I wouldn't have had it any other way . . . unless he could have loved me back again. It's made life more beautiful, not poisoned everything.

And one day maybe I'll find someone I can love in a different way, a new way, not all mixed up with childhood and remembering the fall woods, and growing up together, and then I'll marry him.

I'll try to keep my love for Bob beautiful all my life, and not let it spoil me, or spoil my marriage . . . or even spoil my husband! She smiled very faintly. The corner of Culver and Sycamore Avenues was in sight, and she could see Bob's tall figure waiting. In another moment she stopped the car by him, and he opened the door and got in beside her. He had a small case with him.

'I hope I didn't keep you waiting,' she said. She was so shocked by the change in him that she spoke out of sheer nervousness as she might have to a stranger. His face was drawn and unshaven and there were black shadows under his eyes, but dreadful as his appearance was, it was less dreadful to her than a differentness that hung over him, making him unlike Bob. She felt as if a light had gone out.

'That's all right,' he said, not looking at her.

'Shall we go?'

'Yes, please. I've got to be there by half-after seven.'

She started the car and they moved off.

The spring evening was fading into dusk. The sky was already dark clear blue, but the streets were light with a ghostly reflection from the snow heaped in mounds on the sidewalks, and the branches of the trees, dipping lower than usual with their burden of lightly-frozen snow, sparkled wonderfully in the glow from the electric standards. Helen's old favourites, the white hyacinths, stood up through snow in garden after garden as they passed.

'The poor flowers,' she murmured, after a very long silence.

'What?'

'Only the snow, I meant. It's killed so many flowers.'

But the word 'killed' hung on the air for minutes after she had spoken it; and she became so frightened at his silence and the way he kept his face turned away from her and stared at the houses going past that she could hardly drive.

'I'd better light up,' she murmured, and the next instant the road just in front of the car was lit by a long beam. They were out in the country now, and the road was brown and white with crushed snow. It looked to Helen like the only real object in the world, coming steadily forward to meet the car out of the hushed twilight.

She was wondering in great misery of mind whether it would be better for her to try and make him talk, or to let him sit beside her in that alarming silence. And why was he going to Black Lake? What would he do there at a summer hotel in the mountains that would only just be open, miles from anywhere?

At last she could bear the silence no longer and said:

'Are you going to stay at Black Lake?'

'I don't know. I'm meeting Dan there.'

'Dan?' For the moment she did not know who he meant. She had been away from home so much during the last year that her memory of local characters was a little dimmed, and in any case she had never been interested in local characters whose activities lay, so to speak, south of the tracks. All her folks, her friends and her interests, lay north of the tracks in the pleasant residential district. And Dan had left Vine Falls years ago.

'Dan Carr.'

Then she remembered.

'But——!' she began—and was silent.

'Sure,' said Bob hardly, 'you remember now.'

'But why are you meeting him, Bob? Isn't he dangerous?'

'Yes.'

'What does he want to see you for?'

'We're going on a little trip together.'

She was silent, too appalled to speak. Terrified thoughts whirled round and round in her head as she wondered wildly what to do.

'You see,' Bob went on, in the same indifferent voice, 'I'm not going back to the Owen Vallance next term.'

260

'Because of what's happened?'

'Yes.'

'Bob,' began Helen, trying to speak in her usual voice, 'Everybody knows how bad you feel about this. You *can't* believe anyone thinks you did it on purpose.'

'I don't care what in hell they think.'

'Well, then. Why're you going with Dan? All you've got to do is to go away for a while, and when you come back, maybe—maybe people'll have forgotten——'

Her hands were trembling so, and her voice, that he noticed, and said, 'You'd better let me drive.'

'But you mustn't.'

'Who's to see me, out here?'

Silently she let him get into the driver's seat, and settled herself beside him, pulling her fur jacket tightly round her, for she was very cold. Oh, how she longed to keep silent! To sit beside him as the car went on through the dusk, between the lonely fields covered with snow, and not force herself to speak, and him to answer! But she was so frightened by what he had said that she forced herself to go on. I must find out where he's going, and what he's going to do, she thought.

'Does your father know you're going with Dan?' she asked at last, with an effort.

'Yes.'

'But . . . didn't he . . . what did he say?'

'Told me to quit.'

'Told you to *quit?*' she repeated, slowly. 'But I can't *believe* it! Why?'

'He thinks I'm ungrateful,' said Bob. She could tell by his voice that he was smiling, and turned quickly to look at him. But it was too dark to see his face.

'Why?'

'He fixed up a swell crook lawyer for me, didn't he? I ought to be grateful.'

'But, Bob——' she said, and then was silent again.

'You were going to say I knew what they were up to, and I needn't have stood for it.'

'Well . . . I was, yes.'

'Oh yes, I knew all right. But I couldn't face up to things. So I let Dad and Schroeder fix it.'

She was still silent, for she could not think of a word to say.

'I kept on thinking about the work,' he said suddenly. 'I kept on thinking it would finish me, if I went to prison, and I could never be a doctor. Dad said it would, too. So I let them talk me into it.'

'You don't know that it really was Schroeder who got you off, Bob. The jury might have brought in Not Guilty anyway.' She was trying desperately to persuade him that he was not to blame.

'They were fixed, too.'

'*What*?' Then she really did turn to face him, swinging right round in her seat, and staring at his profile in the dusk, as though she had not properly heard what he said. '*What* did you say?'

'I said, the jury was fixed. Dan did it.'

'But——'

'Francey was with me on the night of the smash. When I came round, she'd gone, but Dan called me up next day and asked me not to say she'd been with me.'

'Why not?'

'He didn't want the police to pick her up and third degree her about him.'

'But he couldn't fix the whole twelve!'

'He didn't have to. There were only two who were likely to want fixing. All the others . . . knew me . . . and of course Judge Bronson was all right.'

She nodded. Judge Bronson was an old friend of Bob's family, as he was of hers.

'Dan said if I didn't say Francey was with me, he'd take care of the jury for me. And I let him.'

'I think you were right!' she cried, with tears running down her face. 'It wasn't your fault. You didn't mean to kill Sally. It's more important that you should go ahead with your work than—than——'

'You think so?' he said indifferently. 'I don't. I used to think I was the type to make a doctor. Now I don't. First I kill a kid speeding, then I can't stand up to a fair trial. Swell doctor I should have made.'

'But what will you do, when—when you come back, if you're not going to be a doctor?'

There was a pause. Then he said:

'I don't know.'

But she knew that he meant—'I'm not coming back.'

For a long time they drove without speaking. She was crying quietly, helplessly. But even while she bit her lips to keep back sobs, and wiped away the tears that seemed as if they would never stop coming into her eyes, her mind was racing wildly, trying to think of a way to help him, to stop him going with Dan. But she could not think of a thing to do, for she was so alarmed by his looks and manner that all her usual ease with him had gone. In all the twenty-odd years that they had played and worked together, he had never once knowingly hurt her or failed to show affection and concern for her welfare; and what really drove home to her, now, the change in him, was the fact that he had not once thanked her for coming out in the snow to drive him up into the mountains, nor wondered if she would get home safely, nor said one word to show that he had ever felt the slightest affection for her. To sit beside him, and to feel that he was unaware of her misery, and would have been indifferent to it had she suddenly cried it at him, was to her the most dreadful part of this dreadful drive.

At last she said:

'Surely Aunt Sharlie doesn't know you're going, Bob?'

He shook his head.

'She was out.'

'But Bob!' she exclaimed, 'you can't let her come home and just find you gone like that! You can't! Think how she'll feel! Please, please, darling, don't be like this! We all . . . love you so much . . .' She stumbled over the words, 'and we'll help you to win through if you'll only stay with us. Please, *please*, don't go with Dan!'

'Oh . . . leave me alone,' he answered in a low impatient tone. 'I'm not going to turn gangster, if that's what you're worrying about. I just want a little holiday, that's all. I'll find a job, maybe. Dan said he's got one for me, as a matter of fact.'

He spoke quickly, almost gabbling, as if his own control was nearly at an end.

'But if we all helped—even if you don't want me—I mean, if you'd only stay with us——'

Then he suddenly turned violently on her.

'Can't you see I don't want to stay with all of you? You'd all remind me all the time how I let Dad and Schroeder fix things. I want to get away. I'll be all right with Dan. I know him and he knows me. Now leave me alone.'

His voice was frighteningly loud, echoing over the dim fields mantled with snow. Helen shrank from the big figure that shouted at her and made uncontrollable movements, as though the misery inside it must escape, and said faintly: 'Don't . . . don't . . .'

She heard a voice in her heart saying reassuringly: 'This is Bob. It's only Bob,' but she could not believe it.

There was a long silence, while he sat staring at his hands on the wheel. She could feel his body trembling and did not dare to speak. At last he started the car and they moved on.

She was very frightened. It seemed to her that Bob had gone suddenly crazy. She still did not believe that he was going with Dan and might never come back; she kept expecting that he would suddenly turn to her and say: 'I must have been crazy. Let's go home.' But the minutes passed, and suddenly she could see lights far ahead on the dark mountainside, and still Bob did not say a word.

So at last they came to the Black Lake Inn, and he stopped the car a little way down the road from the entrance. The hotel was open, and evidently the mild weather before the snowstorm had tempted some visitors to it, for one or two cars were parked outside and the radio was playing in the bar. Black pine forests shut the building in on three sides, and far below in a little valley there was a gleam, where the lake was just beginning to reflect the rising moon. The air was cold and still, yet awake.

Bob groped at his feet for his case, and she suddenly sat up, realizing with a shock that it was here he was going to leave her.

'Please, Bob. Please don't go,' she said, trying to speak sensibly.

He did not answer, and she stared at him while he got out of the car. He slammed the door, and stood for a second with his hand on it. The faint light from the windows of the Inn shone on the line of his cheekbones and the dark patches of shadow that were his eyes and on his mouth, still tender with youth. He was looking at her as though he did not see her.

'Darling,' she said, staring at him, but the word was a whisper lost in the fur of her hood.

'G'd-bye,' he muttered, looking at her. The faint light shone on her beautiful pale face in the raccoon fur hood. It seemed as though he would say something more, but he did not. He turned away, and walked on with his shoulders hunched against the cold, and she saw him go through the door of the bar, and disappear.

Helen sat there for a long time. One or two cars came up and people got out and went into the Inn. It was quite dark now, and the moon was sailing above the pines, making the snow glitter. She wondered if she should go into the bar and look for Bob, but she was afraid. She was afraid of Dan, of the far-off whisper of violence that seemed to hover in the air when Bob had spoken his name. If she went in there to look for Bob, Dan might shoot her. Things like that happened every day.

At last she moved, shivering in her fur, and slid into the driver's seat again and started the engine. I'll drive to Gow Flats, she decided, and call up Uncle Webster from there. That's all I can do.

There was a gasolene station at Gow Flats, a village five miles back on the Vine Falls road, and from there she got through to the town.

'Hullo there,' said Myron's voice, sulkily.

'Myron? This is Helen. Get Mr Webster for me, will you, it's important.'

'He ain't in.'

'Well—Lou, then—anybody. Only do hurry!'

'What's the grief? Everybody's out.'

'Oh——!' Helen swayed from side to side, distracted. 'It's Bob. He's in trouble.' She was thankful to have Myron at the other end of the line, who had known them all as children.

'What kind of trouble?'

'He says he's going off with Dan Carr.'

'Gone off with that rat? He's crazy!' came back the sharp New England voice, suddenly high up in the nose, supercilious yet shocked.

'Oh Myron,' wept Helen, leaning against the wall, 'he isn't! It's true. He's at the Black Lake Inn, waiting for Dan now. I don't know what to do.'

'Well, quit cryin', fer a start. Where are yer?'

'At Gow Flats, at the gasolene station.'

'I'll be right over in the Ford. Wait fer me there.'

She hung up the receiver, and went into the little eating-house attached to the gasolene station, where she sat down and ordered coffee and lit a cigarette. It was comforting to think of Myron hurrying to her in the Ford, but what could they do when he got there? By the time they reached the Black Lake Inn, Bob might be twenty miles away. There was nothing—*nothing*—that she or Myron or any of them could do now.

★

Bob went across to a far corner of the bar and sat down at a table. A waiter came up, and he ordered a drink, and sat there with it in front of him, staring at the wall. The room was empty except for a small group laughing with the bar-tender.

Presently a man came in through the swing doors, and after a casual glance round walked over to Bob's table and sat down opposite to him.

'Hullo, kid,' he said gently.

Bob looked up and nodded.

'Hullo, Dan.'

'Sorry if I kept you waiting. I was just waiting till Helen drove away.'

'That's all right. How about a drink?'

'Thanks.'

The waiter came up again and Dan ordered for them both. When the drinks came he sipped at his glass, holding it carefully in one manicured hand; Bob drained his at once. They sat for a while in silence, Bob looking down at the table and Dan gazing indifferently about the room. The group round the bar had gone, and the bar-tender was reading a magazine. At last Dan said in the same gentle tone:

'I took care of those two for you, all right. Didn't have any trouble, did you?'

'No.'

'That's fine.'

There was silence.

'I didn't have any trouble, either,' said Dan. 'They both wanted to help.' He smiled a little. 'Old Powell's got a little grand-daughter he's very fond of, and Tracey and his wife only opened a cleaning store six weeks back. Tracey's intelligent. He only needed a hint. I had to talk to the old man a little longer. He couldn't get the idea at first. But I told him times had changed, and then he got it, all right.' He took another sip at his drink.

'How about another?' he asked.

'Thanks.' The boy came up, and Dan paid.

'Well, now,' said Dan, 'about this little trip. How about coming up into the woods for a bit? I've got a nice little place up there. We could get some shooting. I've got to lie low for a while, and you need a holiday.'

'Do I?' Bob laughed.

'Now, kid, don't be like that,' said Dan gently. 'You've been crucified. Anybody can see that. But just try and take it easy. Sure, I know how you feel, the first time you ki——' He stopped, and sipped slowly at his glass. '. . . I know how you feel. But try and take it easy. We'll go up to the woods and shoot, and maybe read a bit, and talk.'

'You always liked talking, didn't you, Dan?'

'Sure I like talking.' The gangster began to pull thick gloves of fine leather over his hands. 'You can get drunk on talking, like you can on liquor. You know me. I don't like liquor—much. I only like women sometimes. I like to talk and I like to read and I like to—I like knowing people'll do what I say.' His dark eyes moved slowly about the room. 'We'll go into the woods and rest up a while, and shoot, and then I'll find you a job where you'll see some life. Go places, and learn things. An intelligent kid, like you, going to be a doctor——'

'Keep off that, will you?'

'Sorry, kid. But you won't feel like that in a week or two.' He leant a little over the table to emphasize his words, and Bob caught, together with the faint smell of the good cloth from which his coat was made, the sharp smell of pine from the high woods through which he had been driving.

'The air's always so good up in the woods,' he said suddenly. For the first time they smiled faintly at one another.

'Remember the time I nearly put your eye out, aiming at a killdeer?' said Bob, rubbing his unshaven cheek and yawning.

'Sure. That was the second time we ever went out.'

'Can you still shoot, Dan?'

'I don't have to do my own—now,' said Dan, gently. 'But I can still shoot, if I have to.'

'Let's go,' said Bob suddenly, resting his elbows on the table and putting his face in his hands. 'I'm tired.'

'Sure. We'll go now.'

He lifted his hand, and the waiter came over and Dan paid for the rest of the drinks. He moved compactly, as if he were all made in one piece and very strong. His face was dark and smooth and his custom-tailored clothes, because of the superb material of which they were made, had a bloom on them, sombre yet rich. Bob watched him tucking a silk scarf, exactly the colour of a violet, into his coat. Here was his saviour. If Dan had not taken care of the jurors, he, Bob, might have been in prison now, instead of sitting here. Or perhaps the other ten jurors, who had known the Vorsts for years, before he was born, might have talked them over. Perhaps he had let Dan fix those two, and let Schroeder fix the witness, all for nothing. He didn't know. Anyway, it was done now. He rubbed his eyes, yawning.

'You know,' said Dan, looking down at him and smiling as he tucked in the scarf, 'the boys don't call me Dan any more. They call me Silk. Because of this.' He touched the beautiful scarf with an almost graceful gesture. 'You'd better call me Silk, too, maybe.'

'All right, Silk. I don't mind. Let's go,' said Bob, swaying with weariness as he got up.

He had stopped feeling remorse and shame. He felt nothing except tiredness, and the relief of being with someone who had known him for years, who expected nothing of him. He would go away with Dan and rest, and have a little shooting, and then maybe things would work themselves out. He followed the compact dark figure down the long room, and out through the doors into the spring night.

18

A month later Amy was standing at the window of her flat in Hyde House, Hyde Park, watching the sun go down behind the trees.

The last of the daylight was faintly reflected on a picture where Victorian ladies and gentlemen skated under a yellow sunset, very like the real sunset that Amy was watching from the window. On the other walls were the medieval battle scene with red and blue-clad soldiers, and the Japanese painting of birds on a bough laden with snow and flowers. In the middle of the yellow carpet was a round Victorian table of yellow wood (but without any hot-plate marks). Shelves were built into the walls on either side of the electric fire that lay flat against a sheet of copper, and on them were the solid backs of *Dred: A Tale of the Great Dismal Swamp*, *St Elmo*, *Say and Seal*, and other friends of Amy's childhood. Very out of place they and the old pictures looked in this room, in which the taste of a fashionable decorator had provided the background, and the affection of the owner for her few old possessions had provided the personal touch. The decorator had been so angry when he saw the photograph of Amy's grandparents on the white sycamore-wood desk that he refused to have anything more to do with her, and a mutual acquaintance had repeated to Amy his furious comment: 'The place for *photographs* is the servant's bedroom.' 'You tell him that's his place, too,' Amy had retorted, with one of her flashes.

The room was perfectly quiet, with that padded, luxurious quietness that only money can buy in a modern city. However noisy the streets below may be, noises falter, discouraged, before they can climb to the top flats in such buildings as Hyde House;

like those bees which never discover the luckless virgin flowers in the penthouse gardens of New York. It is not a peaceful silence. There is something drugged and enchanted about it. Conditioned air, central heating, and sound-proof walls are the only magicians employed to produce this hush, yet it gives a strange feeling to a visitor of being cut off from the living world.

A faint smell of Turkish cigarettes lingered in the room and two empty glasses stood on a mirror-glass tray on the table, by a decanter decorated with silver stars. Amy had been entertaining Mr Humfriss, her agent.

Mr Humfriss was a pink young man under thirty, with a classic profile and cold blue eyes, who was most efficient in helping Amy to earn and manage her handsome income. They did not like one another. Mr Humfriss liked young men better than he liked young women, and he liked music better than either; and Amy simply disliked him without knowing why, but their business relations were completely satisfactory because Mr Humfriss could be as impersonal as he pleased with Amy and she never seemed to notice or mind, and Amy could leave her affairs to him with perfect confidence without feeling that she must be nice to him. As she was finding it increasingly difficult lately to be nice to people she did like, let alone those she did not, the services of Mr Humfriss suited her perfectly.

This evening, however, their conversation had not been so completely impersonal as usual. Mr Humfriss, whose standard of good manners was unusually high in a lax age, felt that politeness demanded he should remark upon Miss Lee's extreme pallor. Every now and again, too, as she sat opposite to him at the round Victorian table with contracts and letters and cheques spread between them, she had opened her eyes wide in a strange, strained way and her temples had given a little twitch as though trying to shake off pain. It was evident that her head ached.

'You look excessively tired,' at last observed Mr Humfriss, putting a contract into an envelope and not looking at her and speaking without a shred of sympathy or warmth in his well-bred young voice. 'Are you going to spend the summer in London, as usual?'

'Spend the summer?'

'Stay here, I meant, throughout the summer months.'

'Yes, of course. Why?'

'A great many people,' explained Mr Humfriss carefully, as though enlightening a weak-headed child of six, 'go away in the summer.'

'Yes, I know. The Beedings do.'

'Summer in London is excessively trying,' he went on. 'So cold and wet. A good many people go abroad in August, when all hope of fine weather has been abandoned.' He smiled chillily.

'Yes, I know. I've seen pictures of them in *Vogue*.'

Mr Humfriss ignored this, though he approved of the fact that she had taken to reading *Vogue*. Perhaps that was why she was better dressed than formerly. Or perhaps old Lady Welwoodham had been taking her shopping? Old Lady Welwoodham herself dressed very well (Mr Humfriss was a critic of female dress), originally yet not artily; and Heaven knew that the little Lee, when he first met her three years ago, could have done with as much help about her clothes both from Lady Welwoodham and from *Vogue* as she could get. However.

'It hasn't occurred to you that you might go abroad, too?'

'No, I can't say it has,' she retorted, with one of those commonish turns of speech that jarred upon Mr Humfriss. 'I never thought about it.'

'Well, it is an idea,' he commented. 'All writers' (Mr Humfriss never called them authors) 'travel sooner or later, of course, to get new ideas, and if you are feeling a little tired and even perhaps a little stale in your work——'

'Do you mean my last book was stale?'

'——it might do you good to get away from it all, as they

272

say,' tranquilly concluded Mr Humfriss. 'Have you thought any more about the American lecture tour?'

She shook her head, and her temples, now swept clear of hair so that their tender youthful modelling was revealed, twitched once more as though to throw off a burden.

'I shouldn't know what to say. I told you that before,' she said—helpfully.

'If you decided to go, there would be no difficulty about finding subjects for you to talk about,' pursued Mr Humfriss, who knew from experience that Amy was not cooperative unless matters were made as easy for her as he could possibly make them. 'We are used to arranging tours for our writers, of course, and Mr Aubrett could find you as much material as you would want. I hesitated to trouble you with this letter from our New York agent' (he handed it to her) 'because you were so sure that you did not want to go to the States, but if you are thinking about going abroad, the States would make' (he smiled faintly) 'a nice change for you. There are some dozens of women's clubs that are anxious to hear you.'

Amy took the letter, and shut her eyes as a wave of pain went through her head. Then she opened them again and stared wearily at the list of Clubs and Societies 'in the following towns.'

She had read half-way down the list when she came to a name that she knew.

Vine Falls, Paul County, New Leicester.

She stared dreamily at the name for a moment. Vine Falls—such a pretty name, making her see a picture of a waterfall dashing down through veils of red autumn leaves. Her head ached so badly that she could not think properly. Vine Falls. Where have I heard that name before?

Of course. That's where my American lived.

She sat quite still, staring at the name on the letter. The dim room was quiet, filled with slowly-wreathing smoke from their cigarettes, and Mr Humfriss sat patiently waiting for her to make up her mind, leaning back in his chair in a reposeful attitude. The pain in her head was so intense that she could not think clearly, and she shut her eyes for a moment.

And suddenly she saw in the darkness the face of a young man. He was very pale, and looked ill, and had fair longish hair disordered on his forehead. He was so deeply asleep with his head against a red cushion that he might have been dead. Yet somehow she knew that he was not dead. And his face was older, but it was the face of the little boy she had seen in the courtyard of Kenwood House ten years ago.

The picture only lasted for a flash of time—a long, slow, dreamlike flash. Then she opened her eyes again and found that she was in the living-room of her flat in Hyde House. And she was saying eagerly to Mr Humfriss:

'I'll go to America, Mr Humfriss. It's a real place, you see, and I would so love to see it——' and he was looking at her curiously as he stubbed out his cigarette.

She was trembling with a strange excitement that was touched with fear, and did not want to meet his chill, intelligent eyes, so she got up, muttering, 'I'm cold. I'll just get a jacket,' and went into her room, coming back a minute later pulling on a coat.

'When would you like to go?' he asked.

His tone was not eager, for he did not much care whether the little Lee went to the States or not. But it was always useful for an English writer to make personal contacts in America; and he and his partner, Jeremy Aubrett, did sometimes wonder how long it would be before the deep subconscious conflicts in the little Lee's nature (upon which, they had decided, her talent was nourished) sent her into a mental home. The more holidays, the more changes of scene, she had, the better in health she would be and the less likely to go into a mental home, thereby cutting off a profitable source of income to Mr Aubrett and Mr Humfriss.

'It is now the end of April,' he went on to say patiently, as she did not answer his question, which she did not seem to have heard. 'Would you like to go in about three weeks?'

She nodded, staring at him with a frightened expression. She had suddenly realized that she had never been further out of London than to Bracing Bay, in Essex.

'That will give us plenty of time to make all the arrangements,' he remarked, putting together his papers.

'Yes. Thank you, Mr Humfriss,' she answered in a low tone, holding out her hand. 'Good-night.'

'Good-night, Miss Lee. I will telephone you tomorrow afternoon and let you know what subjects Mr Aubrett has in mind for you to talk about.'

He shook hands with her and went away, a young man pink and cold as a strawberry ice, to snatch a sandwich and a drink before going to the Queen's Hall to hear Schnabel play Brahms's Thirty-Four Variations on a Theme by Handel, and to forget for some blessed hours about women and writing.

And then Amy went over and stood at the window to watch the soft colours of the sunset disappear, and to think with strange excitement and anxiety of the face she had seen when she closed her eyes, and of her trip to America, and of how lonely she was on this exquisite evening of late spring.

The sky was watery blue, with grey clouds above the yellow clouds shaped like a fan. Down in the Park daffodils glimmered between the dark trunks of the trees. People were hurrying homewards from work, just as Amy used to hurry four years ago. She leaned her head on the cold window pane, kneeling in the windowseat of her tower, high, high above London, and stared dreamily down on the little dark scurrying dolls. Behind her the room settled into darkness.

She was hardly recognizable as the dowdy of four years ago, for Lady Welwoodham had indeed been taking her shopping. Her dress of so dark a red as to be almost black, adorned by a necklace of Indian jewelled work, did credit to Lady Welwoodham's taste. Her hair was pulled back from her brow and dressed high, a style which displayed its slight wave (Lady Welwoodham detested what she called The Arty Bun). On the *tops* of her ears Amy wore small earrings matching her necklace; this fashion had only just come in among the fashionables of Rio de Janeiro, where Lady Welwoodham had a correspondent.

All this elegance of person, and the smart flat, and the services of Mr Humfriss, were paid for by Amy's books. She had written seven books in the last three years, and showed no signs, so far, of having begun to outwrite herself. She had a very large public for her stories, and as the latter were also first-rate plots for filming she had added another public ten times as large from cinema audiences all over the world.

Lord Welwoodham, who took the credit for introducing Amy Lee to the world and who followed her literary career with as much friendly and amused interest as his wife took in her sartorial one, said that she was one of those writers who fly full-fledged from the nest, and whose first book is as good as their last. The famous *River Boy*, the film rights of which were bought by London Films for a handsome sum a few weeks after its publication in *The Prize*, was as good as *By Night*, Amy's first full-length novel, and *By Night* was no better than *The Desperate Gentlemen*. The rich yet quickly-moving style, the simple and vivid characters, the sense of danger and the nearness of death which haunted her books were Amy's special gifts and could not be confused with the gifts of any other living writer, but they were gifts that had been marked as hers from the opening sentences of *The River Boy*, and the books which followed on her first story showed no deepening or broadening of her talent. It was the talent of a wonderfully gifted and ageless child, who could neither grow up nor lose its powers.

Her stories spoke with one of the voices of the modern world, and thousands of readers were quick to hear. The modern world is becoming used to images of danger and death, and to desire the excruciating thrill which only fear can give; it is as if the readers and cinemagoers 'escape,' not into dreamland, but into the heart of horror itself and there find what they want. They are less and less able to look at the images of peace and beauty because there is no peace and little beauty in the real world. Beauty and peace have become unbearable because they are unattainable. Amy's stories fed the craving for excitement that is felt by most readers under forty; and the films made from her books, which heightened their tension and sense of danger, fed the same appetite in millions of cinemagoers from London to Buenos Ayres. The desire to watch excitement rising, to admire an outlaw who defies the massed forces of Danger, is one that an unemployed cabinet-maker in Wolverhampton can share with a half-breed in Mexico City. Amy's talent was fed by, it pandered to, the oldest of the passions: Fear. It was no wonder that she made a lot of money; the panders to lust and greed are equally prosperous.

But the great difference between Amy and the writers who consciously pander to the destructive passions in humanity was that she did not know she was doing it. Her stories were natural flowers growing from the soil of her mind, which had been saturated with fear since her childhood. She had always been afraid of size, afraid of noise, afraid of people shattering her secret world, and she could only get rid of this fear by pouring it out on paper, and unconsciously identifying herself with the brave and honourable hero who was not afraid of anything.

In all her books the pattern, if not the actual plot, was the same. It was disguised with different settings for the action of the story, which took place in Stalin's Russia or in Nazi Germany or in the underworld of London, but the same design always emerged. A hero, embittered by injustice, defied the forces of Law and proved himself a better fighter and man than the Law's supporters. He was a modern Raffles, harder and more bitter and ruthless than the amiable gentleman cracksman of pre-War fancy. He took what he wanted. He knew no laws but the two which he imposed on his own nature: he never betrayed a friend, he never gave in to his enemies. He was, of course, Amy herself; the child alone in the world, defiant yet secretly desperately afraid.

But her books were not gloomy or sadistic. If they had been, they would never have secured their great success, for though the contemporary world craves its danger-thrill it has not yet sunk so far that it can take it absolutely neat (when that happens, readers will go to watch parachute descents and dirt-track racing instead of sitting at home reading) and the popularity of Amy's stories was due largely to the glamour that they cast over violence and horror. She had the gift that makes a writer popular: *a clear picture of a world*, and although it was a picture seen by someone who was unhappy and afraid, it was as unmistakably an *Amy Lee picture* as the stories of Edgar Allan Poe are pictures of *his* world. She also had the gift of making the reader feel that life in her world was more exciting and desirable than life in the actual world. She was a natural writer, expressing herself in words as inevitably as an actor does in gesture or a composer in music, and even the intelligent literary critics admitted as much. Jeremy Aubrett and Giles Humfriss sometimes thought that her books might change in theme if she became a happily married mother, but they never imagined that she would cease to write. A natural writer stops writing only when dead.

As for the girl inside the elegant shell of clothes that Lady Welwoodham's taste had suggested and Amy's money had bought, she was not so much altered by money and fame as might have been expected.

It is commonly admitted that money is delightful: but it must also be admitted that money is not much use if you happen to want things which money cannot buy. There is no extraordinary merit in wanting such things; to want them does not give you the right to despise other people who want the things that money can buy; it only means that your money, though useful, will not be more important to you than anything else in the world. Amy did not know what she wanted; but she was already sure that money could not buy it. She was deeply unhappy, and her unhappiness grew deeper every week. Her luxurious home, her lovely clothes, the charming and intelligent people to whom Lady Welwoodham had introduced her, did not make her one atom less unhappy.

Her experiences in the world in which Lady Welwoodham moved had been such as to drive her back, bewildered and unhappy, into her own secret world. She had begun by despising her new acquaintances as Sops and Chin-Waggers, Mind-Pokers and Bossers who could not write stories. She had gone forth to their dinners and parties feeling defiant yet wary, like Buck Finch, that oldest of her friends, among the cannibals. But everyone was so kind to her that she soon stopped feeling like Buck Finch, and as the little door in her mind refused to open and let her escape through it, she found herself only a nervous girl without social background and without anything to say to some of the most intelligent and charming people in London. Her fourth book, *The Soldier of Misfortune*, had pleased a more varied public than any of the others, and all that world which is known to the irreverent as Arty-Smarty, from alarming old judges to delicious silly débutantes, wanted to meet the writer who had created Ted Cassiter, the limping ex-service man who died so gallantly in the end of the book.

Lady Welwoodham arranged for any number of people to meet her. But after Amy had been to two or three grand parties at which she never opened her mouth except to mutter, 'No, thank you,' or 'Yes, please,' in an accent not ripe enough to be interesting; and had once or twice broken amused silences by such observations as, 'It must be awful in Russia now, I think,' or 'There was an exciting bit in the *Daily Express* this morning from India about a postman who was a dwarf, an *Indian* postman,' at the same time fixing her companion with a stare in which alarm and suspicion were hardly concealed by a glazed, polite smile—the fashionable world which had been so eager to meet Amy Lee decided, though reluctantly, that she really was very dull, poor little thing. Clearly, It All Went Into The Books, and there was nothing left over with which to entertain the Nobility and Gentry, the Screen and the Stage (for *The Soldier of Misfortune* had been dramatized with Ralph Richardson as Ted Cassiter and the Stage was also eager, in its rich warm way, to slap Miss Lee on the back).

But it was Mr Antrobus who finally convinced Amy that the world of fame and fashion was not the world for her. She had been to a dinner given by a literary society at which he was also present, and had been excited and shy at the sight of him, for she always felt that it was he who had fired her ambition and made her into a 'proper writer.' No-one had presented her to him, for the members of the society were many of them his friends and knew that George detested meeting promising young writers. He would grace the dinner with his presence, but be nice to promising young writers he would not. So Amy looked at him reverently from her place lower down the table, and was not in a mood to observe that he was drinking a good deal of burgundy; she only observed that he was making his neighbours laugh a lot and did not stop doing so during the speech made by the guest of honour.

The dinner and speeches were boring. Both Amy and Mr Antrobus decided to leave early, and as she was coming down the wide marble staircase of the restaurant, who should she see but the god himself, coming out of the gentlemen's cloakroom and furling himself into his opera cloak with a dreary look on his face.

At once she saw herself, as she so often did, going up to him and saying, 'Mr Antrobus, do you remember me?' and then she saw him put his parrotty head on one side and cry: 'Why it's little No-Boy-and-No-Brothers! Of course I remember you.'

All the time she was thinking this she was flying down the steps after Mr Antrobus with her cloak billowing out, and by the time she got to the foot of the stairs she caught up with him.

'Mr Antrobus!' she said eagerly.

He turned, mechanically pulling off his hat.

'Do you remember me?'

Mr Antrobus put his head on one side and considered a tiny, glowing, romantic girl with diamond stars in her hair and a red satin dress under a dark blue cloak like a soldier's.

'Of course,' said Mr Antrobus, speaking carefully in a thick voice. 'Of course I remember you, very well. How are you?'

'Oh, I'm very well, thank you.'

'Still living in the same———?' inquired Mr Antrobus, swaying.

'Well, you see———' she began, but Mr Antrobus went on, swaying even nearer towards her:

'How about dining with me? Would that amuse you?' And he put out his hand, gropingly, towards her bare neck.

Amy suddenly remembered Old Porty, her father, and Mr Beeding.

'No thank you. It doesn't matter,' she said very politely, and ran away from him, across the empty hall and out into the rain, where a fatherly commissionaire got her a taxi and was made even more fatherly by a five shilling tip. Because he's got such a nice face, thought Amy confusedly, sitting back in the taxi. Beastly old Mr Antrobus, I hope he's sick. And she began to cry.

After this incident she became quieter and less easy to entertain than ever, and as even the most intelligent and charming people in London could not go on entertaining a wittol and moron for ever, gradually, though it continued to read her books, Lady Welwoodham's world lost interest in Amy Lee.

She was deeply troubled by her failure to get on with people.

She was intelligent enough to see that it was her own fault, and she began at last to wonder if she were very different from everyone else, and why. She had never thought much about her own character until this, her twenty-third year; she had identified herself with the people in her dream world, and had loved the memory of her mother, and had enjoyed her writing and occasionally (when she saw a man buying one of her books from a railway bookstall or a woman reading one in the tube) her fame. But she had never thought of herself as the outside world might see her until that sad, disappointing summer last year when Lady Welwoodham had tried to launch her into a circle of delightful new friends.

That summer seemed a long time ago. For the last year she had been out hardly at all, and had seen fewer and fewer people. She had told Mr Humfriss that she did not want to attend literary luncheons nor to make speeches to women's clubs, and Mr Humfriss protected her very thoroughly from all such activities. He realized that she was not one of those writers whose income is increased by their social life; it did not matter to the audiences who flocked to see the film of her latest book whether she went out or stayed at home. She was rich enough and well-known enough, as a name, to afford the last luxury of a successful writer in the modern world: she could be private. Besides, the literary luncheons and women's clubs did not want her, for she had no glamour and nothing to say. Mr Humfriss's own opinion of Amy was that she was a fool with a gift. He did not mind how quiet she kept, and neither did Jeremy Aubrett.

She was also secretly troubled by her failure to attract a proposal of marriage. It was not that she wanted to be married; she had never thought much about marriage or about love, and her new way of living had not made her think more. But it upset and annoyed her because a certain kind of witty and elegant young man, which was the only kind she had met at Lady Welwoodham's parties, did not trouble to conceal his dislike of her books and, it was sadly plain, of their writer. This young man (he was all rather alike, and it was difficult to remember him apart) was often a balletomane or an interior-decorator or a dress designer. He accused Amy's books of being subconscious Fascist or Communist propaganda, according to which way his own political dislikes lay, and when he had no politics but was a classless, nationless Artist, he accused her stories of being insensitive and brutal. It hurt Amy's pride as a girl, as well as her pride as a writer, that these exquisite, goddish creatures should so clearly find her unattractive. And she was so lonely!

In fact, the only bright spot about Amy's venture into the great world was the way she got on with His Majesty's Fighting Forces.

At Lady Welwoodham's parties she had more than once met military men in high positions and Air Force officers and important sailors, all of whom enjoyed her books and were prepared to admire their writer, and these admirers had offered to let her into all sorts of places where the general public never got.

'Might be useful, perhaps?' diffidently suggested the soldiers and sailors and airmen. 'If ever you're writing about that sort of thing . . . Getting copy, I believe you writers call it, don't you?'

These offers pleased and flattered her very much, and she had made careful notes of the names of the authoritative creatures and had later written polite letters asking if she might come to see whatever it was they commanded, as they had so kindly suggested, on such and such a day. She had always received a cordial permission, and had enjoyed tea after the visit in all kinds of Messes with demure Ranker-Members of H.M. Forces to hand the toasted scones and go off at the double for more hot water.

Her hosts in the Services enjoyed these visits as much as she did. When they found that the writer of those grand yarns *China Walk* and *Make Way for Death* was a little girl just as high as their hearts, pretty in an unusual way and well-turned out, whose shy but polite manners did not conceal her interest in everything they had to show her and her admiration for themselves and their calling, the soldiers and sailors and airmen could hardly do enough for her.

Amy came as near losing her heart as she had ever done to a young naval lieutenant. He had the bluest eyes she had ever seen in a human head, and he never took them off her own while he murmured at her.

All through tea he gazed into her eyes between half-closed lids, and murmured. His favourite word was *wizard*. ('I hear Buda-Pesth's a wizard place.') He was rather like a very young wizard himself, in his blue-black and gold, with those eyes and that murmuring incantatory voice, and Amy dreamed about him for two nights.

But on the second night the blue eyes looking into her own changed to grey, and the face that came suddenly nearer her own was not the face of the young lieutenant. Yet it was a real face; it was not the vague face of a dream. She had awakened with her heart beating fast, and had lain awake for some time, listening to the low sleepless roar of London far in the streets below, and trying to remember the face in her dream.

But in spite of her enjoyable excursions with the Forces, she made no friends and found no sweetheart among the soldiers and sailors and airmen, and gradually, after the first public interest in her as a person had died away, she found herself almost as much alone as she had been before she became famous. The dark-red satin evening dress, the three diamond stars for her hair, were put away in wardrobe and jewel-box and had not enjoyed an airing for months.

Her days were passed in work. She discovered that it set her imagination dancing to wander through districts of London that were unfamiliar to her; and once or twice a week she slipped out of Hyde House, dressed in garments saved from the old days before Lady Welwoodham took her clothes in hand, and took the bus to Clapton or Southall or Manor Park, Alperton or Walthamstow or Catford. There she idled along the streets, letting the people, the sights and sounds and smells, strike upon her senses while her mind was in a dream. She would have her tea at an A.B.C., or even an eating house frequented by lorry-drivers and bus-conductors. No-one took any notice of a smallish dark girl in a shabby fawn tweed coat, a fawn hat, and horn-rimmed glasses. She managed to look like a nothing; she was hardly there at all. But the strongest, strangest feeling of all came to her when she strolled past some gigantic cinema, blazing with lights and flaring with posters proclaiming:

GARY COOPER
in
'The Soldier of Misfortune.'
The world-famous novel by
Amy Lee

She would stand in the dusk, staring up at Gary's lean delightful face next to the name of her story—the name that she had invented, and fierce delight would overcome her. At last the Hurrying People had been made to stop! *Listen . . . I will tell you a story . . .* and the Hurrying People who had haunted the dreams of her childhood faltered in their haste, turning curiously to hear what Amy Lee had to say. In every city in the world they stopped to listen to Amy Lee. It was wonderful, it was like one of her own stories, to stand among them, unknown and unrecognized in her shabby clothes, and watch the crowds moving in to see *The Soldier of Misfortune*, by Amy Lee.

On the days that she was not wandering through London, learning the city, she went to the London Library or to the British Museum Reading Room and read up facts to weave into the backgrounds of new stories. She had discovered that her imagination worked best upon facts, stated in books of reference. On the few occasions that she had attempted to report, rather than to imagine, an incident, she had done bad work; once, in the middle of writing a book, she had gone to watch a liner sail, but the description she had afterwards written had been spoiled by too much detail. She used to think: *I only need a touch, to set my mind off*, and experience had proved to her that this was true.

When she was not learning the city of London, or reading up facts, she was writing, high in her room above the Park, in that unnatural silence in which she was now kneeling at the window watching the last of the sunset. She wrote quickly and for hours at a time, emerging, when the inspiration suddenly failed, cold and ravenously hungry and sleepy. She would either go down to a meal in the restaurant on the ground floor of Hyde House or send down to Service for whatever was on the menu; and sometimes she did not exchange a word all day with anyone except the maid who came in to clean the flat in the mornings and the man who brought dinner at night. Sometimes Lady Welwoodham rang up, or Mona Beeding (now married to a spotty young man connected with the London Telephone Exchange, and mistress of Trevarra, Parkview Avenue, Berrydown Estate, Esher) telephoned to say that she was Up for Swan and Edgar's sale and could she pop in for tea? And Amy was always secretly ashamed of being so glad to see her. Mona never got tired of poking round the flat, examining Amy's clothes, spraying herself with *Blue Grass*, telephoning down to Service for two Clover Clubs, pumping Amy to find out how much she earned, and generally bringing a breath of Highbury into Hyde House. But Mona did not often come to town, and Lady Welwoodham spent much of the year gardening down at the house in Hampshire, and Amy could not always be over at the Beedings—it would look so funny, they would think she wasn't happy in her beautiful flat, if she went over to Highbury more than once every few weeks. And not to anyone would she admit how lonely—how frighteningly lonely—and unhappy she was.

But in fact, Mrs Beeding and Lady Welwoodham and Miss Lathom (with whom Amy still kept in touch) could see that everything was not right with her. All three women realized how unnatural her life was for a girl of twenty-three, even a girl with genius. All three, too, were sure that the terrible headaches that had lately been torturing her were due in some unexplained way to her unhappiness. She wore glasses while she wrote, and an oculist had assured her that the trouble did not lie with her eyes, so on Lady Welwoodham's advice she went to the Welwoodhams' pet nerve specialist. He told her that the headaches might be due to half a dozen causes. He saw that she did not want to be asked if she were unhappy, and would not enjoy talking about herself, and he therefore asked her only the simplest questions. ('You have no worry, nothing is troubling you, that you're aware of?') He finally observed that more fresh air, light exercise, plenty of rest and sleep, could do no harm, and might do good.

But he told Lady Welwoodham (whom he regarded as he would have Amy's mother had she been living) that Miss Lee's peculiar upbringing and lack of healthy family and social relationships, together with her super-developed imagination, causing what might almost be called mild delusions, and her strong sense of inferiority battling with an equally strong consciousness of unusual gifts, was quite enough to cause headaches and anything else from which Miss Lee might suffer. But he was as near certain as he could be of anything that the headaches would disappear when once Miss Lee had adjusted herself to a more normal way of living.

'I suppose that means a husband and six babies?' tinkled Lady Welwoodham acidly; she was no feminist, but she knew more than one pastime that she preferred to husbands and babies.

'A husband and six babies could do no harm and might do good,' smiled Sir Parham Blaine, indulgently.

So that spring Amy walked alone in the woods, where yellow catkins trembled in the wind and the green leaves unfolded, and the sprays of beech were beginning to spread themselves in the warm sunlight. But although the delicious moist air of April brought colour into her cheeks, the woods made her so miserable that she wanted to die.

She walked alone, crying noiselessly as she used to when a child, the tears running down her face and the same frightened loneliness on her spirit that had oppressed it in the dream of the Hurrying People.

But when she was a child she had been able to retreat from loneliness and fear into her secret world; and now, when she was grown up and famous and rich, her secret world was becoming unreal to her, as if shafts of sunlight were breaking through the tattered walls of a sorcerer's tent. Outside was the real world, covered with millions of people with homes and families, with their work troubles and their money troubles; millions of people loving and suffering and working under the blazing light of the sun as the Earth whirled round in space. And she knew nothing about any of these people, nor about the things they cared for. She did not like them and they did not like her. They liked her books (*listen . . . I will tell you a story*) but she was a nothing, a ghost in the sunlight.

The power to love, that had slept in her nature since the death of her mother and fed in its trance upon the beings in her dream-world, moved in its slumber and wept. She did not know why she was miserable; she only stood staring at the green slope of a meadow with one golden tree in it, the clear blue sky above, the rich white masses of a hawthorn hedge lifted to the sun, and wished that she could die. *Oh, what's the matter with me? I'm the dreamer whose dream came true, and I wish I was dead.*

★

It was nearly dark, but she still sat at the window, staring unsee-ingly down at the people and wondering in a confused way why she had said that she would go to America. The romantic interest she had felt in that country as a child had faded, and the prospect of lecturing to hundreds of people terrified her, and so did the thought of leaving London, the only place where she had memories and friends. I must have been mad, she thought, to tell Mr Humfriss I'd go.

And suddenly, just as if a light had been struck in a dark room, she remembered that she was going to Vine Falls. She would not be utterly without memories in America. In the beautiful sycamore desk she still had the five-cent piece with the buffalo on one side of it and the Indian head on the other, wrapped in the original piece of paper with the name and address of the American boy who had given it to her ten years ago. She murmured the words over to herself as she sat there in the twilight:

Robert . . . Somebody . . . (some name like Frost), Vine Falls, Paul County, New Leicester, America.

I shall see the town where he lives.

But I expect he's left there long ago, it's eleven years. Eleven years on my birthday this year.

That *was* a queer picture I saw when I shut my eyes. It wasn't like a dream, or the sort of picture I get when I'm seeing a story in my head. It was real.

He was like my American, grown up. Only he looked ill and unhappy, and my American looked so happy, the only time I ever saw him.

He was so kind. I do hope, wherever he is now, he's all right and not (the words came unexpectedly into her head) *in danger.*

She moved stiffly, and found that she had pins and needles. The window pane was cold against her forehead, and her head-ache was getting worse. Below in the streets the poor, the unlucky in love, the cruel, the disillusioned, and the mediocre, hurried past to their homes, and Amy, who was none of these things, stared down unseeingly at them from her tower.

Some days before she sailed for America she went to a farewell supper with the Beedings.

She got there about half-past six. It was May Day, and Mrs Beeding was indignant because on her way out to buy sausages she had been held up by a procession of Communists and on her way back from buying sausages she had been held up by a procession of Fascists.

'Seems a long time, don't it, luv, since all we used to look at on May Day was the carthorses done up with their brasses and ribbons?' observed Mrs Beeding. 'I used to like that, when I was a girl first come to London. Me and Mr Beeding used to go every year to see the procession in Regent's Park.'

'And a long time ago, Mrs Beeding,' said Amy, eagerly yet dreamily from her seat at the kitchen table, 'they used to go out (Londoners, I mean) into the fields before it was light and bring home the May and decorate their houses with it.' Amy still dispensed tit-bits of legend and history to her foster-mother, just as she used when she was a little girl.

'Did they, luv. I reckon the country was nearer to London than it is now.'

'Yes. There were fields in Westminster then,' said Amy, in the same low dreamy tone. 'It's queer to think of, isn't it, Mrs Beeding?'

'There's a lot of queer things in this world, luv.' Mrs Beeding was making pastry for apple dumplings, and conversation was carried on to the comfortable sound of the roller on the pasteboard.

'That's a new fur, isn't it, luv?' said Mrs Beeding presently.

Amy glanced at the rich brown jacket hanging carelessly on the cupboard door.

'Yes. I thought it might be cold on the boat.'

Then silence settled over the kitchen once more, broken only by the quick ticking of the clock and the soft thumping of the roller.

But on Amy's side at least it was not altogether a peaceful silence. Her glance had happened to wander from the fur jacket to Mrs Beeding's worn and knotted hands, moving capably as they kneaded the dough, and the contrast between the luxurious, inanimate object hanging against the cupboard door and the two lively objects turning and pressing the white mass, had started thoughts in Amy's mind that kept her very quiet for some moments.

The insolent way the coat hung against the door made it a stranger to everything else in the kitchen. The price of it would have bought up the kitchen's furnishings ten times over, including that New World gas cooker on which Mrs Beeding was anxiously yet proudly paying instalments. And especially was it a stranger to Mrs Beeding's hands, wrinkled by years of washing, already the hands of an old woman. The coat, for all its silky springy surface, looked a dead thing beside Mrs Beeding's hands. And Amy suddenly realized, as she sat there, how delicate Mrs Beeding had always been about Amy's change in fortune; and how the whole family, so soon as they realized that Amy was going to become famous and rich, had let her leave them, in body and in spirit, with never a word about what they had done for her when she was poor and unknown. It was true that Mrs Beeding had been paid twelve and sixpence a week for Amy's bed and her food, but no money could pay for the natural kindness with which the whole family had taken Amy in, and let her shelter among their casual daily life like a storm-weary bird in a warm quiet room. Why, this was the only place in all London where she felt at home! Her mother had sat at this very table shelling peas and talking to Mrs Beeding; her father's ghost, with greying gilt hair and charming smile, walked the stairs. She could come here whenever she liked; whenever her head ached and she felt frightened or lonely or depressed by her failure to talk to people at a grand party, she could come here and be a child again.

And what had she done for the Beedings, ever since she had been rich, to show her love and gratitude for what they had given her?

She had done nothing. Oh, they had had seats in the dress circle whenever a film made from one of her books had its *première* in London, and she sent them pretty scarves and elegant trifles at Christmas ('Give them something *useless*, my dear. People who live that drab sort of life adore useless pretties,' Lady Welwoodham had advised) but she had done nothing that really showed how much she loved the Beedings and the house in Highbury.

Now that she was going so far away from them, she realized for the first time what they meant to her, and she was suddenly, deeply ashamed.

I take all and give nothing, she thought. I'm selfish. In all the books I ever read when I was little, it said Think of Others. But I only think about stories and myself. Perhaps that's why I'm so miserable?

A door slammed upstairs and a shrill voice called:

'Hullo—ee? Anybody home?'

'Aye. Aime's here,' called Mrs Beeding.

'What, again?' Dora's voice came more faintly as she went upstairs to her room. 'Sure the Duke of Westminster can spare you, Aime? I'll be down in a minute.'

'Where's Baby?' inquired Amy.

'Out with them Brownies of hers. She doesn't half love them. She's going to camp with them in June. Pity the poor soul that has them little monkeys to keep out of mischief, I say. A whole fortnight of it!' Mrs Beeding gave one of her rare laughs and put the dumplings in the oven.

'Mr Beeding'll be in presently, luv.'

'Oh, I'm glad. I was hoping I'd see him.'

Quick light steps pattered down the stairs and Dora came in.

'Hullo, Aime!' The two girls exchanged a peck of a kiss. 'My god, poor pussy's copped it at last!' Dora went on, catching sight of the fur jacket. 'What a beauty! I say, can I try it on?'

Amy handed it to her and she slipped it on, turning this way and that, her thin plain clever face sparkling above the glossy fur. She was thirty now, and secretary to a director of her firm and earning five pounds a week, one of which went regularly into the Post Office Savings Bank every Friday evening. Tailored, neat and astringent in personality, she seemed settling into spinsterhood without regrets. Her 'steady' had long since drifted away, discouraged by her efficiency and power to earn more money than he could, and she did not seem to mind his going. She had two or three close friends of her own age and type; thin, caustic girls with such nicknames as Slugs, Potty and The Marvel, who seemed bottled into an eternal Upper Fifth. They wore good classic coats and skirts with good silk blouses, and went cycling at week-ends in *culottes* (none of those shorts, thank you). She had done very well for herself, Dora had. So thought her mother, looking at her with a placid pride. Well, all the girls were doing well, come to that. Not like poor Maurice—and Dad. Mrs Beeding shut off her thoughts at this point; and began to slice potatoes into fresh cold water while the girls gossiped.

'You're in luck tonight, Aime; the Old Guy's making a Personal Appearance,' said Dora presently. She was perched on the table, swinging her legs.

'That's not the way to speak about your own sister.' Mrs Beeding was setting the cloth as well as she could round her eldest daughter's seat.

'Where's Artie?' demanded Amy. She wanted to see them all.

'He'll be in presently. They don't shut till nine on Saturdays. He likes it all right. He's had a cold ever since he's been there, but he'll be all right when the warm weather comes.'

Artie had just started as what can only be described as an

outside-egg-boy at a big grocer's in the High Street; a post which his mother announced at intervals would lead in time to his being a Branch Manager.

Then Mr Beeding came in, and smiled at Amy tenderly out of his wet dark eyes, and asked eagerly if she was writing another book. He was the only Beeding who did not say her stories were a bit far-fetched; his starved yet lively Welsh imagination seized upon their strong, strange plots, their rich satsifying glow of atmosphere and colour, and relished them to the last page.

'Oh, yes, Mr Beeding. I've nearly finished the one I told you about last time I was here. *The Fire Walker*, you know.'

'I must look out for it.'

'Oh, I'll send you one, of course,' she murmured, rather embarrassed. She had not forgotten her remorseful thoughts of a little while ago; indeed, they lingered at the back of her mind throughout the visit.

A loud sniffing from Dora now heralded the arrival of Mona, the Old Guy in person, who came carefully downstairs on very high black suede heels accompanied by a strong blast of *Mischief*.

'Hullo Mum, hullo Dad, hullo Dora, heart alive, girl, you're skinnier than ever, how do you manage it? Hullo, Aime. Mum, I'm going to take my shoes off, they do fit me but I haven't broken them in.' She sat down and kicked them off, her eyes fixed on Amy's jacket, which Dora had replaced on the cupboard. 'Heart alive, Aime Lee, is that yours?'

Amy nodded.

'I say, do let me look.' She hobbled over to the coat and fingered it. 'I say, what is it? Mink?'

Amy nodded again.

'Good heavens alive, Aime Lee, however mu——' She stopped, gulped, and bent closer over the jacket. 'Isn't it *gorgeous*! Do let me try it on.'

Unfortunately the mink jacket would not meet across Mona's mauve jumper, for Mona was going to have a baby in four months and had got exceeding fat, and as this failure made her rather cross, a slight gloom fell over the proceedings. If everyone had not been used to the Old Guy it would have been more than slight. However, they all knew her little ways, so the cloud soon blew over; and when they drew up their chairs to the table, where the tasty brown sausages sizzled in savoury-yellow batter, supported by two dishes of crisp yet fat golden chips, everyone was cheerful. Mr Beeding sat in silence, but a faint smile some-times passed over his tallowy face, and Mrs Beeding poured out the strong tea and ladled the potatoes, listening to the chatter of the three young women and occasionally putting in a down-right, sensible word, and the big kitchen rang with laughter as it used when Amy was a child.

Artie came in half-way through the meal, his face rosy and pleasing to look upon in spite of his cold and some spots, and announced that Maurice wouldn't be in till late, he'd gone off with the Fasheest marchers.

'Sloppy ha'porth,' commented Dora. 'No sugar, Mum. I'm slimming.'

Everybody laughed except Mrs Beeding. She was thinking how Maurice would look at her sometimes under the brim of his jaunty, greasy hat when she ticked him off, and say jeeringly: 'Yes, it's Dad and me're the unlucky ones in this family,' and that would always shut her up. Then he would go off to the Dog Racing track, swanking up the street in his shabby overcoat with the big padded shoulders and the buttonholes worn and dragged into strings. He had some mysterious half-time job up there, that kept him in money for cigarettes and the Pools. Them Pools! What with Dad having his bit every now and then on the horses, and Dora always joining in her office sweepstakes for the Derby and the Oaks and the Grand National and the Lincoln, and Artie doing the same with the staff at his shop, and Mona going in for those competitions in the picture papers about Can You Choose Clothes with huge cash prizes—it seemed to Mrs

Beeding that her family, together with most of England, was turning into Something-for-Nothingers; gamblers, eager to make money without working for it. Poor Maurice. Her boy. But he was bone lazy, as well. Funny; the boys seemed all wrong nowadays; it was the girls who had the grit and got the brass, too.

It was nice having old Aime to supper in the kitchen again, thought the Beedings in their different ways. The mink jacket, the West-End flat, the posh parties, had not pepped up old Aime at all. She still said Yes, Mrs Beeding, and No, Mrs Beeding and giggled at Dora's jokes. Even Mona had to admit, when tackled by Dora after Amy's first visit to the family since her installation at Hyde House, that Aime did not stick it on at all.

And they were all so used to her that it was easy to forget that she was Amy Lee, whose photo was always appearing in the papers (quite a thrill, seeing old Aime's pan in the *Daily Express!*), whose books were always being filmed. Amy Lee? Oh yes, we know her awfully well, my Mum practically brought her up. And they were all so proud, the self-respecting, independent Yorkshire strain of their mother's blood so dominated the emotional Welsh strain of their father's, that they never said, even among themselves, '*She might have done a bit more for us now she's got all that money.*' Even Maurice never said it, even Mona, with her envy of Amy's clothes and her supposed hobnobbings with film-stars.

After supper they sat in the Lounge, talking and laughing, and the rest of the evening passed very pleasantly. Baby came in later, having been seen to her own door by a conscientious Brown Owl who lived a bit further down the Walk. Her thick gold curls bobbed under her Brownie hat just as Dora's and Mona's used to when they were her age, but she was far prettier than her sisters had ever been. She turned her head away with an embarrassed grin when Amy greeted her, for she had been only six years old when Amy left Highbury and she was a little shy of her.

'Go and get yer supper, luv,' said Mrs Beeding.

'Oh, Mum!'

'Now, don't be silly. They won't hurt you, they're more afraid of you than you are of them. Go along now, a great girl like you. What would yer Brownies say?'

'Well, can I bring it upstairs to eat?'

'You go along, now. Artie, you go with her and kill the beetles for her.'

Artie got up grumbling from the wireless cabinet and went after his sister. How wonderful that lemon yellow Beeding hair was! Amy watched the light on Baby's head as she went out of the room, and thought that their curls were like three magic wigs; only Baby's seemed to belong to her face, Dora's and Mona's seemed dropped above their plain countenances by a spell.

Dora and Mona had gone upstairs together and Mr Beeding had descended to his hell in the bakehouse, so Amy and Mrs Beeding were alone when Amy, gazing at her foster-mother, suddenly saw that she was old. Her cheeks were sunken and her broad back stooped. Amy experienced such a shock that she could not control herself, and she exclaimed impulsively:

'Dear Mrs Beeding! I *shall* miss you when I'm away!'

'That's real nice of yer, luv,' answered Mrs Beeding, looking up from her knitting. 'I'll miss you too, Amy, you're like one o' me own.'

There was a little silence.

'Did yer ever go to that place in the country, where yer Dad and Mother was born, Amy? You was talking about going last summer.'

Amy nodded, staring into the bright red stove.

'I didn't find anybody. I hoped there might be someone, some relations perhaps, belonging to Mother, but there weren't. My grandfather's offices had just been pulled down, a week or two before I went. The chemist opposite remembered him. He told me—he said he remembered him quite well.'

She would never forget the contemptuous pity in the old Scots chemist's voice when he spoke of her grandfather. But then, too, she would always remember how his tone had softened when he spoke of 'the daughter—that was a bonny girl, it did you good to hear her laugh. Did you know her, perhaps?' But she would never tell that to Mrs Beeding, nor to anyone.

'It was a lovely place,' she said, leaning back in her chair. 'The bells kept ringing; near, you know, and then far away, all day.'

'Give you the miseries, bells,' said Mrs Beeding severely. After a pause—

'Amy, you must be right lonely up in that place o' yours. When're you goin' to get married?'

Amy stared at her, then opened her mouth, but could think of nothing to say and so was silent. Mrs Beeding went on.

'Me and Miss Lathom both think the same about you. I was up at the School the other day. They had a Bazaar to get money for that Missionary Society o' theirs that they are always going on about, and I went along to see if there was anything would do for Baby. I had quite a long talk with Miss Lathom about you.'

'Did you?' said Amy feebly.

'Aye. She's an educated woman, Miss Lathom is (though she's that sensible with it you'd never notice it), but she agreed wi' me. She thinks you ought to get married.'

'I'm not lonely, Mrs Beeding, honestly I'm not,' protested Amy. Not even to her foster-mother could she tell her vague, nameless troubles.

'Oh, yes you are. And lookin' peaky, too.'

'I'm all right, really.'

'When did y'have a headache last?'

'Oh . . . day before yesterday . . . but——'

'And cried, too, I'll lay.'

'Oh, well . . . not much, truly. At least——'

'There y'are. I can see, I'm not blind, like some. Now what

you ought to do is ter find some nice young man at one o' those posh parties you go to, and marry him.'

'But I don't want to, I'm all right, I don't want to marry anybody, it 'ud be awful, I shouldn't know what to do, with somebody there all the time,' Amy said, a little wildly.

'Everybody ought to get married,' pronounced Mrs Beeding, 'because it's natural. It's good for human beings like rain's good for the plants. Look at Mona, she's twice the girl since she married Syd. Not that she ever was much, Mona,' she added, after a pause in which the knitting stayed suspended, and its owner reflected.

'Oh, well, p'raps you'll find someone in America,' she concluded, glancing keenly at Amy's troubled face. 'Anyway, that's what you ought to do, so you keep it in mind.'

'Have you seen Old Porty lately?' said Amy quickly, determined to change the subject.

'There!' Mrs Beeding excitedly raised the knitting and lowered it again. 'I knew I had something to tell yer! He's lost his job.'

'Porty has?'

'Aye. He met Dora in the High Street one night last week and told her. After fifteen years. No pension, not even a bonus. Just told him he was too old and packed him off with a month's pay.'

'Good, I'm glad,' said Amy, fiercely, yet with a dreary ring in her young voice. 'Beastly old thing, serve him right.'

'Aye. And 'tisn't as though he hadn't had all the fun he wanted while his money lasted, the wicked old sinner. I'll lay he never put a penny by, neither.'

'What'll he do, Mrs Beeding?' Amy was trying not to think about Porty's ageing, veined hands on the wheel of his car, as she had seen them four years ago. I'm not sorry for him, wicked ugly old pig, he deserves it, she thought hardly.

'I don't know, Amy. It's difficult enough for the young ones nowadays, let alone old ones.'

'Oh, well . . . we don't care, do we, Mrs Beeding?'

'It's a judgment on him, there's no doubt about that,' agreed Mrs Beeding.

But her eyes, lifted from the knitting, rested just for an instant on the mink coat.

Amy rode home in a taxi that night after the good-byes, the kisses, the good-luck wishes had been exchanged, leaving the Beedings grouped on the doorstep of 5 Highbury Walk waving her farewell. She leant back with a sigh, recognizing with dread the creeping onslaught of a headache, and shut her eyes.

Now she had said her last good-bye. Lord and Lady Welwoodham were coming to the train to see her off, and she had looked in at the offices of *The Prize* yesterday to bid farewell to Mr Danesford and Miss Grace. They had both been rather surprised to see her, but Mr Danesford had given her his good wishes with the touch of condescension that he always kept for the former office-girl, poor Lee's daughter. He had never quite forgiven her for deceiving *The Prize* about *The River Boy*, and only seemed pleased at her success because it was well known that *The Prize* had published her first story, and any fame belonging to Amy must indirectly belong also to *The Prize*. Amy always felt a little envious and depressed after she had seen him, because he was so plainly a contented man. She suspected him of having some private grief that darkened his life (though he had never once uttered a word that gave her cause to suspect as much), but his work on *The Prize* and his attachment to the paper seemed to make up for it. Amy was young, rich and famous, but she was less content with her lot than Mr Danesford, the ageing sub-editor on a slowly dying magazine.

Miss Grace had filled the office on the occasion of Amy's farewell visit with the familiar hot-vinegar odour of envy. The words *Upstart* and *Cheat* seemed to hover in the air above Miss Grace's elaborately curled head, and she could barely bring herself to give Amy a sour farewell smile. Miss Grace had worked off her feeling about Amy by building up an elaborate theory among her friends that Amy had a man friend who wrote all her books, based on the fact that Maurice Beeding had once rung Amy up at the office with some information about dog-racing which she wanted to work into a story. Miss Grace's friends used to nod their heads and compress their lips and smile whenever Amy's books came up in conversation, and if envy and hard work on the Man-Friend theory could have miraculously procured Miss Grace a mink jacket, Miss Grace would have had more mink jackets than she knew what to do with. But as she said good-bye to Amy Miss Grace had to face the fact that she had only a squirrel coney collar on a three and a half guinea coat. Small wonder that the vinegar boiled and seethed.

I hate making people jealous, suddenly thought Amy, leaning back with her eyes shut as the taxi rattled through Islington. Miss Grace was awfully jealous yesterday because I've got a fur jacket. I liked thinking she was jealous, too, because I've always hated her, but tonight I feel miserable myself and everything's in a muddle and beastly and I'm so lonely I wish I was dead.

It serves Porty right. Why should I do anything for him? He's never done anything for me. Why should you feel sorry for people who've always been beastly to you, and been wicked, too?

But on the emerald walls of the Snow Queen's Palace, that had never reflected any light but the lonely flashing of the Aurora, there must have gleamed faintly for an instant the common gold of daybreak. Before Amy sailed for America, accompanied by some smart new pigskin luggage, the kind farewells of Lord and Lady Welwoodham, and a lecture-schedule drawn up by Mr Humfriss, she had put in the post two cheques. One was for a hundred pounds 'for dear Mrs Beeding with love from Amy,' and one was for twenty pounds, and made out to E. Talbot Porteous, c/o Murray's Hotel, King's Cross. With it went this note:

'DEAR PORTY,
I am sorry you are down on your luck. Please accept this.
Wishing you good luck.

AMY LEE.'

Ungracious, stiff with dislike as the note was, all the icy bastions
of the Palace trembled. For about its walls swept the first warm
breath of the conquering spring.

19

At four o'clock on a June afternoon Lou was still trying to make up her mind whether to go to Mrs Boadman's reception.

She was sitting at the table in the sewing-room finishing the hem of a dress by hand, and thinking what a nuisance it was that a reception for an English writer in Vine Falls (where receptions were rare and English writers even rarer) should have to be held at the Boadman home. There were so many other homes to which Lou would sooner have gone!

Since she had had to give up all hope of two years at a dress-designing school in New York, she had made it a practice to accept every invitation she received, sensibly deciding that a full social life in a small town was better than no social life at all. Parties in Vine Falls were dull compared with those imaginary parties in New York about which her fancy had played, but at least she was Somebody at the parties in Vine Falls, and it was more satisfying to be a big fish in a little sea than a frustrated fish who refused to swim in any social ocean. And, quite apart from her habit of accepting local invitations, she had wanted to meet this English writer; the dress she was finishing had been designed and made for this very ocasion. Oh, yes, she had been looking forward to it; it was only an hour or two ago that the quietness of the empty, sunny house had begun to creep over her spirits in a vague sadness, and then her depression had ended (as all depression did nowadays) in thoughts of Bob, and she had remembered how inquisitive and cruel Mrs Boadman could be.

'The hell with the old battleaxe,' thought Lou, reaching for the cotton. 'I feel just like going out. It would take me out of myself, as they put it. There certainly is nothing like a quiet summer afternoon alone in the house for making a girl realize that time is fleeting. But if I go, that old heel is sure to ask if we've heard from Bob lately, and I know Miss Cordell will ask me right out where he is; she doesn't believe a word of that Down South story, she as good as told Mother so. Oh, well. Maybe if I don't open my mouth and stay all evening behind the radiogram . . .'

She sighed. Her nature from childhood had been curiously without illusions or dreams. She had never been unthinkingly happy, as most of the young people in Vine Falls were happy, but she had had a cool appreciation of the good things of life and the climate of her spirit had been equable, dry yet bright like a pleasant day in any season of the year. Now even this moderate happiness (Greek in its natural wisdom, although Lou did not suspect it) had been driven away by Bob's disappearance; and when his sister sighed it was because she could not imagine ever regaining her former ease of mind. She had always loved Bob deeply, as a naturally sophisticated nature will sometimes love a simple one, and her distress in watching the misery that was torturing her mother, and the helpless rage that was making an old man of her father, was increased by her own ceaseless anxiety.

But she did not believe that Bob would never come back to them. She had said to her mother, in the first dreadful days after he had gone:

'I'm sure he'll come back. I've got a cast-iron hunch he will. He's so good, naturally good, like a dog or a nice kid. Life doesn't smash up that sort of person. He'll stop being crazy and then he'll come home.'

And this had been all the comfort Mrs Vorst had been able to find in the three months since Bob had disappeared.

For all efforts to trace Dan Carr by private detectives had been useless; and Mr Vorst had been hindered by the fact that he did not dare to inform the police. If he had told them that his son was last heard of in the company of a small time gangster who had promised him 'a job,' he might draw Bob into a net that would end in his ruin and death. The father raged, but he raged helplessly. The boy was of age and could do as he chose. So long as he did not drive a car in the State of New Leicester he was on the right side of the Law, and if he wanted to run with mobsmen, neither his father nor the police could stop him. He had chosen to share the gangsters' dangers and if he came up against the police in doing so they could shoot him, but they could neither arrest nor kill him so long as he did not break the law. A father could not say to the police: 'I think my boy is in bad company; find him and save him for me.' And his family did not even know if he was still with Dan.

Since the night that Helen had watched him walk through the doors of the Black Lake Hotel, silence had fallen over him, and not a word nor a glimpse nor a rumour had broken that silence. He might have been dead—except that had he been dead they might sometimes have spoken of him only with love and sorrow.

The family had prepared a story that he had gone South to continue his medical studies in Louisiana, where Mrs Vorst's brother, the doctor, lived; and most of their old friends and neighbours pretended to believe it. But gradually Vine Falls as a whole had come to realize that something mighty queer had happened to Bob Vorst.

This was the fault, naturally, of Myron.

Myron had been surprisingly moved out of his usual malicious detachment by Bob's disappearance, and he had not been able to hold his tongue after years of letting it wag. His contempt for his buddies in Vine Falls and his grudging loyalty to the Vorsts had prevented him from telling everything that he knew to the pool-rooms and bars, but he had not been able to prevent himself from hinting. The story had spread from south of the tracks to the residential district, and it was too good a story for people not to listen to it. Many kind neighbours disbelieved it, but many others did believe it and were both shocked and sorry, while a minority was eager to find out as many facts as possible and to enjoy a thrill.

The Boadmans came in this last class; and that was why Lou did not want to go to their home to meet the famous English writer Amy Lee.

But towards five o'clock, when the dress was pressed and hanging by the window in the sunlight, Lou's desire to exchange the quiet of the sunlit house for voices and company proved too strong for her, and she went upstairs to put on the new dress. After all, she thought, if I'm there I can at least quash any stories that old battleaxe spreads around, and maybe she won't say so much if I'm there, either. I'll go.

Amy stood in the centre of a group with a polite serious expression on her face, listening. In one hand she held a glass full of golden drink and in the other a cigarette from which a piece of ash occasionally fell to the ground. The large room was full of people and the air was thick with smoke, and if anyone there had had ears sufficiently sensitive to mind an ugly noise they would have noticed the ugly noise of voices talking foolishly and fast, like ghosts gabbling in Hell. But no-one noticed the uproar except Amy, and she was getting used to it, for it seemed to her, as she stood there politely listening and sometimes sipping her golden drink, that for the last two months she had lived in an uproar and had never been away from crowds of people.

Her heart (already troubled by its own coldness before she left England) had been touched by the admiration, the kindness and hospitality which she had everywhere found in America; and she felt that she was a kinder, friendlier person than she had been two months ago because of the welcome she had received; it was impossible not to be warmed by so much kindness. But she had made no friends, although she had made many pleasant acquaintanceships which might have ripened into friendships had they been given time, and there had been times when she had found herself wishing rather drearily amid the clamour and the crowds that she had never come to America.

It was not the America she had loved in the stories of her childhood; the Land of The Free, where the feathered headdress of the Indian and the black face of the negro were woven with the white hood of the prairie schooner and the dull gleam on the rattlesnake into one marvellous tapestry, bordered with the red maple leaves of the fall. It was just a country new to her, where she liked the people and enjoyed the novel food and the sense of great tracts of country lying all about her; but where her chief happiness, so far, had been in those moments when she had recognized some custom or object (distorted by time but still identifiable) that was dear and familiar to her from the pages of American books she had loved in her childhood. And there had not been many of those moments.

The tour had seemed like a confused and noisy dream in which she, its central figure, obediently read aloud the lectures prepared for her, and was afterwards applauded, fêted, and asked questions which she found it simplest to answer by a shake of her head, a nod, or a smile.

But it had been a comfort to realize that the Americans whom she met at receptions seemed to like her better than the English people she had met at Lady Welwoodham's parties. The remarks that she made about her stories or about the news of the day, her mild little jokes and her shy inquiries about those things in American life that interested her, were received by Americans with attention and apparent pleasure, and she had found, with a heartening sensation of being understood, that she could talk as 'ordinarily' (as she called it) to most Americans as she did to the Beedings.

Her only encounter with that doubtful and amused expression which had disturbed her when she saw it on the charming and intelligent faces of Lady Welwoodham's friends had been in New York, where her agent gave a party for the Press to meet Amy Lee. Some of the smart newspaperwomen had looked at her knowingly, as if they could see that she was playing a joke on them, and some of them had been condescending, as if she had been a soppy kid. And when the interviews appeared in the New York papers some of them had had headlines like: SO SIMPLE: AMY LEE RIBS NEW YORK, and others had said: JUST A DAISY IN THE FIELD: AMY LEE CAN'T TALK. It had been unpleasant, and had cast a shadow over the beginning of her American tour which had only been dispersed by the simple kindness she had met in the smaller towns.

(The newspaper-women, in fact, were still wondering whether Amy was too green to be real or whether she was the most sophisticated thing that had hit the city since Dorothy Parker. Their experiences had prepared them for reporting every type of publicity-hunter except a person who never thought about publicity at all, and it was not unnatural that they had fallen down on the story.)

Amy's childhood interest in America had revived at the prospect of visiting the country, but it had again faded as the weeks went on and she did not find her dream-America except in the kind hearts of its people. Her itinerary took her from cities to small towns and back again to cities, and she could never stay long enough in any one of the places she visited to absorb its special atmosphere; therefore all American cities and small towns seemed much alike to her. Only New York had seemed different from all the other places. In spite of her unfortunate experiences with the newspaper-women, she had liked the sparkling streets of New York under its hard blue sky, and had been sorry to leave it. And now the tour was nearly over, Vine Falls was the last town but two on her itinerary, and here she was in Vine Falls, the only town in America which was linked with her childhood, the only place where someone had once lived who had seen her and talked to her when she was a little girl living in a secret world.

She had looked forward all through her tour to visiting Vine Falls, hoping wistfully that there, in the town with the pretty name where her American had lived, she might find the America of her childhood. But on alighting from the train at the depot she had been gushingly received by a large smart woman called Mrs Boadman and a committee of ladies, who at once whisked her off to the hotel where the lecture was to be given; she had barely had time for a glance through the windows of the car before they arrived.

However, she had seen a brightness in the air, a profusion of snowball bushes and lilacs in the gardens, a glimpse between the houses of distant hills lending mystery to the view, that made this town seem different from all the other places she had visited; and all through the lecture, and even now as she stood in Mrs Boadman's apartment listening politely to an elegant middle-aged man talking about American literature, she was wishing that she could slip away by herself and explore Vine Falls. She wanted to wander through its streets as she did in London, unrecognized and in old clothes, watching and listening and remembering that day long ago when she had talked to the American boy outside Kenwood House. He would be grown up by now, of course, and gone away; Americans did not live in the same place for years as English people did, but it would be delightful to wander through the streets where he had walked to school and think about him.

I suppose (Amy lifted her glass and took a sip, her light brown eyes fixed steadily upon the face of the elegant elderly man) the way I've always felt about that American boy is the nearest I've ever been to being in love. It's awfully queer. And it was queer, too, seeing the picture of that young man with his head on the red cushion looking just like my American grown up.

I do wonder what my American looks like now?

And then she happened to glance away from the elderly man for an instant towards the crowd in the background, and gave such a start that she nearly dropped her glass.

A face, smiling under a slanting grey hat like a young man's, was moving slowly towards her.

Her heart began to beat fast. She could not take her eyes from that face—so strangely familiar and dear!—whose owner was working her way through the crowd. *Her* way, for Amy could now see that the face belonged to a girl of her own age, elegantly dressed in dark grey. But the high cheekbones, the shape of the grey eyes, the sweet wide mouth, were those that had haunted Amy's imagination ever since the evening in her flat when she had seen the picture of the young man asleep on a red cushion. And as she stared, she realized that this was the face that had come between her own face and the blue eyes of the young lieutenant in her dream; it was the face of her American, Robert Somebody, grown-up!

The girl had now got clear of the crowd and was approaching their little group, with a faint wary smile. She held a pair of dark red net gloves in one hand and was swinging them gently as she came up.

'Hullo, Mrs Boadman,' she said in a high, soft voice, holding out her hand.

'Why, Lou, dear,' replied Mrs Boadman absently, taking the hand for a moment and continuing to give most of her attention to the elderly man. 'So glad you could make it. I'm sure you're just crazy to meet Miss Lee. Miss Lee, this is Lou Vorst, she's just crazy to meet you, she's a clever girl, too, she was going to do dress-designing in New York, weren't you, Lou, only——'

Amy held out her hand. She heard nothing of Mrs Boadman's speech except the name. Lou Vorst. VORST. She must be his sister, she thought, beginning to tremble. It's the same name. It sounds just the same as when *he* said it that time; and then her hand was taken in a cool clasp for a second, and the girl said:

310

'I'm very pleased to meet you, Miss Lee.'

'I'm very pleased to meet you, too, Miss Vorst,' said Amy faintly, and perhaps that sentence had never before been said in Mrs Boadman's drawing-room with such complete truth.

'You weren't at the lecture, you bad thing!' continued Mrs Boadman, pulling Lou's slender arm within her fat one. Her tone made the words offensive. 'Miss Lee told us all about her methods of work. So original. You missed quite a treat.'

'I couldn't make it. I'm sorry,' lied Lou, gently withdrawing her arm from Mrs Boadman's and reaching out to take a canapé from a tray which was being carried past. She addressed Amy, looking at her with interest. She's a funny little number but there's something cute about her, decided Lou. She certainly does stare. I wonder if maybe my hat is on crooked? Amy smiled vaguely, but did not reply and continued to stare.

At this moment Mrs Boadman was called away by her daughter Elenor to greet some important new arrival. Amy, Lou and the elderly man were left alone, and he was just opening his mouth to continue his lecture on American literature when he was hailed by an acquaintance and, excusing himself with a smile, turned away. Amy and Lou were now, by one of those chances which sometimes occur at crowded receptions, left facing one another in a corner which was sufficiently apart from the rest of the room for them to feel themselves alone, and to carry on a conversation in comparative comfort.

They looked at one another in silence for a moment. Then Amy began to say something but Lou began to speak at the same instant, and they both laughed.

'I'm so sorry—you were going to say something.'

'No, do go on.'

'It wasn't anything original,' said Lou. 'I was only going to ask you the usual question about this being your first visit to Vine Falls?'

'Yes, it is, but I was so looking forward to coming here,' replied Amy, so earnestly that Lou was surprised.

'Mighty nice of you,' she said a little drily; she had taken a fancy to Amy, and it was disappointing to hear her making the type of remark usually made by visiting celebrities.

'You think I don't mean it, don't you?' Amy had gone pink with distress, but for once she did not take refuge in silence when confronted by a suspicious, yet amused glance. She was so anxious to talk to Lou, and to find out if she had a brother!

'Why, Miss Lee—surely—I didn't mean——' Lou felt that she had been rude, and was embarrassed.

'No, I'm sure you didn't, it's only that people don't always believe I mean what I say. I don't know why. I suppose they think a person can't write books and be sincere at the same time. I really did mean it. I *did* want to come to Vine Falls. I—I had a special reason,' ended Amy, suddenly feeling so desolate that tears came to her eyes, and she turned away to hide them, putting her glass beside Lou's on the piano.

'Why, I'm so sorry, Miss Lee,' said Lou gently, not knowing quite what to say but feeling more interested in Amy every moment. 'It's just that Vine Falls is a small town, you know, and we live in it all the year round, and I guess it seems strange to us that a writer like yourself, who goes places and gets around, should want to come to a place like this. But maybe if you had a special reason——'

Lou was as sophisticated as a small town society girl could be, but she had never lost one of her childhood weaknesses: she liked to find out. The little girl who had gossiped with Myron was now grown up, but she still enjoyed hearing secrets and getting sidelights on the odd corners in human nature. She was longing to know Amy Lee's 'special reason' for wanting to visit Vine Falls.

'Well, I had. Only when I come to—to tell somebody (you

see, I've never told anybody before) it seems—soppy,' said Amy, staring at Lou desperately. 'Crazy, you'd say, if I told you.'

'Oh, *do* tell me!' coaxed Lou, lowering her voice a little and moving her charming face, so like Bob's with its faintly Indian look and thick fair eyelashes, a little nearer to Amy's own.

But at that moment——

'Miss Lee, here's Miss Cordell just crazy to meet you,' announced Mrs Boadman, coming up with a small old woman. 'Miss Cordell's a great reader, she read *Gone with the Wind* three times. Miss Lee, Miss Cordell.' And Mrs Boadman, waving to someone, rushed away.

Amy held out her hand, but Miss Cordell did not take it. Instead, she gave a stiff little bow and folded both her own tiny gloved hands upon the tall ivory handle of an antique sunshade. She was nearly seventy, and very ancient indeed by American standards. She wore the dim nondescript clothes worn by unfashionable old women all over the Western world and a hat with squashed tremulous roses on it, but her back was straight and her eyes were sharp and her voice was firm.

'Well, Miss Lee (*no, Lou Vorst, don't you try to get away from me, you stay right here until I'm ready to talk to you about that brother of yours, I want to know all about it and I want the truth, this time*) I liked your lecture, Miss Lee, but I don't like your books.'

And Miss Cordell, settling her hands more firmly upon the handle of her sunshade, unhurriedly surveyed Amy from head to foot, at the same time moving across the corner so that Lou could not escape.

'Don't you?' said Amy faintly. What was that remark to Lou about *that brother of yours*? She looked steadily at the old woman, but her thoughts were not on what she was hearing.

'No, I don't, and what's to stop me saying so in spite of Nell Boadman pulling my jacket' (here Miss Cordell twitched herself free from Mrs Boadman, who had grasped the situation in passing, seized the old lady's tail, and was agitatedly jerking at it), 'No, my dear, I don't like your books. You write about people on the wrong side of the law, and we've still got quite enough of that right here in New Leicester without the children reading about it in books.'

'Oh, come now, Lucy, you'll have Miss Lee thinking we're overrun with gangsters right here in Vine Falls,' protested another lady pleasantly; she had already been introduced to Amy as Mrs Jonas Frankwood Senior. 'Why, I think it's wonderful the way the G-men have cleared things up.' She was about to join their group, which she had paused to address on her way to some friends at the other end of the room, but at that moment she caught sight of Lou, and looked a little embarrassed. 'Why hullo, Lou dear, I didn't see you there,' she murmured, and continued on her way.

'Still plenty of rats about, and we don't want 'em glorified in our books,' persisted Miss Cordell with a sharp glance at Lou. 'The business of literature is to elevate and improve, not to make bad men and bad ways fascinating to our boys and girls. You're a young girl, Miss Lee, and I can see you don't know much about life and you don't mean any harm, but one day you'll learn that evil can't be played with.'

She paused, putting a tiny hand in a grey glove gently on Lou's arm, but continued to address Amy, looking severely yet sorrowfully into her eyes:

'Why, haven't I seen one of the dearest boys in the world, this girl's own brother . . . my cousin Amalie and I have known him since he was born and she taught him to play the piano . . . a fine young man, going to be a doctor. Now he's got into bad ways, running around with gangsters . . .'

She suddenly turned on Lou, who was watching her with a pale but composed face.

'Isn't that so, Lou?' she said sharply. 'Doesn't everybody know it?'

Lou said nothing, and Miss Cordell went on.

'And now his own mother doesn't know where he is. Your books won't help him to come to his senses, nor help people like me to pray for him . . . as I do every night of my life. He comes of a fine old family, too. One of the oldest families in New Leicester.' She drew Lou a little closer, and her expression softened. 'Been settled here since the War.'

'The War?' To Amy, the Englishwoman, there was only one War. But Lou explained, her face a study in amusement and resentment and another feeling that Amy, with a shock, recognized as grief:

'*Our* War, Miss Lee. The one between the North and the South.'

'*You're* one of the forces, Miss Lee, that's helping to break up civilization,' concluded Miss Cordell firmly. 'Anyway, your books are, and it comes to the same thing. You think it over. Try and write something sweet and homey that the women'll like. Good-day to you,' and she gave Amy another stiff little nod and turned towards Lou. But the expression on Lou's face, and the sudden recollection that they were not alone, and that Mrs Boadman and her daughter were gossips—seemed to change her mind. All she did was to take Lou's hand again, give it an affectionate squeeze, and look at her for a moment. Then she smiled painfully and turned away.

Lou took a glass from a passing tray and held it out to Amy, but Amy shook her head.

'Well, I will. I need it.' Lou drank half the contents, and set it down beside the other on the piano. She looked as if she were trying to put something out of her mind.

'Miss Lee,' she said, 'you've got me all worked up about your special reason for wanting to come to my home town. Are you in a hurry to get away after this show? If you could spare the time I'd just love to drive you round and show you places. And then,' she smiled charmingly, 'maybe you could tell me what the special reason is?'

'I should love to come,' stammered Amy, more confused and excited every moment. 'My train doesn't go till nine o'clock, so I should have time. The only thing is, I'm afraid someone on the Committee, Mrs Frankwood, I think, was going to drive me to the station.'

'Tell them you'd rather go with me,' said Lou coolly. 'What's the use of being famous if you can't throw a temperament?'

'But wouldn't that seem rather——' Amy was beginning doubtfully, when there occurred another interruption.

'Miss Lee,' announced Mrs Boadman, bustling up, 'I'm so sorry. It really is too bad, but our Committee member who was going to drive you to the depot, Mrs Frankwood, has just been called up to say she must go into Morgan, her daughter's sick.'

'I'm so sorry,' murmured Amy.

'Isn't it just too bad? I'll find someone else, of course. I'd have been honoured if I or my daughter could have driven you down. We have two cars. But unfortunately we've both got engagements for later this evening (you know what girls are for going places evenings! and I'm nearly as bad!). Now I wonder who would——'

'I'll be glad to drive Miss Lee to the depot,' said Lou quickly. 'She wants to see something of the town, too. We can take a little run around.'

'Why, that's sweet of you, Lou. I'm so pleased. You two girls have got quite a crush on each other, isn't that nice.' And Mrs Boadman glanced from Amy's face to Lou's. Her own expression was not made less acid by the conspiratorial solemnity of theirs. After exchanging one lightning glance on her approach which said *Oh Lord Here Comes The Old Trout Again*, they had composed their faces, but unfortunately they had composed them so well that Mrs Boadman was quite sure they had been tearing her apartment and her character to shreds.

'Well, that's fine. Now, Miss Lee, Lou has had you quite long enough. I've got two perfectly lovely people here I'd love to have you meet.' And Mrs Boadman hurried away to get the two perfectly lovely people.

'All right, then,' said Lou. 'As soon as the party breaks up, we'll go. It won't be long now. How about eating somewhere? Or would you sooner eat on the train?'

'I'd sooner eat with you, if you'd like to?'

'Fine. We'll go to Roselands. That's a place where two females can eat alone. They've got a terrace over the lake there, where my brother used to take his dates.'

Amy nodded. She could hardly speak. The American boy was coming nearer every moment. His presence (an unknown personality, but the eyes were like this girl's eyes and the mouth smiled in the same way) filled the room. That old woman had spoken of him, and Lou had looked so sad, and now she had spoken of him herself. So he used to take girls to dine on a terrace above the lake! Amy saw a fair head and wide shoulders leaning towards a dark head and a white frock, and the sheen of moonlight on water, and suddenly experienced a novel and disagreeable emotion. It was her first attack of jealousy, and none the easier to bear because she was jealous of a kind of ghost! I must be going mad, she thought wildly.

'I'll come and fetch you a bit later on,' smiled Lou, and moved away across the room, which was already growing less crowded.

Left alone for a moment, Amy looked about her in search of a chair, and when she discovered one, close to her, she sat down, suddenly feeling so tired that she could not stand up a moment longer. The large room with its modern wallpaper in a design of blue and grey tulips on a red ground, the late afternoon sunlight pouring through the open windows, the blue haze of the cigarette smoke, the chairs covered in red, blue and grey striped satin, the laughing faces and the sound of the shrill voices, all became dim and faraway. She shut her eyes.

At once she saw a picture.

*

But it was not a coloured and moving copy of an actual scene. It was a blurred photograph in a newspaper, and she was looking down at it as it lay on the floor at her feet. She could make out a kind of cabin made from rough-hewn logs, and some trees with pointed tips that looked like pines, and there was a group of men standing round something—it looked like a heap of dark clothes—lying on the ground. She gradually made out a streak of white between some dark shapes in one corner, and somehow she knew that it must be a swift mountain river rushing between large boulders. And as she looked, a horror of the scene came over her; the dark pines, the blurred group of men looking down at the motionless object on the ground, and the half-ruined cabin in the background were horrible; they were wicked, and they terrified her.

'Miss Lee! Here are two lovely people who are crazy to meet you!'

She opened her eyes, and looked dazedly into Mrs Boadman's smiling face. Only the picture and that sense of wickedness were real, and she could not realize where she was. Then, as Mrs Boadman stared at her curiously and the man and woman standing just behind her began to look surprised, she collected herself and stood up hastily, murmuring polite phrases. Her agitation and inexplicable alarm were by now so acute that she hardly knew how to reply to the friendly questions of her two new acquaintances, and the party suddenly became unendurable to her. The loud voices of the few people left in the room, the smell of smoke, the strong taste of alcohol in her mouth, all increased her nervous distress, and she longed for fresh air and silence and an opportunity to confide her recent extraordinary experience to Lou.

The liking which Lou had at once felt for her had been mutual; it was more than a fanciful wish to spend an hour with a girl who looked like her American that made Amy wish Lou would hurry up and get them both away from the party. I'll tell her all about it, she thought. I'll tell her how he gave me the coin, and how I've always remembered him, and how I saw the picture of that young man with his head on a cushion, looking so like my American grown up. I'll tell her everything queer that's ever happened to me about the American boy, and then I'll ask her if she thinks he's her brother and if I'm going crazy. I shan't mind telling her, because I like her. She reminds me of Dora (only she's younger, of course, and smarter) and I'm sure she'll be sensible about it all.

Amy had fastened upon the quality of Lou which, next to her haunting likeness to a memory, was the one most likely to attract her. Amy herself was the least sensible of girls, ridden by a violent imagination and made unhappy by strong and unexpressed feelings whose existence she only half-suspected and for which she had no outlet. It was inevitable that the good sense in Lou's manner should charm her as much as the cool friendliness. Lou, on her side, was equally charmed by the child-like earnestness and strength of emotion which she divined in Amy. These qualities, so different from her own, were not common in the girls of Vine Falls, and for Lou they had all the attraction of novelty.

Therefore, when the two girls drove away half an hour later with Lou at the wheel, both were pleased at having escaped together and at the prospect of enjoying an hour or so's companionship, which might develop into a friendship. Amy's spirits rose a little as they moved off down the wide pleasant road bordered with shady trees through which the sunlight came with tempered heat in long evening rays. There was a spirit of energy mingled with one of tranquillity in the air of this little town which she had encountered nowhere else in America, and it was impossible not to feel happier under its influence. But even her pleasure at being in Vine Falls, even the fairytale delight of driving down Sycamore Avenue with a girl who looked just like Robert

Somebody himself, could not completely banish Amy's agitation. She was unpleasantly, deeply disturbed, and *afraid*.

Presently Lou gave a little laugh.

'What is it?' asked Amy, smiling too.

'Oh, I was just thinking I have a nerve, carrying off a visiting celebrity like this. Mrs Boadman didn't like it at all.'

'I didn't like her. She's got a beastly face,' said Amy.

Lou blinked, then glanced at her.

'Yes, it's downright mean, but we don't usually say so. Miss Lee, do you always speak your mind right out like that?'

'Well——' Amy considered. 'I don't say much, because (since I got famous, you know) people sort of—pay too much attention to what I say. They won't believe I mean just *what* I say and nothing else. I used to get awfully miserable about it at parties in London.'

'Smart Alecs,' murmured Lou. 'So clever they fall right down and go boom. I know.'

'But it's quite easy to talk to you because I like you,' Amy ended.

'That goes for me too,' said Lou cheerfully, turning to smile at her.

'I'm so glad! I've never had a friend of my own age.'

Lou felt a little as if she had stepped into the pages of *Melbourne House*, but her inward smile only added a glint of her dry humour to a situation which she found oddly moving. Amy Lee certainly was a funny little number! But she was very likable. The unexpected thought crossed Lou's mind that Amy was like Bob. She had the same lack of sophistication, yet the same unaggressive confidence in herself. He used to be like a nice kid, thought Lou, and she's rather the same.

It seemed to Amy that there was no pause before she answered:

'I'd like to be friends with you, too.'

She instinctively chose the simplest words, and was rewarded by Amy's expression.

'Oh, I *am* glad! Because a lot of extraordinary things have been happening to me, and I want to ask your advice about them.'

'I'll certainly be pleased to do what I can, Miss Lee.' Lou answered, with the formality which gives sometimes a quaint attraction to the speech of educated American girls. She added, unable to resist her curiosity:

'Is it something to do with your "special reason" for wanting to come here?'

'Yes, it is.' Amy clasped her hands together. 'Only the whole thing sounds so absolutely barmy—crazy, you know—that I don't like to tell you about it. I'm afraid you'll think I'm going mad, or else telling lies.'

'I promise I won't.'

Amy sighed. 'It *is* such an extraordinary business—and, of course, there may not be anything in it, after all, and then you *will* think I'm mad.'

'I won't. I promise I won't. There are few things I enjoy more than a really extraordinary business. Go on, Miss Lee! Shoot!'

'Well——' Amy hesitated. 'Will you promise not to ask any questions about what I'm going to tell you until I've asked *you* some questions?'

Lou nodded.

'No matter how much you want to?'

Lou nodded again.

'All right, then.' Amy took one rather desperate glance around her at the vacant lots where children were playing past which they were now driving. Then she pressed both hands tightly together and asked quickly in a low voice:

'Have you any brothers?'

'Two,' answered Lou quickly, glancing at her, her face suddenly alarmed.

'Oh, please don't look like that! Did either of them ever go to England?'

'Why, yes. My youngest brother Bob did, about ten years ago. In 1928, I think it was, or thereabouts.'

'Oh!' Amy gave a little gasp. 'And—and did he go to London, do you know?'

'Surely. My mother went on the trip too, and my Aunt Carol Viner. We were all very thrilled about it, because it was the first time any of the family'd been to Europe since my father's people sailed from Holland in the seventeenth century.'

'Oh. Well, I'm sure it must have been your brother I met outside Kenwood House in London when I was a little girl. He gave me a shilling for my birthday. At least, he thought it was a shilling, but it was really five cents. I've still got it. And I've never forgotten him. That's all.'

She was so agitated by this time that she could hardly get the words out, and Lou had to incline her head towards her to hear the end of the sentence.

'But——' began Lou.

'I thought you *must* be his sister, you see, because you're so like him. You *are* like him, aren't you?'

'Oh, yes. We're so alike it's a family joke. But how could you possibly have remembered——'

'Well, that's what's so queer,' said Amy faintly. 'You see, I did remember what your brother looked like as a little boy. I've always remembered his face perfectly. But, of course, I couldn't know what he looked like when he was grown up, because I'd never seen him. But—but just before I came to America I—I did see him. In a kind of dream. Only I wasn't really asleep, I was just resting.'

'You saw *Bob*? But how?'

Amy nodded. 'He was asleep, with his head against a red cushion, and he looked so ill.'

Lou, looking utterly bewildered, could only shake her head. She had stopped the car under a group of trees on the edge of a field, and she now turned to Amy and demanded:

322

'But how could you know it was *Bob* in the dream?'

'He was so like the little boy I remembered, only grown up, of course. And—and I saw him another time, too, in a real dream, that time. His face—was quite close to mine, and he was—smiling.'

'See here,' Lou started the engine again, 'Miss Lee, we can't go to Roselands, we shall only meet half Vine Falls there. Shall we go home? We can hunt in the ice-box for something to eat, and then we can talk this out.'

'Oh, yes, let's go to your home! You're not angry, are you?' she added timidly.

'Of course not. But I *am* just a little bit scared. It's all so creepy. And I suppose you must have heard what Miss Cordell said. You see, Bob isn't with us any more. We don't know where he is. Oh, we can't talk here! Let's get home.'

For some moments they drove in silence. Then Amy said:

'You see, when I saw you at the party, you looked so like him that I knew you must be some sort of relation.'

Lou nodded.

'And—and I was sort of worried about that picture of him I saw on the cushion. I felt I must tell you about it. And when Miss Cordell said he was running around with gangsters, I felt awful.'

'We don't even know if he's still with the gangsters. We don't know if—we don't know *anything*,' said Lou, accelerating. 'That's what's so hard.'

'You see, the only time I ever saw him, he was so kind.' Tears came to Amy's eyes. 'My mother had died about a year ago and it was my birthday and I told him about it, and he said, "*Gee, I'm sorry. That's bad*".'

Lou smiled.

'That sounds just like Bob. He was the nicest kid. Until three months ago, he was the swellest guy around, too.' Her soft high voice played ironically yet tenderly on the slang words.

'Then he had a car smash and killed a little girl and put a boy's eye out. He was acquitted, but my Dad made the mistake of getting a crooked lawyer to help him get off and—and I think some of the jury were fixed too, and that sent Bob quite crazy. He just went off.'

'Ran away, do you mean?'

'He told my cousin he was going off with a small-time gangster, a man we used to know when we were kids. She drove him out to a hotel in the mountains where he said he was going to meet this man, and we've never seen him since.'

'How can you bear it?' cried Amy, so violently that Lou glanced at her, startled.

'It is pretty bad. But I can bear it because I'm sure he'll come back.'

'Are you? Why?'

'I don't know. I just am. I'm not at all a suggestible type, Miss Lee, and I never get hunches. But I just do have a hunch about this. I know Bob as well as I know myself, and I know he'll come back.'

Amy was silent. Her feelings were so confused, and she was so troubled by the dread that had haunted her ever since she had seen the blurred newspaper photograph, that she was glad to lean back for the rest of the journey without saying another word, and to let her mind play over what Lou had just told her. But the situation had developed so uncannily, one piece of it fitting into another like a puzzle with such strange precision, that she could not think clearly nor come to any conclusions, except that she was sorry—so sorry for the trouble that had overtaken her happy young American, and longed to help him. He was now a real person, not a kind of ghost, and so much had her feelings about him deepened and changed since earlier in the afternoon that she no longer remembered, as they drove through Vine Falls, that she had longed to wander through the streets dreaming about the little boy that he had been. Now she was on her way with his sister to the house that had been his home. Had anyone told her as she stepped out of the train at Vine Falls that this was to happen to her, she would have been overwhelmed with excitement and happiness. But now it only seemed the natural thing to be doing. At Lou's home they could talk quietly and perhaps think out a way to help Bob. She thought of him now as Bob, not as My American. The ghost was rapidly becoming real, and with every moment he grew dearer and more important to the girl who had seen him once when they were children.

'Here we are,' said Lou, and drove the car between two low banks covered with long grass, where two opulent bushes laden with snowball flowers made a natural gateway to the drive. The house was white, with a graceful portico approached by three shallow circular steps, and its proportions were so pleasing and so admirably set off by the shady trees grouped at either side of it that Amy could not help exclaiming:

'Oh, what a lovely house!'

'My great-grandfather built it,' said Lou, shutting off the engine, and glancing up at the shabby, charming façade with affection. 'We like it. It's falling to pieces, but we wouldn't live anywhere else. There are only one or two houses like this in Vine Falls; my cousins, Helen and Stebby Viner, live in the one down the hill. Maybe you noticed it on the ride up.'

She opened the front door, and motioned Amy into a wide entrance hall with a small but graceful staircase. An atmosphere at once elegant, shabby and affectionate greeted Amy, which seemed familiar to her. It reminded her of the flat at Five Highbury Walk, and she immediately felt at ease.

'There's nobody home,' said Lou. 'Do come upstairs. My mother and father are away on a trip, to get Mother better from worrying about Bob, and our handy-man's out. Just a minute——' They were now crossing the landing, and she went into a room on her left. 'I'd like to have you see something.'

It was a small room, with books piled on the floor in one corner, a bed stacked with folded blankets, college pennants crossed on the walls. The white frilled curtains hung straight at the closed windows. It looked like the room of somebody who had died. And Amy, who was standing at the open door, suddenly realized with a shock whose room it was.

'Look.' Lou came towards her holding out a photograph which she had taken from the wall. 'Miss Lee—which of these boys is Bob?'

Amy took the photograph in a trembling hand, and looked at it.

It was a group of young men in rowing dress assembled outside a college building. Amy's eyes moved eagerly over the smiling young faces and stopped at last at the young man on the extreme left of the group. She put her finger gently on the picture and said faintly:

'This one.'

Lou nodded. 'Yes. That's Bob. But he doesn't look nearly so like me in this picture as he usually does, and that's why I wanted to have you see it, to see if you'd know which he was. Miss Lee' (she turned away to re-hang the picture on the wall, followed by Amy's rather wistful gaze; Amy would have liked to look at the photograph for a little longer) 'this is the strangest business, isn't it? What do you make of it, anyway?'

Amy shook her head helplessly.

'I don't know, but I think it's frightening, somehow, and I do feel—so dreadfully sorry for your brother. I do wish I could help.'

'That's lovely of you,' said Lou, over her shoulder as she led the way to her room, and meant what she said, for with every moment that they spent together she liked Amy more, feeling beneath her child-like manner a true sweetness and strength, like the taste of honey, which had nothing to do with the determined 'loveliness' that she, Lou, had always despised in women.

Both girls felt too disturbed in mind to talk much while they were freshening up, and their silence lasted while they made coffee and salad in the kitchen and carried two trays into the drawing-room.

It was nearly eight o'clock, and the neglected garden outside the long open windows was beginning to render up fragrance to the evening coolness. Amy's eye was taken by a trellis just outside the window covered with a tapestry of convolvulus (morning glories is the pretty American name), and she continued to stare at the delicate mass of tiny red, white, blue and purple horns while she ate and drank; they were all twisted in sleep now, looking so crumpled among their long pointed leaves that it was difficult to picture them as they would be tomorrow morning, unrolled, without a crease in their fragile petals.

She was also very taken with the room, where old Colonial furniture was blent with pleasant modern pieces, and the whole set off by a wallpaper striped in soft grey and patterned with flowery medallions in green and rosy lilac. The curtains, the chintz on the chairs, matched the wallpaper. White-painted shelves of books, and sketches and paintings of vigorous American faces with old-fashioned collars and out-moded hairdressings gave dignity and a sense of the Past. A grand piano, its shape shown to advantage by the long low shape of the room, shared the musical honours with a radio cabinet. It was a charming room, but its charm was not due to the silent presence of flowers whose strange fringed faces stared out at the evening light, nor to that light itself, nor to the peaceful silence. Here was a room where people had been content, had danced on the shining floor, laughed and made plans for the happy summer, the gay fall, that was coming. In this room, brisk aunts had made plans for the undoing of graceless nieces or the welfare of worthy nephews; the arrival of new babies had been announced, and people had waited to hear of deaths. There had been a proposal or two blurted by the fireplace, and young faces had turned away to the window to hide tears. Amy, sitting in silence, was almost happy—in spite of the vague dread lurking in her mind—to be where she was. This is his home, she thought. He grew up here. I've never been in such a lovely room before. No wonder he was a happy little boy.

And then came the desolate recollection that he was happy no more.

Lou was sitting opposite to Amy in silence, also staring out of the window, and wondering if the whole story were a lie arranged and carried out for some reason which she could not imagine.

Perhaps Bob had met this girl at some place, and they had decided . . .

What had they decided? What could be the reason for telling such an unconvincing lie?

No, I'm sure it's true; it's too queer not to be, decided Lou. Her doubts had only been the natural response of a sceptical nature to an unlikely tale, and she now had no reservations as she turned and said:

'Miss Lee——'

'Do call me Amy, please.'

'I'd love to have you call me Lou, too. Well, Amy, then. What do you think all this means? You must have some notion.'

Amy shook her head.

'No, I haven't. I just think it's queer and frightening.'

'Me too. The only clear thing about it is that you seem mixed up with Bob in some way.'

'Oh, *yes!*' breathed Amy, charmed in spite of her anxiety by this thought.

'You aren't psychic, are you?'

'Oh, no. These pictures of your brother were the first ones I've ever had. That's why I was so frightened.'

'You see,' Lou leant forward, with her elbows on her knees and stared at the carpet, 'it's so maddening because we can't *get* at anything! There doesn't seem to be any reason *why* you should see Bob in a dream.'

'Unless it was meant to show me he was in danger,' said Amy in a low tone.

'But what could you do, even if you did know he was in danger?'

'Well, I've told you, haven't I? And you're his sister.'

'Yes, but I already knew he was in danger. At least, I'm afraid he probably is. He mayn't be in danger of being killed, but it can't be doing him any good, knocking around with those rats.'

'I'm sure he's in danger,' Amy said in the same low voice, speaking as if to herself. 'It's always been in the back of my mind, I know that now. I've been sure of it ever since that night when I saw him asleep on the red cushion.'

'That red cushion!' Lou got up and walked round the room, lighting a cigarette. 'Why *red*? Why not green or blue or yellow?'

'Perhaps it was in some special place,' suggested Amy. 'Do you know any rooms where your brother might be where there's a red cushion?'

Lou laughed.

'America's mighty large,' she said, and sat down.

'No, but I meant a room in some house or flat, belonging to someone you know where your brother might naturally go,' explained Amy.

Lou shook her head.

'Maybe I do, but I can't think just now. I feel all balled up.' She got up again and walked over to the window and looked out at the darkening garden, where the trees were giving their usual impression of nature's indifference to human affairs. 'All I know is, you've made me feel much more worried about Bob than I was before.'

'I'm so sorry,' said Amy earnestly, 'but I felt so bad about it that I had to tell you.'

Lou said nothing for a moment, and in the silence Amy made

up her mind not to tell her about the picture she had seen only that afternoon, the blurred newspaper photograph. It had frightened Amy, but it might have nothing to do with Bob, so there was no point in letting it frighten Lou; Amy would keep it to herself.

Nevertheless, as she made this decision, she wished that she could tell Lou. Her loneliness and fear were increased by keeping this secret.

'You see,' Lou said suddenly, 'I don't like feeling helpless. And I do feel helpless about all this. What can we, you and I, *do* about it?'

'Well . . . I can keep in touch with you,' said Amy after a moment's thought.

'I hope you'll do that anyway.'

'Oh, I will! I want to. But I meant that if I have any more queer pictures I can let you know at once.'

'That's about all we can do, isn't it?'

'Yes. And if you hear anything about him, or if he comes back, you'll let me know at once, won't you?'

Lou glanced across at her, then nodded. The daylight had almost gone and there was not enough of it left to reveal the look on Amy's face, but the sound of her voice was enough to give Lou her final shock for that day. Good grief, she's in love with him, she thought, and feeling herself quite unable to deal with this extraordinary discovery while standing still in the twilight, she moved quickly to switch on the light and blundered noisily into the coffee trays which they had left on the floor, causing Amy to jump almost out of her skin.

Of course, it's only only a schoolgirl crush. She's such a funny, lonely little number, just the kind to get romantic about a man she doesn't know . . . the thoughts went vaguely through Lou's mind as she stood staring down at the upset cups, blinking in the sudden glare of light.

'I'll get a cloth,' she said, and went out of the room.

While they were on their knees clearing up the mess, Lou said:

'How much longer are you staying over here?'

'I've got two more lectures to do this week, one in Pennsylvania and one in Maryland, and then I've got to fill up a fortnight before I do the last two, in Illinois. So I'll be here about another month.'

But even as she spoke, she could not believe that she would ever really go home, back to London and her lonely luxurious flat. London seemed unreal as a dream. She could not believe that she might have to go back to England without any more news of Bob. She longed so strongly for the story to go on, to come to a middle and then to an end, that she could not face the idea that it might drag on drearily without either.

'And where're you going to stay for the fortnight?'

'New York,' answered Amy at once. 'I liked it. I want to start my new story.'

'Have you got a place to stay?'

'No, I'll have to find somewhere. Why?'

'Well, I was thinking . . . my other brother, Boone, and his wife have got an apartment in Greenwich Village that they want to let for the summer. If you stayed there, you'd feel in touch with us, wouldn't you?'

'Oh, yes, I should! I'd love to!'

'And my cousin Helen and I are going on a little trip to New York in a week or so and we could look you up.'

'That would be lovely. Perhaps you could both come and stay there with me?'

America had undoubtedly changed Amy's habits; in London it had never occurred to her to invite anyone to spend so much as a single night in her flat, and here she was extending hospitality to two girls, one of whom she had never met. But then, she did not feel that Lou was a stranger, and any cousin of Lou's must be nice.

'Thanks a lot, but we couldn't do that,' answered Lou firmly and promptly. 'My brother's wife would be mad. She doesn't like his relations. We aren't progressive enough for her.'

'She sounds horrid.'

'She is. But she can't stop us coming in for a drink sometimes. Now how about it? I'll write to Boone's agent tonight, shall I?'

'Oh, yes, please, if you would, and then he'll know I'm all right.'

'He'll feel that instinctively when I tell him who you are,' said Lou dryly.

'I wish you needn't tell him. It *is* such a nuisance. People are sure to come bothering.'

'Very well, if you'd rather not. I'll just say you're Miss Lee, a friend of mine from England. He's sure to find out and never forgive me for not stinging you for treble rent, but never mind. I'll write him tonight.'

She glanced at her watch.

'Mercy! If we're going to make your connection we'll have to hurry!'

Dazed by the crowded events of the day and by the sudden need for haste, Amy put on her hat and jacket and went upstairs to fetch the small case containing her needs for a night on the train. When she came down again Lou was speaking to the handyman in the hall. He fiddled about with some letters on a table, apparently listening to what Lou was saying, but keeping a stare of sour, piercing curiosity fixed on Amy, who was too tired and agitated to notice it. She stood in a patient attitude, gazing dreamily up the shallow white staircase and wondering if she would ever see this house again, and meet the young man whose presence seemed to haunt its rooms? Sadness and tenderness crept over her, she did not know why, and made her want to weep.

'Let's go,' said Lou coming quickly over to her. 'I certainly am sorry to hurry you off like this, but I was so taken up with what we were saying that I never noticed the time. I suppose you *must* make this connection?'

'Oh, yes. It's the only one that will get me to Bardsville in time for my lecture.'

'I was wishing you could have stayed the night here,' said Lou, getting into the car.

'Oh, I wish I could have; I do like your house so much,' and Amy turned, as the car passed between the two snowball bushes, to take a last look at the white columns glimmering through the dusk.

'You must come and stay when you've finished your lectures.'

Lou's voice was not exactly absent; Amy could tell that she was not merely being polite; but it was plain that she was thinking of something else as she spoke. She went on: 'I'm just wondering whether to tell Mother about all this. On the whole, I think I won't. It would only worry her worse than ever.'

Amy said nothing. She was suddenly wondering if there was someone else whom Lou ought to tell about 'all this'—the girl Bob was engaged to. The thought was painful, so painful that she was alarmed. I simply must stop feeling like this about him, she thought. Why, I may never see him again! A person *can't* be in love with a person they've only seen once, when they were twelve years old! It would be soppy. If only I didn't feel that he's *my* American, and nobody else's! That's what makes it so difficult to be sensible about him. Oh dear, it's all so frightening and queer, I don't know how I'm going to think about anything else for the next three weeks.

They only just made the connection. Amy had to run, and was swung up on to the train by a grinning negro porter, with wonderful animal strength, as if she had had no weight. She turned back to wave to Lou, looking as if there were a thousand things she wanted to say, but the train moved off, faster and faster, into the darkness. Lou called 'I'll write to you,' and stood waving until its lights had vanished, then walked back to the car feeling as if she had had an unusually vivid dream.

Myron came out to help her put the car away, and while they were doing so, she said:

'Dan Carr hasn't been around lately, has he?'

'Well, fer cryin' out loud! Wouldn't I hev said so, if I'd heard anythin'?'

'Yes, of course. I was only wondering . . . Myron, you think Bob'll come back, some time, don't you?'

'He'll come back if that big-mouth don't get him shot up.'

'Do you think Dan's all that dangerous? I thought you always said he was yellow.'

'So he is, yeller. But that sort, yeller an' always shootin' off their mouths, they're the sort that is dangerous. They talk so big, everybody believes 'em, an' when the time comes, they ain't no manner of use. He's the kind that gits folks into trouble an' then can't git 'em out again. Dangerous! He's dangerous like some yipping little dawg that runs under an auto an' gets the driver killed. That's all. No, he ain't been around, Lou. I'd know, if he had. I know a place up in the mountains where he hides. I was there yesterday, but he ain't been there for months.'

'Do you, Myron! Where is it?'

'Never you mind, Lou. I'm keepin' a watch, that's all. Now you go right in, I waunt to rest up fer a bit, I got to mow that lawn termorrer, and I got ter be up early.'

He went off towards the kitchen and the radio, and Lou went in to write to Boone's agent about the flat.

20

For the next three weeks Amy had to deliver her lectures, to chat pleasantly with the hundreds of people who were introduced to her and answer their questions politely and with intelligence, while it seemed to her that nothing was important except what had happened to her that afternoon at Vine Falls.

While she was staying in Illinois for the two lectures she was giving there, she was delighted to get a telephone call from Lou, who wanted to tell her that all arrangements about the apartment were now completed and that she could move in whenever she liked.

'Seen any more pictures?' inquired Lou, when they had finished talking about practical details.

'No. I've been trying to, but they won't come.'

'How do you mean—trying to?'

'Lying in the dark with my eyes shut. But it's no use. I suppose you haven't heard anything?'

'Not a thing. If I do, I'll call you up at once. There doesn't seem anything more to say, does there? I'll see you at the apartment, then, on the seventeenth. Take care of yourself, honey,' and she rang off.

The affectionate little name cheered Amy, who was feeling lonelier than usual because she was bored with lecturing, with the crowds and long railway trips, and only wanted to get to New York and settle into the apartment and wait for Lou's visit. She was also irritated because the unsettled life she was leading prevented her from starting her new story, which she could feel growing in her mind, and which was almost ready to be put into words. She promised herself that she would

335

begin it on her first evening in the apartment, and in spite of her disturbed and unhappy state of mind she looked forward to doing so.

The lectures, the parties, the long railway journeys, went on. She played her part in them docilely, like the good child she had promised her mother she would try to be, but she only longed for the times late at night when she was alone, and could lie awake in her Pullman sleeper and begin to dream. Outside, America went past in the darkness. Behind the train lay the cold hills of Vermont, and it was thundering towards the rich woods of the Carolinas. Amy played the old train-game of wondering how near, or how far, the train-traveller is from the person loved best in the world. Now the train descends a long curve; I am farther away from him. Now it is climbing a hill; perhaps I am half a mile nearer. But then she would suddenly remember in the middle of the game that she did not know where he was, and that he was in danger. He was in danger. The thought was always at the back of her mind, a warning whisper. *Danger.* The train thundered slowly through the night, and she fell asleep.

The apartment was in a shabby brownstone house in a street that was quiet, for New York. Its windows looked across roofs to a wide avenue where traffic hummed and roared, and neon lights shone with their insanely steady glare. Amy liked to sit at the living-room window in the twilight and silence, watching the glow that came up from the avenue as if from a witch's cauldron. When she sat there, listening and dreaming, she thought of her tower over Hyde Park in London and experienced the same feeling of loneliness and power. A picture-house on the avenue had revived *The Soldier of Misfortune* in the slack summer season, and her own name shone high above the dark roofs in scarlet fire. But it was not possible for her to believe that that was her name, the name of the girl who sat here in the dusk, reading it over and over again until her eyes were dazzled. It was the name of someone who did not seem real, and Amy could feel no excitement about it.

She had started her new story, but it was not yet Beginning to Run. She was enjoying the writing of it, because she always enjoyed writing, but she could not lose herself in it as she usually lost herself in a story. For the first time since she had been a child writing *The Wolf of Leningrad* at Highbury Walk, she could not give her mind utterly to her writing. The deep current of her thoughts turned steadily and persistently to the young American who was in danger. Her thoughts of him were not ordinary thoughts, but resembled dreams or moods, influencing everything she did and colouring all her everyday thoughts as if with a strange dye. I am a different person, she thought, over and over again during her long, lonely day. It's as if I were under a spell or something.

She had plenty of time to write her new story, for her only daily visitor was a coloured girl named Myrtle, who cleaned the flat for Boone and his wife, and had been taken on by their tenant with the flat. Myrtle only came in for two hours in the morning and for an hour at night in order to prepare the supper. In her first week at the flat Amy had had one or two callers; people whom her American agent thought might amuse her or be useful to her. They were electrically lively New Yorkers, capable of amusing anyone who was not already dead on their feet, but it is well known that when someone is under a spell, nothing but the counter-spell will free them. These people did not happen to have the counter-spell; and therefore Amy had no use for them. They found her nice but dull, and having decided that she wanted to be left alone to work, they did not call or telephone again.

'The States don't seem to have stimulated the little Lee much,' said Giles Humfriss discontentedly, handing Jeremy Aubrett a letter from their New York representative. 'Apparently all she does is to sit in a room in the Village and write. That's all she does in London.'

'I think it was Montaigne (or was it Pascal?) who said that all man's misfortunes arise from his inability to do just that one thing,' observed Mr Aubrett. 'How I wish some of our other writers would follow her example!'

Sometimes Amy explored New York. She went to all the places that were utterly unlike London: walked down Fifth Avenue, went out to Coney Island (where the noise and glare and smells stunned her), or sat in Childs (the New York equivalent of Lyons) eating sundaes and watching the people. But even in Childs, where she felt more at home than in any other part of New York, she could not fall into that daydream, that fruitful trance, which comes to some writers when they sit silent and observant in a crowd, and which until now had never failed to come to her. When she awoke in the small hours, and lay staring into the dim summer dawn and breathing the cool wind sweeping through the city from the sea, she was still aware of anxiety at the back of her mind, a feeling of trouble and pain, like nothing so much as a motionless dark cloud. It was a dreary, heavy, *waiting* feeling. She explained it by admitting her impatience to see Lou again, and hear her talk about Bob.

In this lonely dreamlike time, alone save for the haunting presence of a young man in danger, Amy thought more about her own feelings and character than she had ever done before, and came to the natural conclusion that she was a very queer person indeed. One night she made a list of the ordinary things she did not like, and also a list of the things she had never done, and to her amazement it covered two sheets of notepaper. She sat staring at it for a long time, feeling rather frightened, and her dismay increased when, her thoughts turning to Bob as an escape from their own uneasiness, she suddenly realized how very unusual were her feelings about *him*. I'm very queer, there's no doubt about that, she decided, standing up at last and crumpling the paper with a sigh. Perhaps I'm going mad? Thank goodness Lou will be here the day after tomorrow, and then I can talk to her about Bob and she'll make me feel he's a real person again, not a kind of dream. But I *must* be a very strange person, to feel like this about someone I've only seen once when they were a little boy.

That night was hot, and she slept badly because she was disturbed by the crying of some children in a tenement house across the road who could not rest for the heat. She awoke at six o'clock from a troubled slumber and after lying for a little while listening to the morning noises in the street, she got out of bed and went across to the window and leaned out into the air of early day.

At once she knew that it was going to be very hot. Heat came up from the sidewalks and off the roofs as if the stone and metal were burning, and the sky was already white, as if the cool blue of the night had all been scorched away. She stared down dazedly into the street, yawning and closing her heavy eyes for a moment. She felt as if she had not been to sleep at all. In the very hot weather, day and night seem to be one, undivided by the beautiful coolness of dawn and evening. Heat binds them helpless in a long period of time for which no name had yet been found, and everyone who works and suffers in the heat feels this mysterious suspension of ordinary hours. Today, Amy knew, was going to be one of these unnamed, weary spells. She yawned again and drew in her head.

It was too hot to go out. She had a shower, and settled down after breakfast to write, while Myrtle moved about the flat, cleaning and tidying and sometimes glancing at Amy, sitting at the table, writing. Amy found Myrtle romantic, for was not Myrtle black? and the very tones of her voice were unfamiliar, as if a glossy cat should begin to talk. Just because she found Myrtle so romantic, she found it even more difficult to talk to her than she did to most people, and so she kept up a grave polite way with her which impressed Myrtle but also rather awed her. She saw Amy as a tiny scribbling witch with never a dark hair out of place on the hottest day, who moved lightly about in Mexican sandals small as a child's and owned a cupboardful of wonderful clothes at which she seldom troubled to look. But she liked the way Amy spoke to her; the natural graces and good manners of the negro, which spring from a poet's heart, found their echo in Amy's frequent 'pleases' and 'would you minds,' and Myrtle told the sister with whom she roomed in Harlem that Miss Lee surely had lovely English manners.

Myrtle walked about in white shoes with high heels and a white skirt and frilled pale pink blouse, washing the dishes and sometimes humming to herself, and Amy sat writing away for dear life, never lifting her head, sometimes stretching out her aching wrist to rest it, in her old childish habit, sometimes groping for the glass of ice-water that always stood beside her on the table and taking a sip at it while she read through a few lines, then settling to write again.

Two hours passed. Then Myrtle, pausing at the door with her white straw hat swinging in her dark hand, said softly:

'Miss Lee, it's all cleaned up now. Ah'm gwine.'

Amy nodded, without looking up.

'Good morning, Miss Lee. Sure is going to be hot!' and Myrtle went out, quietly shutting the door after her.

Amy wrote on. The ice-box, turned full on to freeze the ice-cream Myrtle had made for her lunch, hummed distinctly in the stillness. A shrill roar which made the air seem hotter came across from the avenue, but the street below was drowsily hushed in the noonday heat, and in the apartment was silence, made more silent by the tiny domestic sounds threading through it. Amy forgot the ice-cream, and ate two thickly buttered slices of rye bread and two tomatoes and drank a glass of milk for her lunch, took another shower (absently, because the story was unfolding itself in her head all the time she stood under the spray of water) and then went back to her writing. Vaguely she felt glad that it was so hot, and that the flat and the streets outside, quivering with heat haze, were caught in this unnamed, timeless period; it was a wonderful day for writing! With her nerves slightly on edge from sleeplessness, and this hot, hushed silence all about her, she could write as if there were no pen, no symbols, between the paper and her thought. For the story was 'Beginning to Run' at last, and the pen raced, and Amy's bare ankles were twisted uncomfortably round the legs of her chair and a piece of hair had come loose from the mass coiled on the top of her head for coolness, and her fingers were damp and aching with their grip on the pen. For the first time since that afternoon at Vine Falls, she had forgotten everything except her story, and she was happy.

It was called *The Tower of the Wicked*. It began with the brother and sister, waiting for their train in the old Swiss town asleep in the noonday heat. They strolled about the deserted squares and peered into the cool gloom of old churches to fill up time while they waited, and then, on the outskirts of the town near the bridge across the rushing mountain river, they found a tall old tower of crumbling brown stone, with one window looking away towards the mountains, and the brother pulled the bell that hung on the rusty chain outside the weed-grown door . . .

It was an exciting beginning; Amy had not enjoyed writing a story so much since *China Walk*, her own favourite among her books. The hours flew by, and at five o'clock she made some tea and absently drank it, filling her mouth with bread and jam while she read through what she had written and finally setting the cup down on the clean sheets of paper where it made a moist ring. She pushed the cup aside and settled to write again.

It was a long time later (but she did not know how long, for she had been unconscious of time) that a sound, an irritating and familiar sound, broke through the mist of imagination that was shutting her away from the world. The noise must have been going on for some minutes, but she would not let it come in; she would not listen to it, nor realize what it was, nor even lift her eyes from the paper in front of her. Then it stopped, and she thought thankfully: *that's all right*. But a minute later it came again, steady and persistent, cutting through the silence in the hot room, coming past the people in her mind to her ears. She leaned back, flinging down her pen, and looked angrily towards the door of the apartment.

Someone was ringing the bell.

She waited a moment, but the noise went on, so she got up, muttering crossly, and walked across to the door and flung it open.

21

A big young man stood there, leaning against the wall and staring down at the floor in a strange, intent way.

'What is it, please?' asked Amy sharply, looking up at him with eyes still half-blind to the real world.

The big young man took off his hat. That is, he put up his hand and sketched exactly the movement a man makes when he takes off a hat, but his hat was not there, and so his hand dropped uncertainly to his side again. His thick fair hair looked as if it had not been covered by a hat for days; it was dusty and tangled and—Amy's eyes travelled slowly to his feet—the white tennis shoes he wore were split at the toes. He had a windbreaker jacket zipped up close to his throat and grey trousers ragged at the hems, and all over his clothes lay the white dust of midsummer. He was very pale, with white lips and sunken cheeks.

He leaned a little lower against the wall and said very quietly, almost in a whisper:

'I'm sorry if I disturbed you. Does Mr Boone Vorst live here?'

'Yes, but he's away.' Amy's own voice sounded strange, low as his own, faint and quiet. She was staring at him as if she could not take her eyes from the unshaven face, the lock of hair over his forehead, the dusty thick eyelashes lying on his cheek as if he were asleep.

'Do you know when he'll be back?' Now his voice was actually a whisper, but as if trying to convey his meaning by another messenger he slowly lifted his head and looked straight at her with grey eyes sunk deep in their sockets.

'I'm awfully sorry,' Amy began, also in a whisper—when the young man said distinctly:

'I'm very sorry. I'm afraid I'm going to faint,' and slipped to the floor.

Amy was terrified. She dropped on her knees and crouched beside him, looking wildly round for help.

He had fallen just inside the door. Desperately, with every scrap of her strength, she pulled and hauled him into the room, and shut it. Then she darted across and snatched up one of the cushions off the divan and put it under his head. He lay still, not seeming to breathe, and she sat back on her heels, staring at him and trying distractedly to remember what you did to bring someone out of a faint. Brandy! Brandy, of course!

She ran into the kitchen and hunted frantically through the little cupboard that was fitted up as a bar. Bourbon—rye—gin—tomato juice—vermouth—lime—no brandy! Whisky would have to do.

She carried the bottle back into the living-room, tearing at the foil cover with her teeth. Where was the corkscrew? She looked round dazedly, then smashed off the head of the bottle against the edge of the table, poured some whisky into the glass that had contained her ice-water, and knelt down beside him. She lifted his heavy head and forced the liquid between his lips.

Then she saw what she had so often described in her stories but never seen in life—a man choking under the reviving power of spirit. She was alarmed, but forced more between his lips until he moved, opening his eyes, and caught at her hand, dragging it down and shaking his head.

'That's enough!' he gasped.

His head fell back, and he sighed deeply and shut his eyes again.

Amy knelt beside him, staring at the big, still figure sprawling on the floor, looking so strange in its dirty clothes against the clean white matting.

Suddenly his eyes opened and he stared at her, but with no

344

lively natural interest in his look; it was the grave exhausted stare of a man who is very ill. She bent over him, murmuring:

'Do you feel better?'

'I shan't faint again,' he answered hoarsely. 'I'm sorry if I frightened you. Can I have some hot milk with whisky—if it isn't too much trouble?'

'Yes, of course!'

She ran into the kitchen and heated the milk on the electric stove as quickly as she could for the shaking of her hands, and poured a lot of whisky into it. He watched her come across the room, still with that grave, exhausted stare, and said suddenly:

'Haven't I seen you before?'

Amy nearly dropped the glass. She could not speak. She knelt beside him, trembling from head to foot, and set the glass on the floor.

'Haven't I?'

'I don't know . . . I don't think so,' she muttered. 'Here's the milk. Hadn't you better get on to the divan?' He raised himself on one elbow, shut his eyes and shook his head impatiently, then got up and walked unsteadily across to the divan and fell forward on it.

'I'm sorry to give you all this trouble,' he said a moment later.

'It's all right, really. Can you drink this now?'

'Yes.' He held out his hand for the milk and she gave it him.

He leant back against the wall, sipping the drink and not lifting his eyes from the glass while she sat on the extreme edge of the divan, watching him.

'I'm sorry I fell over your doorstep like that,' he said presently in a stronger, more natural voice. 'I guess I must have frightened you.'

'Well, you did, a bit.'

'I shan't do it again.' He drained the glass and she took it from him and put it down on the floor.

'My brother lives here—I was expecting to see him,' he went on. 'How long is he away for, do you know?'

She shook her head. She could not speak.

'Oh, well——' He was quiet for a moment, staring down at his broken shoes; then he said, 'My name's Robert Vorst.'

The room went dark to Amy, yet she managed to say faintly but naturally:

'Oh, then you must be Lou's brother!'

'Yes, I'm Lou's brother,' he said shortly. 'Why? Do you know Lou?'

'Oh, yes. It was Lou who told me about this flat.'

'I see. I supposed you got it through Boone's agent. I didn't take in that you're a family friend.'

He was looking at her with a touching little expression of polite interest, that did not in the least conceal his exhaustion and misery.

'Well——' Amy laughed nervously. 'I've only known your sister for a little while, but I like her very much.'

He said nothing.

'I was lecturing in Vine Falls about a month ago and I met your sister at a reception Mrs Boadman (I think it was) very kindly gave for me.'

'So you're a lecturer. And you're English, aren't you?'

'Oh, yes. Well, I'm a writer, really, not a lecturer. I live in London. My name——' she stopped. Her breath seemed suddenly to have gone away and she could not speak properly. 'My name's Amy Lee,' she concluded, not daring to look at his face.

'*The Soldier of Misfortune*,' he said at once. 'Pleased to meet you, Miss Lee,' and his unshaven lips twisted in a bitter little smile.

Amy continued to stare at the empty glass standing on the floor.

'I expect that's why you thought you'd seen me before,' she went on in a low tone, after a pause. 'There were quite a lot of pictures of me in the American papers when *The Soldier of Misfortune* was filmed.'

He shook his head. 'No,' he replied, looking at her steadily. 'I've never seen a picture of you. But I know your face. I knew it the minute you opened the door, only I didn't get a chance to say so before I passed out.'

'Oh, well, that's funny, isn't it!' she said, still looking away from him and then she went on quickly.

'How do you feel now?'

'I'm all right. I'm not ill. That was just hunger that made me pass out.' He spoke without emphasis.

'Oh,' said Amy faintly. 'Have you—come from far?'

'Central Park. I slept there last night.'

She said nothing, but got up and slowly walked across to a table and chose herself a cigarette, so that he should not see that her eyes were full of tears. She held the box out to him, without looking at him, but he shook his head.

'Wouldn't you like some supper?' she managed to say at last.

'No, thanks. I must be getting along.'

'Where to?'

He moved his big shoulders indifferently.

'I'll see when I get there.'

'I was hoping you'd stay and see Lou. She's coming here tomorrow,' said Amy.

'Lou? Is she in town?' he asked quickly.

'She will be tomorrow morning. With your cousin—Helen, I think she said.'

'Helen Viner, yes. Well, I may as well see Lou. Maybe I could call in tomorrow—if you wouldn't mind?'

'Oh, please do. But won't you stay to supper now? I wish you would. You did say you were—hungry, and if you were sleeping in Central Park—and you said you didn't know where you were going——' she stammered.

He did not answer, but looked at her steadily and gravely.

347

'And stay the night, too. I wish you would,' Amy ended, forgetting certain warnings from Mrs Beeding and only wild with anxiety to keep him from going back to sleep in Central Park.

'Miss Lee, it's very kind of you, but I can't do that.'

'Why not?'

'Well . . . you're all alone here, aren't you?'

'Yes, but nobody in this house'll mind you staying. I expect they won't even know about it. This is a funny sort of place, people go in and out and don't take any notice of each other at all. I don't know any of them.'

'It's mighty kind of you. You're quite sure you don't mind?'

He was still looking at her steadily as he spoke, trying to make out what kind of a girl she was. She seemed a funny little thing, sweet and sensible, almost like a child, but most girls were more than ready to meet a man half-way. He knew that now.

'I'm quite sure I don't mind. I'd like you to stay, please,' answered Amy, returning his look as steadily and still completely forgetful of Mrs Beeding.

Then he demanded suddenly:

'Did Lou tell you all about me?'

She shook her head.

He smiled and said bitterly:

'Do you mean to say that you went to a reception at Mrs Boadman's and nobody told you about me?'

'Well—Miss Cordell said—and Lou did just say that——' faltered Amy, wondering in much distress whether to tell him the truth. She wanted to! She could not bear the thought of lying to him; but then, she did not want to hurt him, either.

'So Miss Cordell was there too, was she? You seem to have had a regular Old Home Week. And I'm sure Lucy Cordell told you all about me, if Lou didn't?'

'Oh, no, not everything,' replied Amy, picking at the fringe on one of the red cushions. 'Only that your own mother didn't know where you were. And—and she said she prayed for you every night of her life.'

He was silent.

'I only wanted you to know what kind of a person you've invited to spend the night here,' he said at last.

'That's all right,' she said at once. 'Please do stay.'

'All right then, Miss Lee. I guess I will, and thanks a lot.'

He leant back against the wall, and suddenly a feeling of deep relief came over him. Tonight he need not face the hot sidewalks that he had tramped all the afternoon; he need not watch faces drifting past him, the curious, pitying or indifferent faces; he need not breathe the faint sickening smell of the withered grass on which he had slept last night. He could shut himself into a quiet room, and go to sleep. And tomorrow he could see Lou and Helen. The longing to see them both, and to feel through them the peace and tenderness of his home and the happiness gone for ever, was too strong for him to resist. He would not go back with them, because he was never going back, but see them he must.

Amy sat in silence, watching the ash gather on the end of her cigarette. He was going to stay! He was going to stay here all night, and she would be able to get supper for him. The ash fell to the floor, and Bob moved, and glanced down at his hands.

'Do you mind if I take a shower?'

'No, of course not,' she answered, and at that moment the telephone bell rang.

'Miss Lee,' began Myrtle's rich voice, 'Ah'm mighty sorry, Ah can't get up to you this evenin', mah sister's tuk sick.'

'Oh, I am sorry, Myrtle. Is that the one that's going to have a baby?'

'Yes, Miss Lee. Mah sister Louella. She's mighty bad, Ah'm gwine to take her down to the hospital right now.'

'All right, Myrtle. Can you come in tomorrow?'

'Sure I can, Miss Lee. Ah'll come in first thing, moment the baby's bo'n.'

'All right, Myrtle. I hope your sister'll be all right.'

'She'll be all right, Miss Lee, she don't have no trouble with her babies once they'se started. Ah surely am sorry to put you out so, Miss Lee. G'd-bye, Miss Lee.'

'Good-bye, Myrtle,' and Amy hung up the receiver.

'That was the coloured girl who comes in to do the cleaning. She can't come tonight, her sister's having a baby,' explained Amy. 'So I'll get the supper while you have your shower.'

'Won't it be a trouble to you? Don't you want to go on writing?' And he glanced at the papers scattered over the table.

'Oh, no. I've been writing all day. I'm tired now. I'd like to get the supper; it'll be a change.'

'Right.' He spoke with a little restraint, as if the unusualness of the situation had suddenly struck him, and went through into the bathroom without saying anything more.

Amy quickly set the table and got the food out of the ice-box, pushing her frightened happiness away to the back of her mind. He's hungry, he's starving, I must make him eat as much as possible, and then he must get a good long sleep, she thought as she hurried between the living-room and the kitchenette. She was so bewildered and disturbed by his presence there that she could not realize that the dream, the legend, which had haunted her memory for twelve years, had walked into the room an hour ago. He was no longer My American; he was a young man in trouble, and every feeling of tenderness in her nature that had been denied expression for the past twelve years turned yearningly towards him.

He was so long over his shower that she took her scribbling block on to the kitchen table, among the lettuce leaves and discarded cellophane wrappers, and started writing again to fill up time. When he came out, he paused at the door of the living-room for a moment to look at the picture before him. It was exactly like a picture, with the wonderful lights of New York, sparkling and glowing through the open window in the clear hot twilight, as a background.

Amy was sitting in a magician's circle of light with everything about her in shadow. Her intent, foreshortened little face, bent over the paper and crowned with its heavy knot of dark hair, her small moving hand, were strangely beautiful. But the strangest thing about this picture, to Bob, was the fact that *he had seen it before*. He knew the ring of radiance from the lamp set upon the table, the whiteness of the paper over which the pen hurried, the green of the wilted lettuce leaves and the sparkle of crumpled wrappings, the silver bubbles in the glass of water standing at the writer's elbow. He knew just how she would look when she glanced up and smiled, gazing beyond the circle of light into the dusk—

'Hullo? Supper's all ready.'

He came slowly across to her, and stood looking down at the page covered with round untidy writing.

'Don't you ever use a typewriter?'

'No, I hate them. Shall we have supper now?'

'If you're ready.'

He set a chair for her at the table and they sat down, facing one another across the bowl piled with fresh leaves and yellow fruit, and the sophisticated squat shapes of the alcohol bottles. He poured out two drinks, then leant back and sipped his own in silence while Amy put the food on to the plates.

He was soothed by the shower and the rest, but he was still deathly tired; too tired to talk; certainly too tired to notice how unlike the usual meaningful silence of a man and a girl in an unusual situation was the unembarrassed quietness in which they were eating. They might have been two old friends seeing each other through a bad time. And although he had lifted his glass— how many times!—in a toast to how many pretty girls in the past, tonight it never even entered his head to raise it to her in

351

silence, with a smile. Yet dimly he felt grateful to her for not talking, for moving so quietly and being so pretty, like a bright-eyed little bird.

She's nice to be with. Kind of restful, he thought, slowly and dazedly eating his food.

The clock softly struck ten as Amy got up.

'Do sit on the divan. I'm only going to make coffee,' she told him.

The strong coffee roused him a little, and when they had been sitting on the divan drinking it in silence for a while, he said:

'I came here to borrow twenty dollars from Boone. That was all I could think about. I just thought: I'll get twenty dollars from Boone, and eat, and get some shoes, and then maybe something'll turn up. Now he isn't here, I don't know—I can't think ahead. I suppose it's because I'm so tired.'

'Please, may I lend it to you?'

'No, thanks, Miss Lee, I guess not.'

'But *why* not?'

'Because you're a girl.'

'I can't see that that matters.'

'Well, maybe it doesn't. I don't know. All I know is, I've done a lot of darn queer things in the last few months but I haven't taken to sponging on women—yet.'

'I think that's silly. A . . . a friend is a friend, whether they're a woman or a man.'

'So you're my friend, are you?'

'Well, please, I'd like to be,' said Amy, turning red but speaking composedly. 'I like Lou so much, and you're her brother. I should like to help you, if I could.'

'That's fine of you,' he answered, while his sad young eyes rested steadily upon her earnest face. 'But I don't think anyone can do anything, now. Nothing seems to matter. I'll see the girls tomorrow, because—well, there doesn't seem any reason why I shouldn't see them. But I don't know what I'll do after that.'

There was a lengthy silence, during which he leant back against the wall with his arms behind his head, staring past Amy at the sparkling lights and scarlet neon signs above the avenue. But she had a strong feeling that he wanted to talk, and presently she said timidly:

'Why didn't you come to see your brother before?'

'I only got into New York yesterday morning. I hitchhiked from Harrisburg. I had a job there, but I walked out.'

'Why?' she ventured to ask, still timidly.

'Well——' He suddenly took his arms from behind his head, and folded them as he turned to look at her. 'Miss Lee, please tell. Just how much do you know about me?'

For the first time in years Amy resisted the instinct to lie, for she longed that there should be nothing between him and herself but the truth.

'I only know what Lou told me,' she answered at once. 'She said that you—you killed a little girl in a car smash and injured a little boy, and then you went crazy because the trial wasn't a fair one. She said you let a gangster fix the jury, so that you got off, and then you went away with the gangster afterwards.'

'I was yellow,' he said in a hard voice. 'I couldn't go on living in Vine Falls, knowing I'd got off through a crook lawyer and a fixed jury. So I went off with Dan Carr. Yes, that's right.'

'Is that the gangster?'

He glanced at her quickly. 'That's a big thrill for you, isn't it? For weeks I lived with gangsters. Now you feel you're more my friend than ever, don't you?' And he gave her a miserable smile.

'It doesn't make any difference at all to the way I feel,' she answered quietly. 'But I can't help wondering what the gangsters are like. Anybody would.'

'Oh——' he said impatiently. He got up and helped himself to a cigarette, then sat down beside her again. 'They aren't so different as all that from ordinary people. There's only one big difference.'

'What?'

He glanced at her in surprise. 'Why, they kill. They don't care if they kill. That's the big difference, isn't it? You needn't be afraid' (she was watching him with her eyes widened and her lips parted) 'I didn't kill. I didn't see much of that sort of thing while I was running around with Dan, either. Dan's a particular kind of guy; he has his killing done for him. He doesn't like things all mussed up; he likes things tidy.' He spoke almost indulgently, as if making excuses for someone he knew well whose peculiarities he had learned to accept.

'You don't hate him, then?'

'Why should I? He can't help being what he is. Nobody can.'

'Well, you said you walked out of a job in Harrisburg. I thought you might have had a row with him.'

'That job wasn't with Dan. It was playing the piano for two bucks a night in a dive. I left Dan weeks ago. I haven't seen him since.'

'Why did you leave him, if you don't hate him?'

He did not answer for a minute, but sat staring at the cigarette he held, moving his lips once or twice as if he were trying to find his way to the expression of a difficult thought. At last he said:

'Have you ever seen anyone dead?'

Amy started.

'I saw my mother, when I was a little girl.'

'Oh, I don't mean dead like that, lying tidily in a coffin with everybody upset and people praying. I meant just dead. Alive one minute, and then dead on the floor. Smashed up, and nobody taking much notice.'

She shook her head.

'I have.' He bent forward and knocked the ash off his cigarette. 'I saw a man killed. That was what made me leave Dan.' He was quiet for a little while, then he said as if to himself:

'*All that marvellous machinery, smashed up. That was what finished me.*'

'Did Dan kill him?'

'No. (I told you Dan never kills.) He and I were in a joint one night run by a pal of Dan's, and a man got bumped off for squealing. He was sitting at a table with a girl, laughing, and a man walked in and shot him through the face.'

Amy leaned a little closer. She did not shudder.

'They pulled him out of the way behind a curtain in a corner and put a tablecloth over him. He wasn't dead. We had to sit there as if nothing had happened. We sat there for half an hour, while he was dying. I heard him. It was the first time I'd ever heard a man die. I wanted to do what I could for him. You see, my job is—my job was going to be saving life. That's a doctor's work, isn't it? So I guess that made me want to help, even more than just a natural instinct. But Dan wouldn't let me.'

'Wouldn't *let* you?'

'He covered me with his gun until the man was dead. He said he deserved to die for squealing, and he'd die anyway, whether I helped or not. So we sat there staring at each other for half an hour, until the man was dead.'

'I'm glad you didn't try to help. You might have got killed yourself.'

'Oh, Dan wouldn't have killed me. He was laughing. I think he enjoyed the whole thing. He used to like watching the way I reacted to the things they took for granted. He's a queer guy.'

'I think he sounds horrible,' she exclaimed violently.

'Well, he had a raw deal as a kid. He was clever, but there wasn't anyone to do anything for him. He wanted power more than anything in the world and the only way he could get it was by turning gangster. He quite understood how I felt about that man dying. The next day I said I was going, and he never even tried to stop me.'

'Wasn't he afraid you'd tell the police about him and the gang?'

'Of course not. Why should he be? He and I were kids together; I couldn't squeal on Dan.'

'But you won't go back to them again, will you?' said Amy, comforted by the detached way in which he spoke of his life with the gangsters but longing to hear him say in so many words that he would never return to it.

He shook his head.

'I told you, seeing that man shot finished me. I talked with Dan for hours (he talked, rather, and I listened. He loves talking). I made him see I wasn't their sort and never could be. He was sorry. He wanted to make a super-crook out of me, I guess. He says crooks only fail because they're stupid and uneducated. He's got a great respect for education and culture. It's queer.'

'I think he sounds a beast,' repeated Amy stubbornly.

'We're all beasts,' he said gently, leaning back and looking at her. 'But don't worry. I'm never going back.'

'Oh, I *am* so glad,' she said, curling her feet under her, with a long sigh.

'Are you?'

His grave, lingering gaze travelled slowly, with a pleasure that he had not known for months, over the fineness of her white skin and dark hair, her tiny ear, the brilliance of her long-shaped eyes. And she was so clean! like a freshly-washed and powdered child.

'Yes. I was so afraid you'd go back.'

'Well, you needn't be.' And suddenly he put his hand over her own and held it tight, and they stayed like that for a moment, quite still.

Amy knelt like a Japanese girl, her eyelashes lowered, staring at the big hand with unkempt nails that covered her own. The whole side of the divan sagged under his weight, though hers hardly moved it, and all his manhood, the strangeness of his presence there, seemed concentrated in that heavy clasp on her hand. It was the first time that a young man had ever touched her, and yet she was not trembling. Her hand crept out slowly until her fingers lay on his wrist, and then she made a little stroking movement as though trying to comfort him but still she did not look up, and when he began to pull her gently towards him, at the same time making room for her, she turned her head away; and when, trembling at last, she lay down against his side and he drew her close so that her head rested on his shoulder, she had not once looked at him.

'You don't mind?' he asked in a low voice.

She shook her head. He could see her heart-beats shaking the dark red silk of her jacket.

'Are you comfortable like that?'

Again she nodded. The room was very quiet. Outside, the lights flashed and quivered through the weary summer night and there was no slackening of the noise in the streets, but the room only seemed to sink deeper into its enchanted hush because of the city's sleeplessness.

After a little while he went on softly, as if he were beginning to feel drowsy:

'When Dan and I were kids (you don't mind if I talk, do you? I haven't talked in weeks, not to anybody) he lived back of our place, and there was an old rail fence round their cabin, with a hole in it. I used to go through there when I wanted to go shooting with him. I was always crazy to get on the other side of that fence. Dan's folks were bootleggers; I was only a kid, and that thrilled me. I've often thought about that hole in the fence since everything went smash. I'm on Dan's side of the fence now, and I can't get back.'

'But you haven't done anything. You did go away with Dan, but you didn't kill anyone.'

'I only killed one kid and put out another's eye,' he retorted bitterly.

'You didn't mean to. And *anyone* can see how sorry you are!'

'It wasn't killing the little girl that put me on the wrong side of the fence. It was letting my father hire a crook lawyer to defend me, and letting Dan fix the two people on the jury who didn't know me and might be difficult. I'm not a balanced enough type to be a doctor. That's why I can't ever go back to my home town, or study to be a doctor again.'

'You could if you tried. If you went back now——'

'It would be hell.'

'But you won't feel better until you *have* gone back!' she cried, suddenly lifting her head and looking up at him. '*Nothing* can ever make you feel better except going back to Vine Falls and being with all the people who know you, and working to be a doctor again. That's the only thing to do.'

'I know it!' he answered violently. 'I've known it ever since that night when I went off with Dan. But if I did go back——'

He paused, and a long silence followed.

'Nothing could ever be the same,' he said at last.

'Why not?'

'Because I'm a different person. I used to have everything worked out so neat and tidy. Now I'm not sure about anything. I'm not even sure about what's right and what's wrong. I've been on the wrong side of the fence, and I can't be comfortable on the right side any more——'

Then she interrupted him, sighing and moving a little closer to him because she was beginning to feel sleepy:

'*But a doctor has to know about everything, doesn't he?*'

After the words had sounded through the hush in the room, there was a very long silence. He sat quite still, holding her against his breast and staring across her dark head at the restless quivering lights, and the simplicity and truth of what she had said sank deeper and deeper into his soul, until the words reached the beautiful truths that he himself felt lingering there in the darkness, the truths that he could live by. He continued to stare at the harsh lights with eyes that found it more and more difficult to keep awake, and suddenly the sweetness of hope broke over him, and he caught Amy close and put his face against the black softness of her hair.

The movement awoke her from a light sleep, and she opened her eyes to see above her the face that had come to her in the dream in London. It was smiling at her, as it had smiled then, but now the eyes were wet.

'It's you,' she murmured, putting up her fingers and gently touching his cheek. 'How lovely. I was dreaming.'

'Go to sleep again, darling. I will, too.'

And the last thing she saw, before she lay down beside him and fell into sleep as deep and peaceful as his own, was his arm stretched over her head to put out the light. The long cool wind from the sea, blowing the torn paper along the deserted streets in the blue light of early morning, did not awaken them.

22

At seven o'clock the noises in the street roused Amy. She cautiously moved her cramped limbs and turned to see if he were awake, but he was still deeply asleep, breathing heavily with arms flung behind his head, looking exhausted and young. She slid carefully off the couch and went into the kitchen to put the coffee on over a low current, then to the bathroom to take her shower. All the time she was washing and dressing she thought of nothing but being quiet, for he was so tired! he must have his sleep out; but while she was brushing her hair in the bedroom a muffled shout came from the next room, and she dropped the brush and ran in to him, her black hair floating loose.

'What is it—what's the matter?' she gasped.

He was crouching on the divan, staring at her dazedly.

'Do you feel bad?' She knelt beside him and put her arm round his shoulders.

'I dreamt I was fighting,' he answered hoarsely, and turned his face against her breast. After a silence he sighed deeply and said:

'I'm sorry I frightened you.'

'That's all right. Are you better now?'

He nodded, smiling faintly up at her. She moved away and got off the divan.

'I'm so hungry again. Sorry.'

'The coffee's nearly ready.'

'Don't you have tea for breakfast? I know English people usually do.'

'Oh, I like coffee sometimes. This morning I'll have it.'

While she spoke she was twisting up her hair, holding the

360

pins in her mouth, and he was leaning back, watching her with eyes that were still dazed from his nightmares. Suddenly he said:

'I know who you are now, you're the Swimming Girl, of course, that's who you are.'

'Pardon?' said Amy, dropping a coil of hair and staring at him, while her voice, in her alarm, went straight back into the thin polite cockney accent of twelve years ago.

'It's all right. Nothing; I guess I was still dreaming,' he answered more naturally but with a little embarrassment. 'Can I take a shower now, if you've had yours?'

'Oh, yes, and then breakfast'll be ready,' she answered, and was making for the kitchen to finish dressing herself and sort out her feelings in solitude, when he picked up a tress of her hair and kissed it without looking at her.

'Please kiss me, will you?' he muttered and suddenly put his arms round her.

'I'm sorry, I can't help it, you've been such an angel to me, you're so sweet and lovely,' he said, kissing her mouth and eyes and hair.

'It's all right——' she said breathlessly, 'I—I like you too, as a matter of fact——'

'Do you? Oh, darling!' And he lifted her off her feet.

'The coffee's boiling over!' Amy twisted round quickly, suddenly overcome with shyness and fear. 'Oh, please let me go!'

He let her go at once.

'You aren't mad at me, are you?'

'Oh, no,' said Amy, retreating backwards into the kitchen, 'only you see, nobody ever kissed me before and—and it's all a bit strange at first, that's all,' she ended in a mutter, snatching the coffee off the stove.

'Oh, I guess I frightened you, then. I'm sorry. You just tell me another time when I'm kissing you too much and I—well, I guess I'll take my shower now.' And he turned away. Amy continued to pour milk into a saucepan, staring at it.

'That doesn't mean you won't ever want to kiss me again, does it?' he asked, lingering at the door.

'Oh, no! I said I liked it—only *do* please go and have your shower now!' she implored and still without looking up she waved the empty milk carton at him. He went off to the bathroom, and then the telephone bell rang.

'Miss Lee,' announced the cheerful voice of Myrtle, 'mah sister's done had twins!'

'Oh, Myrtle! Is she pleased?'

'She sho' is, Miss Lee, only mah brother-in-law, he's on Relief just now, so they won't have much fo' the babies. They'se lovely babies, Miss Lee, they done weigh seven pounds each!'

'Fancy, Myrtle! I'm so glad.'

'Thank you, Miss Lee. Miss Lee, Ah was wonderin'—there's such an old muss-up down here, all the little ones hoppin' about without their breakfasts 'cause me and mah brother-in-law we been up all night at the hospital—Ah was wonderin' if you could manage without me this mornin'? So's Ah could stay with the little ones?'

'Oh, yes, Myrtle, that'll be all right, I can manage,' Amy answered eagerly. Indeed, she was relieved, for the tocsins of Mrs Beeding had suddenly sounded in her memory, and what would Myrtle think if she arrived and found a young man breakfasting there? (People Are Always Thinkin' Somethin' had been one of Mrs Beeding's warnings. There may be nothin' in it, but People Always Get Talkin'.) Amy shrank from having herself and Bob talked about.

'You call me up again, will you, Myrtle, if you can't come in tomorrow?' she added.

'Mighty kind of you, Miss Lee, Ah surely will. How will yo' manage fo' yo' marketin', Miss Lee?'

'Oh, I'll call up the delicatessen, I'll be all right. Good-bye, Myrtle,' and she hung up the receiver.

She finished getting the breakfast, moving about with light steps in a happy dream. She had not known that it was possible to be so happy. She did not want to talk, not even to him; she only wanted to move about, lightly and silently, preparing the breakfast and feeling happiness in herself and all about her.

Presently he called from the bathroom:

'I wish I had a razor. Boone hasn't got one stowed away, has he?'

'I don't know. There are some drawers and cupboards locked up. I should look, if I were you.'

After a pause filled with the discontented rattlings of drawers—

'No.'

'Can't you get a shave at the shop over the way after breakfast?'

He did not answer.

'You might let me lend you a *dollar*!' cried Amy, coming exasperated into the living-room with the grapefruit, and meeting him face to face as he came out of the bathroom. 'Lou could pay me back this afternoon. Won't you?'

'Not a cent,' he said firmly.

'Well, I *owe* you five cents, anyway!' she said recklessly, putting down the grapefruit on the table. 'You might let me pay you back what I *owe* you!'

He stood in the morning sunlight and stared at her.

'You owe me five cents? What the heck do you mean? How can you owe me five cents?'

'Well, you gave me a five-cent piece in mistake for a shilling twelve years ago, and I've still got it,' she cried, shaking from head to foot. 'It was at Kenwood House in England one very cold Saturday afternoon in 1928, and it was my birthday and I asked you to lend me sixpence to get home with and you said you'd give me a shilling for a birthday present. But it wasn't a shilling, it was five cents, with an Indian and a buffalo on it and I was *so* disappointed, I thought you'd done it on purpose. But you didn't, did you?' she ended imploringly, standing on tiptoe and gazing up at him.

He sat down heavily on the edge of the divan, and demanded:
'Are we both crazy? I know you're my Swimming Girl, and now you say——'

'Wait—wait—I've still got it—I'll show you——' and away she flew into the bedroom, leaving him staring after her.

In a minute she was back at his side, eagerly showing him something cradled in her hand. He bent his head, taking her hand in his own to steady it, and saw with an ever-deepening astonishment an Indian's head five-cent piece, dulled with age. It lay in a piece of crumpled paper on which was written, in a hand that he recognized as a more youthful version of the one he had seen last night on Amy's manuscript:

American coin given to A. Lee as a birthday present by Robert Somebody, an American boy from Vine Falls, Paul County, New Leicester, America, on the said A. Lee's birthday, October 31st, 1928.

'That was you, wasn't it?' she demanded.

'We certainly were in London in 1928, but I can't remember—where did you say it was?'

'At Kenwood House,' she said eagerly. 'It's a big historic old house on Hampstead Heath, just outside London.'

He shook his head. 'I don't remember a thing about it, but it must have been me, because there couldn't have been two of us, could there?'

'And the address is right, isn't it? I couldn't catch your other name so that was why I put Robert "Somebody".'

He was silent for a little while, studying the coin and the paper while she wistfully watched his face.

'I do wish you could remember if you gave it me for a joke,' she said at last.

He smiled, still looking at the coin as if he were trying to make it show him the past, and put his arm around her.

'It's no use, I'm afraid I don't remember at all. But what were you like, all that time ago?'

'Oh, sort of little and thin and I had a white tam-o-shanter and I was very lonely and miserable.'

He held her closer and said decidedly: 'Then I'm sure I didn't mean it as a joke. It was just a mistake. My mother always made us behave properly when we were kids and my father lammed the daylights out of Boone and me if he caught us hazing Stebby (that's my cousin).'

'So you wouldn't have done a thing like that to a girl, would you?'

'No, I don't think I would. I was probably a fresh sort of kid, but I wouldn't have played a lowdown trick like that on a little girl, especially a miserable little girl,' and he drew her gently to him and kissed her cheek.

'Oh, I am so glad,' she murmured, 'I've always wondered about it. Now you tell me why you said I was the Swimming Girl—oh, the coffee'll be cold. Let's have it now, and you can tell me while we're having it.'

'It's so darned queer,' he muttered, pulling up a chair for her. 'This time yesterday I'd never even seen you, and now I seem to have known you for ever.'

'Do you take sugar?' said Amy quickly, looking across at him where he sat, a big, gaunt, drawn-faced young man, opposite her. 'I feel like that about you, too,' she added. 'And—and I like being with you very much, as well,' she ended shyly. She suddenly felt so happy that her happiness must find expression, and the only way she could show it was in this prim and childish phrase.

'So do I.' He was staring at her as if he could never tire. 'You can't imagine what it's like, being with you after the last weeks.'

'I wish you'd tell me what you did after you left Dan. My mother used to say it did people good to talk about things.'

'Oh——' He drank some coffee and began to eat. 'I walked

365

about the streets all that day. I had ten dollars I'd won playing poker. Then I joined up with a man who was hitch-hiking to Saint Louis looking for work. He was very religious; every time we thumbed a car he prayed it would stop! Then I caught him trying to get away with money one night.'

'What did you do?'

'Shook him.'

'I hope you hurt him,' she said fiercely.

He glanced at her, a little surprised. 'Well, I was pretty mad. But he was't a bad little rat. We got on all right after that.'

'After he'd tried to steal your money?'

'Surely. We got to laughing about it. You get like that when you haven't anything. I kind of despised him because he was a small time crook and he didn't like it because he said I hadn't any use for religion, but we got along.'

'You don't seem to hate *anybody*!' she burst out, clasping her hands together and raising her voice. 'I can't understand it! If anybody'd been beastly to me, the way Dan has to you, and that man, trying to steal your money, I'd——'

'You can't be mad at people when you haven't got anything. You both feel helpless together, and weak, somehow. I can't explain it. It's just the other side of the fence, that's all. One side, you can be quite sure what's right and what's wrong, but on the other side it isn't like that. I can't explain properly, even to you, because you haven't been on the other side.'

'Well, I haven't always had a *lot* of money, you know.'

'Haven't you?'

'No. My father used to earn six pounds a week. That's quite a lot, but I didn't get any of it.'

'Thirty dollars. What did he do?'

'He was in the advertising department on a boys' paper.'

'I thought—well, you're so elegant, I thought you'd always been rich.'

'Oh, no. I was very poor. Mrs Beeding brought me up; she's

the baker's wife, whose house we lived in. I worked in an office when I was fifteen.'

'Did you?' he said gently, studying her. 'Wasn't there anyone to look after you?'

'Oh, well, there was Mrs Beeding and the girls, but I was fearfully lonely. As a matter of fact, I still am.' And Amy hastily drank some coffee.

He said nothing, but continued to look at her as if he had not heard what she had said and as if he had forgotten that she was a human being, who could respond to his look with surprise at its length and intensity. Amy spooned the last drops of juice from her grapefruit without once looking up, but she was very conscious of his look, and at last she said:

'I wish you'd tell me about the Swimming Girl.'

'Oh!' Bob filled his mouth so that he need not answer at once. Then he said:

'Well, it's mighty queer, but you're exactly like a girl I've dreamt about ever since I was a kid. We were always swimming together in a very blue sea.'

'How lovely' she said dreamily.

'It certainly was.' He drank some more coffee, deciding not to tell her that the Swimming Girl was naked. He could still see the fine black hair floating across her breast, sprayed out under the blue water. 'I used to wake up very happy from those dreams.'

'It's all awfully queer, isn't it?' Amy, turning quite pale, suddenly put down her fork. 'Our meeting like that at Kenwood all those years ago, and my always remembering you, and your dreaming about someone just like me. It makes me feel rather frightened.'

'It's the queerest thing that's ever happened to me,' he answered in a low voice. He suddenly looked deadly tired. 'But don't let it scare you. I'm glad about it, it makes me feel as if we belonged to each other.' He stopped suddenly. 'I'm sorry, I guess I'll have to lie down again for a while. I don't feel——'

He got up unsteadily and went over to the divan and lay down on his face. She half rose from her chair, but did not go over to him; she stood there, troubledly watching him, wondering what to do. Presently he lifted his head and smiled at her.

'It's all right. But I haven't been leading a very healthy life lately, and I'm still starved. It'll take time to get me right again.'

'Oh!' she cried with a radiant face, clasping her hands. 'Then you're going home!'

He nodded, watching her, smiling faintly.

'Yes.'

She came over and sat beside him, looking earnestly down at his fair untidy head.

'Oh, I can't tell you how glad I am! Now everything will be all right.'

'Will it? I'll be a mighty queer kind of doctor, if ever I get through my examinations.'

'You'll be a very good doctor,' she said confidently. 'Because you'll know how those poor people feel without any work and any homes.'

'And the gangsters. I'll know how they feel. And I'll know that all the people with jobs and homes are just lucky, not hard-working or good. So what'll be the use of trying to be hard-working or good, when it's all luck?' he asked, his smile changing to a mocking one while he watched her.

'Oh, no!' she exclaimed, shocked. 'It isn't luck. God looks after the good people and punishes the wicked ones.'

'You're mighty down on the wicked ones yourself, aren't you?'

'People shouldn't be wicked,' said Amy.

'Hardly anyone is.'

'Not even Dan?'

'Dan! I told you, Dan's all right. It's all luck. No-one's bad and no-one's good. That's the worst thing I've found out in these last weeks. That's why I haven't anything to hang on to now, except my work. People always get sick, and they've got to be cured. I don't know why. I just feel that they have.' He was speaking half to himself, staring down at the cover on the divan.

'Well,' said Amy, thinking hard, and also frowning down at the red cover on the divan without in the least realizing that it was red, as was the cushion under Bob's shoulders, 'if I were you, I should just hang on to that. That's something you *feel*.'

He nodded and moved a little towards her. 'Right now I'm so tired I can't feel anything except that you're lovely.'

Amy put her arm round his shoulders. 'Let's sit here quietly for a little while,' she whispered, putting her cheek to his.

There was a long silence. Sounds came up clearly from the streets already burning in the sunlight, but the room, as it had been last night, was hushed as a tower in a fairy tale. The pictures on its white walls—a black and red lyre, some pale stone ruins where horses caracolled, a plate of dim fruits—glowed strangely with a life of their own, uncomforting, like windows opening on to uncanny landscapes. The real window, that had given last night on a witchlike panorama of quivering crimson lines and glittering symbols, now showed only ordinary roofs and walls against a dull hot sky where an aeroplane droned. It was nine o'clock in the morning in a modern city, where fear and money ruled the people as they have always ruled, yet along the hot ugly streets, side by side with the fear and the power of money, beauty and mystery walked as they have always walked, and at any moment a human being might step aside into them and stand still to dream, as Bob and Amy were dreaming now. But they only knew that they were in the midst of peace and silence and that it comforted them to be together.

At last Bob moved, sighing, and said:

'When did you say Lou was coming?'

'I don't know. She said she'd telephone me this morning about ten o'clock to arrange things.'

'It's a quarter of ten now,' he said, glancing at the electric clock. 'I'll speak to her when she does call up, if you don't mind.'

'Oh, do! It'll be such a lovely surprise for her!'

He laughed for the first time and asked, surveying her:

'How old are you?'

'I'll be twenty-three in October. How old are you?'

'I was twenty-three in January.'

They looked at one another for a moment, then Amy glanced away and said:

'I'd better wash up. Myrtle can't come in, her sister's had twins.'

'Don't you want to write?'

Amy shook her head. Never had she been less anxious to write.

'I'll help do the dishes.'

'You'd better rest, hadn't you? There isn't much to wash up, really.'

'No, I'll help.'

While they were washing up the telephone bell rang, and Bob went quickly across to answer it. Amy came and stood at the kitchen door, with a cloth and a half-dried cup in her hands, and listened. A girl with knowledge of the conventions would have stayed in the kitchen, and a girl with natural tact would have found some task to occupy her in the bedroom, but it did not occur to Amy that she should not stand and listen, for Lou was about to have her delightful surprise; it was a happy occasion, not one for hiding in the kitchen.

'Lou?' said Bob, and then Amy heard an excited exclamation at the other end of the line, sounding clearly in the quiet room.

'Yes it's me,' said Bob. 'Yes, I'm all right.' His voice went on, replying in monosyllables to her questions, sounding tired and discouraged in contrast to his sister's excited high tones. He did not turn to smile at Amy, and she began to feel that the occasion was not so happy as she had thought it would be.

At last he hung up the receiver and turned to her. 'They're coming right over,' he said. 'Helen too.'

'I'm glad.'

'Sure. I want to see them both. And then I can fix about going home.' But he began to wander round the room, looking at the dim or brilliant pictures as if he were not really seeing them, and Amy went back into the kitchen and went on with the drying-up. She was trying to control her jealousy. She did not want to share Bob with anyone, for it seemed so long since he had knocked at the door last night that she felt she had always known him; she had forgotten that he had once been only a childish memory, and it seemed so natural for him to be alone with her that she dreaded the arrival of other people, even the members of his own family.

Soon he came and stood by her as she was polishing the last plate.

'I want to ask you something.'

'All right,' said Amy, beginning to tremble as she carefully put the plate on to the dresser. She kept her back turned to him because she was afraid to look round, but he gently put his hands on her shoulders and turned her about until she faced him and stood looking up seriously into his serious face.

'It's so queer about you and me,' he said in a low tone, 'that I can't begin to talk about it, there's so much to say. We'll have to talk about it some time soon. But never mind that now. I must ask you something. I've never felt about anyone like I do about you. Do you feel like that about me? As if we belonged to each other?'

She nodded. He looked at her for a moment, and then he put his arms round her and gave her a kiss.

It was so wonderful a kiss that she felt it to be a gift, even in the confusion that filled her mind. Forgotten memories of her mother's good-night kisses came back to her, as if they were the breath of spring flowers rather than thoughts; and memories of the long afternoons when she had been contentedly alone in the little room at school, writing with the solemn moon looking in at her; she remembered rare moments as a child when she had felt safe and surrounded by love; and moments after she was grown-up when she had been sure that one day she would be happy, as if an angel had told her so in a dream. Peace and sweetness came to her from the gentle embrace in which he held her and the firm tender touch of his mouth on her own; and as she shut her eyes she felt veils falling and falling away in her mind and heart and soul, revealing deeper beauty and peace. These veils were years, she suddenly knew, falling and falling away into the past, and in each year he and she would belong to one another, and in each one they would learn to love one another more. *And they lived happily ever after* came into her mind; the lovely ending to all the fears of the fairy tale, the desire of the world. *And they lived happily ever after.* She opened her eyes, and she was crying.

'Darling, it's all right. Don't cry. I feel it too. It's real. Whatever happens, you and I belong to each other, don't we?'

'Oh, yes, yes!'

They held one another in silence for a little while, and then he said:

'Now I can go home and try to work. I had to ask you.'

'I'm so glad you did. Oh, I am so happy! I didn't know people could be happy like this.'

He smiled, murmuring to her and kissing her. 'Neither did I. But it's real—can't you feel it is?'

The bell of the apartment rang, making her start, and he gently released her from his arms.

'That's Lou. I'll go.'

He went quickly across to the door, Amy following him more slowly, wiping her eyes.

When he opened the door she had an instant's impression of the two girls standing there on the landing in the dusty sunlight pouring through the windows, both of them bending forward eagerly; and then the picture broke up as Lou came forward and put her arms round Bob's neck. The other girl, who was staring at Bob, did not move but her handbag fell to the floor. Amy picked it up, and the other girl made an uncertain little movement with her hand. 'Thank you,' she said, slowly turning her eyes away from Bob and looking at Amy. 'Oh, thank you.' They looked at one another for a moment and then Amy said: 'You're Miss Viner, aren't you? I'm Amy Lee. I expect Lou told you——'

'Yes, she did. I'm very pleased to meet you, Miss Lee,' said Helen, smiling; and as she spoke Bob put out his hand to her and drew her towards him.

'Hullo, Helen. I'm glad you——'

'Bob,' she said, as if to herself, and they exchanged an affectionate kiss; then all moved forward into the room and Amy shut the door.

'I'm so glad to see you,' she said at once to Lou, beginning to pull up chairs for everyone and to hand cigarettes with a natural wish to make them feel more at ease; the moment was so full of emotion that no-one found it easy to begin talking, and they sat down amid half-finished remarks and polite little exclamations of 'Let me——' 'No—you sit here——'

'I'm glad to see you, too. I'll sort everything out presently,' answered Lou, leaning back and lighting a cigarette. 'In a minute or two, I expect, only I'm so knocked endways over Bob. It certainly is good to see you again!' she ended cheerfully, turning to her brother. But Amy, with her perceptions made more sensitive than usual by the experiences of the morning, could tell that she was so deeply shocked by Bob's appearance that she found it difficult to talk to him naturally; and when she stole a glance at Helen, while busily mixing drinks at a side table, she saw on her face, uncontrolled, the same shocked, incredulous look that Lou was trying to hide.

Of course, she thought, shaking the mixer, I don't know what he was like before he went away, but he must be dreadfully changed, to make them look like that.

'I came to borrow twenty dollars from Boone,' said Bob, leaning back on the divan with his arms behind his head and beginning to talk with an effort. 'I had a job in Harrisburg, playing the piano, but I walked out of that and hitch-hiked here. Miss Lee very kindly asked me to stay.'

'We thought you were with Dan,' murmured Lou, wondering how soon she could get a doctor to him.

'So I was, until three weeks ago.'

'Have you called up Mother yet?'

He shook his head.

'She's been away with Dad on a trip, but they get home this afternoon.'

'All right; I'll call them later. Where are you staying?'

'The Abraham Lincoln, on Lexington Avenue and Twenty-third.'

'I'll come back with you, if they've got a room? Is it very full?'

'No. They're sure to have one. When are you going home?'

'When I've talked to Dad. Tomorrow, if I can.'

The conversation between the brother and sister went on in quiet tones, as if they were in a sick room. Bob was very tired. He lay back with his head on the red cushion, looking wearily at Lou, or sometimes turning to smile at Helen, and then moving his head to watch Amy as she went about the kitchen getting crackers out of the cupboard. Lou continued to question him cautiously about his plans and to make arrangements for his return, but she found it difficult to talk naturally, as Amy had seen, partly because she was so shocked at the change in him and partly because she was fascinated by the red cushion behind his head! She kept staring at it and noticing every detail of its appearance; the thick white fringe that decorated it, the different shade of whiteness in Bob's cheek, the dent his head made in

374

its fullness. In this state of her feelings she was grateful to Amy for busying herself calmly with the ordinary duties of a hostess and thus helping to create a more natural atmosphere in the room, and she unconsciously began to think of Amy as less of a child and with more respect.

Helen sat in silence, sipping her drink while Lou and Bob talked. All the time their quiet conversation went on, her eyes were moving slowly about the room; from the white matting on the floor to the Spanish leather screen, then to the picture of the caracolling horses, past them to the window with the dull view of roofs and distant walls. Her gaze went searching desperately, like someone dying of thirst, for one drop, one sparkle, of beauty to comfort her. For weeks, ever since Bob disappeared, beauty had been her only refuge; and now that he had come back and she had seen how he looked at Amy, she knew that she was going to need its help (but she had not thought that *possible!*) more than ever.

At last her eyes rested on a Japanese painting of water and moonlit islands, and slowly the pain lessened until it was bearable once more.

She managed to smile naturally and to answer Amy's shy question as to how she liked New York, and gradually the conversation grew more normal, as Lou joined in with comments on Amy's trip to Illinois. Presently a discussion was going on, and they were even smiling a little over Amy's discoveries about America. But in spite of their efforts the atmosphere was a strange one, subdued and almost exhausted, as if these four handsome young people under twenty-five had just escaped some peril of which they did not wish to speak. Each one of them, too, was busy with strong feelings to which they could give no expression, and their voices were slightly absent-minded and their glances kept straying.

I'll go crazy with curiosity if I can't get her alone and hear all about it soon, thought Lou. It's the weirdest thing, his turning up here—and yet I suppose that's perfectly natural, really; why shouldn't he come to Boone's for money? It's those dreams of hers, and that red cushion! Oh, that cushion! If she hadn't had the dreams she wouldn't have recognized me at the party; and if she hadn't told me about them I shouldn't have advised her to take the flat; and if strangers had been here, instead of Amy, Bob would have gone away without knowing that we were going to be in New York today, and we should none of us have been here now. Everything goes back to those dreams of hers. It's getting creepier and creepier, like an Alexander Woollcott story, and I don't like it, decided Lou, the calm climate of whose mind had no natural sympathy with 'creepiness.' It's grand to have him back, of course (though I'm afraid Mother will get a shock when she sees him) and I like that funny little number better every minute. But it *is* creepy! I'm glad I didn't tell Mother about those dreams.

She was also conscious that Helen was suffering, and this gave her pain. She was the only one of the Vorsts who had guessed the depth of Helen's feelings. Though the rest of the family had always vaguely thought that 'it would be grand if Bob married Helen,' and had realized that Helen and Bob had a special feeling for one another, they had never become aware that Helen loved him. But Lou had known it since she was a child, and now that she, too, had seen how he looked at Amy, she knew how Helen must feel, and she could not console herself by thinking easily, 'Oh, she'll find someone else.' Helen was beautiful and good and men loved her; she would certainly marry, but Lou was sure that she would not find someone else.

'I'm sorry, I feel bad,' said Bob suddenly, during a pause in the talk. 'It's nothing much, don't worry.' But he looked so ill that Lou said rather quickly to Helen:

'I should think he'd better come back with us now, hadn't he? And he can rest in the hotel while I call up Mother and break the news to her.'

'He could stay here, if you like?' suggested Amy timidly, seating herself upon the edge of the divan with her little hands locked over one another, and looking at him in deep distress. The innocent possessiveness in her voice, the look with which he met her glance, made their feelings about one another so plain that Lou hastily glanced away from Helen's face.

'No, I'll come with you,' he said decidedly to his sister. 'And I'll call up Mother, too; I'm not so sick as all that. Then I shan't be any more trouble to you,' he added to Amy.

She shook her head.

'I'll get a taxi,' said Helen suddenly, going over to the telephone.

While she was dialling the number and Lou was painting her mouth in front of the mirror, Bob said to Amy:

'I'll call you up later. Will you be in?'

Again she moved her head, looking at him.

'I must go with them now,' he went on in the same low voice, 'because there are so many things to fix up, now I'm going home to get on with my work. I want to stay with you, but I can't, I've been crazy enough. But don't feel bad about it, darling, it's real, remember. And I'll call you up tonight.'

In the midst of a little pause during which they looked steadily at one another Helen announced that the taxi was coming round the block. Bob got up and they all moved towards the door.

'I'll call you up early tomorrow,' said Lou meaningly to Amy, as they all went down in the lift. 'Maybe we could meet for coffee in the morning?'

'I should love it,' replied Amy, but without enthusiasm.

She did not want to talk about what had happened; it was already sacred. Lou gave her a dry look which she did not see, and thought, *Relatives Keep Off.* Well, I'm glad it's her, for it might have been Francey Carr or something from the Ecstasy Club. All the same, she must know where he's been and every-thing, and tomorrow I am going to have a bare outline. I don't want to probe their feelings, but a bare outline I must and will have. Myron will want to know all about it when Bob gets home and of course Bob won't tell him one thing and probably he won't tell us much, either. If I don't tell Myron something when I get home he'll make it all up as he goes along, and people will be talking quite enough, without Myron's help. Besides, I want to know.

The lift stopped in the lobby and they went across to the door. Bob took Amy's hand for a moment and smiled down at her and said, 'Good-bye,' and the girls made friendly farewells, and then the three Americans went quickly down the steps to the waiting taxi.

Amy was startled for a second; the contrast between the girls in elegant dark summer dresses and the big fair young man in broken shoes and stained jacket made the group look so dramatic as to be unreal. They're going, and I shall never see them again! she thought. But the taxi driver scarcely glanced at the three, for the Village was the Village, and full of odd sights; and as the taxi drove away Bob leant out of the window and moved his hand to her, while the girls waved and smiled.

She went slowly back to the lift, seeing nothing but his smiling white face, and the little movement of his hand. She stood quite still as the lift climbed to the sixth floor, staring at the wall and feeling desolate, for suddenly the events of yesterday evening were no longer real; and she already knew that her heart was a prisoner and could only be comforted by realizing that the words he and she had said to one another, the slumber they had shared on the red couch, were true.

In the apartment, cigarette smoke lingered on the air and the glasses stood about on the arm-trays of the chairs. The sunlight poured in with a steady look, as if it would burn the walls and floor. She moved from room to room emptying ashtrays and tidying the glasses away, plumping the cushions and arranging the chairs, while an aching lump grew in her throat and a painful feeling of confusion and loss, as bodily as a headache, slowly overcame her. Presently, while she was getting out her manuscript and putting her glass of water ready, she began to cry, and though she sat down and prepared to write she could not stop crying. She got up and wandered round the room, rubbing the tears from her eyes, and at last lay down on the divan, still impressed by his body, and cried for a long time. It was while she was lying there, wearied out, that a large box of pale yellow roses arrived, with a card:

'For my Swimming Girl'

An American courtship had begun.

'She isn't a bit what one expects a writer to be, is she?' said Helen suddenly, as she and Lou were going up in the lift to their room, having left Bob asleep in his.

'No. Most writers are nuts,' answered Lou, not aggressively but as one who refers to a fact. 'She's inclined to be jittery but she's not nuts. Did you like her?'

It was the natural question to ask and therefore Lou asked it, for she was determined that there should be no meaningful silences, no sympathetic glances, between herself and Helen. She knew that if they were distasteful to herself they would be unbearable to her cousin.

'There's something striking about her, but I can't truthfully say I liked her,' replied Helen, going pale but also speaking naturally. 'She has that very unforthcoming British air—you know. It doesn't attract me. But if I knew her well I should respect her. She's single-minded, I should think.'

'Knows what she wants, do you mean?'

'No. I meant that she only likes a very few things and people, and is faithful to them. Most people have so many loyalties and interests that they're all tangled-up. She's restful, somehow.'

The words *what she wants—faithful*—lingered on the air with a faint sadness after they were spoken, and for a moment both girls were silent, thinking about the same thing, of which they would never speak to one another. Then Helen added:

'She doesn't sparkle at all——'

'Thank God.'

—'And her books don't either, do they? I was surprised by the one you lent me, it was so childish.'

'It was a swell story, I couldn't put it down.'

'But *only* a story, Lou. No deep psychological problems or social analysis, and nothing mature.'

'It did make you feel you were in the story yourself, though,' said Lou thoughtfully, as they walked down the corridor. 'I really felt I knew that queer old house in whereisit——'

'. . . Lambeth. In London, south of the Thames.'

'. . . and that creepy old guy and his cats. I got a kick out of it.'

Helen shook her head.

'I guess I'm too old for fairy tales,' she said gently. It was the first bitter sentence Lou had heard her speak in the twenty years they had known one another, and she had to resist an impulse to take her arm and give it a loving pressure, but she did resist it, and they went into their room in silence.

I must get away, thought Helen, beginning to brush her hair. Miles away to California, or Florida—and stay there. If I'm to make anything of my life, if I'm not to go rotten with dreams, that's what I've got to do, and quick.

It's tough on her and she's being grand about it, thought Lou, sitting on her bed and carefully examining her stockings for runs. I wonder if Mother and Dad put Bob off by dropping hints? That's what everyone has always done to me and Stebby. Maybe we'll walk in married one of these beautiful spring mornings, we must be pretty attracted or we wouldn't fight the way we do, but I'm darned if I marry Stebby—the fresh thing!—until the old folks give up hoping I will. Nudge—hint—wink, until I could howl like a timber wolf!

She walked over to Helen's bureau and looked at a photograph of Helen's dark, slender, conceited brother while she took off her hat. Pleased with yourself, beautiful? She made the faintest face at his laughing face before she turned away.

This time last night he was here. Amy was sitting at the table late that evening trying to write, but every few sentences she stopped and began to draw doodles on the blotting paper, while her mind went spinning away into memories and dreams. *This time last night he was here.* She was also waiting for the telephone to ring. (Ah, that sound! which is usually an accursed nuisance but can be romantic as any *lieder*) and fearing that soon it would be too late, for it was ten o'clock, and in the circles in which she was most at home in London people did not ring up after ten o'clock, any more than they sent telegrams unless something was wrong.

Then it rang, making her start violently. It sounded actually beautiful to her, and she had come so far in self-examination that she thought how strange that was, as she took up the receiver, clumsily, because she was trembling.

'Hullo there?' said a young man's voice, unrecognizable.

'Hullo?'

'Is that———? This is Bob.'

'Oh, yes! Your voice sounds different.'

'So does yours.'

'Are you—how do you feel now?'

'Much better. I've been———'

'Oh, I'm so glad. I was—what did you say?'

'I only said I've been asleep ever since I left you.'

'I'm glad. That'll do you good.'

Pause.

'I called up my mother. I'm going home tomorrow morning.'

381

'Oh. I'm—that's good. Isn't your mother glad?'

'Yes. How are you?'

'Oh, I'm all right. I was just writing.'

'I'm not interrupting, am I?'

'Oh, no! I wasn't really doing much—only just——'

'Have you got the lamp on the table?'

'Yes. Oh—and the roses! Oh, I meant to thank you! Thank you very much. I never saw anything so beautiful!'

'I'm glad you liked them.'

'The stems are so long! I never saw——'

'Listen, I want to ask you something. Will you come and stay with us?'

'Stay——?'

'At home. In about a week? Lou says you're going to Marydale. That's only fifty miles from Vine Falls. I could come and meet you.'

'Oh, yes!'

'I'm sorry. I'll have to come by the bus. I mustn't drive a car, you know.'

'I don't mind a bit. It would be simply lovely.'

'All right, then. I'll write to you as soon as I get home and fix it up.'

'Wh—what time are you going tomorrow?'

'Half-after seven.'

'Oh. That's very early, isn't it?'

'Yes. Maybe I could call you up at six, if that isn't too early? Just to say good-bye.'

'Yes. I was hoping——'

'I will, then. Just to say good-bye.'

'Yes.'

Pause.

'Amy.'

'Yes.'

'That's the first time I've said your name, isn't it?'

'Yes.'

'Say mine.'

'Bob.'

'Amy, I only wanted to tell you that all the things we said were real.'

'Oh, I am glad you said that! I've been feeling bad, because——'

'I know, so have I. I'm glad you felt like that too. When you come to visit, we can talk.'

'Yes.'

Pause.

'Amy.'

'Yes . . . yes, Bob.'

'I—you've made me much happier. I'm feeling better about things—you know.'

'I'm so glad. You—you've made me much happier, too.'

'I wish I could see you.'

'Yes.'

'But I'll call you up at six tomorrow.'

'Oh, yes. I'll be awake.'

'Well. Well, good-night.'

'Good-night.'

'Good-night, darling.' The word came softly over the wires.

'Good-night. Oh—good-night——' She heard a faint click.

Slowly, as if it were something sacred, she replaced the receiver.

23

The long, low, cool house—how pleasant it was, with the country silence that was half-wild, the sharp silence of American woodlands, all about it and the killdeer's clear note coming from the woods! Bob leant out between the gently-moving white curtains at his bedroom window and looked at the familiar view; the lawn and the old elm and the tennis court and beyond the trees, the glimpse of blue hills. Then he turned back and looked at his room, where the textbooks from his chambers in Morgan had been hastily piled. It was familiar yet strange, like the photograph of a room he used to know; and as he surveyed it he felt like two people; the happy young man who had slept here for twenty-two years and taken the whole of life for granted, and the dishonoured coward who could never as long as he lived take anything for granted again.

It was his first evening at home, and he had already realized that it was going to be very difficult to get back on his own side of the fence.

His mother was so glad to have him back that she could not be angry with him (a state of affairs which made him feel worse than if she had been) but his father was very angry, and hardly attempted to hide his bitter disappointment. Bob was wondering how he and his father were going to live in the same house together for the next two years without continual quarrels.

I was a kid when I went away; I'm a man now, he thought, sitting on the window seat and staring out at the distant woods. Mother can see that, but Dad can't. I know it's tough on him; he's lost a packet, and can't afford to send Lou to New York, and he's had to sell the old newspapers, and he's seen men who've worked for him and his father before him sacked by this syndicate. I guess the state of the country must seem like the end of the world to him—all this unemployment and the New Deal and everything—and then I go crazy and ruin my career and come back different—and he's got to keep me for two more years! I don't wonder he's bitter. And he can't understand how I feel, and why I don't hate Dan and despise all the bums I ran around with because they're 'failures.' You can't get his generation to see that hard work and putting money by isn't enough nowadays. Something's slipped, but they can't—or won't—see it. And why should they? They've always been on the right side of the fence.

He stood up, sighing, as his mother came into the room.

'Bob, I was wondering—I think we'll have a little party on the day Miss Lee comes down, just a few old friends for cocktails. I just want people to know you're back from the South.'

'Myron will have told them, don't worry,' he said dryly. 'He's had his ears buttoned back ever since I got here.'

'He's very inquisitive, but he's been with us for twenty-seven years,' she reminded him, coming across and fondly putting her hands on the lapels of his old jacket as if she must touch her regained treasure. 'He's very fond of you, in his way. Vermont people aren't like other people, you know. He knew you were with Dan, but he won't talk, I'm sure.'

'Everybody here's lovely,' he said suddenly, bending his head to kiss her. 'You can't possibly know how lovely you all are.'

'I'm so glad to have you back, son,' she answered softly. 'I've been praying and praying ever since you went away; and ever since you called up yesterday I've been thanking God.'

He patted her hands as they lay on his shoulders, studying her face that had been an elegant middle-aged woman's when he went away, and now was old.

'Bob, I'm sure your father's come round,' she said next, confidently. 'He feels bad now, but he's glad to have you back.'

'Is he?'

'Surely, son! Only you must give him time; the last few years have been so hard for him.'

'Things won't ever be the same again,' he suddenly warned her, turning to look out of the window at the darkening garden, where the morning glories were closing for the night. 'Maybe we'll all be happy again some day, but not like we used to be.'

'Oh—I think everything's going to be fine,' she said, with the unconquerable Southern optimism, lazy and sweet like that of a flower which cannot tell it is dying. 'Irene'll have a baby, maybe, and you'll get through your examinations and get your degree, and Lou'll marry Stebby——'

'Will she?'

'Surely she will,' said Lou's mother tranquilly. 'I've planned the grandest apartment for them on Sunset Heights—just a small one, at first, until Stebby gets on and they can afford a house in Goldenwood.'

'Stebby likes women,' said Bob abruptly.

'All boys like girls; it's natural. He'll be just fine when they're married,' said Mrs Vorst, dismissing Stebby's weakness with an indulgent smile.

'Not just girls, Mother; women. And they like him. That doesn't matter, of course, unless he marries Lou, but I can't see her standing for that.'

'Oh, I'm sure he and Lou'll be wonderful together. He'll settle down when they're married. Now I was wondering—who shall we ask on Friday? Miss Cordell and Amalie (Lou said Miss Cordell has a real crush on Miss Lee since the reception) and Judge Van Damm——'

She stood by the door for a moment, looking down at him as he knelt beside his textbooks and sorted them into order, but for the first time since his return she was not thinking about him. She had a dreamy manner, but she had the natural cunning in the management of emotional affairs that belongs to very feminine women, and at that moment she was thinking about this Miss Lee.

Lou and her mother had had a long talk on the telephone about Amy, before the cousins left New York to visit Irene at Cape Cod. Lou had explained that Amy had let Bob stay the night at the flat, trusting to her mother's common-sense as well as to her habitual delicacy of thought to avoid suspicions that a coarser mind might have felt. She had ended her story by warning her mother that Bob had fallen heavily for Amy and she for him. It's a case; let's face it, had been her last words. We'll just have to see how it turns out, thought Mrs Vorst, soothing herself. I wish she was an American girl, but maybe she's not so starchy as most of the British. And Lou said she has some money. I don't want Bob to live on his wife (American boys don't do that) but it's better that she should have some money of her own. Maybe she's a sweet girl. Anyway, I'm glad she's coming on a visit; I can make up my mind about her then.

'Miss Lee'll be here to lunch on Friday, Bob?'

'No, I guess not; I'm going into Marydale to meet her and we shan't be back until afternoon.'

'Just as you like, son. I'm always glad to see your friends.' And she smiled absently at him and glided from the room, leaving him feeling soothed, he did not know why.

He finished arranging his books, then rolled up a stained windbreaker jacket and a pair of trousers ragged at the hems and some broken white shoes. He could burn those in the furnace, one day when Myron was out. His mood as he did so was neither depressed nor exalted, but only dogged. Everything was the same at home; and yet all was changed; it was like living with dearly loved ghosts in a dream. Nothing was real to him now, except memories of the broken luckless people on the other side of the fence, and the faint sweet smell of Amy's hair.

★

When Amy climbed down from the train at Marydale on Friday morning, looking eagerly around for Bob, her first impression was that the tall young man striding towards her with a light belted coat flying and one hand up, saluting her, was a stranger. She had not, of course, ever seen him in a hat and a collar and he looked younger and less pale than she remembered him. Deep shyness overcame her.

'Hullo!' he said, taking off his hat with exactly the same gesture he had made on that first evening, and coming to a halt in front of her.

'Hullo,' she said faintly.

'Let me have your grip.' He took her case and they began to walk down the platform towards the exits. 'Did you have a good trip?'

'Oh, yes, very, thank you.'

'The bus is waiting over there. It's hell, my not being able to drive a car. I'm sorry.'

'I don't mind buses at all. I quite like riding in them, as a matter of fact.'

'Do you? I certainly am glad to hear that. Mother suggested Myron driving us back, and I said no.'

'Who's Myron?'

'Myron Blodgett, our handyman. He's a character; comes from Vermont. He's the original sourpuss, I should say. He's been with us twenty-seven years.'

'Before you were born.'

'Yes. He was a printer out of a job, and he walked across three States (they didn't hitch-hike in those days) to get away from his folks; said they plagued him. Dad hadn't a job on any of the papers but he took him on at home to drive the buggy and cut grass and run errands. And he's just stayed.'

They climbed into the bus, and as he followed her up the steps he could not take his eyes off the upward sweep of her dark hair on the white nape of her neck. He liked to look at it in exactly the same way that he liked watching the katydids when he was a boy; they had their own way of doing things; cunning and quite different from humans, and Amy's hair, on the head of a girl, a creature so different from himself, had just the same look of demure yet abundant life and fascinated him in the same way. He wanted to take it down and play with it and kiss the back of her neck, but there was more than this in the charm it exercised over him, and he knew it.

They sat down in the front part of the bus.

'It's funny,' he went on after a pause, 'I never *think* about Myron, but it wouldn't be the same at home without him and his old hickory rocker, croaking and creaking round the place and saying, "*So-and-so hain't got no fa-a-a-culty*".' (Bob drawled it through his nose, New England fashion).

'What's faculty?'

'New England for doing a thing the best way possible.'

Amy thought for a moment.

'Horse-sense, would it be, in English?'

He laughed.

'That's about it.'

The bus was slowly filling up behind them, and as Amy still felt painfully shy, she listened for some time without speaking to the unfamiliar buzz of conversation, quicker and higher-pitched than that of an English bus-load. She heard the thick, slow, flattened tones of a Pole talking English, striking heavily across the piercing chatter of women; and she remembered how beautiful the negro voices had sounded to her in the streets of Harlem, the only voices she had heard in New York that seemed to come straight from the humanness of the speakers; sounding as the voices of Adam and Eve might have sounded as they talked in the Garden of Eden. *De goole bug*, she thought, imagining Jupiter saying the words in the negro voice that was now familiar to her, *de purty goole bug*.

It makes a difference, having heard and seen and smelled

things, she thought. Books come more alive. Now I know what a drug store is like and a porch, where Meg used to 'rest and read.'

But her thoughts were only half with the voices in the bus, for she was so strongly aware of the young man sitting beside her that she could not go off into the dreamy state of mind that usually crept over her in public places; she could see his big hand (the nails were clean now) lying across his knee, the fingers impatiently rolling their tickets into a tiny baton, the knee-cap itself under the grey flannel trouser leg, a few inches of blue sock and a long shapely foot in a subtly but completely unEnglish brown shoe. I don't know any of his clothes today, that's why I feel he's a stranger, she thought. I got to know that old jacket and those white shoes and I miss them.

He turned suddenly to her and, catching her gaze fixed curiously on his shoes, went a little red.

'I wish all these people weren't here,' he said.

'Yes.'

'I've never been so sorry I mustn't drive a car. I didn't hire one, because the driver'd be there all the time, and——'

'Please don't mind. I would rather have had a car, of course, because——' And then she stopped, realizing what her words implied, and unable to continue because of her shyness.

'If you'd rather, that's enough—well, not quite enough, but it's pretty good.'

At that they both laughed a little, the first time they had ever laughed together, as the bus moved off through the pleasant uptown district.

Amy was very happy. She always enjoyed riding in buses, and with Bob sitting beside her, looking happier and healthier than when she had last seen him, she felt she had very little left to wish for. It was not quite true that she would rather have had a car, for she was so shy of him, in spite of her delight in being with him, that the prospect of a ride alone with him was alarming.

It was only a week since their first meeting, and in that time she had exchanged two telephone conversations with him (one a mere murmur of 'Good-bye, then' at six o'clock in the morning), and had received one letter, chiefly concerned with arrangements for their meeting on Friday. But although it had begun 'Dear Amy,' it had ended (as if the short sentences found it difficult to leave the pen because they meant so much to the writer) *I am getting a little better. You have helped me so much. I think about you all the time. I hope you do sometimes about me.* And then some words tantalisingly scratched out and the signature 'Bob.'

If she had been violently and consciously in love this letter would have been disappointing to her. But she was not consciously in love, and in her complete inexperience of men she took the letter to mean exactly what it said. *I think about you all the time. I hope you do sometimes about me.* Sometimes! She never stopped thinking about him except when she was asleep, and then she dreamt about him. And, as he said as much, she took it that that was how he thought about her. Even at this moment, as he sat beside her while the bus moved past vacant lots towards the open country, he must be thinking about her—just as she was thinking of him!

Bob was thinking about her. He was as bewitched as she was, but his reason for not writing a letter saying: 'I love you' was a simple one: he had realised after some conversation with Lou that Amy must make a large income from her writing, and though his reason told him that money should not keep a man and a woman apart when they loved one another, his natural American instinct to 'make good' and not to offer marriage until he could offer a sufficient income with it made him hesitate to write, 'I love you'—although he longed to write it, and even more to say it.

That was how he had felt before he saw her again; but he had not been with her for more than ten minutes before he was once more under that peculiar, unspoken, intimate spell which had held them both in the flat; that feeling of *belonging* which made the question of money seem unimportant. *Of course she'll understand*, he found himself thinking, *what am I worrying about?*

He had been fretting over this money question ever since he left New York, but now he suddenly ceased to worry. Unconsciously, under the spell of Amy's presence, he applied to the question the wisdom he had learned on the other side of the fence, the touchstone of reality. Money was useful, whoever it belonged to, and if two people loved each other it did not matter whose the money was.

Besides, he thought, I'll be working in a year, and earning some myself. I guess she'd live in a shack in the Polak quarter if she feels like me. Anyway, I'm going to ask her. *After all that's happened I'm not going to let her go.*

Amy suddenly took off her hat and put it on her lap, and he started, realizing that they had not exchanged a word for a long time.

'Headache?' he inquired anxiously.

'Oh no, I just like being without a hat. You can see better, I always think.'

Her eyes, brilliant as topazes, looked up at him from under eyebrows which had not been plucked and had the dusty winglike look which nowadays only children's eyebrows have. He said—

'Yes——' but did not realize that he had said it, for they continued to look at one another, and he saw Amy's expression slowly change to one of intent, wondering happiness. Her gaze slowly moved over his face, until at last she came back to rest in his eyes, and stayed there lost in their clear grey, with a gaze naked in its unconscious avowal of love. Then the blood came up quickly into his face and he saw it come as quickly into her own.

'Of course, in London you have to wear a hat,' she said quickly, looking away.

'Yes, I suppose you do.' He could not look away just yet; for he had never seen anything so delicate as the line of hair on her high forehead, and the curve of her cheek.

'I'm a swell guide to New Leicester,' he said presently, 'but this part isn't very interesting—there's the farm I had my first pony from when I was a kid.'

'Oh, where?' she said eagerly, and kept her gaze steadily fixed on the low wooden buildings, yellow as cream against the deeper yellow of maize fields in stook, until the dark elms that overhung the farm, the golden pumpkin heap beside the stream, were lost to sight.

'We're just getting into Alva,' he said as the bus went round a clump of trees and they came on the big highway sign—

WELCOME TO ALVA

'That's so nice and polite, you know,' observed Amy.

'Don't you have them in England?'

'Oh, goodness, no! We just have a notice, all black and yellow like a wasp, with the name of the village on it. Nothing like "Welcome".'

'Nobody but a sucker would come to live here, though,' said Bob, as the bus drew up in Main Street opposite a movie house. 'The branch line closed down two years ago because of competition from these cross-country buses, and that half-killed the place. Alva was put up in the real-estate boom ten years ago but it isn't a real town.'

'How long has Vine Falls been there?' asked Amy, thinking dreamily how strange, how frighteningly strange, it was to be sitting here beside *my American*, asking him a question about the town whose name had been a charm to her imagination for eleven years. She waited happily for the sound of his voice in answer. It was a voice with some of his mother's Southern softness, unaffected, warmer than most American voices, with the unfamiliar burr of the New World muted by education and tradition.

'Oh, we've got roots!' he said with a touch of pride. 'Vine Falls is a real town; we've been there nearly eighty years. My great-grandfather, Boone Vorst, helped to build Vine Falls.'

'Oh, do tell me about him!' cried Amy, turning on him the face of a child asking for a story.

'Well, he must have been as crazy as a coot, but he was a grand old boy, too. He'd read a lot of European writers and he had some notion of building a city in the West and spreading culture among the Redskins. He owned a printing business and a small newspaper in New York and he was doing well there, but he got together a bunch as crazy as himself and they collected tools and corn-seed and all the things you want to start a city with, and he piled Great-Grandmother and the eight kids and the printing presses on a covered waggon, and off they went.'

'Brave,' said Amy softly.

'It certainly was, especially Great-Grandmama, with a new baby every year! But they never got to the Golden West, because they found Vine Falls and settled there and Great-Grandfather helped build the town. He founded the first newspapers in the State, too. He left them to Grandfather, and *he* left them to my dad. But they're all gone now. We were never sorrier about anything than when Dad had to let those three old papers go to a syndicate.'

'Don't you think he might ever be able to buy them back?' she asked, thinking affectionately of *The Prize* and hoping Lord Welwoodham would never have to sell that.

'No. Not now. You see, he lost a pile when the market crashed in '29.'

'Tell me some more about your great-grandfather.'

'Oh—well, there's one story that always thrilled Helen and me when we were kids. When he was a young man, before he had his own press and paper, he worked on a little weekly in New York. There were dozens of them, round about that time (somewhere in the early eighteen-thirties, it would be), little rags full of dirty politics and local scandal. This particular little one-horse affair was got out by the editor and Great-Grandfather and a boy in two dirty rooms at the top of a crazy old building, and the editor drank like a fish, especially on press nights, so Great-Grandpa was often left to put the paper to bed with only the boy to help, because the editor had passed out in the inner office. He used to say he learned everything there was to know about running a newspaper that way.'

'What was the paper called?'

'*The New York Watcher.* We've got some copies of it at home; I'll show you. Well, one bitter night in the middle of winter the paper was due to go to press in a couple of hours when the editor suddenly passed out. He'd been drinking hard all day and cussing and swearing at Great-Grandpa and the boy, so they weren't sorry when he collapsed. They hauled him into the next room and pitched his tall hat in after him (everybody wore tall hats to work in those days) and shut the door. Then Great-Grandpa sent the boy out for some coffee and sandwiches and settled down to wait for the last bit of copy they were holding the paper back for; something about a local meeting.'

'How do you know about the coffee and the tall hat?'

'Great-Grandma. She wrote it down, years afterwards, just as he told her. Well, after the boy had gone (he used to say) *it was so quiet you could hear the snow brushing against the windows*. The room was warm and Great-Grandpa was beginning to feel sleepy when suddenly he heard the front door slam, and then someone began coming up the stairs. At first he thought it was the boy back again, but then he listened, and he knew it wasn't the boy's step. *It was a kind of a proud step*, he used to say, *slow and proud, like as if some Southern gentleman was condescending to climb our stairs and not thinking much of 'em while he climbed*. Great-Grandpa didn't move, he just sat listening, and the steps reached the landing, and came across it, and suddenly the door was flung open. It went right back on its hinges, and there was a young man standing there, looking in at Great-Grandfather.'

'Oh, who——?' she cried.

'All right, all right,' smiling down at her. 'Don't spoil the story! Well, he was very pale and dressed all in black with an old cloak with capes on it and a shabby tall hat and black gloves. That's what Great-Grandpa noticed most of all, somehow, his small thin hands in black skin gloves with the fingertips worn white. His coat was all plastered up with snow and he was breathing quickly as if he'd been running.

'They stared at each other for a minute, and then Great-Grandpa said:

'"Well, and what do you want?" He didn't like the way the stranger was looking him up and down so he didn't trouble to be polite. The young man said haughtily:

'"*Good evening, suh. Is your editor at liberty?*" (Bob's voice turned to a Southern drawl.)

'My great-grandfather jerked his head at the door of the inner office and said, "*He's in there. What do you want?*" and the young man answered: "*I hesitate to intrude upon him in the midst of what, I was informed below, is the busiest evening of the week, but I have here——*" and he began fumbling in his pocket. "*He's drunk. Mostly is on press nights,*" said Great-Grandpa. "*And I'm in charge here. If it's copy, you're too late for this week.*" And then the stranger drew himself up in a high and mighty style and said: "*I regret, suh, that I cannot submit my contribution (it is a poem) to the consideration of anyone but your editor, presumably a man of culture and sensibility. I thank you, suh, and I wish you good-night.*" And he turned and stalked out of the room *like a great black bird*, Great-Grandfather used to say. He had half a mind to run after him and kick him in the pants. But just as the stranger was crossing the landing the boy came up with the coffee and sandwiches, and the young man stood aside to let him pass, and my great-grandfather saw him fix such an awful look on the food, *kind of scornful and starved, both at once,* that he never forgot it. Then he went slowly downstairs pulling his cloak round him, and presently the front door slammed.'

'So what happened?' asked Amy breathlessly.

'Nothing. They never saw him again. But eighteen years later when Great-Grandpa was settled in Vine Falls and running his three newspapers, he opened a bundle of papers from New York one morning, brought in by the Wells and Fargo messenger, and stared for a long time at a picture on the front page, and at last he said to Great-Grandma: *I never forget a face. That's the fellow who came into the offices of* The Watcher *that night in the winter of '31 and wouldn't show me his poem.* And Great-Grandmother looked, and under the picture it said that Edgar Allan Poe had died that week in the Washington University Hospital at Baltimore. Peach of a story, isn't it?'

She nodded, for the moment too entranced to speak. The story had revived all the spell that Poe's tales and poems had exercised upon her childhood.

'I love his stories,' she said at last. 'Do you like them?'

'Used to when I was a kid. Not so much now.'

She did not ask him why. She felt he was trying to tell her that Poe's beautiful trances of horror were as nothing beside the body of a dead child, limp in the arms of the man who had killed it. There was nothing more to be said.

The effort of telling the story had tired Bob, who was not yet completely restored to health, and he said no more for a long time. The silence between them gradually grew more intimate and tender.

Presently, by the sleepy hush which seemed to flow in from the quiet, almost uninhabited landscape going past the windows and creep over the few passengers, Amy became aware that they were passing through a region of uncultivated fields and isolated patches of woodland. Lonely, unfenced, a-nod with golden rod and tall sprays of coarse flowers, the neglected fields rolled away on either side to the horizon where the hills began, blue-grey with distance, and on them the sunlight blazed. A shabby, unimpressive land overgrown with the commoner wild blossoms, where Nature seemed in undress, not troubling to compress her powers into anything strikingly beautiful, and even the trees, which will appear beautiful in the most unpromising landscape, had a raggedy look. A shirt-sleeved, reach-me-down, cornstalk-in-mouth, apple-barrel-seat country—but over it sailed the enormous bright white clouds, the primitive sky-scrapers 'that are said to be seen nowhere but in the skies of America,' glorifying the scattered, untidy, shiftless-looking wooden houses as they slowly towered above them and sailed away under pressure of the wind towards the South.

'Can you remember the English country?' she asked suddenly after a long stare through the window.

'Very green. Small fields like they have in New England,' he said at once. 'Very tidy. Brick farmhouses looking kind of sunk in deep grass. Little hedges. Red apples on the trees.'

She nodded.

'This is so absolutely different, so wild and lonely. I can imagine Indians here.'

'There were Indians in the hills, years and years ago. We've got some houses in Vine Falls with holes in the walls for the men to fire at the Indians when they raided the village. But maybe Lou showed you.'

'I was only there a day and there wasn't time to see anything. I'd have liked to get up into the woods; they looked lovely.'

'I'll take you,' he promised, feeling relieved that she liked that kind of thing, which cost nothing, and which he liked too. He would be spared the shame of telling her that he could not afford to take her into Morgan to dance. 'We'll make a fire.'

'But won't you have to work?'

'Not all the time,' smiling. 'I don't go back to the Owen

Vallance for another two weeks; there are all kinds of things to fix up first.'

Then they both thought: *what will have happened in another two weeks?* but neither spoke, until Amy said:

'I brought my book. I thought your mother wouldn't mind? I'm so used to doing a bit every day.'

'She'll be mighty proud—a book being written under our roof. It'll be the first ever.'

It was then that Amy summoned all her courage and asked the question she had been longing to ask ever since they left Marydale.

'Bob?'

'What?' bending a little towards her. 'I like to hear you say my name, your accent's so pretty. What did you want me to tell you?'

'Have you read any of my books?' and Amy nearly shut her eyes with anxiety while she awaited the answer.

He nodded. 'Oh, yes. The first thing I did after I got home was to get *China Walk*.'

'And—did you like it?'

After a lengthy pause, in which her apprehensions increased and she clenched her hands so tightly that they ached, he said reluctantly—

'I thought it was wonderful that someone like you should turn out such a swell thriller. No-one would think you could do it.'

'But did you *like* it?' she persisted, increasingly troubled.

He shook his head, looking as distressed as she was.

'No. I'm sorry.'

'Oh, why not?' and her eyes suddenly filled with tears.

'Well, you see, fighting and death aren't like that and criminals aren't. You don't tell the truth about them.'

'It isn't meant to be true, it's a *story*!' she cried.

'I know. But it's a story glorifying criminals. Perhaps people who don't know what criminals are like might like it. But it just seemed silly to me.'

399

Amy was silent. It seemed the sun had gone in and she was sitting in a dreary vehicle going through drab country beside a stranger.

'I'm sorry,' he said again. 'But you wouldn't want me to say I liked it if I didn't, would you?'

'No, I suppose not. But I can't help wishing you did like it.'

'I'm sorry. I was hoping you wouldn't ask. Maybe I'll like some of the others better. But it doesn't make any difference to—to—how we feel, does it?'

She shook her head. She was bitterly disappointed, but she was quite sure that it did not make any difference.

'Tell me about when you were a little girl,' he said suddenly. 'That first time we met, when you had the white beret. You said you were miserable.'

So for the remainder of the journey she talked to him about the Beedings and her mother and father and London. The picture she painted was without self-pity, but even so it showed a childhood so different from his own that he found himself in the unexpected position of being sorry for her. It was plain that in spite of her success as a writer she had not shaken off the memories of ten lonely and frightened years and that she badly needed someone to take care of her. The realization brought him as near happiness as he could get, in his present shaken and embittered state of mind. She was not a wealthy and condescending angel; she was a little girl with no father and mother and no . . .

'Have you ever been engaged to be married?' he asked suddenly. He blurted out the question because he could not keep it back.

'Oh, no!' She turned right round and looked at him, startled out of her thoughts of far-away London. 'No-one ever—until the other day——' She broke off, but continued to look at him, confused, but so anxious to reassure him that she could ignore her confusion.

'You didn't mind my asking?'

'Oh, no. Have you?'

'I've never been engaged to be married. I was—with Dan's sister, some of the time I was away.'

'You don't love her, do you?' she whispered, looking down at her hat.

'No, of course not—it's quite different—I'm sorry about it now——'

'It's all right,' she said quickly. 'Truly. Please don't mind about it.'

A few contemptuous sentences of Lady Welwoodham's about 'men being different' now returned to her; she remembered Mrs Beeding saying more than once of some murder in the papers: No Doubt She Led Him On. That was what Dan's sister had done to Bob; and Amy immediately hated her with all the jealousy in a passionate nature. But she said no more on the matter, and her hatred did not spoil the happiness of being with Bob, for, after all, he had said that he did not love Dan's sister, and she believed him.

The bus was now entering a more prosperous-looking country with big farms and orchards, and the distant blue-grey hills had come near, revealing themselves as thickly covered with maple. 'WELCOME TO VINE FALLS, FRIEND,' said the sign some way outside the town, 'YOU ARE NOW APPROACHING THE BIRTH-PLACE OF JABEZ ELDOR, NOTED ABOLITIONIST AND FRIEND OF LINCOLN.' Presently they passed the beautiful campus of Eldor College, whose white buildings gleamed among shady trees with an Athenian dignity hardly sustained by its standards of learning; and then the bus went through some attractive new suburbs and stopped at last in the Square, still after eighty years the centre of life in Vine Falls.

Bob seemed completely at ease as he helped Amy down, and walked beside her carrying her case to where Myron had parked the Packard and was waiting for them, but his lips were compressed and he did not glance about him. Everyone who had business downtown that afternoon would notice his arrival by bus with an elegant girl, and everyone would talk. It was only part of the talk which would go on for the rest of his life, but this realization made facts no easier to bear.

Myron, for one. Myron, who wore an ordinary blue suit but somehow conveyed the impression that he was dressed in dungarees and a farm straw-hat, sat looking in their direction without a flicker on his wooden face, but Bob knew that no movie-camera could have recorded their appearance, their very thoughts, more mercilessly.

'This is Myron Blodgett. Myron, this is Miss Lee,' he said shortly, dumping Amy's case beside the handyman.

'Pleased to meet yer, Miss Lee,' snapped Myron, out of a dry square mouth suggesting that of a tortoise. Amy's hand was already held out and he gave it one quick, firm shake.

'Bob, yer maw says will we go in yer uncle's for some tomayto-juice, they ain't sent.'

'Couldn't you have done that while you were waiting?'

'Me? I hain't but just come.'

'Get along, then; we'll wait,' and as Myron climbed out and walked stiffly away he glanced apologetically at Amy, and suddenly exclaimed, with the youngest intonation she had yet heard from him:—

'Gosh, this is pretty awful for you—coming here by bus and me not being able to drive and Myron running errands and everything!'

She looked so elegant, standing by the car in her dark suit and blouse of fine French embroidery, that he had been overcome by a purely American feeling of shame. If only he had met her before they had lost their money, before he had gone crazy and run away with Dan and ruined his career! He stood under the ancient hickory trees whose shade had fallen upon three generations of Viners and Vorsts crossing the sidewalk to enter the stores of the Square, and the very homeliness and familiarity of the scene were hateful to him. Once it had been his kingdom and he had been happy in it, but now it was only an ordinary shabbyish square in a small town, shut in by houses where people lived who loved to gossip.

But Amy was looking about her, and for once hardly heard what he said. She had felt a tender interest in Vine Falls because it was Bob's home, but now there was more than this: the spirit of the place had suddenly fallen upon her, as a place-spirit will invade the imagination of a writer, and she heard the creak of waggon wheels, the solemn lowing of herds retreating into the afternoon light; she saw in fancy the clouds of dust moving slowly Westwards, leaving a man and a woman and their children camped beside the waterfalls of the Mooween. Her only answer was a dreamy:

'Oh, that's all right, I don't mind a bit. Bob, I do think this is a lovely place! Where's the Indian house?'

'South of the tracks. I'll show you tomorrow. Let's get in, shall we?' and he opened the door of the car, feeling ashamed of his outburst.

'You won't mind this party, will you?' he said presently, as they sat side by side in the back of the car. 'My mother wanted to have a few old friends to meet you and say hello to me. I'm supposed to have been visiting with my uncle, in the South.'

This time he spoke quietly, but Amy knew at once that he was very unhappy. She put out her hand and covered his, saying impulsively:

'I know it's awful for you, but try not to mind. I'm here, and I'll try to help. *Let's stick it out together, shall we?*'

'God, that's a wonderful thing to say,' he answered unsteadily, and the hand she held gripped fast on her own.

Simultaneously with the appearance of Myron at the door of Viner's stores and his slow approach across the road, a voice said:

'Hello there, Mr Vorst!' and a round whitish head, in shape and colour suggesting a mop, came over the side of the car. The flaxen hair crowned a boy's face on which a shocking network of fading white scars and the dirt of a day's activities were mingled, but no-one looking at him for the first time could see anything in that face except the reddened and sunken eyelid covering the socket where an eye, fellow to the blue one that was now looking steadily at Bob, should have sparkled.

'Hello, Joe.' Bob leant forward and smiled, but Amy saw his expression change. 'Hey, where's your shade?' he added quickly.

'Traded it to George Mooney for nuts.' The eye turned towards the hickory trees, then back to Bob. 'And a catapult,' he added. 'Aw, I can get along without a shade fine now, guess I don't hardly miss that old eye at all, Mr Vorst.'

The tone was casual, but Amy, listening and watching intently, heard something else in it: a desire to comfort.

'Go over to the drug store and get yourself another one,' said Bob, feeling in his pocket. 'That place still needs protecting,' and he gave him a half dollar.

'Gee, thanks a lot, Mr Vorst!'

'How many shades have you traded this week?'

'Only three, honest!'

'Well, don't trade any more.'

Joe laughed, and his eye moved past Bob's face to Amy's and stayed there, steadily watching her while the laugh faded to a mischievous smile. She was fascinated by the beauty of his teeth and could only return his gaze helplessly. That face, where childhood lingered like a prisoner behind the network of scars, filled her with unfamiliar emotion which she did not know was mother-love.

'She your girl?' demanded Joe suddenly, jerking his head at Amy.

'Scram!' Bob playfully lifted his arm, while Myron, climbing into the car, echoed hoarsely and as if to himself, 'Scram!'

Joe continued to look steadily at Amy, and at length pronounced:

'She's swell.'

'Thanks!' said Bob, glancing at Amy with a smile half-amused and half-painful. 'There'll be ice-cream at home if you come up round about five, Joe.'

'Gee, thanks a lot, Mr Vorst!'

He jumped off the running board just as Myron started the engine and observed in the same low hoarse absent voice:

'Git out of here, will yer, we don't want no more accidents.'

Joe waved and ran off towards the drug store as the car moved away.

'He's about the most popular kid around town,' said Bob presently, staring down at his shoes. 'Everybody made a hero out of him after the smash but it hasn't spoilt him at all.'

'He likes you,' she said.

'Does he?' He glanced at her.

'Yes, I'm sure he does.'

'Oh, well . . . I'm going to do something for him later on, when he's decided what he wants to do. His folks are very poor; the father's a truck driver but he's been on Relief ever since the smash, my mother says. I don't want the kid to get taking laundry round and losing his job in the next slump. He's smart and he's got guts. When I'm qualified I'm going to take care of him.'

Oh, you're so kind, you're so good, and you don't even hate Dan! thought Amy. I am a beast, hating people and never doing anything for anyone; if you knew what a beast I am you wouldn't want to kiss me.

'I'm very selfish,' she said suddenly with an effort, staring straight in front of her.

'You're lovely,' he answered gently, putting his hand over hers for a moment.

'Truly I'm not. I never do anything for anybody.'

'Never mind. We'll do things for people together, won't we? I'll get better, maybe, and I won't feel it's all luck, and we'll be together——'

405

(The beautiful hopefulness of a young people, his gift from his race, sounded in his voice.)

'Oh, yes! We'll be together,' she breathed. (They were almost whispering, because of Myron there in front, driving carefully but listening to every word.)

'Tomorrow we'll go up into the woods, shall we? and make a fire.'

'That would be lovely.'

They said no more for a while. Amy watched the white houses going past, set back from the road with wide lawns in front and large lilac and rose bushes in their unfenced gardens; and thought of the thick hedges, the gates and discreet net curtains that make privacy for the same type of house in English suburbs and seaside towns. Here, everybody seemed to live their life on the porch; there was none of the secrecy and rich atmospheric patina that glosses any European house over thirty years old.

But she liked it, she liked it all so much! The candour and hospitable kindness of Americans had charmed her by its contrast with the glum manner of Londoners (a disillusioned race of people, imbrued with the secret grumbling charm of their dark purple and grey city, sprawling on its ancient marsh) and American houses delighted her in the same way. And this was his home, and she loved the houses and the people because they belonged to the place where he had been born.

'We're nearly there,' he said presently, and she smiled, but did not answer.

She was naturally nervous of meeting his parents, but not as nervous as a conventionally brought-up girl would have been. It did not occur to her that her position as 'Bob's friend, Miss Lee,' was ambiguous. She was simple in such matters; her ingenuous upbringing by Mrs Beeding had preserved her social innocence while her fame had given her confidence, and her present apprehensions only took the shape of the thought: oh, will they like me? A fleeting recollection of Buck

Finch among the cannibals did just cross her mind, but she severely dismissed it.

'Here we are,' he said, as the car turned in at the drive between the two snowball bushes, 'and there's my mother,' he added a little nervously.

A tall woman was standing on the shallow circle of steps, smiling with eyes screwed up against the afternoon sunlight, and Amy, with awe, recognized her as one of the two ladies who had been with Bob at Kenwood House eleven years ago. It was the strangest moment of her life. She got out of the car and walked slowly up the steps towards Mrs Vorst, who advanced to meet her, and as she did so Amy *felt*, rather than thought, how safe and gracious was the setting in which she appeared. The old house, the steady sunlight, the slight rustle in the trees surrounding the drive, Mrs Vorst's own welcoming look, all breathed of peace and the pleasant procession of everyday affairs. It's all so lovely—perhaps everything's going to be all right now!—what is there that can go wrong, now he's home again? Amy thought, as she took his mother's outstretched hand.

'I'm so very pleased to welcome you, Miss Lee.'

'It's very kind of you to ask me, I'm so glad to come——'

Their voices murmured on, coming without pause after Bob's words—'Mother, this is Miss Lee—this is my mother——'

'Did you have a good trip?' Mrs Vorst continued, leading the way into the house and looking down at Amy with a lazy smile in her dark eyes. 'I dislike travelling by railroad, I find it twice as tiring as a road trip. But flying! I flew down South two years ago. That's the way to travel!——'

They were crossing the hall. Its little air of melancholy had gone, banished by two large vases filled with blazing yet delicate summer flowers, and a pair of worn gloves tossed down on the lowest stair. The only sounds were Mrs Vorst's voice and the distant tinkle made by someone shaking a cocktail mixer behind the half-open door that Amy knew led to the kitchen, but that

407

sound conveyed the renewed cheerfulness which pervaded the whole house, and again Amy thought: Everything feels all right again. Surely there isn't anything that can hurt it, now? Her mind ran anxiously over all the possibilities, just as it used to when she was a child and feared that a visit from Old Porty might prevent her father taking her to the pictures.

And suddenly she remembered something. The dream of Bob's head lying against the red cushion had come true, and the dream of his face bending over her as she awoke from sleep had come true. She and Lou had talked over this amazing fact when they met on the morning of Bob's return to Vine Falls, exclaiming and wondering, feeling frightened and awed. But there was a third dream, the dream of the torn newspaper photograph, of which Amy had never spoken to a soul. That had not come true—yet. But if the other two had 'happened', why should not the third happen? The third, the most frightening of the three? There arose in her mind the exact shape and dark-dotted texture of that squalid fragment of paper. She saw again the wooden cabin and the ring of men staring down at something lying on the ground and felt the evil rising from the scene.

A peculiar horror surrounds newspaper photographs of scenes of violence. The coarse surface of the actual paper, its ephemeral nature, the impression left upon the beholder's mind of a calculated display of horror in order to make money, the knowledge that ever-widening rings of distress, ugliness and morbid attention are spread by the appearance of such pictures, make them one of the few *fully contemporary* horrors of this age. Unsoftened, unheightened by art, reminders of our increasing danger in the civilization that we have made, they are more vile than any demons in stained glass or any figures lost in lust on the frescoes of the Ancient World.

These qualities began at once to press with their full weight upon Amy's imagination and as she followed Mrs Vorst upstairs her spirits sank. Myron followed close behind, carrying her case and conveying so much by his silence that she was as aware of his presence as if he had been a lion; but even Myron, even Mrs Vorst of whom she was so nervous, was better company now than her own thoughts. She was glad when Myron lingered to inspect a window-sash after he had dumped her cases down on the gay colours of the hooked rug, and she detained Mrs Vorst at the door to ask shyly if there was time to take a shower before she came downstairs.

'Mercy, yes, please do whatever you want here, Miss Lee; I want you to have a real rest and just relax. It's only a few old friends coming in to meet you and say hello to Bob.'

'Thank you.'

'You've got everything you want, I hope? Myron, did you fix that window?'

'Sure.'

Myron worked his way past her, with a sidelong glance.

'Then I'll leave you to rest.'

She went smiling away, but she was thinking: I can't quite make her out. She looks rather French, so dark and elegant, and I like her looks, but still I can't make her out. I wish Bob had picked a girl like Helen, someone sweet and lovely, that we could all love. Maybe it's because Miss Lee's a writer; writers are different, I suppose. Or maybe she's shy? She certainly has poise, and taste, too. I like that suit. Well, I'll just have to see how she turns out.

She went downstairs to overlook the preparations for the party.

Amy went slowly over to the bed, and lay down on it and shut her eyes.

Why did I suddenly remember that bit of newspaper (she thought), *unless it's getting near the time for it to come true*? If only I had someone to talk to about it! If only I could tell *him*! Then she remembered that they were going into the woods tomorrow, and decided that she would tell him about it then. I can't keep it to myself any longer, she thought, I'm too frightened.

She lay there for a little while, trying to calm her feelings, and presently the peaceful silence in the room and the small sounds coming in through the open windows from the garden restored her. A shower-bath and a leisurely dressing soothed her still more, and when she went downstairs an hour later she felt more able to face the party.

She came slowly down the shallow stairs, and as she came a curtain blew slowly out in a beam of sunlight and then slowly fell back against the long window. The drawing-room door stood open, and she could see that the room was already full, while the not unpleasant sound of voices (the voices of people who had known one another for years and could therefore address one another naturally and without haste) floated up the well of the stairs. She went down, also without haste, longing for the moment when she should see Bob's fair head above the others, and moving as she used to move when a child through the crowded streets of London, lightly as a leaf from a London plane tree.

Bob's father glanced out through the door and saw her coming down; she seemed very much the famous Miss Lee to him, with her hair done higher than any woman's there that afternoon and wearing a dark red silk dress printed with a Persian design by a famous house. He came quickly out to meet her, thinking that she looked a queer little highbrow stick, but impressive; and he was at once anxious to impress *her*.

Before she reached the foot of the stairs a commotion at the kitchen door attracted her attention and she turned her head slightly to see what it was (for in the Beeding household you had not pretended something exciting was not going on when it was).

'Git away from that door, will yer?'

'Honest, I was on'y goin'——'

'One squawk out o' you and you don't get a mite o' ice-cream, not a mite.'

It was Joe and Myron, wrestling. Myron dragged the boy inside but not before Joe had seen Amy and waved to her. She waved back, laughing, and thereby establishing herself more favourably with Bob's father, who felt a little less anxious to impress her and therefore better disposed towards her. But as he came up to her and said—

'Miss Lee? How do you do? I'm Bob's father. I'm delighted to welcome you—hope you had a good trip?' and listened with relief to the unaffected English voice replying: 'Oh, yes, thank you. Isn't it a lovely day?' he was wondering just what there was between this girl and his son? She looked a dark, secret little kitten, now that he stood close to her; she was too calm, too simple-mannered, altogether too good to be true. She was part of the three months Bob had spent away from home, part of that time about which he would not talk to anyone, in spite of his father's demands to be informed exactly where he had been and what he had done.

Mr Vorst led the way into the drawing-room, giving Amy a good imitation of a simple hospitable American welcoming a distinguished guest. But as he turned away, leaving her with his wife and a group of eager Vinebridge ladies, his handsome silver head was full of unhappy suspicions and he instinctively took a large glass from a tray to comfort himself. He drank half of it, watching his son who was talking with some people at the other end of the room, and then he sighed.

It seemed a long time since he had felt comfortable. Business, politics, the newspaper game, were going from bad to worse; a man could never stop worrying nowadays. It was impossible to realize that only ten years ago America seemed to have entered her Golden Age. Now public and private affairs alike were all confusion, disappointment, uncertainty and bitterness. And bitterest of all to him, though he only vaguely knew it, was the fact that Bob, whom he had loved but always a little despised, should have 'gone off like that,' breaking away from safety and the known ways of living to run with gangsters and down-and-outs. He had seen things his father never had and knew things his father would never know. Mr Vorst was full of secret envy as he stared across the room at Bob. He was angry as a father, but as a man, an individual, he was full of deep envy. Danger, thrills, death, something big to do, a man's job, rugged individualism, rail-splitting pioneers—the phrases went vaguely through his head as he smiled and talked with Judge van Damm, and he took a second big glass from the tray.

'Miss Lee, this is Ellen van Damm—she's just crazy to meet you——'

'Miss Lee, may I present Mrs Eldor—she's read *China Walk* five times——'

'My boys are crazy about your stories, Miss Lee——'

'Miss Lee, have you taken my advice yet, and written something homey for the womenfolk?'

'Well, I certainly am surprised to see *you* again, Bob! We all made sure one of those Southern belles would catch you!'

The old friends, the kindly acquaintances, were all playing the game beautifully.

He and she were separated by the length of the room, and he did not exchange more than a few words and a smile with her the whole time, yet she felt the bond between them grow steadily as the afternoon wore on and the noise of voices, the animation of the guests, the clouds of cigarette smoke, increased. She had been very anxious to play her part well, knowing that this gathering marked his return to the social life of Vine Falls, and she made great efforts; struggling to throw off her ordinary habit of polite silent attention and to give her full interest to whoever addressed her. The effort was something quite new for her, and it gave the deeper note to her voice and brought the colour to her face that only a few of her oldest friends in London, and Bob, had ever seen; and thus for the first time in her life she managed to convey something of her genius through her personality. She talked more than was usual for her, and if it was not in sparkling or profound phrases, her glowing face and steady brilliant eyes gave new meaning to her words and seemed to set them against the horrific and gorgeous background of her books.

The atmosphere in the room went steadily up and up; sober people took an extra glass and glittered; the chaste became flirtatious and the elderly regained the delicious irresponsibility of youth; if no-one said or felt anything memorable, everyone felt that they had: and in short the party was a success. Mrs Vorst was very pleased. Her highest hopes were exceeded, and she felt really warm towards Amy, to whom the success was due. Bob, too, was exactly right in manner. She had not detected one sigh or one fit of abstraction or one bitter enigmatic sentence. He had decided to take up his life where he had left it off, and he was doing so. Mrs Vorst felt happier than she had for months as the rooms began to empty towards seven o'clock, and guest after departing guest assured her, with flattering earnestness, what a wonderful party it had been.

But Amy was very tired. When the last guest had gone she sat down in a chair by the window and looked out into the garden, where the shadows were growing long. Behind her the room was in all the disorder of dirty glasses, crumpled straws, curling sandwiches and stale cigarette smoke. Mr and Mrs Vorst were in the hall saying a few last good-byes, and except for their voices the room was quiet. Suddenly she saw Bob come out through the french windows of the dining-room, and walk quickly across the lawn towards the woods. The sunlight fell on his fair head, turning it to gold. He was swinging his arm, and she could see that in one hand he held a letter. When he got to the edge of the lawn he turned back and looked at the house, and then he saw her sitting at the window. He held up the letter, and then pointed down towards the woods.

'Just going to mail this,' he called. His voice came clearly through the evening air. 'I shan't be ten minutes.'

She waved and smiled, not lifting her head because she was so tired. She was content to sit quiet, watching him, and thinking: Tomorrow—tomorrow we shall be in the woods.

He walked on, and presently she saw him go into the dark trees, and then she saw him no more.

24

Bob walked down the track. That part of the country seldom had a day without clouds, because of the hills to the north, and now there was a gigantic one towering slowly forward over half the heavens, gradually blotting out the setting sun and filling the woods with hush and awe. The south wind was rising fitfully, as it often did at eventime, but it was as yet only in the treetops, and the undergrowth was motionless. He walked quickly, anxious to catch the mail with this letter to the landlord of his former rooms at Morgan; the party had caused him nearly to forget it. He was anxious, too, to get back to Amy, for he felt as if he had not spoken to her for hours. But the party had been an ordeal for him, and he welcomed a walk in the cool evening air.

It was over now. Old friends had seen him and shown him that they were going to ignore the past; and acquaintances had taken their cue from the successful tone of the party and decided not to hint or sneer. His first step back towards his own side of the fence had been taken, and if one part of his nature felt impatient and scornful of the whole business, another side was warmly grateful towards his own family and the friends who had made that step possible. I must be getting better, he thought, striding down towards the steep slope that led to Carr's bungalow; it's a long time since I've felt like that about people. They've taken me back, that's what it amounts to. I can't ever feel better about what I did, but I can feel grateful to them for wanting me back. And I've got her, and tomorrow we're going up into the woods.

Carr's bungalow had been deserted for months. The snows of a long winter had broken the rail fence so that part of it lay on the ground, and the windows of the house were boarded over. A grey rag on the porch flapped in the rising wind, and as Bob came sliding down the slope among the fading briars a chipmunk ran across the yard where he and Dan used to play. It stopped at the edge of the wood and looked back at him, and he halted to return its stare. For a moment they steadily contemplated one another, then it darted off among the trees and he went on down the slope and crossed over to the fallen fence.

The wind was getting into its strength now, shaking the bushes with strong gusts and blowing dust along the ground. He stepped over the fence and walked round the house towards the mailbox on its post, and as he did so he thought again: I'm getting better. For weeks this particular spot had haunted his imagination, with its gap in the fence and its history of commonplace violence and breaking of the law. Here (it had seemed to him in countless miserable fits of brooding) he had taken as a boy the first steps that had led to the wrecking of his life as a young man. But now the spell was broken; he had come down to the mailbox without once thinking: I'll have to go by Carr's—I can't face it; and this evening 'Carr's' was only a squalid little house falling into ruin, with a grey rag flapping on the porch where Dan used to lie on Sunday afternoons and read in the tabloids about Al Capone.

Good luck to Dan; I don't ever want to see him again. The thought went through his head as he came round the house into the road. And then he saw that there was a small black sedan standing opposite Carr's, and a woman in a light coat just getting out of it. She slammed the door and tried it, standing with her back to him, while he stopped, staring at her and recognizing her hair and the beautiful lines of her body with a shock of dismay, and then she turned hastily round as if she were in a hurry to set off somewhere.

It was Francey Carr.

She gasped loudly when she saw him and ran towards him,

while he simply stood there looking at her, with all the night-mare of the last months horribly revived.

'*Bob!* I was coming to call you up!'

'What for?' he said roughly, moving a little away as she came up with him. She was breathing quickly and her face was very pale and for an instant a painful suspicion filled his mind. But it stayed no longer than her next words:

'It's Dan. He's taken Joe Murphy. He picked him up at the crossroads half an hour ago.'

'Picked him up?' he repeated stupidly.

'He's crazy. The kid was waiting for the bus, and Dan and I were riding together. Dan stopped the car and said would he like a ride and the kid said no thank you, he was going by bus. So Dan said, "You're a popular kid around Vine Falls, aren't you, Joe? I guess they'd pay a lot to have you back if you were to get lost," and then he got out his rod and made the kid get in. He told me to go home by the bus. But I went into town and hired this,' she jerked her head at the car, 'and I was coming up to call you from the box on your corner.'

'But he's crazy!'

'Bob, he's been crazy for weeks. A big job went wrong and he had to lie low and he got in with a man who put him on to some drug or other—Mary Warner, may be.' She lowered her voice over the mobsman's name for the drug marihuana.

'Dan never used to be a hophead.'

'Oh, well, maybe he isn't now. I don't know. But he was certainly acting queer this evening.'

'Is he shot up much? Enough to make him hurt the kid?'

'Not much. He said he wouldn't touch Joe unless the bulls came after him. But you know what they're like in this State about kidnapping since the Rhinelander kid got bumped off. If they catch Dan they'll lynch him, and me too.' And she began to cry, getting a cigarette case out of her bag and lighting one with shaking hands.

'But what did you come to *me* for?' he demanded. 'What can I do?'

'Oh, Bob, you're the *only* one that can do anything!' she said, sobbing and choking so over the smoke that he could hardly hear what she said. 'You owe Joe a good turn, anyway, and Dan'll listen to you. And maybe you could fix up about the ransom——'

'But where's he *taken* him?' he asked, his strongest feeling one of fury at being dragged back into the violent unrealities of the life he had just escaped from.

'Up in the woods, he said.'

'The place near Black Lake?'

'No—the cabin, I guess.'

'You mean where we——'

'Sure.' She tossed her cigarette away, not looking at him and he, too, glanced away from her as he spoke.

'You'd better tell the police,' he said in a hard voice. 'Come on, let's go,' and he took a step down the road. But Francey did not follow him.

'Bob, he swore he'd kill the kid if I squawked. He's going to let the town know somehow tonight he's got him, and then——'

'Is he working alone?'

She nodded.

'Was Joe scared?' said Bob suddenly.

'Sure he was, scared stiff, but he tried not to show it, he kinda made a joke of it——'

'*Oh, hell.*' The two words came out in a groan.

There was a pause. The wind blew furiously against them.

'I'll have to go,' he said at last.

'Oh, Bob! I knew you would! Maybe he'll let you have the kid back without any money——'

'How is this off for gasoline?' he interrupted, going over to the car.

'I just filled up.'

'All right.' He was getting into the driver's seat when he

418

suddenly remembered that he was forbidden to drive. But he put the thought impatiently aside.

'Aren't you going home for a gun?'

'I won't need one. If he isn't so shot up as all that he won't kill me. And he wouldn't, anyway.'

'No. I guess it'll be all right,' she said, relieved by his matter-of-fact tone. 'Maybe he just meant it for a kind of joke; you know he's got a funny sense of humour. But the kid was scared all right.'

'Yes. You said so before.' He had started the engine and the regular mechanical noise seemed to add to the violence that had come into the evening with the rising of the wind. He turned the car round while she watched, and set it towards the north.

'Francey.'

'What?'

'Do something for me, will you? Call up home and tell them I've had to go into Morgan and I may be back late. You needn't say who you are.'

She nodded. 'Sure I will, Bob. I'll do that first thing after you've gone, so's they won't worry.'

'Thanks.' The car began to move. She came over and walked beside it, putting her hand for a moment over his.

'Gee, Bob, I think you're swell!'

'I don't feel it. Go home, there's a good girl, and just lie low, will you? The quieter you keep the better.'

'Oh, Bob, I do hope you'll be all right!' She was running beside the car with her red hair blowing in the wind as it used to when they were children, and he turned to look at her. But even the little affection that had been between them was dead now, killed by full bodily knowledge without love. He only smiled meaninglessly at her and said, 'Don't worry, it'll be all right,' and then accelerated. The car moved off into the wild lights and moving shadows of evening.

When it had disappeared she stood for a little while glancing uncertainly about her, up into the woods where the trees were now swaying furiously in the wind, now down the road towards the town, and all the time trying to tilt her hat on her curls at its correct angle. The dust blew against her ankles and stung them. She seemed to be trying to make up her mind about something. At last she shook her head, said something under her breath, and began to walk quickly away towards the town. An expression of shame was on her doll-like face for a few moments; then, as she gave all her attention to increasing her pace and struggling against the wind, it faded. With her coat flapping and both hands holding on to her hat she passed quickly out of sight.

'Where's Bob?' asked Mrs Vorst in a surprised tone, coming into the drawing-room a little later and finding Amy still among the wreckage of the party. 'I didn't know you were all alone, Miss Lee—I'm so sorry! I thought Bob was here.'

'He just went out to post a letter. He said he'd be about ten minutes,' replied Amy. She was quite content to sit there by the window enjoying the restful silence. She turned her head to smile tranquilly at Bob's mother.

'Well, won't you come into the sun-parlour, and rest a little before we go up to change? I feel quite exhausted, don't you?'

When they had been lying on the long chairs in the sun-parlour for a while, enjoying the evening light from the garden with the windows shut against the rising wind, Mr Vorst joined them, and for half an hour Amy had to answer questions about her work. She knew very little about the side of it that most interested him, leaving as she did all questions of contracts, terms and translations to the efficient Messrs Aubrett and Humfriss, and her natural disinclination to talk about the dull side of being a writer was increased by her gathering uneasiness at the prolonged absence of Bob. He had said he would be ten minutes, and he had been gone nearly an hour! It was silly to feel rather frightened, but she did.

At last, after a pause in their talk, she said to Mrs Vorst with an uneasy smile—

'Wherever do you think Bob can be?'

'Yes—he is a long time, isn't he!' said his mother at once, getting up and going over to the window. 'If he's not back soon he'll get wet. Look!' She put a finger against the pane, where a glittering drop had just dashed, and turned to smile at Amy. 'It's going to be a wet night.'

'Where'd he go?' demanded his father, rousing himself from a silence.

'Only out to mail a letter, Miss Lee says.'

'Yes, I saw him,' said Amy eagerly, glad for some reason to be able to put her last sight of him into words. 'I was looking out of the window and he came past with a letter in his hand; he was walking fast, and when he got to the edge of the lawn he turned round and held up the letter and called, "I won't be ten minutes." And then he went into the wood.'

'Oh, then he's gone down to the mailbox by Carr's. Perhaps he's coming the long way home; the road goes round the hill, you know, and turns off up to here by the river. Yes, I expect that's what he's done,' murmured Mrs Vorst, still with her finger pressed against the window pane as she stared out into the garden. The whole expanse glittered with drops now and they were beginning to roll down it.

'Crazy thing to do on a night like this,' said his father, getting up. Amy happened to be looking at him as he spoke, and he suddenly gave her a grudging, amused, sympathetic smile. *But then, the boy is crazy. We know that, don't we?* it said. Amy replied with a shy but eager look, and thus a completely unexpected friendship was formed. The fact was, she had charmed him. Her fame, her simplicity, her feminine ignorance of contracts and her French-seeming elegance was a new combination for him, and its piquancy brought stimulating memories of a time when he was a happier man, with the energy and inclination to admire piquancy in a woman. His suspicions about her relationship with his son had vanished: they were simply not possible in the face of this new liking for her. She's charming, he decided, and she and Bob ought to do very well together; they're both so darned queer! But Sharlie isn't sure about her yet; I can tell that.

'Oh, he'll be in any minute now,' he said, moving to open the door for them.

'Surely,' murmured Mrs Vorst, but for a moment she lingered by the window, looking up at the lowering twilight sky, before she followed Amy out of the room.

When Bob had been driving for an hour and had left the town well behind him, he had an impulse to turn back. He was not afraid of Dan, for he knew him too well to believe that he would be dangerous, but a deep distaste and weariness came over him. He must go on, of course; the boy must be got back as quickly and secretly as possible; and it was quite out of the question to stop on the way to the cabin and tell Joe's parents or inform the police, but he loathed the task in front of him. He could already hear Dan's soft voice, gently justifying himself in sentences full of the long words which helped to hypnotize him when he was in a self-justifying mood. He would have to 'manage' Dan as he had done many times before, exactly as if he were managing an ill-tempered and worthless horse; and this time, too, he might be more difficult to manage than he had ever been, if Francey had not been exaggerating about the drugs and his mood.

Maybe he will shoot me, and the kid too, thought Bob as he turned the car off the main road into one that led up into the mountains. But I guess he won't; Dan isn't a killer. Poor little kid, I bet he's scared! I've got to get him out of this, and safe, too. I've got the chance now to make up for what I did to him. And he drove on, ashamed that he had even let the thought of going back enter his head.

He was now working his way straight across the State by

lesser roads, where the only traffic was an occasional Ford full of parcels and children on its way back from shopping to some lonely farm. The rainstorm that had swept down from the hills with the giant cloud was now over, and had shattered the cloud itself into long banks of grey lying above a serene and gorgeous afterglow of gold. The little faces of some children looking through the windows of an old car which he passed were glorified by this radiance from the west, and their quick smiles and the small hands they waved to him seemed beautiful. But ahead of him rose the barrier of the Gluscap Mountains, spread for hundreds of miles with their sombre woods against the sky of the north. The children's faces made him think tenderly of Amy, and he wondered if Francey had called them up at home yet and given his message? It'll seem crazy to them, he thought, and they'll wonder why I couldn't call them up myself, and who the heck Francey is, but it's better than leaving them without a word.

The road grew rougher and lonelier under the fast-darkening sky as the car steadily climbed. The air was keen here, and he caught wafts of scent from berry-bushes scattered over with little flowers, from patches of wiry grass drenched by rain and from the sombre branches of pines where already the night wind was faintly hissing, from hemlocks and pines standing motionless with raindrops glittering on their leaves from the glow in the west. Tomorrow I'll be here with her, he thought. It's beautiful here—I wish she could see it now. And he thought how different it would look tomorrow, under the hot sun and blue sky, with the katydids fiddling and the morning glories open. His mind went over into tomorrow and rested there in happiness, as if tomorrow were paradise.

He switched on the lights, and turned the car up a track leading to the heart of the hills.

Amy looked out of her window before she went down to dinner to see if Bob might be crossing the lawn. But it was dark except for the faintest streak of light in the west, and she could make out nothing. She drew her head in, disturbed and anxious, and went downstairs.

'Bob back?' inquired Mr Vorst, shaking cocktails in the drawing-room, whence all traces of the party had been cleared away.

'I don't know, dear; I haven't heard him. Myron, is Bob back?' asked Mrs Vorst, as the handyman came in to speak to Mr Vorst.

'Nope.'

'Are you sure?' she asked, startled.

'Yep. He ain't in. Reckon something's happened to him,' retorted Myron with satisfaction.

'Don't be a fool! What could have happened to him? He only went to mail a letter!' said Mr Vorst sharply: Amy had suddenly sat upright in her low chair and was staring across at Myron with a white face.

'Dunno, but it's mighty queer; goin' out to mail a letter and not comin' back,' persisted Myron sulkily, looking at Amy out of the corner of his eye. 'Crazy kind o' thing to do, the first night o' visitors bein' here, and so forth.'

'Maybe he went down to see his Aunt Carol; I might just go and call her up,' and Mrs Vorst went quickly out of the room.

'Mrs Vorst's sister is in bed; had a touch of grippe,' explained Mr Vorst. 'She thought maybe Bob might have gone down to see her. Is that right for you, Miss Lee?' coming across to her with a glass held up and smiling.

'Yes, thank you,' she said faintly, taking it in her cold fingers.

'Don't worry, he's perfectly all right,' he said very kindly completely dropping his pretence of not noticing her agitation. 'It's just some quite ordinary thing, I'm sure . . . only naturally we all still feel a bit jumpy about Bob, because of what happened——'

'Yes!' she said gratefully, looking up at him. 'He's only just come back, you see, hasn't he?'

He nodded, returning her look steadily. Myron was still fussing about the window as they spoke, with his back to them, but listening to every word. Suddenly a telephone bell rang faintly as if from a distant part of the house.

'That's in my study—you can't get through while Mrs Vorst's talking in the dining-room—maybe it's Bob—there now, Miss Lee, you'll have to come and give him a talking-to!' and he hurried, smiling, out of the room. She heard him running upstairs with the heavy step of middle-age, and then there was silence except for the distant sound of Mrs Vorst's low voice through the half-open door as she talked on the telephone to her sister's house.

Myron finished what he was doing to the window and came slowly across the room to the door. To reach it he had to pass Amy, and when he was level with her he suddenly said—

'Worried about Bob, ain't yer?'

'Yes! Oh, yes, I am! And I'm frightened!' she answered at once, turning round in her chair to face him with her hands pressed together. She could think of nothing but that scrap of newspaper! that awful picture of something lying on the ground! The longing to tell someone about it was torturing her.

'So'm I,' he said gloomily, standing on one foot and lowering his queer battered face so that it looked dolefully down at her. 'All very well, but I reckon something *must* hev happened to him.'

'What could have, do you think?' she asked fearfully.

'Well, I dunno. But I reckon Dan Carr's got hold o' him again, somehow. I kind o' feel it. He's been round here lately. Buddy o' mine down at Hannigan's Pool Rooms saw him only yesterday. An' he wouldn't like Bob leavin' his mob an' comin' back home. Jest out o' spite he'd want him ter go back with them again.'

'Oh, what shall I do, what shall I do?' she said quietly, beginning to rock to and fro, staring down at the ground.

'Quit bein' hysterical, fer a start,' said Myron at once—just as he had to the weeping Helen three months ago. 'That don't help any. If Bob is with Dan, I reckon he'll be all right. He's a poor thing, Dan Carr, a poor mean thing. Hain't got no faculty. When he was a kid I used to notice his hands. Like a bear's paws—no good fer anythin'. All talk, he was, an' still is. Now Bob's hands—they're a human creature's hands. Clever. There's a lot in hands, if you notice.'

She nodded, drying her eyes and not looking at him, but she had stopped rocking.

'Yes——' he went on musingly in his unlovely New England voice. 'I reckon that's about what's happened. Now what I'm jest wonderin' is this——'

For the next moment she did not hear what he was saying, for she was wondering whether to tell him about the scrap of newspaper. In spite of his spiteful, inquisitive manner, she felt at ease with him in a strange way, exactly as a child feels more at home with another child, even an unpleasant child, than with the kindest and most intelligent grown-up. She knew that Myron would believe her story about the scrap of newspaper. He might say it was queer, *but he would at once see how queer it was*, and would not try to soothe her by explaining it away.

She came out of her agitated thoughts to hear him saying:

'—An' I reckon ef he's got him anywhere, that's wheer he is.'

'I want to tell you something,' she began at once, not heeding what he said. 'I've had queer dreams sometimes about Bob (he and I are going to get married, you know,' she explained simply, lifting her wet eyes to Myron, whose own dim brown ones seemed at once to blaze with passionate interest) 'and there's one dream I had that frightened me very much. It was about a bit of newspaper. It was a photograph of a cabin in the woods somewhere, and there were some men standing round a—a—dark thing lying on the ground. It might have been someone dead. Do you think it could have anything to do with Bob?'

'Ain't that just what I've been *tellin'* yer?' he said shortly, suddenly stooping to pick up a dirty glass which someone had left down beside a chair. 'Dan's got a cabin he uses up in the Gluscaps, on the Moon River. That's wheer I reckon he's took Bob—ef he's got him. That's wheer you dreamt about. Ah, I believe in dreams. My uncle married a woman from Missouri and they had a darkey servant as used to see hants. (That's what they call a ghost down South; a hant.) He saw a hant in the woods one day when he was out berryin' with my aunt's children an' he fainted clean away. Skeered, you know. Sure, that's wheer you dreamt about. Dan's cabin.' And he began to move towards the door with the usual spiteful yet wooden expression on his face.

'But if Dan really has got him, and taken him there, can't we *do* something?' she exclaimed desperately, getting up and moving after him.

'Oh, maybe it ain't so at all, maybe it's all imaginin' an' so forth,' he said at once, backing out of the room. 'Can't go to the police with a tale like that now, can we? Me thinkin' Dan *may* hev get him, an' you dreamin' about a picture that *may* be Dan's cabin. Why, the police wouldn't go anywheer fer that. Psychopaths' ward, thet's wheer they'd put us.'

'And perhaps Dan hasn't got him at all!' she said, a great relief suddenly coming over her. 'Perhaps it's just some quite ordinary thing, and in a minute he'll come in, and we'll all feel so silly for having been so frightened——'

'Mebbe,' he said, but he said it doubtfully, and just then Mrs Vorst came past him into the room, trying not to look worried.

'No, he isn't down at Aunt Carol's,' she said. 'Didn't the telephone go upstairs?' to Myron.

'Sure. Mr Vorst's up theer now.'

'Oh, then perhaps it's Bob——'

But Mr Vorst was coming down the stairs shaking his head. 'Only *The Sentinel*, wanting me to look in tomorrow,' he said.

Mrs Vorst took up her drink and stared at it. She seemed to have forgotten Amy's presence. At last she said:

'Oh, well. Perhaps we'd better have dinner. Tell Olga, will you, Myron?'

Myron went out, and Mr Vorst drained his glass.

'Another, Miss Lee?'

She shook her head, smiling painfully.

'Sharlie?'

'No, thanks. Webster, do you think he could have fallen and twisted his ankle?'

'In Carr's Wood? He knows it like the back of his own hand. No; there's some perfectly good and simple reason . . . oh, he'll be in any minute now.'

'Maybe Myron ought to go down with a torch and look——'

'Oh, Sharlie!' He dropped his hand affectionately on her shoulder, turning to smile at Amy. 'Be your age! We're getting all worked up over nothing. Let's come in and eat. It's queer,' he went on, as they crossed the hall to the dining-room, 'I always eat everything in sight at a cocktail party and yet I'm never so ready for my dinner as after we've thrown one——'

They sat down, and the Polish girl began to hand the soup.

Out in the kitchen, Myron sat himself down in his old hickory rocker with that morning's *Sentinel* and began to read the first column of the first page. But before he had read half-way down he sighed loudly, crumpled the paper into a ball, and dropped it on the floor. Then he got up and went into the little room opening off the kitchen which was his lair.

Here he hoarded old coats discarded years ago by Boone and Bob, back numbers of *Life* and *The Sentinel*, a buffalo robe worn greasy with age, flattened moccasins, and a drawerful of beautiful and fantastic tiny toys carved out of scraps of wood; fairylike boats with full-rigged sails made from bits of bright stuff discarded by Lou in her dressmaking; models of his own rocker fitted with a minute cushion, cradles with peanut-babies in them, little sofas fitted with roly-poly pillows, and miniature birdcages made from fragments of wire, with tiny birds of cork and killdeer or chickadee feathers inside. No child had ever been gladdened by a present of one of these marvels save Lou; Boone and Bob and Irene had years ago forgotten that they existed, but Lou still possessed a set of doll's furniture, bed, table, chairs and sofa, given to her by Myron when she was eight. He admired her deftness; she had always been clever with her hands, and the elfin furniture was a tribute from one artist to another.

But this evening Myron had not come to admire his drawerful of toys; he had business with the drawer next to it. Then he put on his overcoat and hat and came out into the kitchen.

Olga looked up from the salad she was mixing.

'Goin' to the movies,' remarked Myron, and went out to the yard. Presently, while she was nicely dropping in the oil, Olga heard his old car start up and drive away.

Bob stopped at last at the beginning of a track too rough for the car to attempt, which went up into the woods. All was still, but long streamers of cloud moved quickly across the bright stars as if there was a high wind blowing up there, and far off he could hear the roar of falling water—the Mooween, dashing down between its rocks. He remembered how black they used to look against the white foam, like big animals crouching to drink. The Indians had seen them thus: the river's name meant Black Bear. He shut the door of the car and turned up his collar against the wind and set off along the track.

The wood was full of little sounds and movement, while the clouds moved quickly among the black branches over his head, now hiding a big glittering star, now leaving it flashing clear, and the fresh woodsy smell he so well remembered came out from wet moss and drenched leaves. Once he went past a clearing where trees had been cut down, and their stumps glimmered;

he saw the woodsmen's deserted cabin and the blackened ring left by their fire. He thought vaguely about the woods, rolling away across their mountain-range, always beautiful, full of darting secret life, and able to do without man. It's cold and lonely here but it's beautiful, he thought, glancing away on either side into the confusion of tree trunks now beginning to be visible in the radiance forerunning the rising moon. I wonder where Dan's parked the car? Poor little kid; he must be scared. And by now at home they'll have called up all sorts of folk in Morgan to see if I'm there, and they'll be getting scared, too. *She'll* be frightened. I wish I'd called them up myself, now. It was a fool thing to do. But I had to come. I've got to get Joe back.

It'll be all right, I guess. It's just one of Dan's crazy jokes.

But if they catch him this time he won't get off.

When he had been walking steadily for nearly an hour he came to a place where he stopped, and stared up into the branches overhead.

A white rag hung there, showing plainly even in the confusing gloom, and he at once turned aside and entered the forest.

Soon his shoes and his trousers as far as the knee were soaked in dew as he moved slowly through the undergrowth, with a slightly swaying movement like that of a man wading in deep water. The moon had risen and its light made his way a little easier and the roar of the water sounded loud and very near.

And at last he came out into a glade where old stumps showed grey by the doubtful light from the young moon, and across the far end of the clearing something white moved and splashed among black rounded shapes: the Mooween between its bearlike rocks. A ruined cabin, dark and silent, stood on the far edge of the clearing where the trees began again.

The moon had brought the sense of summer back into the night. Its light seemed to calm the moving tops of the trees. The wind had fallen. Little flowers on a bush showed white as Bob went past and a sweet smell wafted over him. He put his hands in his pockets and, still walking towards the hut with his eyes fixed on its shut door, he shouted:

'Dan! Hullo there!'

The loud sound seemed to have nothing to do with the motionless trees, the rushing water, the faint light from the moon.

He shouted again, still advancing—

'Dan!'

Mrs Vorst said suddenly—

'I can't stand this a minute longer, Webster! Where *is* he? He went out to mail a letter and he's been gone three hours!'

She crushed out her cigarette and stood up quickly, looking wildly at her husband. Amy, too, was looking at Mr Vorst, but with an absolutely expressionless face. Her terror and anxiety had so increased during the last hour that she was now almost incapable of thought, let alone sensible speech, and automatically she had put on once more the mask that had served her so well in her childhood.

'Now, don't worry, Sharlie. Everything's going to be all right,' Mr Vorst said soothingly. 'I'm still sure the boy's perfectly safe, but if it will make you feel better we'll have Myron go down to Carr's and see if he has turned his ankle or met a wild Indian or something—why, you'll give Miss Lee a very poor opinion of Vine Falls if you go on like this——' he went on turning to smile at Amy. But the faint movement of the lips and the agonized stare with which she met his smile stopped him from finishing his speech. Good God, she's terrified out of her wits, he thought, returning her stare and trying to think of something to say. Her terror communicated itself to him, and when he spoke again it was in a changed tone.

'I'll go down with him. It certainly is very strange—Miss Lee's first evening here——' and he hurried out of the room.

'What *can* have happened?' said Mrs Vorst at once in a low

voice, turning to Amy. 'Oh, I'm so frightened! It's crazy of me, I suppose, but I can't help being afraid of Dan Carr.'

Amy made a faint sound in her throat. Her eyes were fixed on Mrs Vorst imploringly, as if asking for mercy.

Mr Vorst came back almost immediately.

'Myron's gone to the movies,' he said angrily. 'I'll go.' He was tying the belt of his coat as he spoke.

Mrs Vorst said slowly—

'Webster, I shouldn't trouble. I'm sure he's not down there with a twisted ankle. You'd better call up the police.'

'The police! Don't be crazy, dear!'

'It's you who are crazy!' she cried, losing control. 'He's been gone three hours—leaving her here without a word on her first evening! Of course there's something wrong—he wouldn't have done that unless there was something badly wrong—I want you to call up the police right away!'

'I'll call up Jacoby; I was playing golf with him this morning and talking about Bob. He won't get talking all over the place——' Mr Vorst muttered, and went out of the room. Mrs Vorst went over and sat beside Amy.

'Ah hate waiting for someone who doesn't come. Ah do so,' she said softly yet violently, the Southern accent coming into her voice as it always did when she was moved. 'Ah hate it worse than anything in this world. And when it's mah own son and— Miss Lee!' suddenly putting her hand on Amy's bare arm, 'what is it? Are you sick?'

Amy shook her head. She was shivering so violently that her teeth were chattering.

'I'm all right,' she managed to say. 'I'm only so worried. You don't think Dan could have——'

'Now, now, I don't think Dan's done anything,' said Mrs Vorst, getting up and going over to the table. 'I only said that because— well, Dan always was a mean creature and I wondered if he might be mad at Bob's coming home—here, drink this; I'm going to have one, too,' and she held out the highball she had been mixing while she talked.

Amy took it and sipped it, but instead of restoring her spirits and courage it went to her head and immediately swept her away into the dreamlike trance of horror against which she had been struggling. She sat there, turning the glass in her fingers and staring at Mrs Vorst; and all she could think was that tomorrow they were to have gone to the woods, and now they would never go. They would never go.

'Joe Murphy's missing, too,' said Mr Vorst, coming back with a white face. 'His father called up the station an hour ago. He's never been home!'

'He was here this afternoon; Bob asked him up!' exclaimed Mrs Vorst.

'Did they go off together?' he asked.

'Bob was by himself, when I saw him,' put in Amy, slowly.

'Do you think they can be together, Webster? Perhaps Bob ran across Joe down in the wood and thought he'd better see him home.'

'It doesn't take three hours to get to Joe's home.'

'No.' Mrs Vorst put her hand against her forehead. 'I wasn't thinking . . . What are they going to do about Bob?'

'Calling all cars to look out for him, and Joe too. That's all they can do, for the time being. Both of them may turn up any minute. I expect they've gone to the movies.' Mr Vorst spoke irritably to hide his alarm and dismay.

'Well.' He sat down heavily, and stared at his wife, and then at Amy. 'Now there's nothing to do but wait. Miss Lee, will you smoke?'

'No, thank you,' she whispered.

Then for a while no-one spoke. A clock somewhere struck ten.

Towards three o'clock Mrs Vorst helped Amy upstairs and made her lie on the bed. She could not stop trembling, and lay shaking in silence while Mrs Vorst found some sleeping tablets and poured out a glass of water.

'Now I want you just to take these, honey. Just be a sweet good child. Come along.' It was the softest, kindest murmur. 'Try to relax and get some sleep.'

Amy obediently swallowed the tablets and drank some water, never taking her eyes from Mrs Vorst's worried face.

'I'm going to sit up with Mr Vorst, just in case there's any news. But I want you to call me at once if you feel bad. Will you?'

Trying to stop trembling, Amy nodded.

'I'm sure Myron's gone to look for Bob. If anyone—I'm sure he'll find him, too.'

Again Amy nodded. Her lips moved and Mrs Vorst bent nearer. She caught a murmur—

'. . . so sorry . . . such a nuisance . . . so worried——'

'Ah, never mind about that.' She gently arranged the eider-down over Amy's shoulders. 'Just try to sleep. Shall I sit with you for a little while?'

On Amy's grateful nod and murmur, she turned out the lights and seated herself in a low chair by the radiator. Presently she got up and crept over to the bed. Hurried breathing told her that Amy had fallen asleep, and she went quietly out of the room.

The hall was still except for the loud slow ticking of the clock, and the flowers looked unreal in the electric light. Her husband had fallen asleep in his chair with his mouth open and looked an old, tired, weak man. She sat down opposite him and shut her eyes, but was at once compelled to open them again: it was impossible to rest. Presently three o'clock struck. She sat quite still, staring about the room with her hands clasped together, and the night crept on.

Amy slept only for a little while. Suddenly she started awake, as if aroused by a shout, and in the very instant of waking, without pause or mercy, fear leapt upon her and she began to tremble uncontrollably. *He hasn't come back. He just went out to post a letter and he hasn't come back. The police are looking for him. It's true. I forgot it while I was asleep, but it's true.*

But her mind would not accept the truth; her mind rushed away terrified, down corridors of hope, of fantasy, of memory. *Tomorrow perhaps we'll go to the woods after all, if he isn't too tired. Perhaps he's come in while I was asleep. No, they promised to wake me up. But perhaps he said no, don't wake her, let her sleep. Then they wouldn't have told me.*

Was that the front door?

Someone talking in the hall?

She started up in the darkness, shaking so violently from head to foot that the bed trembled under her. The room was utterly silent. A line of light lay under her door, but downstairs there was not a sound. She felt as if the house was alive, and waiting, in a timeless trance of horror, for one who would never come.

She lay down again and dozed uneasily for a little while, half-dreaming, half-remembering, the Hurrying People and the Lady Ligeia's Entombment and all the fears of her childhood, and while she was seeing them she forgot Bob. And then for a few blessed moments she would fall dreamlessly asleep—but always at intervals of half an hour or less, she started awake, again, trembling, and at once in the grip, without pause or mercy, of fear.

She did not know how long this went on. Sometimes she heard the clock chime but she lost count of the hours. Fear raced after her terrified mind and seized it and swung it round to face the unbearable fact that must be borne. The only expression she could give to her agony was the ceaseless trembling that shook her body. She lost all sense of time, she could remember nothing. There was nothing in the world but darkness, and fear without pause or mercy, and the shaking of her cold body huddled on the bed.

When footsteps came quickly up the stairs and hurried along the passage just before sunrise, she had fallen into a stupor and could not hear.

'Dan? Hullo there!'

Suddenly the door of the hut was jerked open and a dark figure stood there, motionless, glaring at Bob, with one hand steadily holding a gun against its side. For a moment they confronted one another across the clearing filled by the dim rays of the moon, and Bob heard the noise of the water very clearly and noticed how white Dan's face was; so white that it seemed to draw upon itself all the light in the heavens. Then Dan let his arm sink to his side, dropping the gun into his pocket, and lurched forward.

'How in hell did you get here?' he said hoarsely, and passed his hand across his forehead. 'I was asleep. And I heard someone calling "Dan". Why didn't you call "Silk"? No-one calls me Dan now.' He wiped his forehead again.

'I thought you might know it was me if I called "Dan",' said Bob, beginning to smile. But as he looked more closely at Dan the smile died. He wore one of his thick dark overcoats closely buttoned round him and the scarf of violet silk that Bob remembered so well, and his hair was disordered and on one cheek was a wide smear, black in the moonlight.

'That's right,' Dan said, as if to himself. 'I did know. I knew your voice. I was dreaming we were kids again, shooting together. The woods, I guess. Being in the woods again.' He stopped, and stared down at the ground for a moment, then suddenly lifted his face and stared up at Bob.

'What do you want?' he demanded loudly. 'How in hell did you get here? Who sent you? No-one knew except Gloria.'

'Gloria's dead,' said Bob, and he took one uncontrollable step backwards. 'Francey sent me.'

'I told her I'd kill her if she squealed,' said Dan in a low voice.

'Of course—I meant Francey. Sure, Gloria's dead. I meant Francey. Why'd Francey———?'

'She's scared for you. She's afraid they'll lynch you for kidnapping Joe,' said Bob, slowly and clearly. While he was speaking he glanced, without moving his head, over Dan's shoulder at the hut. The door was slowly swinging to in the wind and as he watched, it slammed.

'*Ah!*' Dan sprang round, his hand on his gun.

'It's only the door. You're jittering,' said Bob, and put his hand towards his pocket for his cigarette case.

Then he stopped dead, staring. The bulge in Dan's coat swung round and covered him.

'The first lesson you learn is *alone*,' said Dan, softly, 'and the last. The psychology of the superman is solitary. Trust nobody. You'll be crucified if you trust anyone. Like Gloria.'

'Don't be a fool, Dan,' said Bob quietly. 'I haven't got a gun, anyway; and I came to get Joe back and get you out of this mess too, if I can. Is the kid inside?'

'In the cellar. I had to dope him.'

'Is he all right?' Bob controlled a movement towards the hut and tried to speak naturally.

'You're lying about the gun, aren't you?'

Suddenly the white face was close to his own and he smelled the sickliness of drugged breath, while two strong, violent hands clapped against his pockets and sides, searching. There was the extreme of horror in this abrupt bodily contact, as if an animal had pounced on him. When Dan stood back, Bob was trembling with disgust and rage.

'Jesus, it's true,' breathed Dan, staring. 'You bloody mug.'

'I didn't think I'd need a gun. I came up here to get some sense into you, not to shoot you,' said Bob, trying to keep his voice calm.

But already the trees against the sky, and the moon itself (now giving a light strong enough to cast their two shadows on the

grass) and the bright stars, and the flowers on the little bush by
the edge of the wood, were assuming to him that unspeakable
beauty which only falls upon natural objects when the human
eyes which look at them are in danger of death. In a few minutes,
perhaps (he thought) I shall be dead. Oh God, please comfort
her and keep her safe, and let Joe be saved. For Jesus Christ's
sake, amen.

Dan was silent, but on the white face lifted to Bob's there
was a faint smile, as if he were listening to something that gave
him pleasure.

'The bulls'll get Francey and third-degree her and she'll talk.
Then they'll get you,' Bob went on in the same quiet reason-
able tone. 'You can't win, Dan. Let me take the kid back
tonight. I'll make up some story—say we've been for a drive
together, or something.'

Still Dan said nothing; only listened, smiling.

'I won't squeal. I give you my word.'

'Go on talking,' said Dan.

'I'm alone. I came up without telling anyone. If you give me
the kid and let us go, you can make a getaway and no-one need
ever know.'

He was interrupted by a deep noise that he did not at first
realize came from the back of Dan's throat. It began as an actual
snarl and slowly turned to words.

'Ah-h-h-h! You—make—me sick! *You came up here alone. You've
got no gun.* And so I'd admire your nobility and let the kid go.
Now get this——'

He stopped and put his hand to his head.

'I forgot,' he said in his usual soft controlled voice. 'The kid's
dead. I forgot.'

After a pause Bob said—

'Are you sure?'

'I felt his heart. It didn't move. He's in there on the bed, in
the cellar.'

'Dan, let me look at him!'

'I tell you he's dead. It's no use.'

'You don't know—you're all in—you may be mistaken. Just let me look at him—for God's sake——'

He started forward as if to move to the cabin, but at once Dan's gun covered his heart, and he stood still.

'Not afraid, are you?'

'Of course I'm afraid, you fool,' said Bob through his teeth.

Dan shut his eyes and his shoulders writhed as if in pain while all the muscles of his face shuddered.

'*Blast you*,' he burst out at last, lowering the gun. 'You're afraid and you don't care if I know it. What can I do? I never had a chance. You had everything.' His face twisted, and suddenly he was choking with horrible tears. 'You think you can come your Jesus stuff over me, trusting me—but I'm what I've made myself—beyond good'n evil——'

The moon had risen above the trees and now sailed clear of cloud.

'Do you know what?' Dan said, gulping. 'I'm going to kill you.'

'Are you?' said Bob stupidly, after a pause. 'What for, Dan?'

'I've always hated you. Ever since we were kids. You had something I hadn't. All the chances I wanted. Christ, I was glad when you killed that kid! I thought I'd get you that time. But you got away. You've always got away. Only this time you won't, because——'

He choked, and shook his head like a beast in a rage, writhing his shoulders again. '. . . but that's not why I'm going to kill you, that's not why——' he went on, speaking lower and faster and moving a little away from Bob and raising the gun. 'Do you know why? *It's because you're sorry for me, you damned Jesus of Nazareth, in spite of everything you've always been sorry for me——*'

A sharp crack cut across the inhuman raging voice. Dan screamed and flung himself, rather than fell, upon his face. As he fell he fired, and Bob saw a spurt of earth go up just beyond his outstretched hand on the grass.

A man was coming slowly across the clearing, holding an old-fashioned revolver loosely in front of him in one hand and wiping his forehead with a large spotted handkerchief held in the other.

He stopped when he came up to the body. It lay still, looking very dark against the silver of the moonlit grass. Black blood was slowly spreading over the violet silk scarf. Like one of the rocks of the Mooween it lay there; the body of a youngish, fattish man; dead.

Myron touched one of the outflung hands with the tip of his shoe.

'Jest like a bear's paws,' he said. 'He never did have no faculty.'

Chapter the Last

Doctor Robert Vorst's house in Alva looked out towards the mountains. The glow of sunset was fading from the fields now beautiful under six feet of snow, and the blue shadows of the trees were fading too. Soon it would be night, lit by the holy-seeming stars of a Christmas Eve some years later.

Amy was going into the living-room to rest, with a batch of unopened letters in one hand. She still had so much to do!—telephone calls to make, parcels to fix for tomorrow, letters to write, cooking, and a bit of her new story to write, and at any moment Lou would be here. She moved slowly across to her special chair, sat down with a contented sigh, dropped her letters down on the table, and shut her eyes for a moment. She felt very well. It was only to please Bob that she took a little rest every day about this time. And today she felt particularly well and energetic; Christmas could not bring enough tasks for her; she felt like turning out the attics as well. Bob had nodded when she said as much at breakfast and had remarked that this was quite normal, the baby should arrive in a few days as expected. All the clothes were ready, and Doctor Lippmann was on call at Morgan, and a nurse from Vine Falls would arrive shortly. Bob had refused to attend Amy. He had supervised the waiting time, but he did not feel himself brave enough to bring his child into the world. Dr Lippmann, aged sixty-three and deliverer of hundreds, could do that.

'Oh, you'll be perfectly all right,' Bob had said; he had said it several times before he went out on his round, and looked at her rather a long time when he kissed her good-bye and then said it again.

I wish he'd come in, thought Amy, glancing out of the window at the darkening fields. Then she tried to check her thoughts (worrying was bad for the baby) and turned to her letters.

There were some old friends in the room with her: the skating ladies, the red and blue Italian soldiers, the birds on their snowy boughs, but in this room for the first time in their lives they appeared at home. They had seemed too elegant for the flat at Highbury and too old-fashioned for the conventional smartness of the one at Hyde House, but here they looked serenely down upon old pieces of maplewood furniture and a green Chinese carpet and were no more than part of a restful room.

Letters from England! Oh, good, thought Amy. Her heart was where her treasure was, in America, but she did enjoy her English mail! She sorted the letters, putting the dullest ones first, and then began to read. Her little hands, grown plumper in the past months, dutifully turned the pages of a long epistle from Mr Aubrett concerned with contracts, money and translation rights; and then she passed on to some fan-mail (which she read with gratified murmurs, for Amy had learned to love her new public as much as her new public loved her). She put by some catalogues and advertisements to be dealt with by her little secretary, a local girl who came in every morning for two hours. And then, her duty done, she opened a fat letter with an English stamp and a Wimbledon postmark, switched on the lamp (for it was nearly dark and the snowy fields outside were one with the deep blue sky) and settled herself to enjoy the sound of Dora Beeding's voice, from three thousand miles away.

'DEAR OLD AME,

'I expect Horatio will have arrived by the time you get this or is about to any minute and you will be up to your eyes in it, so don't sweat yourself answering it until you've got a sec. to spare. But I just had to tell you our bit of bad news so that you shouldn't say anything about Dad next time you write to Mum. He's gone off with that little so-and-so, Mrs Flower (I expect you remember her— very dark and quiet, lived next door but one). He never said a word—just went off one Saturday and we haven't heard a word since. Mum's taken it awfully hard, she doesn't say anything, not even when Flower came round and kicked up a shine. Maurice had to fetch a policeman. Of course I'd sort of felt Dad was working up for something for years but you know how it is, you don't really notice the people you live with. I suppose the work got him down, it's an awful life, as you know. If Mum hadn't got Maurice I don't know what she'd do but he really has settled down at last. (No more Mosley for him, he wouldn't know who you meant if you mentioned the gent!) He's making money, too. He's got two dogs running at the Hillover Track this week—one, Baker's Boy, looks like being a champion. M. has paid back Mum the eighty he borrowed from her (out of the hundred you gave her) and he's buying one of the new little houses they're building out near the Hillover Track, and he and Mum and Baby and Artie are moving out there in the spring. It'll do Mum good to get away from Highbury. She'll put a manager in the business. Notice my new address? I'm sharing this swelegant little flat with Slugs (remember her?). I've just had another step up—secretary to the Old Swine himself now! Can you beat it—and when I think how I used to bleed at the ears every time he walked through the room fifteen years ago!

'Baby started in the Accounts Department at John Lewis's three weeks ago and seems all right. She's a pretty kid and does she know it, too! I only hope she doesn't slip up the stairs with some boy friend or other. Sydney's had a rise and they've just bought a car!!! It'll be fourpence to speak to the Old Guy soon. Both her kids are awfully fit. Artie's been moved up on the butter counter now ('Guns and Butter' we call him, he's just joined the Terriers!). He sends you his love and says I'm to tell you he doesn't like your new kind of book as well as the old kind. Oh, well. Can't please everyone, can you?

'Well, no more now. Give Horatio his Auntie Dora's love when he arrives, and tell him I'm shortly sending him a jacket (knitted with the sweat of my brow in the intervals of A.R.P.).

'You won't mention Dad to Mum, will you? She's wonderful, really, but she feels it. She's getting on; it's no joke a thing like that at her age. I don't know how I feel about Dad really. In a way I'm sorry for him. He always was a bit of a dark horse (like someone else I know!). But I'm much sorrier for Mum.

'Love to you and the gorgeous-looking husband.

'Yours ever,

'DORA.'

Amy was so moved by this piece of news that she got up clumsily from her chair and walked about the room for a moment, staring without seeing them at the gilded branches and glittering Christmas stars adorning the walls. She remembered how old and tired Mrs Beeding had looked when she had last seen her in London two years ago, and how tenderly she had kissed her good-bye and wished her happiness, putting into the embrace all the affection of those eleven years in which she had stood in the place of Amy's own mother. And Mrs Flower! She was as familiar a sight to Amy as the kitchen at 5 Highbury Walk, as taken for granted, as firmly in her place. There she had been for years, part of the background of their lives, and all the time Mr Beeding must have been drawn to her and at last his unhappiness and sickness and longing to escape had mastered him, and her, and they had gone away together. Amy found herself wondering, as she wiped her eyes for Mrs Beeding, whether they would ever know a moment's happiness. She imagined them in Wales, walking along a road in the hills, and Mr Beeding singing once more, deep and sweet and true as the notes of an organ.

But none of them ever saw or heard of him again.

As she was settling into her chair a door opened abruptly and the head of Myron was put round it.

'All right, are yer?' he demanded.

'Yes, thanks, Myron.'

'Ain't feelin' bad or anythin'?'

'Not a bit, thanks.'

'Mrs Vorst Senior jest called up to know how you was. Joe answered. He said you was fine 'n dandy.'

'That's right, so I am. Myron, has the drink come; and the savouries from Kraus's?'

'Nope.'

'Well, get Joe to go down as soon as he's finished whatever he's doing, will you?'

'Okay. Mrs Vorst Senior said they'll be over tomorrow round twelve.'

'Fine.'

'She said Lou'll be here round about six.'

'All right. Did Mrs Vorst say anything else?' (Telephone messages always had to be wormed out of Myron.)

'Only asked was the baby here yet. I said no.'

Amy laughed. It was the laugh that her mother would have recognized, fat and deep like the laugh of a tickled child.

'All your folks all right?' next inquired Myron, jerking his head towards the letters. He took a passionate interest in Amy's English correspondents, while heartily despising all they said and did.

'Yes, thanks.'

She was preparing to defend the contents of her correspondence by a series of elaborate lies when Joe put his head round the door.

It was a tidier head than it had been two years ago. The flaxen hair was plastered back with grease. The scars had faded so as to be visible only in certain lights and the sunken eyelid had lost its redness. A white coat added to the crispness, the efficiency, that made Joe's young personality unusual.

'All right, are you?' inquired Joe, who had developed an admiration for Myron since the shooting of Dan that made him unconsciously copy Myron's style.

'Yes, thanks.' (Blow you both, go away. I want to get on with my letters, thought Amy.)

'Myron, tea's ready.'

'Wash,' grumbled Myron. But he got up from his knees, where he had been tending the coal fire, and went out of the room.

'Mrs Brady's husband called up,' Joe announced. 'He said she guesses she may be taken bad any time now.'

'Oh Joe,' said Amy, dismayed. 'That means tomorrow!'

'Certainly is tough on the Doc,' said Joe, shaking his head. 'Oh, well, maybe it won't happen. You'd think the Doc could have his Christmas Day in peace, wouldn't you?'

'Come on, come on, we gotta get that wash down us and you've gotta go downtown,' muttered Myron, tramping down the passage. Joe smiled at Amy, lingering at the door.

'Will you have tea today, Mrs Vorst?'

'No, thanks, Joe, I'll wait for Mrs Viner.'

'Okay.' He shut the door.

Amy opened another letter from England, one with a Harrow postmark, and read in an old-fashioned masculine hand—

'DEAR MRS VORST,

'Before I turn to this month's Report, may I express my interest and pleasure at the piece of news contained in your last letter. There can be no deeper joy than that bestowed by a happy and united family life, and I am sincerely happy that you have every prospect of enjoying this. Under separate cover I am forwarding to you a Bear which I hope may please the baby later on. The Bear is not new, as you will notice (it was one of the first toys of this kind ever to be introduced into this country by Messrs Gamage, in 1904) but it has not had much wear and I should like to think of its being used again. Now as to the matter of this month's Report . . .'

But here Amy put the letter down and leant back in her chair, thinking about the last time she had seen Mr Danesford. It was an occasion that she liked to remember.

Some years ago, a few weeks before her marriage, she had gone back to England after over a year's absence to settle up her affairs there and to collect her personal treasures to bring back to her American home. On the very first morning of her arrival she had casually opened *The Times* while waiting at the hairdresser's, and read—with how startled a movement of her heart!—

We announce with regret the death of Lord Welwoodham, owner and editor of *The Prize* since 1906. A memoir will be found on page 16.

Shocked, unable to believe it, she turned to page 16, and there looked up aloofly at her the long face and Edwardian moustache of her first and last employer. She slowly sat down, still staring at the familiar face and experiencing the strongest feelings of shock and sorrow; and learned how he had died after a short but severe illness following a chill caught while hunting.

I must write to Lady Welwoodham at once and send some flowers, she thought, and later in the day she did both. In the afternoon, when the short winter day was rapidly turning to dusk, she decided to go down and see them all at *The Prize* and find out what was to be the old paper's fate.

It was half-past three when she came out of St Paul's Station and crossed the crowded noisy street to Rosemary Lane. A cold rose-red sunset glowed between the dark houses in the old quarters of the City. The lights were all glittering in the broad streets, but the lane kept its old look of dimness and crookedness, with faint lights in the windows of its little shops. There were brown chrysanthemums and purple anemones in the flower shop where she had once seen the blue iris hanging in the sunbeam like blossoms made of stained glass. The Chinese wind-bells had been put inside because of the wild winds of the English winter, and there was a grim little notice in one corner of the window warning customers that delivery of goods could no longer be guaranteed because of the War, and advising them to buy while they could. Amy still kept her childish admiration for the Chinese, and she went into the shop for a moment and bought some embroidery and a bunch of charms, beautifully made in flower-coloured glass. Then she went on, with quickly-beating heart, to the offices of *The Prize*.

Nothing was changed. The sign with the boy receiving the casket from the bearded man still swung gently in the breeze above the shop window full of Bibles; there was the familiar doorway and the dark but clean old wooden staircase up which she had gone countless times as a timid child. It was strange to tread those stairs again now that she was a happy young woman about to be married; it was like being two people, the old one and the new. She crossed the landing and saw the familiar door with the notice: *The Prize: Enquiries. Please Knock*; and then she turned the handle and went quietly in.

The room was in twilight, and at first she thought that there was no-one there. The little fire that Lord Welwoodham had always allowed his staff during the winter months was nearly out in the basket-shaped grate, with one dying red coal among the white ashes, and the curtains had not been pulled across the windows; she could see the massive side of St Paul's through them, with some pigeons walking about on its dark columns that had a faint glow from the chilly rose of sunset. An empty cup with an untasted biscuit in the saucer stood on the desk that had always been Miss Grace's. And then she saw that at the other desk an old man was sitting, with his head buried in his hands. It was not white hairs that gave her the immediate impression of age, for the bowed head that caught the last light from the window was only streaked with grey; it was the bent shoulders and the indescribable absence of hope in his attitude. *An old man* she thought at once; and then, peering through the dimness, she recognized to her dismay the shabby frock-coat and striped trousers and high collar worn by Mr Danesford.

Quickly and silently she retreated, shutting the door after her; and stood on the landing for a long moment in the dusk, much disturbed. She had expected to find them all very upset and troubled about their future, but not this—the room in twilight, and no Miss Grace, and Mr Danesford turned into an old man. Some of her former aloofness and inability to communicate with her fellow-beings crept over her as she hesitated there on the familiar landing. Her happiness with Bob and her adoption by his family had almost conquered it, but suddenly she felt again its cold touch. What could she say to him? He had always seemed so remote to her, such a self-contained and awesome figure. It was like finding one of the Amaravati Tope in tears to discover Mr Danesford with his head in his hands!

But suddenly she felt so sorry for him that all her hesitation vanished, and she knocked firmly on the door. After a longish pause his deep voice called calmly, 'Come in,' and she entered for the second time.

The room looked quite different, for he had pulled the curtains and switched on the lamp on his desk, and was now peering across at her from the circle of light, trying to make out who was there.

'Mr Danesford?' she said, coming forward. 'It's me—Amy Lee.'

'Miss Lee!' He stood up and bent a little towards her, still peering. 'Well! this is a surprise. We did not even know that you were back in England.' She held out her hand and took it limply in his cold one for a second.

'I only got in here yesterday. I've just seen about——'

Mr Danesford quickly looked down at the floor.

'I'm so sorry,' she went on. 'It must be——'

'Let me put on the other light.' He crossed to the door with his well-remembered loping walk. 'The evenings are drawing in so quickly, I hardly realized how dark it had grown.' He switched on the light and pulled up a chair. 'Do sit down, Miss Lee.'

She seated herself and loosened the little sable collar on her coat, but she was so disturbed by the change in him that she could not think of anything to say, and he seemed equally at a loss. He sat opposite to her, not looking at her, playing with an old yellow ruler that she had seen him play with a hundred times in the past while deciding some small point of office policy; and did not say a word. She suspected that he was wishing her miles away.

'How is Miss Grace?' she inquired at last.

'Oh, very well, thank you, very well indeed. She is no longer with us. She left us six months ago to be married.'

'Married!' cried Amy—manners, embarrassment, everything forgotten in sheer amazement.

'Oh, yes. Her parents died within a few months of one another last year, and she sold their house at Hendon, and married a Mr Baron, an old friend of the family, so I understood. He has a nurseryman's business at Berkhampstead and they have settled there.'

'Well, I *am* surprised!' murmured Amy. 'Fancy Miss Grace married! Weren't *you* surprised, Mr Danesford?' She was determined to rouse him, for his air of mingled apathy and grief was beginning to alarm her.

Mr Danesford permitted himself a smile. It was a very slight smile, but it encouraged her, for it was the first sign he had given of recognizing that she was not a stranger but an acquaintance of ten years' standing.

'We were all a little surprised, I fancy,' he admitted, 'but very pleased, of course. We gave her a silver teapot, a fine Georgian piece.'

'And Mr Ramage—how is he?'

'Mr Ramage is no longer with us. He went to *The Airwoman* as advertising manager six months ago,' answered Mr Danesford quietly.

'And Mr Cole and Mr Holbrooke?'

'They too have left us. Mr Carter has been doing their work.'

Amy was silent, too distressed to utter a word. The whole sad story was plain to her: the gradual shrinkage in advertising revenue, the cutting of salaries, the departure of younger and more active members of the staff to safer berths, the petty economies, the desperate effort by Mr Danesford to do several people's work, and then the last blow—the death of Lord Welwoodham.

After a long silence she said awkwardly:

'Do you know what will happen to the paper now?'

He did not move a muscle but somehow she knew that he had to summon all his self-control in order to make himself answer steadily:

'Nothing is decided yet, but I have understood for the last

few months that Mr Cavendish will sell—if he gets an offer. If he does not, we shall cease publication.'

'*Cease publication?*' she cried, unable to believe her ears. 'But doesn't he expect to get an offer?'

Mr Danesford shook his head.

'I have been with *The Prize* for nearly fifty years, Miss Lee, and I have lived to see all the qualities it stands for pass away. No-one wants us nowadays. We represent an England that has gone for ever.'

He got up and went over to the window and parted the curtains and stood there, staring out at the columns of the cathedral, now illuminated by the theatrical glow of the street lamps. He added over his shoulder, half to himself—

'Who would buy *The Prize?*'

'I would,' said Amy.

Mr Danesford turned round at that, with a very kind smile, and came over and stood looking down at her. Though her name was as famous in America as in England, though her dark red coat of French cut and her sable muff and the jewels in her ears all quietly indicated that she was rich, to Mr Danesford she was still poor Lee's daughter, who had been considered lucky to get a job as office girl on *The Prize*.

'I am sure you would, if you could, Miss Lee,' he said, 'and it makes me happy (and I am sure it would have pleased Lord Welwoodham, he always took such an interest in you and your work) to know that you are still loyal to the paper.'

'But I mean it.' Amy clasped her hands inside her muff and looked steadily up at him. 'I really will buy it.'

'But you haven't the money!' bayed Mr Danesford, his usual full rich tones coming back to him under the stress of mingled amazement and hope and doubt, while he stared at her with his bloodhound's eyes as wide open as they would go.

'I've got a great deal of money,' she retorted. 'It's been coming in for six years, you know, and I haven't spent a quarter of it every year. I don't know quite how much it is right now but I'm sure it's enough to make an offer to Mr Cavendish.'

'It seems impossible!' said Mr Danesford abruptly, sitting down and staring at her almost suspiciously. '*You* buying *The Prize*!'

'Well, perhaps I shan't have *enough* money,' she said more cautiously, 'but at least I can *try*. Is Mr Cavendish still at his old address? I'll call him up tonight.'

'But you can't do it like that, over the telephone!' he protested, shocked. 'Those are American methods, Miss Lee!'

'Well, I've been living there for over a year,' she reminded him (and indeed, she had a charming slight accent to prove it) 'and I like to get things settled.'

'Just as if it were a packet of cigarettes———' he muttered, and took out his handkerchief and blew his nose.

'Mr Danesford,' she went on, leaning a little towards him and speaking warmly and eagerly, 'if Mr Cavendish accepts my offer, please will you stay on as Editor?'

There was a pause, while she looked at his face and he looked at the floor. Then he said unsteadily without raising his eyes—

'I am nearly seventy, Miss Lee. Would you not want—a younger man?'

'But no-one knows so much about *The Prize* as you do now,' she said. 'I shall be in America, you know. I'm going to live there. I'm going to be married very soon, as a matter of fact.'

'Indeed? I congratulate you—I wish you every happiness,' he put in, courteously but quite mechanically, while he kept his anxious gaze fixed on her face.

'Yes,' she nodded. The thought of that happiness made her smile a little and brightened her eyes. 'So you see I shan't be able to keep an eye on things. I shall want you to do that for me.'

'I appreciate that . . . very much, Miss Lee. If all turns out well and Mr Cavendish accepts your offer I shall be more than honoured—Lord Welwoodham hinted more than once to Mr

Cavendish, I believe, that I—but of course, everything has happened so suddenly—I never imagined ——'

The yellow ruler slipped between his shaking fingers and fell to the floor.

'I have been worrying about the future a great deal lately, as a matter of fact' (he was stooping to look for the ruler, out of the light) 'because of my own private responsibilities. My only son' (he straightened himself and put the ruler carefully on the desk without looking at her) 'is—an invalid. He has never been able to take his place in the world as an adult, and he needs constant care. So you may imagine——'

His voice died away; and she did what he had given her permission to do. She saw herself six years ago, sitting opposite to Old Porty in the teashop, telling him of her imaginary romance with Mr Danesford's broad-shouldered, grey-eyed young son; and for a second she felt bodily sick, while for the first time in her life her power of making up stories seemed a horrible thing. She stood up rather quickly, buttoning her fur collar, and said—

'I'll call you up in the morning, then, shall I, to let you know what's happened?'

'I shall be most anxious to hear, Miss Lee.'

He moved to the door with her, but he did not at once hold out his hand in farewell and she could tell that something was still troubling him.

'Excuse my asking, Mr Danesford,' she said, and her voice unconsciously dropped into the flat, polite, little-girl tone of her office days, 'but is there something you're still worried about?'

'Yes, there is, Miss Lee,' he answered at once. 'It is this. If your offer is accepted by Mr Cavendish and you become the owner of *The Prize*, shall you make drastic changes in our policy?'

'Of course not!' she cried at once. 'I want it to stay as it is!'

'You will lose money,' he warned her.

'I'll write a serial for it—then I shan't,' she promised confidently.

Mr Danesford looked taken aback: Amy's new kind of book was not at all traditional *Prize* material. But he was considerably relieved by what she had said, and when they shook hands his clasp was no longer limp but firm and strong.

'Good-bye then, Mr Danesford. I'll call you up tomorrow about ten.'

'Good-bye, Miss Lee.' He hesitated. 'I am sure that you must know how much I feel—it is so difficult to express——'

She smiled at him, then bit her lip, shook her head, put up her muff to hide her mouth, and almost ran from the room.

To the extreme horror of Messrs Aubrett and Humfriss, her offer was accepted only too willingly by the exquisite Rupert Cavendish and she became owner of *The Prize*. Their horror was justified, for the paper not only took most of the money she had saved but proved a steady liability; under her and Mr Danesford's careful nursing it stopped actually losing money, but it only just paid its way, and anything like a European crisis or a heavy fall of snow sent its sales down at once. Finally she was compelled to make some changes in its Late Victorian policy and make up or abandon it to its fate, for she had already spent so much on it that she could no longer be called a rich woman and could afford to spend no more; her new kind of book did not immediately prove so popular as her former kind, and while she was making considerably less money from her writing she had had to live on her savings.

So *The Prize* was forced to take a story in her new 'domestic' vein (with Mr Danesford fighting every inch of the way) and Amy gradually broadened the paper's scope so that it appealed to girls as well as to boys.

She always guiltily felt that Mr Danesford would never forgive her, but there was no doubt that from the first issue in the new form the paper began to do better. Now, in Mr Danesford's latest report, the news from Rosemary Lane was cheerful. (Lady Welwoodham always swore that the improvement was due not so much to her serial and the change of policy as to a delightful third leader that appeared in *The Times* a few days after the new *Prize* had made its bow: every reader of *The Times*, she vowed, had at once decided to take in *The Prize* on reading what the third leader-writer had so charmingly said about the transformation. Be that as it may, *The Prize* was prospering.)

She remembered (leaning back in her chair with Mr Danesford's letter on her lap) how she had glanced back at the windows of the old office as she hurried down Rosemary Lane, and seen the light in Mr Danesford's room suddenly go out. Mr Danesford, like millions of other Londoners, would soon be on his way home—to his son. She had remembered that he lived in Harrow and used sometimes to come to work in the summer with a small red rose in his buttonhole. He had been a widower for twenty years, Miss Grace had once let drop.

And now he was no longer an austere, terrifying Presence; he was only a shrunken, loyal old man, old-fashioned and prejudiced, who was in her employ. How strange was Time, that brought such changes about! And (she remembered) she had suddenly felt frightened of the mysteriousness of life and longed for Bob, who was three thousand miles away.

She heard the Ford come out of the yard and drive off, and then Myron suddenly stuck his head round the door again.

'Joe's gone,' he announced.

'Didn't you want to?'

'Aw—no. I gotta whole heap of things to do. It's half-after five. Folks'll be comin' in soon, too.'

She nodded, smiling. She knew that he had stayed behind because he had remembered that Bob did not like her to be alone in the house in case the baby started to come—a fact which she herself had forgotten in the press of Christmas duties.

'Feelin' all right, are yer?'

'Grand, thanks. I—Myron, Bob didn't call up, did he?'

'Now—now! Quit that, will yer? Yer know he can't never say what time he'll be in; a doc. never can.'

She nodded again, meekly.

'I know, Myron. It's awfully silly of me. I wasn't worrying, really. It's only just——'

'Lou'll be here any minute; cheer yer up. Well——'

He vanished, slamming the door after him, and after a moment or two she struggled out of her chair, gathered up her letters, and climbed slowly upstairs to Lou's room to see that everything was ready for her.

The house was warm and quiet, tidy and decorated, as if waiting for the spirit of Christmas to descend and fill it. There was a tree glittering and sparkling at the dining-room window where everyone passing in the street could see it, and a thick circle of glossy holly leaves and scarlet berries hung on the front door. Christmas cards, frosted, gleaming with fantastic angels or entwined with wreaths made from silvered shells and musical instruments were arranged on the chest in the hall. Dozens of unopened parcels were piled in the drawing-room. Myron's radio in the kitchen was softly giving, 'Stilly Night, Holy Night,' by the Dixie Chocolate Cookie Choir; the lovely tune crept wistfully up the well of the staircase, making her pause with her hand on the bannister to listen. From where she stood she could see the nursery with the crib, draped in white, glimmering through the dusk. One star, a huge star that seemed full of meaning and message, shone steadily through the window panes. She went slowly into Lou's room and sat down on the bed. Everything was ready, even to some roses which had arrived for Lou that morning. Amy had not been able to help seeing the card tucked among their thorny stems, which said only 'Forgiven? Bless you.' And over that she had pursed up her mouth.

It was so warm and quiet and peaceful everywhere. I'm so happy I can't believe it's true, she thought dreamily, sitting on the bed with the letters from England spread about her. If only he'd come in! Shall I *never* get over this feeling when he's away? Shall I always be afraid he won't come back—even when I'm an old, old woman?

Then she resolutely picked up a fat letter addressed in a hand which she had good cause to know only too well and opened it.

Out fell a very large Christmas card with a crimson and green coach careering gaily across it, cheered on by a group of ladies and gentlemen dressed in what is popularly known as Jane-Austen-sort-of-costume. Inside was written—'Wishing You Both All the Best from E. Talbot Porteous (Porty).'

Her present of twenty pounds to Old Porty had had the most disastrous results, unloosing upon her a flood of letters and literature dealing with every imaginable method of making a fortune, from Pools to Orange Farming, that a florid fancy could suggest and a distaste for hard work could encourage. Porty, after many ups-and-downs, had finally established himself with a luckless distant male relative who kept a small family and commercial hotel at Castleford in Yorkshire, and had at once undertaken a series of reforms in the management of the establishment, described by him as *'overhauling the whole bally place, lock, stock and barrel,'* apparently with the object of saving the luckless relative from bankruptcy . . .

Downstairs the telephone bell rang. In a moment Myron called up—

'It's Ma Boadman. She says has the baby come yet? Shall I put her through?'

'Oh *no!*' cried Amy, glancing in alarm at the telephone by the bed. 'Give her my love and say I'm resting. (And Myron, *don't* call her Ma, *please!*)' She waited, her peace of mind disturbed.

Presently he shouted—

'She says you're a bad thing an' she don't believe you want to talk to her one bit but all the same she loves you and how's that man of yours. I said we all had plenty to do, it being Christmas. O.K.?'

'O.K.' she called back, laughing, and picked up the mass of literature on silver fox breeding that was enclosed with Porty's card.

She and Bob had often said to one another that Porty's relative would probably prefer bankruptcy and ruin to the continual presence of Porty, but as he never seemed to make any attempts to get rid of Porty (and they felt sure that Porty's letters would have said plenty about it if he had) perhaps he did not mind having Porty about the place so much as they would have done. Bob had forbidden her to send Porty one halfpenny more, and as she obeyed him in money matters as she did in all matters, she often found it difficult to think of convincing excuses for not sending money for investment in one of Porty's gorgeous schemes. Her correspondence with Porty, in fact, was more than a nuisance in a life already full. But she kept up with him because he had known her mother and because he was part of her memories of London.

She liked to remember London, and thought often and with affection of her friends there, but she did not miss the city painfully or long to live there with Bob. She had always been unhappy in London, whereas her happiness in Alva was so new, continuous and delightful that she never ceased to wonder at it. On her last visit to England two years ago she had revisited all her former haunts with the kind of fearful pleasure that a freed prisoner might feel as he curiously turned over in his hands the chains that had bound him. She had been Up Highgate, too, and noticed the blue Air Mail box in the village opposite the butcher's shop that has been there for two hundred years; and had seen a neat official plate with AIR RAID WARDEN on it outside one of the familiar shabby houses in Fortress Road. But the really exciting event had been her encounter, during her visit to Kenwood House, with a large portly dignified black cat whom she found on inquiry had been living round the House for eleven years! Could it be the kitten she had been carrying on the afternoon that she first spoke to Bob? It might be, admitted the waitress in the tea-rooms, cautiously. But Amy was sure that it was.

She put down the pamphlet about fox-breeding with a little sigh. I ought to go down and do a bit of my story, she thought, arranging herself more comfortably on the bed.

She was no longer able to give whole days to her writing, for looking after Bob and managing the house took up most of her time. But fortunately she no longer needed to retreat into a long trance of concentration and excitement in order to create; her books were now the kind that can be written in time snatched from domestic affairs. She had almost forgotten the frightening morning some years ago, when she had sat for an hour, in silence, staring at a blank page on which she was unable to write a word.

After the night when Bob had gone out to post a letter and had not come back, she had had a nervous collapse in which all the suppressed fears and unhappiness of years had come to the surface of her mind. And when her health returned, restored by happiness, she found her secret world had vanished. Not even its ruins were left. She opened the unfinished manuscript of *The Tower of the Wicked*, staring at the last words she had written before her illness and could not remember writing them, nor believe that she had written them. She knew, as she stared at the words, that never again would she be able to make stories out of danger and fear. In the hours of that night when she believed that Dan had found Bob and killed him, she had come face to face with reality at last, and had been powerless to defeat her fear by making it romantic. She had been forced to accept it, in its unutterable horror, and the acceptance had almost killed her and had shattered her secret world for ever.

For weeks after her marriage she had put off trying to write, and when at last she did try, urged by Mr Humfriss and her publishers, this blankness and despair was all that she could feel. Her power to tell stories seemed dead.

Bob had come in and found her sitting there, white and silent. He gathered from her confused explanation what had happened and gave her the first piece of advice that came into his head, for he was late for a lecture and in a hurry.

'Well, darling, maybe you could write something more homey,' he said, and he gave her a tender kiss and hurried away.

When he came back that evening, two chapters of *On the Porch* were written and Amy, with flushed face and the little bump on her third finger once more reddened by the pressure of the pen, had started upon the famous 'second manner' that was to bring her in time nearly as big a public for her stories of domestic life in England and America as she had once had for her stories of danger and death. The new public did not come all at once, for readers (bless them) do like to know what to expect from a writer, but it came. Her stories of family life communicated (because she herself felt it) to the passing of an examination or the breaking of a betrothal the excitement she had once given to escapes from death and last-minute rescues, and she charmed her readers by showing them the variety and interest of every day. (Mr Humfriss and Mr Aubrett had now outwardly recovered from the shock, but they occasionally told one another in confidence over their morning Sanatogen that they would never, never have believed such a thing could happen, and added in a kind of Tibetan-prayer chorus that never, never could they feel *quite* safe about a writer again.)

Miss Cordell took to herself the entire credit for the change and never hesitated to tell Amy as much.

In the kitchen Joe was unwinding his muffler while he argued with Myron.

'It was mighty like her, anyway,' said Joe.

'Mebbe. But she married a sales representative for Sweetbriar Toothpaste an' went to Wisconsin with him. It couldn't hev been Francey,' said Myron, shaking his grey head. He was on his knees stacking bottles for tomorrow's festivities into the ice-box.

'She might have come back.'

'Not she. Skeered.'

'She didn't do anything. The bulls hadn't anything on her; they let her go. What's she got to be scared of, anyway?'

'Mrs Doc might shoot her. Fer not calling us up that night when Bob told her to.' Myron got up, rubbing his knees, and gave one of his loud quick laughs that did not seem to disturb his face.

'Myron,' coaxed Joe, settling comfortably in the old hickory rocker that had come with the handyman from Vine Falls, and stretching out his legs and beginning to rock, 'tell about the time you shot Dan. Aw—go on! The sicks won't be here yet.'

'There's a sick at the door right now, so you git up an' let him in,' said Myron threateningly, as the front door bell rang.

It was not a sick, however, but Mrs Stebby Viner, who gave him her usual cool smile.

'Hullo, Joe. What's new? Baby here yet?'

'No, mam,' said Joe, grinning. 'Will I fetch your grips in and put the automobile away?'

'Do, will you? Mrs Vorst up there?' and then, as Joe nodded, she began to mount the stairs calling ironically:

'Yoo-hoo! Vicky?'

'Hullo, Lou darling!' called Amy, coming out of the bedroom with a slowness that contrasted with her eager voice.

They met at the top of the stairs and kissed.

'Where's Stebby?' asked Amy as they went into the bedroom. She had not yet learnt the finer shades in dealing with her fellow-beings, though she was learning fast. 'Isn't he coming?'

'Stebby,' explained Lou, arranging her fur coat on a hanger

and speaking with her back to Amy, who had reseated herself on the bed, 'is staying over Christmas with some other friends. He sends you his love and a rather filthy bracelet he chose when he wasn't quite sober and says will you forgive him for being so rude.'

'I'm awfully sorry he can't come, because it would have been so much nicer for you,' said Amy soberly.

Lou came over to her and gently patted her cheek.

'One day, honey, you'll get a prize,' she said. Her eyes moved to the roses by the bed. 'And how's Albert?'

'Oh, he's quite well, thanks, only he's still out on his visits and I do wish he'd come in. They've got 'flu down in the Polak quarter. Oh, those roses came for you.'

'So I see,' murmured Lou, who was reading the card. Then she tore it into bits, but she was smiling.

The telephone bell rang downstairs.

'Perhaps that's Bob!' said Amy eagerly, but a minute later Myron called:

'Ellen van Damm called up. She says is the baby here yet.'

'Oh . . . thank her and say not yet and wish her a Happy Christmas, will you?'

'O.K.'

'Do you still have that habit of worrying yourself sick every time Bob's a bit late?' inquired Lou, addressing the reflection of her sister-in-law which she could see in the glass. Amy's face was fuller and rather tired. She wore an ample house-coat of dark material richly striped with satin. (This was left from her pre-*Prize* wardrobe: she could no longer afford expensive clothes.) She looked plain, but more dignified than she would ever look until the one thing that it seemed to lack was added to the picture she made: the child in her arms. She nodded, smiling shamefacedly, and Lou smiled at her in the glass and went on making herself a mouth in silence, while Amy listlessly glanced at two Christmas cards; a severe fourteenth-century Adoration of the Magi (British Museum, price twopence) from Miss Lathom; and a frivolous ballet scene by Degas (Heals, price a shilling) from Lady Welwoodham, who clung to the atheism that had been fashionable and advanced in her girlhood.

Presently Lou said:

'Helen called up this morning from San Francisco. She's going to be married in the New Year.'

'Oh? Who to?' Amy's tone was no more than polite, for her increasing nervous anxiety about Bob made it difficult to give her full attention to anything, and she had seen Helen only once, on that morning at Boone's flat.

'A barrister out there. Much older than she is. Plenty of potatoes, Aunt Carol says. He's got two ex-wives.'

Amy pulled a face.

'Oh, well, maybe it wasn't his fault, he sounds the idealistic type, from what Helen said,' soothed Lou, feeling a second's impatience with Amy's schoolgirl standards.

'Where'll they live?'

'In San Francisco. He's got a ranch out there, too.'

'I'm glad,' said Amy, trying to remember Helen's face. She made an effort to show more interest and went on, 'She's absolutely beautiful, isn't she?'

'She is.'

'You'd think she'd have got married before.'

'You certainly would,' said Lou quietly, shutting the lid of her flapjack.

'Well, I hope she'll be happy, anyway.'

'I hope so, too,' said Lou, turning away from the mirror with her face finished.

'Look——' said Amy, struggling off the bed. 'I must go down and write a little bit of my story; you don't mind, do you?'

The telephone bell rang downstairs.

They waited, smiling at one another in silence, until the shout came up the stairs—

'Miss Julia Cordell called up. She said——'

'Is the baby here yet——'

'Is the baby here yet——'

chanted Lou and Amy together, laughing.

'Give her my love and say not yet, and wish her a happy Christmas, please, Myron.'

'O.K.'

'I want to make a call,' said Lou, lying down on the bed and picking up the telephone. 'You go down and write your little bit and I'll be right down.'

Amy went slowly out of the room; leaving Lou to make her call. To talk in the new voice that she had acquired in a year of marriage, while she swung one foot, and stared at the roses beside her bed. So what? she thought, listening to another voice, charming and indistinct, speaking from two hundred miles away. I always knew it would be this way, and it's lots of fun sometimes, and anyway it'll never be any different. So what?

But Amy went slowly downstairs to the little room with walls covered with books where she usually wrote, switched on an electric plate which stood in one corner and put a saucepan on to heat; and then sat down, with a sigh, at the Heals desk which had come from London and opened the scribbled folder of blotting paper that held her Story, and tried to write.

Every two or three minutes the bell rang, and Myron or Joe, functioning in strictest rotation, came up to let in the Sicks. *There are a lot tonight, he'll be busy when he comes in,* thought Amy. *Perhaps he won't have time to sit with me as he usually does. It is Christmas Eve, but I'll try not to show I mind about it.* Half of her mind was on her story and half was darkening beneath an oppression of anxiety, the legacy from that night when Bob had gone out to post a letter and had not come back. She heard the tramp of heavy boots in the lobby, and excited Jewish voices (operatives from the big new clothing factory recently opened in Alva which was helping to give

465

the town the beginnings of civic self-respect), and the thick voices of Poles, and through all the confused sounds the voices, like flutes, of young children. Alva had already christened Bob 'The Kiddies' Doctor.'

Amy realized that the life led by Bob and herself was a most unusual one. They were young, gifted, healthy, and had some private means, yet Bob had chosen to set up in practice in a half-derelict town where the people were uneducated, narrow-minded and suspicious; and where his work was as hard as it was apparently unexciting. They lived in a comfortable but ugly and ordinary house, run with the help of an old man, a boy, and a temperamental Jewish girl who was often ill, and Amy did much of the cooking herself. 'They have no real culture, no useful contacts, no social life, no *fun*!' Mrs Boadman never wearied of saying with her eyes getting rounder and more spiteful at each 'no.' 'Crazy! They're just two crazy people.'

But Amy and Bob were so busy and happy that they did not notice the lack of useful contacts and social life. Though at first they had found the Alvarites puzzled and prejudiced against them because, possessing most of the equipment for a good time, they did not want one, the Alvarites were gradually won over by Bob's care of their sick children and by Amy's simplicity. They knew who she was, of course, for the papers had made a two days' wonder out of her marriage to Bob following on the shooting of Dan; and at first the women especially could not understand why she did not start a literary circle or otherwise try to raise the cultural standards of the town. But at last it dawned upon them (as it had dawned upon Lady Welwoodham's set in London) that apart from her books Amy was dumb; a homey little thing; just folks; and they left her more or less in peace. It was all she wanted, for she was happy. Their love had survived those small shocks of discovery that must follow such romantic beginnings as theirs had been, and now Lou's name for them, Victoria and Albert, was amusingly apt.

Much of Bob's natural cheerfulness had returned to him, and his example, rather than his persuasion, was making Amy into a woman. His sweet temper inspired her to control her own passionate one, and his unsuspicious friendliness helped her see the best in people. Sometimes he gave her a gentle, laughing little lecture when she had been bitter over some betrayal or slight; and did not fully know how this hesitant advice penetrated her nature and drew its suppressed sweetness, in an agony of love and remorse, to the surface. With every day and night that they were together, her character settled more certainly in those lines leading towards 'an old age serene and bright And lovely as a Lapland night.' How beautiful this slow but steady disentangling of the knots in the human spirit can be, only the priest and the true lover know.

They often talked over the strangeness of their story and wondered at it, and always came to the same puzzling question that stopped all further speculation: did the things that had happened to them happen because they would have happened anyway, or did they happen because the Three Dreams had come to Amy and caused her to act in a certain way?

And all the dreams came true in time, including the dream of the Swimming Girl. On the first day that Amy went out alone after her illness, a torn piece of newspaper had blown against her ankles as she stood waiting to cross the road, and as she glanced down she had seen the loathsome speckled photograph of Dan's cabin on the month-old page, and had fainted. That had been a moment! Never would she forget it. And on the delayed honeymoon that they took after Bob was qualified, they had motored down to Florida and swum naked from an island in the warm blue sea. ('*But are we doing this because we'd have done it anyway, or because I had the dream and that made us want to make it come true? Oh heck! it's crazy!*' and Bob had dived under water, shaking his head in utter bewilderment.)

Whatever the explanation was, they felt that it could not be so important as the fact that their story made them feel that in a special way they belonged to one another.

'Fated,' Lou would say, looking at them with her philosophical smile, carefully untouched by wistfulness. 'It was Meant. Even I, corrupted as I am by the life of Morgan café-society, can see that it was Meant. Vicky and Albert! Bless you, my children.'

As she sat awkwardly at the desk trying to write, Amy suddenly put her head down on her arms and stayed so, trembling.

It was thus that Bob, a few moments later, found her.

She started up and glanced round as he came into the room, then turned away with an attempt to pretend that she was writing, but it was too late; tears were running down her face and he had seen them. He came straight over to the desk, put his arms round her, and half-led, half-carried her to the couch.

When he had comforted her in silence for a little while, he said gently but in a troubled tone—

'Darling, you promised, you know.'

'I know, Bob. I'm awfully sorry. I couldn't help it,' she answered in a stifled voice, not lifting her face from his shoulder.

'I'm not mad at you, but you must try to get a hold on yourself or where'll we be when the baby comes?'

Then she did look up, and answered quickly and proudly, 'I can manage that, I'm not afraid of that a bit. I'm longing for the baby. It'll be a part of you and me, and then if anything happened to you or to it, there'd always be the other one, you see.'

'But darling' (he leant back against the wall and put his arms behind his head, with the briefest glance at the clock on her desk: the waiting-room was already full of patients) 'why should anything happen to me or the baby?'

'Oh, I don't know, but things do. Everything's so dangerous nowadays. And we're so happy that I'm afraid sometimes it seems too good to be true.'

He shook his head.

'I'm not. Whatever made the world meant men and women to be happy together with a home and kids. We're lucky but we're normal, too. Everybody ought to be like us. That's what was meant.'

She listened, her fear already retreating to the back of her mind because of the comfort of his presence. If only he need never go out again! she thought; and then smiled at her own absurdity. He smiled too, and let his arms fall tiredly.

'Is that my soup?' he said, glancing at the little saucepan on the electric plate in the corner.

'Oh, I'm so sorry: you must be starved:' She got up and went over to the plate and poured out the soup, while he watched her. 'That was getting into such a state—I forgot. I'm an awful wife to you.'

'Queer to think the baby might be here this time tomorrow,' he murmured, as she came slowly over to him with the tray.

She sat down beside him and lovingly watched his face. It was already losing the indefinable charm of first youth, but it was gaining the rarer charms of maturity and peace. Presently he said:

'I can't think how to get you out of this worrying about me.'

'I'm all right now, darling, truly I am. I'll try not to be like that again.'

'Yes, but——' he shook his head, and finished the soup. Then he said, leaning a little towards her:

'See here—suppose we admit we're happier than most people, and so we've more to lose. Perhaps we'll even have to pay for our happiness. All right, then. So what? We'll have had it. Isn't it better to realize how happy we are, and take the risks that may go with our happiness, than never have anything—get lost, go rotten, want the wrong things? We've *had* the right things. Nothing can ever take that away. Does that comfort you?'

She nodded, but absently, for she was looking at his face.

'I do love you,' she said at last in a low tone.

He caught her hand and held it.

'And I love you,' he muttered, returning her look. 'So much.'

There was a long silence; and to both of them there seemed to grow in the room a spirit of deep happiness and peace: the spirit that can never leave the world while men and women love one another, and love the children that they make.

THE END

THE HISTORY OF VINTAGE

The famous American publisher Alfred A. Knopf (1892–1984) founded Vintage Books in the United States in 1954 as a paperback home for the authors published by his company. Vintage was launched in the United Kingdom in 1990 and works independently from the American imprint although both are part of the international publishing group, Random House.

Vintage in the United Kingdom was initially created to publish paperback editions of books bought by the prestigious literary hardback imprints in the Random House Group such as Jonathan Cape, Chatto & Windus, Hutchinson and later William Heinemann, Secker & Warburg and The Harvill Press. There are many Booker and Nobel Prize-winning authors on the Vintage list and the imprint publishes a huge variety of fiction and non-fiction. Over the years Vintage has expanded and the list now includes great authors of the past – who are published under the Vintage Classics imprint – as well as many of the most influential authors of the present. In 2012 Vintage Children's Classics was launched to include the much-loved authors of our youth.

For a full list of the books Vintage publishes,
please visit our website
www.vintage-books.co.uk

For book details and other information about the classic authors we publish, please visit the Vintage Classics website
www.vintage-classics.info

www.vintage-classics.info

Visit www.worldofstories.co.uk for all your
favourite children's classics